"INCOMING FIRE!" XAV SHOUTED ABOVE THE DIN. "SOME KIND OF FOCUSED ENERGY PLASMA."

His fist dropping to smack the intercom button on the arm of his chair, al-Khaled had just enough time to relay a warning to the rest of the ship to brace for impact before whatever had been launched at the *Aephas* slammed into the science vessel's deflector shields. Everything trembled around him, and al-Khaled gripped the arms of his chair, feeling his stomach lurch as the ship absorbed the sudden attack.

"Stand by all weapons!" al-Khaled snapped. As he surveyed in rapid fashion the different bridge stations in a hasty attempt to determine the status of the ship's major systems, he saw Lieutenant Rodriguez wrestling with her helm console. Her fingers moved almost too fast to follow as she punched and stabbed various controls, her efforts translated to the viewscreen as the alien ship seemed to bank to starboard and out of the frame.

"_____" _____ called out.

"_____ his l_____ Xav g_____ bent over the unit's viewscreen. "_____ken! If they hit us again like that, they may go altogether!"

Al-Khaled asked, "Can you find the source of that dampening field?"

"Negative. Our scans are being reflected back!"

"They are firing again!" Xav warned.

Read more adventures of the starships
Endeavour and *Sagittarius* in the saga of

VANGUARD

Harbinger
David Mack

Summon the Thunder
Dayton Ward & Kevin Dilmore

Reap the Whirlwind
David Mack

Open Secrets
Dayton Ward

Precipice
David Mack

Declassified
(anthology)
Dayton Ward, Kevin Dilmore,
Marco Palmieri, David Mack

What Judgments Come
Dayton Ward & Kevin Dilmore

Storming Heaven
David Mack

In Tempest's Wake
Dayton Ward

SEEKERS

Seekers #1: Second Nature
David Mack

Seekers #2: Point of Divergence
Dayton Ward & Kevin Dilmore

Seekers #3: Long Shot
David Mack

STAR TREK®
SEEKERS

ALL THAT'S LEFT

DAYTON WARD
& KEVIN DILMORE

Based upon *Star Trek*
created by Gene Roddenberry

POCKET BOOKS

New York   London   Toronto   Sydney   New Delhi   Tài Shan

Pocket Books
An Imprint of Simon & Schuster, Inc.
1230 Avenue of the Americas
New York, NY 10020

™, ®, and © 2015 by CBS Studios Inc. STAR TREK and related marks and logos are trademarks of CBS Studios Inc. All Rights Reserved.

This book is published by Pocket Books, an imprint of Simon & Schuster, Inc., under exclusive license from CBS Studios Inc.

First Pocket Books paperback edition November 2015

POCKET and colophon are registered trademarks of Simon & Schuster, Inc.

For information about special discounts for bulk purchases, please contact Simon & Schuster Special Sales at 1-866-506-1949 or business@simonandschuster.com.

The Simon & Schuster Speakers Bureau can bring authors to your live event. For more information or to book an event, contact the Simon & Schuster Speakers Bureau at 1-866-248-3049 or visit our website at www.simonspeakers.com.

Manufactured in the United States of America

10 9 8 7 6 5 4 3 2 1

ISBN 978-1-4767-9860-8
ISBN 978-1-4767-9861-5 (ebook)

IN MEMORIAM

Harve Bennett
August 17, 1930–February 25, 2015

Leonard Nimoy
March 26, 1931–February 27, 2015

Grace Lee Whitney
April 1, 1930–May 1, 2015

They're really not dead, as long as we remember them.

Historian's Note

The events of this story take place in late 2269, a few months after the events of *Star Trek: Seekers* #2—*Point of Divergence*, and five months after the *Enterprise*'s mission to Camus II (*Star Trek: The Original Series*, "Turnabout Intruder").

1

It was going to be a very busy day, Colleen Cook decided. That was a good thing.

Standing at the edge of the wide, shallow crater that was the focal point of Beta Site, the latest excavation area assigned to her team, Cook surveyed the area and noted that even now, less than twelve hours after the most recent earthquake, things were returning to normal in rapid fashion. Heavy equipment had been brought over from the main encampment to assist in the moving of excavated soil and larger rocks that had shifted during the quake and its handful of aftershocks. All four of the temporary shelters that formed the base of operations for her team at this location were once again standing upright, though Cook noted a new fissure that had opened in the ground at the dig's far end. Several people—a few like her wearing olive-green Starfleet utility coveralls but most wearing civilian attire—were moving about the narrow crevice that snaked for almost a hundred meters across the crater's floor.

"Lieutenant Cook," said a voice from behind her, and Cook glanced over her shoulder to see her friend and colleague T'Naal walking toward her across the rocky terrain separating the crater from the larger encampment that was home to Cook and her team. A civilian member of the archaeological team, T'Naal wore a gray jumpsuit that sported several pockets and was similar in design to her Starfleet coveralls, and she carried a black satchel slung over her right shoulder and across her torso so that the bag rested along her left hip.

"Good morning," Cook offered as the Vulcan moved to stand next to her at the crater's edge. She then gestured to the scene before her. "You know, even though we've been here a month, I still stand here at the start of every day, look around, and get excited about what we might find." As she spoke the words, Cook felt her cheeks warm in embarrassment. "I'm sorry, T'Naal. I know I must sound silly."

Her companion shook her head. "You need not apologize, Lieutenant. I have worked alongside humans for many years, and I am familiar with a broad range of emotional displays. Compared to others I have witnessed, yours was most restrained, and oddly . . . refreshing." She raised her left eyebrow, which Cook had come to learn was T'Naal's way of conveying her various attempts at humor. The silent punctuation to her reply made Cook chuckle before she redirected her attention to the vista before her.

Beyond the crater and extending for several kilometers in all directions were the ruins of what Cook thought had to have once been a beautiful city. When an unmanned probe, three years earlier, had reconnoitered this planet, Cantrel V, its sensors had recorded images and evidence of nearly thirty such developed areas scattered across its three primary landmasses, along with numerous other smaller concentrations of industrialization. Landing parties from the first Starfleet ships to investigate the planet had come away with volumes of information hinting at the civilization that once had thrived here, including evidence of the global conflict that doubtless had precipitated its demise. Sensor scans indicated that the war which had ravaged Cantrel V had taken place more than four centuries earlier, and medical and forensic teams from those initial exploration efforts had collected and studied remains of beings believed to be members of the planet's indigenous humanoid population.

As for the war, evidence of orbital bombardment was everywhere, leading to speculation that two or more factions may have utilized long-range or intercontinental ballistic missiles, or perhaps even space-based weapons. The latter theory received an intriguing twist when the excavation of another dig site revealed a new set of remains that—while humanoid—appeared to be a different species from those previously retrieved and studied. Had the planet been home to more than one form of higher-order life? Perhaps one species had come here from some other, distant world. If that was the case, which race was native to Cantrel V?

"Every morning I come up here," Cook said, "and every morning I ask the same question. What happened to these people, that war on such a scale was the answer?" She gestured toward the ruins in the distance. "It doesn't make any sense. Based on everything we've found so far, this was a civilization that seemed to be doing everything right. Technological advancement, rudimentary space travel, the works." She cast her gaze toward the horizon, where gray-white clouds were gathering and contrasting with the brilliant blue sky. "It doesn't make any damned sense."

"Agreed," replied T'Naal, "particularly in light of our recent discovery." The Vulcan paused, and Cook watched as she studied the devastated city beyond the dig site. "These people were on the cusp of faster-than-light travel. Our scans confirmed the presence of antimatter, still in a protected underground storage facility, and the remnants of a spacecraft fitted with a primitive warp engine not at all unlike the prototype developed by your Zefram Cochrane. The similarities are actually quite remarkable, though Doctor Cochrane's design actually was more efficient than what we found here."

The lieutenant could not resist a teasing smile. "You sound surprised by that."

"It was not my intention to slight Doctor Cochrane's work. On the contrary, his accomplishment is all the more impressive given the environment in which he was forced to work and the resources at his disposal."

Nodding, Cook said, "Which makes what we've got here that much more bizarre. Unless we're just totally misreading everything, these people were far better off than Earth was in the twenty-first century, so what the hell happened?" It was a common question put forth by members of her team, usually as part of spirited discussions over meals at the end of long days spent exploring the different excavation sites. For her part, the mystery was what had driven Cook to take this assignment, rather than one of the others calling for her particular skills. The planet teemed with questions in search of answers.

Following the discoveries made by the original survey teams, Starfleet had devoted personnel and resources to further exploration of Cantrel V, aided in no small part by the civilian colonists and scientists who now called this world home. While the colony itself had taken advantage of the planet's temperate climate to build what was fast becoming a formidable agricultural community, archaeologists like T'Naal as well as specialists from numerous fields of scientific study sought answers to the mystery of the planet's past and the people who once had lived here.

"Any news from Tài Shan?" Cook asked.

T'Naal replied, "Administrator LeMons sent an updated status this morning. She reports that they ultimately were unable to repair the faulty generator and were forced to replace it. However, work on the three buildings damaged during the quake is under way, and she expects those to be completed by tomorrow."

"What about their casualties?"

"The four colonists who suffered minor injuries have all been treated and released to their homes. The colony's primary physician has forwarded his report along with Administrator LeMons's, and I have prepared all of that for your review once you return to base camp."

Cook smiled. "What would I do without you, T'Naal?"

"You likely would perform all of these required administrative tasks yourself," the Vulcan said, "but perhaps without my level of efficiency." Once more, she arched her left eyebrow, and Cook fought back another laugh.

Though she was the officer in command of the Starfleet contingent assigned to Beta Site as well as overall leader of the entire combined team, it had taken Cook almost no time to form a productive collaboration with T'Naal, the civilian group's senior member. They worked well together, helping one another as they each oversaw their respective personnel, and the Vulcan had gone to great lengths to ease Cook's logistical burden as she dealt with all manner of reports and other administrative trivia as required by Starfleet Command. This also entailed doing what she could to support Morgan LeMons, the administrator of Tài Shan, the colony established eighteen months ago on Cantrel V.

One of numerous such settlements founded as part of the Federation's exploration of and expansion into the Taurus Reach, Tài Shan was one of several success stories in this region of space. It had thrived even as other colonies encountered challenges ranging from disease and harsh environmental conditions to attacks from Klingon forces or other renegade elements. Cook knew from personal experience that Starfleet's attention had been occupied by other concerns elsewhere in this contested wedge of space, whereas Tài Shan was one of several outposts that had managed to escape being impacted.

Reaching into her satchel, T'Naal extracted a data slate and handed it to Cook. "We have also received a preliminary report from Ensign ch'Dran. He and his survey team have completed a sweep of the underground caverns and prepared a list of those areas that currently are unsafe for our people. Those sections are being cordoned off until such time as Commander al-Khaled can dispatch engineering teams to assist us."

"I was figuring as much," Cook said. The earthquake had come early the previous evening, after everyone had cleared the subterranean areas of the excavation site for the day, and with only a few stragglers left in the crater itself. All the team members had escaped injury, left instead to deal with the cleanup. "I'll take a little extra digging over broken bones or worse any day."

T'Naal replied, "We were most fortunate. There are two tunnels that will require clearing, after which Ensign ch'Dran can continue his safety inspection to the rest of the cavern, but the delays should be minimal."

"I'll contact the *Aephas* when I get back to camp and ask Commander al-Khaled to get his engineers and their big toys down here. They'll love being able to dig around in the dirt for a while." Cook had not had the opportunity to speak to Mahmud al-Khaled, the commanding officer of the science ship *Aephas*, since the vessel's arrival at Cantrel V two days earlier. He and his crew had spent the bulk of that time with the transfer of supplies they had brought with them, as well as assisting with various tasks in support of the Tài Shan colony. LeMons had doubtless been keeping al-Khaled and his people busy with the sizable list of necessary repairs or infrastructure enhancements, along with whatever desired or "nice to have" requests the *Aephas* and its crew could accommodate.

"You know the commander?" T'Naal asked. When Cook eyed her with a quizzical expression, the Vulcan added, "Your comments made it seem as though you were acquainted."

Cook shrugged. "We served together, briefly, a few years ago." In truth, she had only met al-Khaled once, three years earlier, on the planet Erilon. She had been an ensign assigned to the science department of the *Starship*

Endeavour, and the commander had been serving as the leader of a contingent from Starfleet's Corps of Engineers detached to the *U.S.S. Lovell*. The frozen world had been the site of a most unusual and classified archaeological expedition sanctioned by Starfleet as part of its larger exploration of the Taurus Reach. While Cook, at first, had considered the duty boring if not pointless, that opinion had been shattered once . . .

Now's not the time to be dwelling on that again. You've got work to do.

She was reaching into a pocket of her coveralls to retrieve her communicator when the device emitted a pair of beeps, indicating an incoming call. Extracting the unit from her pocket, she flipped open its gold antenna grid.

"Cook here."

"This is Ensign ch'Dran, Lieutenant," said the voice of the Andorian officer who served as one of Cook's team leaders when her contingent of Starfleet archaeology and geology specialists were scattered across the different dig sites. *"We are still conducting our safety sweep of the area, but we have found something you will want to see. The quake caused a new sinkhole to open approximately five hundred meters from the crater, and if our tricorder readings are correct, it may provide us with access to an entirely new area of the subterranean ruins."* Cook noted that he sounded somewhat out of breath, as though he had been running or climbing or performing some other rigorous activity.

"Ensign, are you all right?"

Ch'Dran replied, *"Yes. I attempted to climb down into the new opening to determine if there was a safe means of entering the new cavern, and part of the hole collapsed even farther. Two of my people had to help pull me clear."*

"Well, stop doing that," Cook said, her tone growing harder. "Nobody goes down there until we verify its safety. That means you too, Zet." She should have known he might attempt to check things out for himself. Despite all his training as a field archeology and anthropology officer, Ensign Zeturildtra ch'Dran possessed a penchant for taking unnecessary risks while performing his duties. His one saving grace was that he limited the straining of protocol to himself, rather than risking the safety of his team members, but she had counseled him twice on this behavior since arriving at Cantrel V. Cook made a note to revisit the subject with ch'Dran at the next available opportunity.

"Understood, Lieutenant," replied the Andorian. *"I have already established a security cordon around the new site, and we are in the process of scanning for possible cave-ins as well as the threat of toxic gases that might have been released from underground pockets. So far, we have found nothing. However, you should be aware that my civilian counterpart is most anxious to investigate the new find. Despite my warnings, Mister Gillespie is most insistent that he and his team be allowed to descend into the cavern as soon as possible."*

Rather than responding to ch'Dran, Cook instead directed an exasperated look to T'Naal. As much as the ensign might irritate her with his occasional need to strike out on his own, James Gillespie had proven to be a monumental pain in the ass since his arrival on Cantrel V. Headstrong and possessing an impressive list of credentials following decades of work as a field archaeologist and professor at one of the most prestigious universities on Mars, Gillespie harbored almost no patience for protocol, bureaucracy, and even—on occasion—civility. He also made a habit of reminding all who might hear him of this disdain, and Cook in particular had been on the receiving end of his ranting more than once.

"Your boy's acting up again."

T'Naal replied, "He is not my offspring." Stepping closer, she directed her voice to Cook's open communicator. "Ensign ch'Dran, this is T'Naal. Inform Mister Gillespie that he is to refrain from entering the new cavern until further notice."

"Acknowledged. Thank you for your assistance. Ch'Dran out."

No sooner had the conversation ended and Cook was about to contact the Tài Shan colony administrator than her communicator beeped again. She frowned at the device in her hand. "Seems I'm popular this morning."

"It would appear so," said T'Naal.

Cook tapped the control to switch the communicator to the new frequency. "Cook here."

"Al-Khaled here, Lieutenant," replied the voice of the *Aephas*'s commanding officer. *"I've already notified Administrator LeMons about this. Alert all your people that our long-range sensors are detecting the approach of an unknown vessel."*

Frowning, Cook asked, "Unknown? As in it's too far away to identify?"

"Unknown as in it's like nothing on file anywhere in our computer's memory banks. Whoever's flying it isn't responding to our hails, and they're definitely heading

for us. We're heading out to meet it before it gets here, but until we can get some idea of who they are or what they want, make sure all of your people are on full alert. Start moving them to designated emergency stations and await further instructions."

Her mind already racing with the various orders to be issued and tasks to be performed, Cook said, "We're not set up for any sort of defensive action down here, Commander. This is a civilian colony, and we're just guests in their house." Tài Shan, while possessing little in the way of weapons, had constructed a series of underground shelters to serve as a degree of protection. It was a practice mimicked by many colonies established in the Taurus Reach after a few such settlements had fallen victim to Klingon or Tholian attack. Would such defensive measures prove sufficient, if the situation came to that? "All we can really do is just hunker down and hope for the best."

There was a brief pause, and Cook thought she could almost hear al-Khaled release a small sigh, before he replied, *"Then start doing that."*

2

There was a time when Mahmud al-Khaled had enjoyed the thrill of solving a mystery. Once, not all that long ago, he would have reveled in the excitement of repairing some bit of malfunctioning or misbehaving equipment, understanding the motivations of a previously unknown culture, or attempting to put back together the scattered remnants of some ancient alien technology. Solving such puzzles and learning something new had been a reward all its own, the very reason he had joined Starfleet in the first place.

A great deal of that enthusiasm, born as it was from youth and naiveté, had been tempered when reality saw fit to show him that some mysteries preferred to remain unsolved, certain puzzles favored ambiguity, and there were definitely questions that were better off unanswered.

Did the ship now approaching Cantrel V fall into any of those categories?

I'd really rather it didn't, al-Khaled thought, offering a silent plea to any deities, real or otherwise, who might at this moment be watching these events unfold.

Seated in front of him at the large helm console she operated by herself at the center of the *Aephas*'s bridge, Lieutenant Sasha Rodriguez said, "Commander, the vessel's speed is decreasing. Estimated time to intercept is two minutes, twenty seconds."

"Thank you, Lieutenant," replied al-Khaled. "Let's see it. On-screen." A moment later, the image on the viewscreen changed to display the approaching ship. Even from its current distance, it was obvious that it was a massive vessel, consisting of five enormous spherical sections sporting blue-gray outer hulls and each connected to the others by an intricate web of cross pieces that were darker in color, contrasting with the spheres and almost disappearing against the backdrop of open space behind the craft.

"Those support struts look pretty large just by themselves," said al-Khaled. "Do you think they're just for connecting the spheres, or serviceable hull sections, or both?"

"I would speculate that they are used for both," replied Lieutenant Molan lek Xav, the *Aephas*'s Tellarite science officer. "They are certainly large enough to serve that purpose, and it would seem to be a waste of material and useful interior space not to utilize them in that matter." He grunted as he shifted in his seat. "Though a logical design feature also would see to it that each of the spheres is capable of functioning on its own."

Turning his chair to face the bridge's communications station, al-Khaled asked, "Any responses to our hails?"

"None, sir," replied Ensign Folanir Pzial, the Rigelian female serving as the *Aephas*'s senior communications officer, as she shifted in her seat and looked in his direction. "I am unable to determine if they are even receiving our transmissions, or simply ignoring us."

Pushing himself from his chair, al-Khaled moved to stand at the curved red railing separating him from the science station along the bridge's starboard bulkhead. "Tell me you have something new," he said, placing his hands on the rail. "What the hell is this thing?"

Swiveling his stout frame in his seat so that he faced al-Khaled, Xav's eyes narrowed as he released a derisive snort. "I cannot tell you what it is, Commander, though I can tell you what it is *not*: It is definitely not like anything on record, *anywhere*. A few references are somewhat similar, but only in the most superficial sense, if our scans are any indication."

"Any idea where it came from?"

Xav replied, "Based on its course, I would guess it traveled a route from somewhere out near the Taurus Reach's outer boundary. It may even have come from beyond that point."

Given the sheer number of star systems that lay in that direction—far beyond territory claimed by the Tholians, Klingons, or even the Gorn Hegemony and that remained unexplored even by automated survey probes—al-Khaled thought it almost a certainty that the ship now before them represented a heretofore unknown species. What were its intentions?

"You mentioned that you thought it was similar to other vessels in the memory banks," he said. "Like what?"

"Earlier this year," said Xav, "the *Enterprise* came across an alien vessel of unknown origin that, according to their sensors, had been orbiting a dead star along the Beta Quadrant's outer rim for three hundred million years." He gestured toward the viewscreen. "Like this one, it consisted of several spheres or pods, all connected by a series of support structures; however, unlike this one, that ship looked like it might have been grown rather than built. It also was much larger than this ship. Whereas this one is just over eleven hundred meters in length, the one the *Enterprise* found was more than twice that. The alloys used in their construction also are different from each other."

Eyeing the mysterious vessel, al-Khaled nodded in understanding. There was no denying that the ship they now faced had been constructed from individual components in accordance with whatever design aesthetics and practical needs had driven its creators. His reaction upon getting his first look at the immense craft was that it had been built with a utilitarian purpose in mind, with function taking priority over form.

"And before you ask," Xav continued, "I have no idea how old this ship might be. I doubt it is three hundred million years old, but until we can investigate it more closely, anything I offer at this point would be conjecture." He grunted in what al-Khaled took to be annoyance. "Its hull composition is interfering with our scans, so I am presently unable to provide any information on the vessel's interior."

"Hull composition?" asked al-Khaled. "What's it made of?"

The science officer said, "An amalgam of several minerals, including at least one I have never seen. I suspect it may be a synthetic compound, but for the moment, I cannot be sure. The cumulative effect is that we are unable to penetrate the ship's outer hull."

"What about life signs?"

"Inconclusive, sir," Xav replied. "Again, due to our sensor issues."

Turning so that he could lean against the railing, al-Khaled crossed his arms and directed his attention to ponder the unfamiliar craft highlighted on the bridge's main viewscreen. It was a fascinating configuration, he decided. Who had built it? From where had they traveled? What about this world in particular had attracted their interest? No answers to these and the numerous other questions he might conjure appeared to be forthcoming. For the moment, al-Khaled was satisfied that the vessel had not opened fire, though he knew such a turn of events remained a distinct possibility. That threat potential also served to remind him yet again that the *Aephas* was alone here and if this situation escalated, the closest ship available to provide reinforcements was ten hours away at minimum.

So, let's try to keep things under control, shall we?

Behind him, something on Xav's console beeped, and al-Khaled shifted his stance to watch the Tellarite as he pressed several controls before rising from his seat to peer into the workstation's hooded sensor viewer.

"Interesting. Our sensors are picking up indications of a dampening field in operation." Without looking up from the viewer, Xav tapped several controls on the adjacent console. "I am attempting to compensate, but so far the field's proving surprisingly resistant."

Al-Khaled returned his attention to the ship displayed on the viewscreen. "What about weapons or defenses?"

"There are weapons ports on each of the spheres as

well as the connecting struts, but none of them are active." Pulling back from the viewer, Xav turned toward the screen. "Its power output is actually far less than what I would expect for a vessel of this size." His face seemed to stretch as his mouth broadened in a wide grin.

"I know that look," al-Khaled said, fighting the urge to smile. "You want to go over there, don't you?"

Xav released a boisterous laugh that was forceful enough for al-Khaled to feel reverberation in the railing. "You know me all too well, Commander."

"Occupational hazard, Lieutenant."

Like Pzial, Rodriguez, and a few other members of the *Aephas*'s crew, Xav had agreed to al-Khaled's request for a temporary transfer with him to the *Miranda*-class science ship while he and the rest of his detachment from the Corps of Engineers awaited permanent reassignment to a new vessel. Their previous ship, the *Lovell*, had been lost several months earlier during events that had preceded an explosive battle between Starfleet and an armada sent by the Tholian Assembly, which had resulted in the loss of Starbase 47 and marked the end of the tumultuous, top-secret project known as "Operation Vanguard." Following that incident, the *Lovell*'s commanding officer, Captain Daniel Okagawa, had been reassigned to Starbase 11, where he now oversaw that facility's starship maintenance and repair depot. According to the latest rumors floating between the different Corps detachments, Okagawa was being considered for command of the entire starbase, and a promotion to commodore also appeared likely.

A more deserving man, I've never met, al-Khaled mused.

As for the *Lovell*, a near relic from the twenty-second century and already operating well beyond its anticipated life expectancy, it had been one of three *Daedalus*-class ships returned to active duty several years previously when the Corps of Engineers had requested a trio of vessels it could dedicate to its specialized mission requirements. With no other starships available that could suit its needs, the Corps had been authorized by Starfleet Command to pull from mothballs any inactive vessel it was believed could be sufficiently refurbished. The three *Daedalus* ships—the *Lovell*, the *Masao*, and the *Zander*—all Starfleet workhorses that had earned storied reputations a century earlier during the Earth-Romulan War, were retrieved from the storage depot at Qualor II and returned to service. The ships had undergone extensive modifications and retrofitting, due in no small part to the expertise and creativity of each vessel's contingent of engineers, who devoted much of their spare time between assignments to the ongoing effort. The *Masao* and the *Zander* remained active, and the Corps currently was in the process of finding a suitable replacement for the *Lovell*.

I miss that old bucket.

Though most of its crew had survived that tragic incident at Starbase 47, the ship's first officer, Commander Areav zh'Rhun, and Lieutenant Kurt Davis, al-Khaled's own second-in-command of the *Lovell*'s Corps of Engineers detachment, had sacrificed themselves to save their shipmates.

I miss both of you, as well.

At the helm station, Lieutenant Rodriguez said, "Commander, the ship is altering its trajectory and continuing to slow its speed. I think it's moving to settle into orbit. Judging by their course, they haven't even noticed us. At its current velocity and rate of deceleration, it will be in position to assume a standard orbit in just over an hour."

"That's rather impolite," al-Khaled replied, returning his attention to the enigmatic vessel on the screen. "Ensign Pzial, hail them again. They can't ignore us forever." He cast a glance over his shoulder at Xav. "Can they?"

"My wife has successfully disregarded me for years. This is nothing."

A moment later, Pzial reported, "Still no response, sir."

"Any idea what it's doing, Xav?" asked al-Khaled.

Once more occupied by his sensor controls, the science officer replied, "No indications of increased power output. No weapons, no scanners, nothing. At least, that is what I am able to determine so long as our scans are being interfered with."

"What do you suppose they want?" Al-Khaled had pondered that question himself before inviting other discussion. "I mean, whoever's aboard that thing, they came from somewhere, and they came to this planet for a reason, right? Is it because they find it interesting the way we do? Could they be looking to it for resources to exploit, or to establish a colony or military presence? Does that make them friend or enemy?"

Xav grunted. "It could be any or all of those."

Shaking his head, al-Khaled pushed away from the railing. "I'm not waiting around to find out. Sound yellow alert." As he returned to his seat, he gestured toward Rodriguez. "Helm, take us in a bit closer. Intercept course that puts us between it and Cantrel V. Maybe that will help with Mister Xav's sensor troubles. Let's still keep a respectful distance, though. Just inside our transporter range should suffice." He had no way to know whether the alien vessel possessed its own transporter technology, or how close the *Aephas* needed to be before it might be threatened by the other ship's weapons, but sitting here idle was getting them nowhere.

"Aye, sir," replied the helm officer as she input the necessary commands to her console.

Al-Khaled watched as the enormous vessel on the viewscreen continued its approach, as though oblivious of the *Aephas* as it maneuvered toward whatever orbital path it would soon assume. Despite its size and lack of any notably pleasing aesthetic features that might denote agility, the ship seemed to move with a grace that belied its unremarkable configuration.

"Something appears to be happening," Xav reported a moment later. "I am detecting indications of scanning activity, directed toward Cantrel V."

Al-Khaled frowned. "Not us?"

"Not yet," replied the science officer. Then, he uttered something al-Khaled could not hear, punctuating the inaudible comment with a grunt of annoyance. "That dampening field I mentioned earlier? It appears to be increasing in intensity."

"Helm, hold this position." Even as he gave the order, al-Khaled heard the slightest change in pitch to the ship's engines, an instant before every light and console on the bridge faded before returning to their normal illumination levels. "The field's causing that?"

Xav said, "I believe so, sir." When an alert tone sounded from his console, the Tellarite scowled as he studied the reading. "Our shield strength is decreasing. It is already down to ninety-four percent."

No sooner did he reply than the ship's intercom whistled for attention, followed by the voice of the *Aephas*'s chief engineer, Commander Moves-With-Burning-Grace.

"Engineering to bridge. Be advised that we are experiencing a power drain in all systems. It is minor, but the decrease is steady."

"He is correct, sir," Xav added. "The drain is consistent, and continuing, and appears to be connected to the dampening field surrounding the alien vessel. The closer we get to it, the greater the field's effects on us. Left unchecked, it represents a significant risk to the ship."

Leaning forward in his chair, al-Khaled said, "Rodriguez, back us away."

Another warning, this time in the form of the red alert klaxon, erupted on the bridge, and al-Khaled flinched as it began wailing.

"Incoming fire!" Xav shouted above the din. "Some kind of focused energy plasma."

His fist dropping to smack the intercom button on the arm of his chair, al-Khaled had just enough time to relay a warning to the rest of the ship to brace for impact before whatever had been launched at the *Aephas* slammed into the science vessel's deflector shields. Everything trembled around him, and al-Khaled gripped the arms of his chair, feeling his stomach lurch as the ship absorbed the sudden attack.

"Stand by all weapons!" al-Khaled snapped. As he surveyed in rapid fashion the different bridge stations in a hasty attempt to determine the status of the ship's major systems, he saw Lieutenant Rodriguez wrestling with her helm console. Her fingers moved almost too fast to follow as she punched and stabbed various controls, her efforts translated to the viewscreen as the alien ship seemed to bank to starboard and out of the frame.

"Initiating evasive maneuvers, sir!" she called out. "But the helm's sluggish!"

On his feet at the science station and using one of his large hands to anchor himself against the console, Xav gripped the sensor viewer with his other hand as he bent over the unit's viewfinder. "Shields continuing to weaken! If they hit us again like that, they may go altogether!"

Al-Khaled asked, "Can you find the source of that dampening field?"

"Negative. Our scans are being reflected back!"

They needed distance from the alien ship, but that came at a price, al-Khaled knew. If the vessel was here to take some form of offensive action against the planet, then the *Aephas* was all that stood between it and the Starfleet and colony personnel on the ground.

"They are firing again!" Xav warned.

In front of him, al-Khaled saw Rodriguez hunched over her helm controls, doing everything she could to keep the *Aephas* from suffering another direct hit. Her efforts were successful, as when the ship was hit this time, he was certain the impact was not as severe. Despite his instincts and even wishful thinking, new alert indicators began sounding and flashing at multiple workstations around the bridge.

Tossed back toward his chair, Xav called over his shoulder, "Shields at twenty-three percent!"

"Target their weapons ports and fire!" al-Khaled ordered. "Helm, get us out of here!"

Behind him, Ensign Pzial said, "Damage reports coming in from all departments, sir. Engineering reports continuing drain to main power systems."

"Our phasers took out a couple of their weapons ports, Commander," said Rodriguez. "There's also damage to their hull from our first spread of torpedoes."

"Maintain evasive and fire again. Phasers and a full spread of torpedoes. Let's see if we can't give back some of what they're dishing out."

On the viewscreen, al-Khaled saw the massive alien ship's weapons ports flaring as they unleashed pulse after pulse of roiling red-white energy. Rodriguez's piloting skills continued to be tested as the helm officer maneuvered the *Aephas* in the face of incoming fire while trying to affect a strategic retreat. The starship's every phaser strike and launched torpedo was marked by the flickering of numerous lights and workstations around the bridge, telling al-Khaled that even at this distance, the alien ship's dampening field was still a factor.

We need to get clear and regroup.

It seemed like a simple enough notion, withdrawing to a safe distance to make repairs to the ship's damaged systems, but al-Khaled knew that he could not afford to wait to see what the alien vessel might do if it continued on its apparent course to assume orbit over Cantrel V. For the moment and based on its actions, there was no reason to believe that the ship was anything but a threat to the colonists and his people on the surface. Retreat, even now with the *Aephas* in deteriorating condition, was not an option.

"More hits on their hull," Xav reported. "At least two more weapons ports disabled, and additional hull damage." Looking up from his sensor viewer, he added, "Of course, that still leaves them with about three dozen more ports to shoot at us."

As if to emphasize his point, the ship shook yet again under the onslaught of a third salvo striking home. This time the impact was powerful enough that al-Khaled felt himself lifted from his chair.

"Shields are down, sir!" Rodriguez warned. Her words were followed by an audible warbling in the omnipresent hum of the *Aephas*'s warp engines along with a new round of alarm indicators wailing from multiple consoles. "Power drain is increasing!"

That's it.

"Get us out of here, now!" Pushing himself from his seat, he lunged forward and gripped the back of the helm officer's chair. "Lay down covering fire and move us out of range of their weapons, before we lose everything." He reached forward and stabbed the console's intercom control. "Bridge to engineering. We need those shields back, now!"

"Working on it, Commander," replied Moves-With-Burning-Grace over the speaker. *"Power readings are*

leveling out, but we still have significant damage to several systems."

Al-Khaled gritted his teeth before replied, "Shields and weapons are the priority, Grace." Turning toward the science station, he asked, "Xav, what's that ship doing?"

His attention once again focused on his sensors, the Tellarite replied, "It is continuing with what can only be a course for orbital insertion." A moment later, he added, "Commander, it has also renewed its scans of the planet, and if I am correctly interpreting these readings, it is focusing much attention on the colony."

Oh holy hell . . .

"Pzial!" al-Khaled shouted. "Flash every communications station and personal communicator on the planet. Broadcast on every frequency, and tell everyone to get to cover, now!"

Turning back toward the viewscreen, he saw the image of the alien vessel, now with the curve of Cantrel V in the background. In about an hour, the ship would be in position, but to do what?

Whatever it is, there's not a damned lot we can do about it.

3

One kilometer to go.

The sun was bright, bringing out the brilliant scarlet tinge of the Martian sky and highlighting the red-brown terrain all around her. Despite the heat, a gentle breeze wafted through the canyon, cooling her sweat-soaked running attire and the perspiration on her exposed skin. None of that mattered, though; not now, when she was in the home stretch.

Could she break her previous record? The question taunted Atish Khatami as she crested the rise and caught sight of the familiar U-shaped rock formation. She would pass it on her right once she reached the curve in the well-worn path, after which there was nothing but the winding trail and its six-percent incline separating her from the finish line. The route was so familiar to her by this point that she could run it with her eyes closed, uneven landscape and snaking curves be damned. A glance at the chronometer in the lower left corner of her heads-up display told her that she had reached this point nearly a minute ahead of her previous time running this route. Four kilometers into the run and her breathing remained even and controlled, and she felt no ache in her legs or chest. She could do this with time to spare.

Then everything went blank.

"What the hell?"

Khatami only just avoided tripping over her own feet as the dusty path through the Martian desert vanished and was replaced by the dull gray surface of the curved viewscreen. She slowed her pace, feeling the treadmill decelerating beneath her feet now that the simulation had reached its abrupt end. Now proceeding at a walk, Khatami reached up to remove the clear glasses that provided her with the HUD information.

"Did I break it?"

"Sorry, Captain!"

The new voice called out from somewhere behind her, and Khatami stepped down from the treadmill to see Chief Petty Officer Lanier Wimmer, a member of the *Endeavour*'s recreation contingent, crossing the gymnasium toward her. Unlike Khatami and everyone else in the massive, curved room, Wimmer wore not athletic attire but instead an olive-green jumpsuit of the sort favored by working parties and smaller vessels that tended to operate on the borders of Federation space, far away from the prying eyes and immaculately tailored uniforms found on ships of the line.

"This is my fault," Wimmer said, gesturing toward the simulator. "I just installed a new software upgrade that included some new location options and enhanced customization features, but it's giving me fits." He frowned, stepping around Khatami and kneeling next to the treadmill so that he could open an access panel on its side. "Either they didn't test it before they sent it out, or else I messed up something when I put it in."

Khatami, still drawing deep breaths as she wound down from the prolonged exertion, reached for a towel she had placed on a bench next to the simulator. As she wiped her face, she replied, "It was working fine right up to the moment it cut out. I've used it three times this week and there were no problems then."

Reaching up to scratch the bare spot on the crown of his head, which was surrounded by hair that was more gray than brown, Wimmer said, "I'll redo the installation this morning. I'm sorry your run was interrupted, Captain. I was looking forward to giving the new features a try myself."

Though treadmills had been standard equipment aboard ship for ages—including models with viewscreens that attempted to simulate different locales and terrain features for the runner—the model installed last month in the *Endeavour*'s gymnasium was a newer model, featuring a larger, curved screen that helped with the immersion process. Glasses such as those Khatami had worn during her run enhanced the effect, working in tandem with the screen and the treadmill itself to complete the illusion of running somewhere other than in place in a room in the bowels of a starship. The treadmill reacted in real time to the runner's choice of speed, while simultaneously introducing resistance effects like inclines and slopes to further simulate various environments. Though Khatami had always preferred running out in the open over treadmills, she had grown to like this particular model, as it was more effective than the older versions in letting her run at her favored pace.

"I'm sure it's just a glitch," she said, wiping perspiration from her arms.

Wimmer gestured toward the unit. "Sometimes I think

they overcomplicate these things just to make my life difficult."

"If you're looking for excitement, security could always use someone with your skills and experience," Khatami said. "I know for a fact that Lieutenant Brax would love to have you. He's mentioned it to me several times, in fact."

Casting what Khatami took to be a knowing grin toward the deck, Wimmer replied, "I'm sure he has, and I'd be lying if I said I wasn't flattered by the offer, but I'm a little past my prime for wearing the red shirt, Captain. Better to let the younger, stronger folks handle that."

"Younger and stronger?" Khatami asked, reaching for a bottle of water she had left on the nearby bench. "Chief, you can outrun, out lift, and outfight nearly everyone aboard this ship, and probably without breaking a sweat." A human male in his late forties, as she recalled from his service record, Wimmer looked even younger thanks to what the ship's gossip mill had reported was an all but obsessive physical fitness regimen that encompassed running, resistance and strength training, yoga, and at least four different styles of martial arts, including jujitsu and *Suus Mahna*. He competed in marathons and martial arts tournaments, and though he tended to affect a humble persona, the trophies, certificates, and other awards filling his office did a fine job of validating the man's skills, accomplishments, and dedication.

Wimmer had reported for duty aboard the *Endeavour* while the starship was still undergoing repairs at Starbase 12 following the "Battle of Vanguard" in the Taurus Reach. When reading his service record while preparing for the usual "welcome aboard" meeting she held with each new crew member, Khatami had been surprised to note that the chief had served distinguished tours as a security officer aboard four different starships over a career spanning almost twenty years. Now he reported to Doctor Leone, and Wimmer and the rest of his department oversaw the *Endeavour*'s recreation areas along with its physical fitness and training facilities. Wimmer was also a licensed field medic and physical therapist, and Khatami knew he had spent time in sickbay assisting Leone as appropriate.

What had prompted this career change? One item in Wimmer's record offered a clue to his decision to transfer from security, which was listed as having taken place three years previously while he was assigned as a security officer to the *Kongo*. The file entry was redacted, and Khatami's attempts to obtain further details from Starfleet Command had been rebuffed due to "security concerns" that were outside the scope of her own clearance for sensitive information. She had received similar responses first from the *Kongo*'s commanding officer and later Wimmer himself when she asked about it during her first meeting with him. The chief had been more than apologetic about his inability to answer her questions, and Khatami knew better than to press the issue, as Wimmer likely was under orders never to discuss the matter without authorization.

Doesn't mean I can't be curious.

"If you change your mind," Khatami said between sips of her water, "don't hesitate to tell me. I'll have the transfer approved before you finish making the request."

Smiling, Wimmer nodded. "I'll remember that when my midlife crisis shows up, Captain." Once more, he gestured to the treadmill. "But first, I should probably fix this thing. I'm due in sickbay at eleven hundred hours to help Doctor Leone review physical therapy and exercise procedures. Starfleet Medical's distributed some new guidelines, and I've been helping the doctor go over it."

"I can only imagine how pleasant that's been," Khatami said. "If there's one thing Doctor Leone hates, it's paperwork of any sort."

"You should be happy about that," said a new voice, echoing across the gymnasium, and Khatami looked over her shoulder to see Anthony Leone walking toward them. "If I was better about keeping my files updated, I might notice that you still haven't shown up for your scheduled vaccinations." His dark, thinning hair was wet and slicked back, and he wore a robe of the sort available in the ship's locker rooms while carrying a damp blue towel in his left hand. Pale, almost skeletal legs extended from beneath the robe and ended in a pair of wide feet sheathed in a pair of sandals.

Khatami eyed him with amusement. "Did you get lost coming out of the shower?"

"On my way there, actually." Glancing to Wimmer, Leone said, "Chief, when you get a minute, can you check the pool's thermostat? I mean, unless you're trying to recreate the North Atlantic in there?"

"That cold?" Khatami asked. She knew that the *Endeavour*'s chief medical officer's preferred method of exercise was his almost daily visits to the ship's pool, where he was known to swim laps for more than an hour at a time.

"There are polar bears warmer than I am right now." The doctor nodded in the direction of the locker rooms. "If anybody's looking for me, I'll be spending my next shift in the sauna."

Wimmer chuckled. "I'll take a look as soon as I can, Doctor. Meanwhile, I just did a maintenance check on the UV beds, if you wanted to get a little sun."

Making a show of gesturing toward his pallid legs, Leone replied, "Thanks, but there's only so much skin I can expose to sunlight before I burst into flames." He indicated the treadmill simulator with a wave of his hand. "I see you've found a new toy, Captain."

"I like it, but we still have a few kinks to work out," Khatami replied. "Right, Chief?"

"It's on my To-Do List, Captain," replied the recreation officer, offering an informal salute. "I'll have it ready for you tomorrow morning."

Eyeing the treadmill, Leone said, "At least you're in here, rather than endangering innocent bystanders running through the ship without a shirt like some crazy person." As he spoke the words, his expression softened, and he released a small sigh. "There are days I really miss him."

"Me too," Khatami said.

"Do you mean Captain Zhao?" asked Wimmer. When Khatami nodded, the chief offered a single, solemn nod. "I served with him several years ago, when he was first officer on the *Excalibur*, and I was a junior security grunt."

He smiled. "He was doing that shirtless running thing even before he showed up there. That man could run you until you cried for mercy, and then he'd run you some more." Shaking his head, the chief looked away as though recalling a fond memory. "It was because of him that several of us started training and competing in marathons." With another laugh, he added, "Of course, he always beat us at those too."

Khatami found herself smiling at the chief's recollection of her friend and former commanding officer, Zhao Sheng. There still were times when she found it hard to believe that she had succeeded him as captain of the *Endeavour* after he was killed during an as-yet-classified mission to Erilon, a remote planet in the Taurus Reach. That ice-bound world had proven to be a key piece in the puzzle that was the mystery of the Shedai. An ancient race that had once ruled over a significant portion of the region located between the borders of Federation, Klingon, and Tholian territory, the Shedai were believed to have been extinct for millennia, but that turned out to be incorrect when evidence of the incredible technology the Shedai had once commanded came to light.

After the discovery of what had come to be known as the "Taurus Meta-Genome," a complex strand of artificially engineered DNA that was the source of the Shedai's unmatched grasp of genetic manipulation on a staggering scale, Starfleet had ordered a comprehensive investigation of the region and a search for anything connected to the enigmatic race. What no one had realized until it was far too late was that the Shedai, or at least representatives of their species, had lain dormant in a form of hibernation for thousands of years, and were angered by an abrupt awakening at the hands of interlopers into their realm. Operation Vanguard, the top-secret project that had resulted from that mandate, had exacted a steep price—lives lost, careers ruined, ships and entire worlds destroyed, political tensions between the Federation, Klingons, and Tholians heightened. Following the loss of Starbase 47, Starfleet had classified everything pertaining to the Shedai under the tightest security restrictions. As far as the general public was concerned, Operation Vanguard had never happened.

Except, of course, that it had, and many of those who knew most or all of the facts surrounding the project, including Khatami, questioned whether learning the Shedai's secrets had been worth the cost. She knew that some of what had been learned already was informing other research and development efforts, most of those also classified for this or that reason, but none of that would replace or repair the lives lost or permanently affected by what had happened here. Zhao Sheng was dead, and all that remained in the wake of the Shedai's apparent defeat at the Battle of Vanguard was to explore the region of space the mystifying civilization had left behind in the hopes of imparting some lasting worth to all the sacrifices made to get here. That was what had driven Khatami to accept the assignment, and she knew that similar motivation drove many among her crew, who had lost friends and shipmates as a consequence of the project.

And so it goes.

"I'm sorry about that," Leone said after the silence between the three of them had grown long enough to border on awkward. "I didn't mean to stomp on everyone's good mood."

Khatami shook her head. "It's okay, Tony. We should remember him, maybe honor him in some substantial way." She looked to Wimmer. "Perhaps a memorial marathon in his name?"

"I like it," replied the chief, nodding in approval.

"Do we all go shirtless?" Leone asked. "I'm asking for a friend."

Before Khatami could respond, either verbally or by reaching out and clapping her friend on the back of his head, the whistle of the ship's intercom sounded in the gymnasium, followed by the voice of Lieutenant Katherine Stano, the *Endeavour*'s first officer.

"Bridge to Captain Khatami."

"You just can't hide from these people, can you?" asked Leone.

Ignoring the doctor, Khatami crossed the gym floor to a nearby communications panel and thumbed the unit's activation switch. "Khatami here."

"Sorry to bother you before your shift, Captain, but it's important. We're receiving a distress call from the Cantrel system."

It took Khatami a moment to recall the name from the unrelenting stream of status reports flooding her desk and computer terminal on any given day. "We've got a colony there, right? Fourth or fifth planet? Along with some kind of long-term archaeology project?"

Stano replied, *"That's the one. Cantrel V is where the colony is, but the distress call's coming from a Starfleet science vessel, the* Aephas. *They report they've been attacked by an unknown alien ship that did a number on them."* After providing a summary of the information provided by the *Aephas*'s message and bringing Khatami up to speed on the current situation at the distant planet, the first officer said, *"Guess who's the closest ship?"*

"If you say the *Sagittarius* I'll give you a week's leave on Arcturus," said Khatami.

"No such luck. I've already computed course and speed; at warp six we can be there in less than nine hours."

Nine hours? If the colony was under attack, that interval would seem like nine centuries. Khatami asked, "Who's the captain of the *Aephas*?"

"Commander al-Khaled, from the Lovell," said Stano. *"He and some of the crew from that ship took a temp assignment while Starfleet figures out what to do with his Corps of Engineers detachment."*

"Lucky him," said Leone, who had moved to stand beside Khatami at the comm panel. "Nice quiet assignment after Vanguard. Somebody in personnel owes him a big fat apology."

With the towel she still held, Khatami wiped her face once more before saying, "Notify the *Aephas* we're on our way. Take us to warp six, and tell engineering I'm going to want more and I don't care how I get it. I'll be there in twenty minutes, and I'll want regular updates from all departments on our preparations until we make orbit."

"Aye, Captain," acknowledged Stano, her voice crisp. The first officer was in full attack mode now, and Kha-

tami pitied anyone who got between her and the tasks she was setting out to complete. *"I'm on it. Bridge out."*

Pressing the switch to deactivate the panel, Khatami turned to Leone, who had dropped his usual sardonic expression. Before she could say anything, the doctor held up a hand.

"I'm already thinking about a trauma team and making up a list of what we'll probably need from ship's stores. Until I hear otherwise, I figure we'll be setting up a full-blown field hospital down there. We'll treat the worst casualties on site and get them stabilized, then beam the ones needing more comprehensive care to our sickbay." He pursed his lips. "It could get pretty crowded."

"We'll worry about that when the time comes," Khatami said. Looking over her shoulder, she saw Wimmer still standing behind them, near the treadmill. "Sorry, Chief. Duty calls."

The recreation officer turned to Leone. "We're not going to be needing any gym equipment fixed, Doc. Put me to work."

Leone grunted. "Gladly. I'll let you know." As he and Khatami turned to head for the locker rooms, he said, "The marathon was a great idea, by the way. Too bad it'll have to wait until we're done with whatever this is."

"Yeah," replied Khatami, her mind already racing as she considered what the next several hours would bring to *Endeavour* once they reached Cantrel V and got their first look at the situation. It was almost a given that time would be a valuable commodity, and few if any of them would be getting much sleep in the coming days.

With that in mind and before she had a chance to forget, Khatami reached over and gave the back of Leone's head a playful slap.

With a sidelong glance, the doctor eyed her with confusion. "What was that for?"

"You and *your friend* know what it's for."

4

"We need to go, Morgan. *Right now!*"

Morgan LeMons felt herself more dragged than escorted from her office, her upper arm gripped by her assistant, Ethan Barbree, as he all but pulled her into the narrow hallway. There, LeMons saw other members of the Tài Shan colony's administrative and support staff leaving their own offices and other workspaces and heading for the exits.

"Did the evacuation order go out?" she asked, talking to the back of Barbree's head as her aide guided her down the passageway. "Are the ships preparing to leave?"

"Most of them are already gone," Barbree replied without looking at her. "They're heading for the other side of the planet for the time being, where their captains will wait for further instructions. A couple of shuttles are still at the landing port."

LeMons said, "Tell them to get clear. I'm staying here."

"Morgan," Barbree said, now turning to regard her even though he kept them both moving. "We have to get you—"

"I'm not leaving," she snapped. "There aren't enough ships to get everyone clear, so the rest of us will just have to use the bunkers." Her statement drew some looks from others in the hallway, and LeMons saw the expressions of appreciation and even a smile, as though the stress they all were feeling was being held at bay if only for a fleeting moment.

At twenty-eight, LeMons was one of the youngest administrators overseeing an active Federation colony. Having grown up on Ophiucus III, she and her family were no strangers to "life on the frontier," and even as a teen she had been interested in the logistics of overseeing such outposts. After attending university on Mars, she had volunteered to be a part of the established Mantilles colony, undergoing an internship under that outpost's administrator and eventually succeeding him in the role. When it was announced that the Federation would be expanding into the Taurus Reach, LeMons had applied to be an administrator to one of those proposed colonies, and a recommendation from her former mentor on Mantilles had seen to it that she was appointed to Cantrel V. She had arrived here two years ago with the initial pair of ships, and she was the first to set foot on the planet as a representative of what would become the colony of Tài Shan.

And nobody's chasing me off.

"Are people getting into the bunkers?" she asked as they made their way along with other members of her staff into one of the stairwells leading from the administration building's third level and, in this case, outside to an entrance allowing access to one of the emergency shelters that had been constructed in the bedrock beneath the colony.

"Yes," Barbree replied, and for the first time LeMons heard tension in her aide's voice. "I'm getting constant updates from each shelter's manager, as well as from Commander al-Khaled." He turned, and his gaze locked with hers. "We don't have a lot of time."

It took LeMons an extra second to comprehend the implication behind his words. She stepped to one side of the narrow stairwell, allowing others to pass as she pulled Barbree close and spoke in a low voice into his ear. "How many?"

"Close to a hundred, at last report," replied her assistant. "Most of them are trying to secure or protect fragile equipment, and others are coordinating the clearing of the landing port."

"Get them into the bunkers, now," LeMons said through her clenched jaw, mindful of the echo in the stairwell. "Tell them to drop everything and go. That other crap can wait." The network of underground shelters, installed by Starfleet's Corps of Engineers before the first permanent buildings had been erected on the planet's surface, were designed to withstand everything from harsh storms and even earthquakes up to and including orbital bombardment. In the wake of attacks on Federation colonies across the quadrant, and in particular the Taurus Reach, Starfleet had insisted on providing the hearty structures. Though similar facilities of varying effectiveness had been constructed on other colony worlds, including one or two she had visited in her travels, LeMons had never given serious thought to their use. Her feelings on that had changed upon learning about the political tensions between the Federation, Klingons, and Tholians as each side fought to assert influence within the Taurus Reach. While that reality had not dissuaded her desire to head up one of the colonies to be established in the contested area, she was not a fool.

Starfleet, despite its best intentions and the resources at its disposal, could not be everywhere. Not for the first time since its arrival, she was grateful for the *U.S.S. Aephas*, in orbit above Cantrel V and at this moment facing off against the mysterious alien vessel.

Holding his personal communicator to his ear, Barbree divided his attention between making sure LeMons stayed with him and getting updates from situation managers across the colony who were charged with overseeing a particular shelter or other area of the outpost.

"We've still got stragglers," he reported after a few moments. "Another all-call's been sent colony-wide."

LeMons paused as they reached a landing. "What about the *Aephas*? Any word from Commander al-Khaled?"

"Not since he sent that last warning." The most recent updates sent by Commander al-Khaled indicated that his ship had sustained considerable damage and was attempting to provide whatever cover or distraction it could even as the alien ship maneuvered into position far above Tài Shan.

With Barbree leading the way, LeMons descended the last of the stairs and the pair made their way out of the administration building and into the large courtyard dominating the settlement's north end. Almost a dozen members of her staff were already moving toward the nearest underground shelter, the entrance to which was a reinforced pressure hatch set into a collar of thick thermo-concrete. Shelter Alpha, designated for LeMons, her staff, and everyone else working in the main building, was one of seven such bunkers scattered around the colony's perimeter. The structure was connected to the others by subterranean passages put into place by the Corps of Engineers teams. Each shelter was designed to hold fifty people, with enough supplies to last two weeks. The Tài Shan settlement was home to more than four hundred people, but the evacuation and emergency plan called for nearly seventy-five colonists to be aboard the transport ships and shuttlecraft supporting the colony.

"Everybody inside!" LeMons shouted, gesturing toward the now open hatchway, where a member of the colony's security detachment stood waving for people to proceed to the entrance. Despite the urgency of the moment, she could not help looking around the courtyard and at the buildings flanking it. A mixture of residential and work areas, the "town square" had become the heart of the colony, a gathering place for festivals, parties, and celebrations of every sort. The care with which the grass, trees, and other foliage were treated had turned the quad into a sanctuary of hope and promise that was mirrored by the rest of the settlement and the people who called it home. Would any of this be here in a few hours? Would everything she and her friends and colleagues had worked for during the last two years be for naught?

LeMons felt a hand on her arm and turned to see Barbree, his expression now more fearful as he held his communicator out for her.

"Commander al-Khaled," was all he said.

Taking the communicator, LeMons held it close and asked, "Commander?"

"Morgan! The ship has settled into orbit. They're arm-

*ing weapons and it looks like they're targeting the colony.
There's nothing we can do to stop them from firing. Are
your people under cover?"*

Instead of replying, LeMons ran toward the shelter entrance, grabbing anyone still standing nearby and shoving
them in that direction. "Everybody inside! *Get inside!"*
Even though she knew she likely would not be able to see
the alien craft hovering somewhere high above the planet,
she still looked upward, searching for this invisible threat.
There was nothing but crystal blue sky and powder white
clouds, reminding her of those first moments on Cantrel V
two years ago. Her ship had landed not far from where she
now stood, and she had looked to the sky, smiling at the
promise this world held, along with the secrets she hoped
one day to uncover.

Then something flashed in the sky, and a heartbeat later
thunder roared in her ears as the first energy burst drilled
into the middle of the courtyard. Dirt and rock along with
trees and grass exploded outward in all directions from
the point of impact, revealing a crater ten meters wide.
Screams from those colonists still on the surface pierced
the air and LeMons turned to see the security officer
grabbing at people's arms and pulling them toward the
shelter entrance.

"Move!" the man was yelling. "Move move *move!"*

Another ball of crimson fury rained down from the
sky, tearing into the two-story dormitory that provided
temporary housing for transport ships and other visitors.
Glass from every window in the structure burst outward,
and every door was ripped from its frame. The building
began collapsing in on itself, joined seconds later by the

smaller one-level structure that had housed the colony's security office.

"Morgan! Come on!"

Barbree's hand was once more gripping her arm, and LeMons felt herself being pulled toward the shelter's hatch. In her peripheral vision, she saw the security officer reaching toward her just as something bright and hot flashed behind her, blinding her as a rush of displaced air howled in her ears.

Her lungs burned. Her legs cramped. Her entire stomach felt as though it might erupt up and out through her mouth. Despite all of this, Colleen Cook ran.

"Everybody into the cavern!" she shouted between huge gulps of air as she crested one of the small hills at the far end of the ancient crater, gesturing toward the dozen or so people she saw scrambling for cover. Ahead of her, other members of the archaeology team were plunging into the three tunnels that had been dug into this part of Beta Site, while others stood at the entrances and waited for their companions to reach safety. To her right, Cook caught sight of T'Naal, sprinting across the open ground like an Academy marathon finalist toward the farthest of the tunnels and gesturing with both hands for people to get to cover.

"Lieutenant!" a voice shouted, and Cook saw Zeturild-tra ch'Dran standing at the mouth of the tunnel closest to her, waving toward her. The ensign held a communicator in his other hand, its antenna grid open. "Hurry!"

Stopping just outside the entrance, Cook gasped for air

and resisted the urge to bend over and put her hands on her knees. Instead, she turned and checked the crater and the nearby shelters, looking for stragglers. She saw no one else out in the open. From her jumpsuit's pocket, she extracted her communicator and flipped it open.

"Cook to T'Naal!"

A moment later the Vulcan replied, *"T'Naal here, Lieutenant. Everyone here at the site has taken shelter underground. I am getting reports from the base camp that our people are evacuating in the shuttles."*

It was an imperfect plan, but for now, it would have to do. Making her way toward the tunnel where ch'Dran waited, Cook asked, "Any word from Tài Shan?"

"Only that the colonists are seeking shelter in the underground bunkers. That process is still under way."

"Take everyone with you and head for the main cavern," Cook said. A base of operations, similar to the one in the crater, had been established there a week earlier to provide support for team members working underground. It had some rations and water, and would serve as a rally point once the current situation—whatever it turned out to be—had passed.

Gesturing to ch'Dran, she said, "Make sure everyone's accounted for." She then tapped a control on her communicator. "Cook to *Aephas*." A moment later, the voice of the science vessel's commanding officer replied.

"Aephas here. This is al-Khaled. The alien vessel is firing on the colony, and we've been severely damaged. We're trying to get back into the fight, but it's taking us time. Be aware that our sensors have picked up the ship scanning the surface, and your area might be a target."

"You're sure, sir?" Cook asked.

"As sure as we can be with compromised sensors." There was a pause, and Cook heard an alarm klaxon through the open frequency before al-Khaled came back. *"Where are your people?"*

"We're all underground, except for our shuttles, which I've sent away from our base camp with instructions to rendezvous with the colony support ships."

"Okay. Keep your heads down until further notice. We're ready to make another run at that ship. Al-Khaled out."

The link was severed, leaving Cook to stare at her communicator. How dire was the situation up there, and what about Tài Shan? If it was being attacked at this very moment, how were the colonists faring? Had they all made it to the emergency shelters or the ships being dispersed to the far side of the planet? Should she attempt to make contact?

Such thoughts were shattered as a string of energy blasts slammed into the bottom of the crater, shaking the ground beneath her feet and sending Cook dashing heading for the relative safety of the tunnel and the caverns belowground.

"All right, people," al-Khaled said, sitting ramrod straight in his command chair. "We've got one last shot at this. Let's make it a good one."

Once more, the image of the enormous alien ship loomed on the bridge's main viewscreen. Damage to three of the vessel's five spheres was evident, testifying to Lieutenant Rodriguez's earlier targeting prowess, though that was small comfort as al-Khaled considered the onslaught to which the Tài Shan colony and a few of the outlying archaeological sites were being subjected. Behind him, Ensign Pzial continued to field the constant influx of status messages coming from the surface as colonists as well as the Starfleet and civilian science teams endured the punishing orbital bombardment.

"Shields at seventy-six percent," reported Rodriguez from the helm station. "And dropping, sir, along with main power at eighty-eight percent and falling. Weapons are eighty-two percent and holding."

The weapons would begin experiencing the same power drain once the shields gave out, al-Khaled knew. Any attempt to force the alien ship to break off its attack had to happen now. "Divert all shield power forward," he ordered, "and be ready to shift to our flanks once we complete our run. We'll just have to make do."

From the communications station, Pzial said, "Sir, Commander Grace is advising that we not spend too long within range of the ship on any one attack run. He reports that our power levels are continuing to fluctuate, and if we sustain any more damage we could end up crippled."

"Acknowledged," al-Khaled replied. After its first skirmish and having to withdraw to a safe distance to avoid further damage, the *Aephas*'s chief engineer and his staff had been hard-pressed to repair even the most critical systems so that the ship could get back in the fight and at least try to defend the colony. Despite valiant effort, Grace had been unable to restore shield power before the alien vessel assumed orbit and commenced firing on the planet's surface. Al-Khaled had been forced to weigh the risks of holding back for much-needed repairs or attempting to confront the mysterious ship at something less than full strength. The dampening field and its debilitative effects had been the deciding factor, as al-Khaled surmised that allowing the *Aephas* to lose all power would only serve to leave it a vulnerable target for further attack.

Tell that to the people down below.

"We're approaching weapons range, Commander," reported Rodriguez.

Standing at his station's sensor viewer, Lieutenant Xav added, "The ship is still firing at the surface. I am detecting multiple strikes both at the colony and the main excavation site."

"So, it is deliberately targeting our people," al-Khaled said. At some point very soon, once this situation had been returned to some measure of control, he vowed that someone on that vessel would answer for the unprovoked attack.

"Initiate your run," al-Khaled said.

The helm officer nodded. "Aye, sir." She pressed several controls on her console in rapid succession, and in response to her commands al-Khaled watched the viewscreen's perspective shift as the *Aephas* rolled into the first of its evasive maneuvers. In orbit above Cantrel V, the enormous alien craft was continuing its bombardment of the planet below, though even now al-Khaled could see that the intensity of the attack had diminished. There was a longer interval between each new strike, and when the ship did fire, it did so with fewer shots. Was its assault coming to an end? Did that mean it had destroyed everything and everyone it had come to vanquish, or was it just having a harder time finding targets now that it had meted out so much wanton destruction?

Focus, Commander.

Leaning forward in his chair, al-Khaled rested his elbows on his thighs. "All right, Lieutenant. Get us clear, quick as you can. No loitering."

"Aye, sir," Rodriguez acknowledged. Following the scheme they had devised while Grace and his team finalized repairs, and using the data provided by Xav to help determine the best points of attack for inflicting the most damage in the least amount of time, she released a barrage of phaser fire. The blue-white beams lanced across open space, flanked by two groups of four photon torpedoes the lieutenant unleashed at the same time. Rather than firing a spread at multiple targets as they had during the previous engagement, Rodriguez now concentrated the entire salvo on one of Xav's selected targets. The results were immediate, with the phasers ripping into the surface of the alien vessel's foremost sphere and the framework connecting it to the rest of the ship as the eight torpedoes hammered at points along the hull encircling the phasers' impact points.

"Nice shooting, Lieutenant!"

Not responding to the praise, Rodriguez instead remained focused on her console, guiding the *Aephas* into another roll that was so severe al-Khaled was certain he felt the strain on the ship's artificial gravity and inertial damping systems. On the screen, he saw several bursts of energy fired in retaliation, and an instant later his chair shivered beneath him, channeling the reverberations coursing through the ship's hull as the shields absorbed the brunt of the attack. Al-Khaled heard Rodriguez utter a rather vile Andorian oath as she fought her console and attempted to guide the *Aephas* to safety.

Xav said, "I am reading power fluctuations over there. That strike must have hit something important." A moment later, he added, "Our shield strength is dropping again, Commander. It is already down to fifty-four percent. Main power at seventy-nine percent and falling. We are still too close."

"One more go," al-Khaled replied. They were here now, and even with shields at half strength, he felt certain they could score more hits on the alien ship. "Besides, look." He gestured toward the screen, where the vessel was hanging in orbit above Cantrel V. "It's not firing at the planet. Take us in for another pass, helm."

More phaser fire and another round of torpedoes streaked toward the other vessel, and al-Khaled saw the damage inflicted on its hull as the *Aephas* whipped past, already shifting into the evasive maneuvers Rodriguez had programmed. Other weapons ports along the other ship's length were coming to life. Multiple shots slammed into the deflector shields with such force that al-Khaled was driven back into his chair, and he felt the deck disappear beneath his feet. Lights flickered all around the bridge, and new alarms began clamoring for attention.

"We're clear, sir!" Rodriguez shouted over the noise.

Calling for the klaxons to be silenced, al-Khaled rose from his chair and turned to Pzial. "Collect damage reports from all departments."

"They are already coming in, Commander," replied

the Rigelian communications officer. "Engineering reports damage to our shield generators and impulse drive, as well as several other key systems. However, the power drain has ceased now that we are away from the alien ship."

"What about the other ship, Xav?" asked al-Khaled, stepping toward the science station.

The Tellarite turned from his console. "According to our scans, our last two strikes inflicted significant damage. I am detecting power loss in the ship's forward sphere as well as some of the framework connecting it to the other pods."

"Is the power loss contained to that one section?" When Xav's eyes narrowed in response to the question, al-Khaled added, "You mentioned earlier that each pod is fairly self-contained, so I'm wondering if damaging or destroying one has any effect on the others?"

Xav replied, "So far, the other pods appear to be operating, two of them at reduced efficiency thanks to our actions, but without more detailed knowledge of the vessel's internal configuration or system dependencies, I can only speculate how this level of damage might impair its overall operation."

"You could've just said you don't know," al-Khaled said, then smiled. "Sorry. Just trying to lighten the mood."

"Which mood?" The science officer grunted. "I have but one mood, and its reaction to gravity remains constant."

Despite the current situation, al-Khaled could not help a small grin. "Well played, Xav."

"Commander," said Ensign Pzial, "we are receiving

new hails from the surface. Administrator LeMons is requesting aid at the colony, as there is much damage and many injuries. She reports that their clinic and medical personnel are among the casualties."

"Damn." The *Aephas*, being a dedicated science vessel and not a ship of the line, was equipped with a decent enough sickbay and a first rate medical staff, but al-Khaled knew that neither was intended for any sort of emergency or trauma situation such as what likely awaited them at the Tài Shan colony.

"Pzial, notify Doctor Sanborn of the situation on the ground, and tell her she's authorized to pull anything and anyone she thinks she needs to aid in relief efforts. It's her show. I know we're not really equipped for this sort of thing, but all we have to do is hold things together until the *Endeavour* gets here."

Xav, still standing at his station, gestured toward the viewscreen and the image of the now seemingly inert alien ship. "What of our friend over there?"

Crossing his arms, al-Khaled leaned against the bridge railing. "Let's just hope it behaves itself until we get things put back together."

"And what if it chooses not to do so?"

Al-Khaled sighed. "One crisis at a time, Xav. One crisis at a time."

5

It was not until Lieutenant Marielise McCormack turned and looked at her that Khatami realized she had been tapping the nail of her right forefinger on the arm of her command chair and that the resulting sound was loud enough to carry across the bridge. When she halted the unconscious movement, Khatami noted several glances from officers at other workstations and even a few knowing smiles. She offered her navigator a sheepish grin.

"Sorry, Lieutenant. My apologies, everyone. It's not my fault that you all do your jobs so well that I'm left with nothing to do here." Her comment elicited a handful of chuckles from around the room. Rising from her seat, Khatami stepped out of the command well and began a slow circuit of the bridge's upper deck stations. Though her people were quite efficient at keeping her informed about the status of every shipboard system, she had long ago grown accustomed to seeing things for herself. It was a habit she had acquired even before her initial tour as first officer of the *Perseus*, but it was her captain who had taught her the critical line to be drawn between wanting firsthand knowledge and micromanaging one's subordinates. She had become quite adept at the latter as a squad leader at Starfleet Academy and later a junior officer and department head.

It was during her first assignment as a starship's

second-in-command that she had refined the art of delegating authority and mentoring those in her charge, trusting them to carry out their duties without constant, unneeded, and likely unwanted oversight. Starfleet did not produce incompetent officers, after all, but it was incumbent upon leaders to remember that as they continued their climb up the chain of command. It was a lesson that was reinforced when she reported for duty aboard the *Endeavour* and observed Captain Zhao Sheng's leadership style. That man had run a tight ship, all the more efficient because he had fostered an environment in which the men and women under his command knew without question what was expected of them, and he allowed them all reasonable latitude to accomplish their duties without his needing to supervise their every move. Khatami and Zhao had meshed as a team from the outset, and his influence remained despite his being dead for more than three years. She had continued fostering that same atmosphere after her own appointment as the *Endeavour*'s commanding officer.

Wherever you are, Sheng, I hope you're proud of our crew.

"Captain," said Lieutenant Neelakanta, her Arcturian helm officer, as he looked over his shoulder in her direction. "We've entered the Cantrel system."

Nodding, Khatami turned from her inspection of the bridge's environmental control station. "Take us out of warp and proceed to Cantrel V at full impulse. Shields up, Mister Neelakanta. I don't want to take any chances."

"Aye, Captain."

From where he sat at the bridge's communications station, Lieutenant Hector Estrada said, "Captain, we're being hailed by the *Aephas*."

Khatami moved back down to the command well to where she could stand in front of the helm and navigation stations to face the main viewscreen. "Patch him through, Lieutenant."

The image on the screen shifted from one of space to that of Commander Mahmud al-Khaled. He looked older than when she had last seen him, with new lines creasing his face and more gray in his dark hair. It took her a moment to realize that her last encounter with al-Khaled had also been with his former captain, Daniel Okagawa, and other members of the *Lovell*'s crew following that ship's destruction prior to the loss of Starbase 47. Al-Khaled and his shipmates had been transferred to Starbase 11 and been dispersed to various other ships and duty assignments before the *Endeavour* had arrived at the space station for its own extended stay.

"Captain Khatami," said al-Khaled, smiling out from the viewscreen, *"it's nice to see you again. I just wish it could be under better circumstances."* He paused and looked at something Khatami could not see before adding, *"You're here faster than we estimated. Thanks for coming so quickly."* He appeared exhausted, with smudges of dirt or grease on his face and gold uniform tunic that told Khatami he had been taking his usual hands-on approach to assisting with the repairs to his ship's systems.

Once an engineer, and all that.

"I'm just glad we were in a position to offer assistance,"

she said. "As for getting here, I had my engineer get out and give our nacelles a couple of swift kicks for good measure."

"A time-tested technique, Captain," replied al-Khaled, offering a tired smile. *"I've used it myself, once or twice."*

Stepping closer to the railing separating her from the main viewscreen, Khatami asked, "How are you and your people holding up?"

"It's been a busy day. My medical staff was down at the colony as fast as we could get them there after the attack, and I have engineering teams assessing damage and determining which structures are safe. An area near the colony experienced a minor earthquake the previous night, so there already were complications from that at the excavation site where the archaeology teams were working."

"How many casualties?"

On the screen, al-Khaled sighed. *"The colony's administrator has reported three deaths so far, and there are between sixty and seventy injured. Another dozen or so remain unaccounted for."* He paused, and Khatami watched his Adam's apple bob as he swallowed. *"The underground shelters Starfleet constructed when the colony was first being set up did their jobs, for the most part, with one exception. We think the alien ship's sensors must have locked on to the life readings inside and targeted its location, because it absolutely hammered that bunker. It held, but there was some buckling inside the structure. That's where the majority of the casualties came from. It could've been worse, but we managed to inflict enough damage for it to break off its attack. For now, anyway."*

"My people are already prepared to beam down to give you some help," Khatami said. Out of the corner of her eye, she saw her science officer, Lieutenant Stephen Klisiewicz, stepping down to stand beside her. Noting his expression, she gestured toward the screen.

"Hello, Commander," said Klisiewicz. "Good to see you."

Al-Khaled nodded. *"Same here. I'm guessing you want to hear about the ship?"*

"Yes, sir," replied the science officer. "Have you learned anything new?"

Blowing out his breath, al-Khaled shook his head. *"Not really. We've been focusing almost all of our people and resources toward helping the colony and addressing our own repairs. I haven't had time to investigate it more. It sustained damage during our fight with it, and the dampening field that was giving us such fits earlier seems to have gone inactive. Their power output has diminished also, to the point that our sensors are barely reading anything. However, we've figured out that the ship's hull contains high concentrations of mendelevium, which is acting to block most of our scans. My engineer thinks he can figure out a workaround, but he's been busy."*

Klisiewicz said, "I'm sure our engineer would love to take a crack at that, Commander." When he noticed Khatami eyeing him, he added, "Once we've addressed your repairs and whatever else might be needed down on the surface, of course."

"We're actually doing okay up here," al-Khaled said, *"but my CMO and her staff could definitely use all the help you can spare."* He gestured to something off screen.

"As for that ship, whatever the reason it's here, it went straight after our people on the ground. It's been quiet since the attacks, but I'm doubting it'll stay that way forever."

Nodding, Khatami replied, "I was thinking the same thing, Commander." Even with the *Aephas*'s pressing repairs and the obvious need for help on the surface, she was not about to let the alien vessel go uninvestigated. The last thing she wanted was for the thing to suddenly come back to life and start shooting again. "Mister Klisiewicz, we'll get you close enough to run some scans, but at this point I'm guessing our best bet for learning anything is to go over there and have a look around."

The science officer said, "Agreed, Captain. I'll get started on that."

"Thank you, Captain." Al-Khaled offered another weary smile. *"We appreciate it. Everything."*

Khatami said, "Happy to be of service, Commander. Tell your people they can rest a little easier. Help's on the way."

Once the communication was concluded, Khatami turned to Klisiewicz. "Have Commander Yataro help you with your initial scans of that ship. I want as much information as we can squeeze out of the sensors before I send anybody over there." She knew that the *Endeavour*'s chief engineer would be more than eager to be on any boarding party she sent over to the mysterious vessel, but she suspected the Lirin's time would become a valuable commodity in short order.

Klisiewicz said, "Understood, though if Commander al-Khaled's right and that ship's hull contains a nice thick plating of mendelevium, we're going to have a hell of a time reconfiguring our sensors to penetrate it. That material is notorious for its resistance to scans and transporters." He paused, and Khatami watched as his gaze shifted to his console as though he were pondering some new thought that had just occurred to him. "On the other hand, if the *Aephas* was able to penetrate the hull with its weapons, it may have weakened it at those points just enough for us to maybe tune our sensors to a narrow, focused beam to get through. I can't guarantee we'll get back anything useful, but it's worth a shot."

"Start shooting, Lieutenant," Khatami said.

Blood, suffering, and death were all around her, closing in and threatening to pull her into the depths of some unyielding abyss. What the hell was wrong with her? Why did it feel as though the very air was fleeing not just from her lungs but the entire room?

Holly Amos was going to vomit.

"Nurse!"

Ignoring the startled cry, Amos stumbled back from the operating table, only just avoiding upsetting a tray of medical instruments as she lunged for the emergency shelter's exit. Another nurse, a male—someone she did not recognize—reached out as though to offer assistance but she staggered past him, through the shelter's front door flap and out onto the open ground. More than a dozen similar structures had been erected here at the center of the Tài Shan colony, the largest open space in close proximity to the settlement's main power generators and water treatment facilities. Crew members from the *Aephas* had made quick work tying into those utilities to establish the first shelters for their temporary camp, with their efforts supplemented by the *Endeavour*'s arrival and subsequent transporting of engineers and other support personnel to the surface.

For all the work those people had done, Amos was only interested in the cargo container situated near the corner of the shelter she had just evacuated, and which was designated for garbage. It was going to be the perfect place to throw up.

Ignoring the curious stares of various onlookers, Amos lurched from the shelter's entrance and all but fell against the container, gulping for air and fighting the urge to unleash the contents of her stomach. Only then did she remember that she was still wearing her field surgical mask, and she reached up to remove it and the cap she wore to keep her hair covered. The need to retch was fading, but she still winced at the knots in her stomach, and she wondered if her lunch might still decide to make a surprise appearance.

"Lieutenant Amos."

Looking up from the garbage container, Amos saw Doctor Leone walking toward her. Like her and the rest of the personnel working inside the shelter, the *Endeavour*'s chief medical officer was dressed in field surgical scrubs, and he had pulled his protective mask from his face to let it hang around his neck. His expression was a mixture of concern and irritation, and she nodded as she took in another deep breath.

"I'm sorry, Doctor. I don't know what came over me in there."

Leone stepped closer, casting an eye into the container. "You didn't throw up?"

"Not yet," said Amos, shaking her head. "Haven't ruled it out, though."

"Well, just wait until dinner. If you can choke one of those down and keep it from staging a mutiny in your gut, you'll be able to handle anything."

Amos blew out her breath. "I've never reacted like that before."

His eyes narrowing, Leone frowned. "Seen a lot of trauma patients, have you?"

The queasiness was fading, and she was feeling more like her old self. "I know you like to give me grief for being so upbeat all the time, Doctor, but I'm a trained nurse. This isn't my first time dealing with serious injuries."

"But it's your first time seeing injuries like this, right?" Leone hooked a thumb over his shoulder to indicate the shelter behind him. It was serving as the operating room for the field hospital he and the *Endeavour* landing party had erected to augment the facilities already set up by Doctor Janice Sanborn and the rest of the *Aephas*'s overburdened medical staff.

It took Amos a moment to realize that Leone might be onto something. "We studied simulations at nursing school, of course, but . . . you're right. I've never had to deal with what we're seeing here for real." She recalled the patient lying on the field surgical table in the shelter—

the one from which she had just fled—with the meter-long metal shard jutting out from his side and the ragged, bloody mess of tortured skin and muscle surrounding it. The man had lost a dangerous amount of blood, and was being kept alive by chemical stimulants used to accelerate the reproduction of humanoid blood cells. Such drugs were still largely in the experimental stage, but Doctor Sanborn had opted to use them on those patients with the most traumatic injuries in the hopes of sustaining them long enough for her and her team to provide the needed surgery.

By comparison, even the most serious injuries Amos had seen firsthand since graduating from Starfleet Academy and her medical training courses had not been as gruesome as what *Aephas* and *Endeavour* personnel were handling right now. The scene around the field hospital was like something out of a war from ages past, with colonists lying about like soldiers and waiting to be treated based on the severity of their wounds. The *Aephas* nurses and medics had conducted the initial triage within the first few hours after the attack, and had been treating patients without pause since then. Doctor Leone and his team had provided a much-needed measure of relief, helping to keep things moving. A post-operative ward had been established next to the surgery shelter, and Amos had already familiarized herself with its layout and the several dozen beds set up there to provide patient aftercare. Even with bone knitters and dermal regenerators to help with the various broken and severed limbs and burns and other assorted wounds, the scene in the post-op area still was grim, with patients forced to stay there until space became available aboard the *Aephas*. With the *Endeavour* now on hand to provide assistance, the starship's sickbay and other large rooms were in the process of receiving the influx of patients. According to the best guesses offered by Doctors Leone and Sanborn, the last of the victims requiring surgery should be treated before nightfall.

Maybe you could help with that, Lieutenant? It's what you signed up for, remember? Though she had joined Starfleet knowing she would encounter such ghastly injuries, she had not expected it to happen so soon, and with such great numbers. Even when Doctor Leone had first told her and the rest of the medical staff what they would be facing once they arrived on the surface, the sheer brutality visited upon some of the more unfortunate colonists was simply more than what Amos had anticipated.

Drawing another deep breath, she reached up to wipe her eyes. "I thought I could handle it, but . . ."

"You can handle it," Leone said. "At least, you will. Now that you've been hit by the initial shock, your brain's already figuring out how to process that kind of information so that next time you can keep moving, instead of freezing up or running away and leaving your doctor in the middle of an operation. Trust me when I tell you that sort of thing doesn't bode well for any birthday presents I might plan on giving you."

Despite her lingering unease, Amos could not help the small laugh the doctor's comments elicited. "Thank you, Doctor. I appreciate it."

"You sure you're okay?" asked Leone.

Amos nodded. "I'm much better now."

"Ready to get back to work?"

"I think so."

"Good." The doctor reached up to wipe perspiration from his forehead. "Then can we go back inside? It's damned hot out here. Besides, we're almost done. Three more patients and then those field rations I promised you. And you say I never take you anywhere."

Laughing again, Amos reached out and landed a playful swat to Leone's arm. "You should be careful, Doctor. Your reputation for being difficult and surly all the time will be ruined."

"Hey, I've worked very hard to cultivate that reputation. If anybody asks, you tell them I chewed you out and dragged you back to work. Let's go."

She turned to follow him, and they were almost to the shelter's entrance when the flap was pulled aside and another figure dressed in field scrubs stepped out. Even with her field mask and cap still in place, Amos recognized her as Doctor Janice Sanborn. When she caught sight of Leone and Amos, she nodded in their direction before releasing a long, audible yawn.

"Sorry," she said as she removed her cap and mask. "Nobody should have to endure that." Now freed, her long, black hair tumbled past her shoulders, and she regarded Amos with blue-gray eyes that seemed ready to drill through her. She had dark circles under her eyes, and she walked with a slight stoop to her shoulders, all evidence to the near-constant strain she had been under since arriving on the surface.

"Lieutenant? You all right?"

Amos nodded. "Yes, Doctor. I sincerely apologize for that. That's never happened to me before. I guess I was just caught off guard." Though she was expecting some form of rebuke, Sanborn instead reached out and placed a hand on her arm.

"We've all been there, Lieutenant. Even Tony here's had his less than stellar moments."

Casting a sidelong glance toward Leone, Amos asked, "You two know each other?"

Sanborn replied, "We were both assigned to the hospital on Starbase 9 about a million years ago." She bobbed her eyebrows. "If he starts riding you too hard, just ask him about the time we had to—"

"Not another word, Janice," said Leone, his eyes narrowing even though Amos saw the hint of a small grin at the corners of his mouth.

Pausing, Sanborn shrugged before looking again to Amos. "If he ever gets too full of himself, just say, 'Rigelian fungus.' I guarantee that'll change the subject."

"You understand that there's an entire planet of undeveloped land around us, right?" Leone asked, shaking his head and gesturing toward the mountains far beyond the colony. "All that uninhabited planet, with countless places to hide a body."

"Ignore him," Sanborn said to Amos, pointing her thumb at Leone. "He'll never admit it, but beneath that gruff shell hides the heart of a big teddy bear. I've seen it with my own eyes."

Leone shook his head. "Not true. All witnesses were silenced."

Any retort Sanborn or Amos might have offered was interrupted by a sudden tremor all around them, and Amos felt the ground rumbling beneath her feet at the same time she saw several of the temporary shelters beginning to sway back and forth. A quick look around confirmed that the rest of the tents were doing the same thing, and one cargo container stacked atop another tumbled to the dirt.

"Earthquake!" yelled someone Amos could not see. All around her, colonists as well as men and women in Starfleet uniforms were running around the courtyard or between buildings or shelters.

Reaching to steady herself against the surgical shelter, Sanborn said, "It's an aftershock. There was one earlier this morning that was about the same level of intensity, and a couple of the colonists tell me they don't last very long."

As quickly as it began, the tremor began to fade, and Amos was already hearing calls for assistance from different locations around the compound. By the time the aftershock had ceased, and with the exception of the increased activity across the courtyard, it was as though the minor quake had not happened at all.

Almost.

"Doctor Sanborn!"

The voice shouting from inside the shelter was enough to send all three of them running for the entrance, and as they drew closer, the sounds of someone crying out in pain grew more distinct. Sanborn was the first inside, and by the time Amos entered the makeshift operating area both she and Leone were hovering over one of the patients who had been waiting for surgery.

"What the hell happened?" asked Leone, not looking up from where he and Sanborn were examining the patient's right leg. Amos recalled that the leg had been broken in three places by falling debris during the attack, but it was obvious by the fresh blood on his dressings that something else had further aggravated his wounds.

One of Sanborn's medics from the *Aephas*, a nurse named Hosking, replied, "It was the quake, Doctor. A diagnostic scanner fell from its mount and onto his leg."

"Okay," Sanborn said. "He just moved to the head of the line. Let's get him prepped for surgery."

Leone said, "Why don't you let me take it? You could use a break."

Blowing out her breath, Sanborn replied, "No argument there. You sure?"

"Yeah, no problem." He waved for Amos to join him. "I've got my number one assistant to help me." When she stepped closer, Leone looked to her. "You ready to get back to it?"

Her feelings of agitation now gone—at least, she sensed no such lingering feelings—Amos nodded. "Absolutely."

It's what you signed up for, remember?

6

"I really hate these things."

Stephen Klisiewicz grunted as he pulled, pushed, and stuffed himself into the environment suit. Prepared by the ship's quartermaster and left for him in one of the equipment lockers of the landing party ready room, the protective garment was supposed to be a comfortable fit for his physique. Groaning as he pulled the suit's upper half past his shoulders, the science officer sighed as the heavy, multi-layered material molded to his body. To call it "form-fitting" seemed a criminal understatement.

Eyeing the lone remaining member of the landing party who like him was in the process of checking and donning the silver EV suit that was a match for his, Klisiewicz released a sigh. "I'm beginning to regret asking the captain to let us get over there so fast. I wouldn't have minded an extra month or so to lose a couple of pounds."

"Would you like to check in with Doctor Leone before we go?" asked Ensign Angela Grammell as she finished sealing the front of her own suit and reached to pull back her long blond hair. "You can ask him to change your diet card. That way, a nice tasty salad could be waiting for you when we get back." With practiced ease, the junior science officer tied her locks into a ponytail, ensuring her hair would remain away from her face. That accomplished, she reached for the helmet sitting on the bench before her, which bore her last name on a small red plate at its base.

"I can't wait." Grabbing his own helmet, he held it up. "I'll check yours if you check mine," he said, referring to the sealed collar that would lock the helmet to his suit once he pulled it into place. Lowering it over his head, he twisted it into its proper position, hearing the satisfying sound of the helmet locking into place. He noticed Grammell stepping toward him, her helmet now in place. She moved her gloved hands over the trio of neon-colored fixtures with corresponding cabling that ran from his suit's collar to its chest-mounted control panel. Grammell reached for one last loose flap on his suit's front, which protected another of the closures. With one last click, he listened to the hiss of air as oxygen filled the suit.

Hermetically sealed and ready to serve.

Lifting one knee and then the other, Klisiewicz grimaced as he felt the suit pull snug between his legs. Without thinking, he reached down and tugged ingloriously at his crotch.

"Oh, damn," he said, feeling his cheeks redden in embarrassment as he noted Grammell watching him with an amused smile. "Sorry."

Instead of replying, Grammell reached up to tap the small control pad mounted just below her suit's collar and its red nameplate. Only then did Klisiewicz realize he had not yet engaged his own suit's communicator. Rolling his eyes, he activated the internal unit. "Am I live?"

Grammell pressed the control on her chest panel to activate the suit's external speaker. *"Loud and clear, Lieutenant. Everything where you want it?"*

Doing his best to put aside his embarrassment, Klisie-wicz attempted a feeble smile. "Thanks for the help. Please pretend I can manage myself better than that."

"*No problem, sir,*" Grammell said, offering another smile that struck him more sympathetic than judgmental.

Now appropriately attired for their forthcoming excursion, the pair made their way from the prep room and proceeded as quickly as their suits would allow them to the transporter room located a short distance down the deck seven main corridor, giving Klisiewicz another moment to acclimate to his suit. During his brief Starfleet career, he still could count on two hands the number of times he had donned such a garment for a mission outside the ship. Typically, when an environment required protective gear during his scientific surveys, he needed no more than a standard hazard suit, which allowed more freedom of movement owing to its thinner material and more comfortable fit.

Then again, Klisiewicz thought, *if something's going to keep me alive, I probably shouldn't complain too much about wearing it.*

They arrived at transporter room two, and the doors parted at their approach, revealing a dozen crew members filling the room. Each wore a suit identical to theirs, and for a moment Klisiewicz was reminded of the deep-space evacuation training exercises he had undergone at Starfleet Academy. The helmets made it difficult for him to distinguish any one person from the group, but the presence of tricorders, equipment bags, and weapons served to distinguish engineers and other members of the *Endeavour*'s science department from the complement of security officers who would serve as their escorts. Standing apart from the group on the first step leading up to the transporter pad was Commander Stano.

"All right, people, listen up," said the first officer, her voice sounding distant as it was filtered through his suit's internal communications system. *"Mister Klisiewicz was able to perform some of that science officer magic he does, and get us a limited peek inside the alien ship by scanning through areas of the hull that were damaged during the earlier firefight. It's not a lot, but at this point, we're taking what we can get."* Turning to Klisiewicz, she said, *"Lieutenant?"*

Nodding, Klisiewicz turned to the group. "Our scans are still pretty muddled, but it was enough to at least get us a picture of the area adjacent to an outer hatch we're going to use to make our way inside. Based on its configuration and the energy readings flowing to and from it, we think it might be a command or control center. We'll know more once we're inside."

"What about life signs?" asked Stano.

"So far, we haven't found anything, but the ship's internal configuration suggests it can support a crew." Klisiewicz shrugged. "I guess we'll know more once we get over there."

"Okay, then," said Stano, *"this is how it's going to go: We'll beam over in two waves. The first group will get us into the alien ship through that hatch. Here's hoping Mister Klisiewicz and his scans don't have us climbing into their waste extraction system."* This remark elicited a few chuckles from the group, which Stano allowed before

continuing, *"Once we're in and determine whether it's safe to stay there, I'll call for the rest of you. Klisiewicz, Gaulke, McMurray, Grammell, and Tomkins are with me. We'll see the rest of you over there in a few."*

There was no small amount of shuffling as the boarding party shifted positions and traded places in order to comply with Stano's division of the group into two teams. Klisiewicz tapped the shoulder of another crew member, one of his junior science specialists, in order to move past her and climb the steps to an unoccupied disc on the transporter pad. Once all six pads had been claimed by the people Stano had designated, the first officer waved to the crew member on duty at the transporter console, Master Chief Petty Officer Michael Hess.

"We're ready to go, Chief," she said. *"Energize."*

Behind the console, Hess nodded. "Happy hunting, Commander."

As he had uncounted times before, Klisiewicz could not help smiling as the familiar tingle of the transporter beam began to envelop him. Out of habit, he drew a breath and held it. There was no logical reason to do so, he knew; it was something he had done out of trepidation during his first experiences with being transported as a child, and the practice had continued into adulthood. He at first thought the ritual might cease after he joined Starfleet and beaming became more commonplace, but here he was, years after graduating from the Academy, holding his breath.

All of that flashed through Klisiewicz's mind in the seconds between Hess engaging the transporter controls and the room around him dissolving into a rush of white energy. Then the walls, floors, and ceilings of the *Endeav-our*'s transporter room were gone, replaced by the unrelenting black of open space and the gray, curved hull of the alien ship.

Touchdown!

Blinking quickly to shake off the last of the transporter beam's effects, Klisiewicz felt the magnetized soles of his boots take hold, anchoring him to the hull plates beneath him. In front of him and to his left, Commander Stano and the rest of the boarding party were standing in the same formation they had assumed on the transporter pad, each held to the hull by their suit's gravity boots.

"Everybody okay?" Stano asked, and after receiving five confirmations, Klisiewicz heard her reporting back to the *Endeavour*, noting the team's successful transport. *"We're proceeding along the hull toward the hatch we marked."*

"Acknowledged, Commander," replied the voice of Captain Khatami. *"Proceed with caution. Lieutenant Klisiewicz, that means no playing with anything until you've had a chance to properly examine it."*

The voice of Ensign Grammell said, *"That's good advice, sir."*

Turning his head so that he could see where she stood, he noted her wry grin through her helmet's faceplate as he keyed his communicator. "Understood, Captain. I promise to behave myself." He noted Stano looking at him and could not help a mock frown. "Where did I get this reputation as a troublemaker?"

"Have you read the logs of our previous missions?" asked the first officer. Directing her attention to the rest

of the group, she said, *"All right, people. Let's move out. Mister Klisiewicz, see if you can't scan inside. Now that we're right outside the hull, maybe we'll get lucky. Besides, if that dampening field decides to act up again, I'm hoping you'll catch it."*

"Aye, Commander." Reaching for the tricorder slung over his shoulder and secured to his hip to keep it from moving about in the absence of gravity, Klisiewicz activated the unit and began tuning its scanning field. Holding the tricorder away from his body so that he could see it through his helmet's faceplate, he fell in behind Stano and the rest of the boarding party as they began making their way along the surface of the alien ship. He lifted the heel of his right boot, an act that felt a lot like peeling it from the skin of the spacecraft punctuated with a quick tug to free the toe. By his count, it took him seven paces before he felt himself getting into something approximating a rhythm as he moved forward. His progress, along with the rest of the team's, was slow and deliberate, with each member taking measured steps across the odd hull plating, which appeared smooth with a dull, almost wine-colored finish.

Now walking with confidence as he followed behind Stano, Klisiewicz could not resist the temptation to look up from the ship's hull and take in the view. Thousands of kilometers away was Cantrel V, curving down and away beneath the horizon provided by the alien vessel and beyond his line of sight. In the distance and hanging above the planet, the *Endeavour* was visible, a sliver of gray contrasting against the blackness of space. Though he looked for it, he could not see the *Aephas*, which he knew could not be too far away, and for a moment he thought about his friend Mahmud al-Khaled and the other members of the crew he had known from their previous assignment aboard the lost *Lovell*. Klisiewicz had not seen any of them since shortly after the destruction of Starbase 47 and the initial debriefings that had consumed everyone involved in Operation Vanguard for weeks. With everything that had happened since the *Endeavour*'s arrival in the Cantrel system, there had been no time to exchange pleasantries, and now with both ships involved either in repair efforts or assisting the Tài Shan colonists, Klisiewicz had no idea how or even if he would have an opportunity to catch up with his colleagues.

Later, Lieutenant.

"The hatch is about ten meters ahead of us," said Stano after the team had been walking for a few minutes. Looking past the first officer, Klisiewicz saw a circular, recessed area in the hull. Stano was the first to reach the hatch, using her own tricorder to scan it. *"Tomkins, scans still are being deflected and scattered. I can't help you here."*

Lieutenant Ivan Tomkins, one of the engineers who had come aboard the *Endeavour* after the ship's last crew rotation, stepped around Stano and took up a kneeling position next to the hatch. From the satchel he had brought with him, Tomkins extracted a squat, rectangular device Klisiewicz recognized as a P-38, a standard Starfleet tool for circumventing the magnetic seals on hatches and other access points. Affixing the unit to the hatch, Tomkins keyed the single control set into its casing. When nothing obvious seemed to happen, the engineer repeated the motion.

"No, joy, Commander," he said. *"I'll have to try something more direct."*

Stano gestured toward the hatch. *"Do it."*

The tool Tomkins pulled from his satchel was much larger than the P-38. It was a cutting laser. Seeing the look Klisiewicz realized must be on his face, the young engineer smiled through his faceplate. *"Commander Yataro told me to be prepared for anything."*

"Excellent," said Stano. *"Just try not to cut through anything important, like a self-destruct booby trap or an intruder alert system. No pressure or anything, Lieutenant."*

After adjusting the laser's power setting, Tomkins aimed the tool at a point along the hatch's edge and depressed its trigger. A bright shaft of amber energy flashed from the laser's barrel, and Klisiewicz turned his head to avoid looking directly at the light while still keeping Tomkins in his peripheral vision. The engineer angled the laser along the hatch's seam, and within a moment, Klisiewicz saw a gap forming as the tool continued its work.

"No escaping air," Stano said. *"That's not too promising."*

"At least the hatch isn't buckling," replied Tomkins. *"And the beam's not encountering any resistance. I'm almost done, Commander. You might want to stand clear."*

Stano took a step back as Tomkins deactivated the laser, and Klisiewicz saw the freed section of hatch beginning to move from its position. Tomkins reached forward and pushed the cut portion back into the ship. With a hand lamp from his satchel, he peered through the opening he had created, which was more than enough for each of the boarding party members to pass through even with their suits.

"Looks like an airlock," he said. *"Big enough for all of us. There's another hatch along the far bulkhead, and a control panel of some kind."*

Stano stepped toward the opening. *"Let's have a look, then."* Taking the lead, she freed her boots from the hull plating and used her hands to maneuver herself through the opening. Klisiewicz waited until Ensigns Adam Gaulke and Carlton McMurray followed Stano inside. Tomkins and Grammell proceeded after them, leaving Klisiewicz as the last one to pull himself through the hatch.

The first order of business upon entering the airlock was reorienting one's self, as they had come through what in reality was the chamber's outboard bulkhead. Once inside, each member of the boarding party took a moment to maneuver themselves so that they were standing on the room's actual deck. As for the room itself, Klisiewicz noted its pronounced lack of features of any sort, with the sole exception of the hatch set into the opposite bulkhead and the odd, ovular control pad positioned next to it.

Unlike the outer door, gaining entry through the lock's inner hatch was an easier proposition, which Tomkins demonstrated with his P-38. When the seal on the door gave way, Klisiewicz noted the small wafts of air escaping around the edges, crystallizing in the vacuum.

"Don't get too excited," Klisiewicz said, noting the readings on his tricorder. "According to this, there are only traces of oxygen inside. However, I'm picking up enough residuals that I'm convinced the atmosphere that should be in there is pretty close to Class-M." Adjusting one of the tricorder's controls, he added, "Still no life signs."

"No life signs, and no atmosphere," said Stano. *"At least, nothing our scans detect. We didn't do this, did we?"*

Klisiewicz replied, "None of our scans picked up any evidence of a hull breach. Whatever atmosphere's in there—or *not* in there—it's been that way since before the ship got here." After a moment, he said, "If I had to guess, I'd say the ship's run entirely by automation."

"And it was programmed to attack the planet surface?"

"It'd have to be a pretty sophisticated computer system, but it's not like we haven't seen those before. As for why it launched an attack, I have no idea." Klisiewicz gestured toward the door. "There's really only one way to find out."

The airlock's inner hatch cycled open, and Stano shone her hand lamp through the new opening. Like the lock itself, the area beyond the hatch was dark. Illumination from the lamp suggested the dull gray bulkhead of a larger room or perhaps a corridor.

"Everybody ready to take a walk?" After receiving a chorus of approvals, the first officer led the way through the open hatch. The team emerged into a large corridor, and once everyone had passed through the doorway, Tomkins closed and locked the hatch behind them before taking a marking stylus from his satchel and applying a large red *X* to the door itself.

"Just a reminder that this is the way out," he said. *"At*

least, until or unless we find a way to activate this thing's life support systems. Then we'll need to make sure we don't open it again."

Klisiewicz nodded. "Yeah, that would be an attention-getter, wouldn't it?"

"That's one way to put it," replied the engineer. Returning his tools to his satchel, he gestured up the corridor toward the rest of the team. *"After you, Lieutenant."*

"Why, thank you, sir." Using his hand lamp to guide the way, Klisiewicz moved to rejoin the boarding party. The beams from the team's lights played across the corridor's bulkheads, which were rounded while possessing a series of flat panels running along the ceiling. With his lamp, Klisiewicz studied the panels and noted what appeared to be lighting elements inside, bordered by long, black cylinders running the length of each section and then continuing on to the next panel.

A few paces away, Grammell said, *"Lights and power?"*

"That's what I'm thinking."

Grammell held up her tricorder. *"I'm picking up power readings from deeper inside this section. If we can find the right controls, we should be able to get the lights on in here, and maybe life support."*

"I love an optimist," Klisiewicz replied.

Ahead of them in the corridor, Stano said, *"Klisiewicz, Tomkins. Take a look at this."* She was standing next to what looked like a bank of control panels set into a recessed area of the bulkhead. The workstation—for lack of a better term at the moment—featured a collection of manual interface mechanisms that included switches, buttons, and levers similar to control inputs Klisiewicz had seen on spacecraft designed by any number of humanoid species. The station also contained a larger, circular depression set into the center of the console's flat workspace area. At the bottom of the depression was a small hole. He ran his gloved fingers across a few of the holes.

"Maybe for some kind of key or stylus?" he asked.

Stano shook her head. *"You're the science officer."*

Retrieving his tricorder, Klisiewicz scanned the workstation. "I'm not seeing any signs of damage, and there's a minimal power flow." He paused, looking back at the hatch they had used to gain access to the ship. "I wonder if this might be some kind of command station for use by a member of the crew using the airlock to enter and leave the ship. Of course, that implies this ship has or had a crew."

"Maybe the crew's dead," said Stano, *"and they've been dead for a while, and the ship is carrying out computer-driven protocols."*

"Seems as good a theory as any," replied Tomkins. He gestured toward the console. *"We can start here, so far as seeing about getting some lights on, and maybe accessing the ship's onboard computer."*

"And some breathable air," added Stano. *"I'd even be okay without artificial gravity for a while if you can make it so I can take off this helmet."*

Standing beside Klisiewicz and studying her own tricorder, Grammell said, *"I've been scanning the atmospheric traces in here. If we do manage to restore life support, the air will be richer in oxygen content than we're used to."*

"I'll take it," Stano said. *"What do you think, Tom-kins?"*

The engineer offered a wide smile. *"I'll have this place smelling as sweet as a meadow once we get rolling, Commander."*

"All right, then," replied the first officer. *"Let's get to work."* She paused, switching her suit communicator's frequency. *"Stano to* Endeavour.*"*

"We read you, Commander," replied the voice of Captain Khatami.

"Captain, we're inside, and so far there are no indications of life aboard, but we're just getting started with our survey. You're clear to beam over the other half of the boarding party. You should be able to pick up the hatch we cut through on sensors. That's our point of entry until we get life support up and running. I'll have our security people waiting at the inner hatch when they arrive."

Khatami replied, *"Acknowledged. The transporter room has been notified. Stand by, Commander."*

Directing his attention to the console, Klisiewicz once more waved his tricorder over its array of controls, studying their layout and analyzing possible commonalities in configuration they might have with systems with which he was familiar.

"So," Tomkins said after a moment, *"you want to just throw some switches and see what happens?"*

Klisiewicz was unable to suppress a small chuckle. "I don't think Commander Stano would appreciate that. Regardless of what you may have heard, I honestly do try to be a bit more deliberate in these kinds of situations."

Several minutes passed in silence as he continued to

study the alien mechanisms before Klisiewicz sensed new movement in the corridor. Turning from the console, he saw that the other six members of the boarding party had entered the passageway through the airlock hatch, and Tomkins was standing in the lock itself, working with another tool from his engineer's satchel to weld back into place the piece of outer hatch he had removed. The new arrivals were in the midst of acclimating themselves to their surroundings as Stano's voice filtered through everyone's helmets.

"All right, I want teams of four. Ensign Gaulke, take your people up the corridor. McMurray, your team will head in the opposite direction. No one goes anywhere alone. Ensign Tropp, you're our medic this time around?"

One member of the new group, a Denobulan, raised his hand. *"I am here, Commander."*

"Stay with me," replied Stano. *"Klisiewicz, you and Tomkins are here too. Keep working on that control station. Everyone else, continue scanning for signs of life or anything else that looks interesting. Maintain this frequency, and report anything you find immediately. Okay, go see what there is to see."*

The two teams moved off in their assigned directions along the corridor, the beams from their hand beacons reflecting off the shimmering bulkheads in a way that reminded Klisiewicz of oil floating atop water. Complying with Stano's order, members of the two teams talked among themselves, sometimes on top of each other, and their voices started to blend as they echoed in his helmet.

"I'm not seeing any intersections," said a voice he could not identify.

"No doors, either," spoke another.

"Looks like we're bending to the right up ahead," said a voice he was sure was Grammell's. *"Any tricorder readings, Hastert?"*

"Some faint power indications," replied Jay Hastert, a young sciences ensign Klisiewicz had recommended for the boarding party. *"I guess this thing is working. At least in here we're getting some halfway decent readings."*

Trying to ignore the chorus, Klisiewicz refocused his attention on the workstation console. A lone control in the panel's upper right corner had caught his attention, and his tricorder seemed to indicate that the minimal power being directed to this location was leading to this particular switch.

"Here goes nothing," he said, handing his tricorder to Tomkins. "I think this is it. Keep an eye on the power readings." Without further preamble, he pressed the switch. He felt it click beneath his fingers even through the reinforced material of his glove. A moment later, the switch illuminated, followed by other controls and indicators beginning to flash and blink.

"There we go," said Tomkins. *"Definitely an increase in the power flow. There are also indications of an attempted connection to a larger internal network."* He paused to adjust the tricorder. *"I'm setting up a data connection with the* Endeavour. *Hopefully our computer can get started on a translation matrix. That should make things go easier."*

"Nice work, gentlemen," said Stano, and when Klisiewicz looked in her direction he saw the first officer nodding in approval.

Klisiewicz nodded, watching the console come to life. A trio of what looked to be status monitors had activated, and within another minute each began displaying a scrolling column of data in unfamiliar text.

It was a start.

7

"Over here!"

Her attention focused on the portable field generator, one of four she and the team of engineers had brought with them from the *Endeavour* to provide power for the Beta Site excavation area, Master Chief Petty Officer Christine Rideout had not heard the first call for help. Only when one of her crewmates sprinted past her did she look up from her attempts to repair the generator, which was damaged as a consequence of the most recent aftershock.

"What the hell?" Rideout said to no one, looking toward the source of the call and seeing another member of the *Endeavour*'s crew, someone in a red tunic she did not recognize, waving with both hands over his head. He stood at the mouth of a tunnel entrance leading from the bottom of the crater into one of the several subterranean caverns found by colonist and Starfleet archeologists beneath the sizable excavation site. In response to the man's summons, a dozen people were running toward him.

"I believe they have found some of the missing persons," said Lieutenant Commander Yataro. Like Rideout, Yataro wore an olive-green jumpsuit. On the Lirin, the garment appeared ready to fall off his tall, lean frame, with his long, thin neck protruding from the uniform's collar and supporting his enlarged, wedge-shaped head.

"I have already summoned additional medical help from the base camp."

"I'm going to see if I can help," said Rideout, pushing herself to her feet and tucking her engineer's diagnostic scanner into the cargo pocket along her right thigh.

Yataro said, "As will I." In the afternoon sunlight, Yataro's bright lavender skin looked as though it possessed an oily sheen, contrasted by his large, dark blue eyes that were set into his oversized skull beneath a wide, pronounced brow. When he spoke, the small mouth at the base of his narrow chin barely moved, giving his face an almost mask-like appearance. Instead of a nose, a pair of small angled openings beneath his eyes served as his olfactory organs.

The two of them set off at a fast jog across the open uneven ground, and despite his seemingly ungainly frame Yataro moved with a speed and grace that surprised Rideout, and she realized she was having to increase her own pace to match his speed. Within seconds they had covered the distance, and as they approached the tunnel entrance, other members of the *Endeavour*'s landing party noticed the chief engineer's approach and stepped aside for him.

"Ensign, what is it?" Yataro asked, gesturing to the young officer Rideout now saw was Kerry Zane, a member of the *Endeavour*'s security detachment. "Have you found someone?"

Standing near the opening and holding a communicator in his right hand, Zane waved toward the tunnel. "That's affirmative, Commander. Four survivors. They're all pretty banged up, but they're alive." He paused, and his expression soured. "There are three others who weren't so lucky."

"We need a hand down here!"

The voice echoed from down the tunnel, and Rideout turned in that direction. "What's going on?"

"I don't know," replied Zane. "A couple of our engineers and security people ran down there to help once we knew there was somebody trapped in there. They were using an antigrav unit to move some of the heavier rubble."

"Master Chief," said Yataro, pointing to Rideout, "you come with me. Ensign Zane, see to it that the medical team from the base camp proceeds here with all due haste."

"On it, sir," replied the security officer, moving aside and allowing Yataro and Rideout access to the tunnel.

Pausing just long enough for both of them to retrieve an emergency light from an equipment container positioned near the entrance, the chief engineer led the way into the narrow passage with Rideout following close behind him. Though she was not claustrophobic, she could not help noticing right away just how close the rock walls seemed. For an odd moment, she felt as though the unyielding stone might be pressing down on her, something she had never experienced even in the cramped confines of a starship's Jefferies tubes, or even within the tighter environs of the access crawlways of the *Archer*-class scout ship that was her previous assignment.

Get your act together, Rideout. Shaking off the unwelcome sensations, she snapped on her light. Shadows retreated as the bright glow of the lamp highlighted the mineral deposits embedded in the rock, flashing in a va-

riety of warm, inviting hues as she and Yataro made their
way deeper into the tunnel.

Within twenty meters, the passage widened into the
first of what Rideout knew was several subterranean
chambers. Unlike some of the caverns found farther
along this path, this area was devoid of anything hinting at Cantrel V's previous civilization. The only lighting
was that afforded by the portable field lamps positioned
around the cavern's perimeter, and the air was much
cooler here than on the surface or even in the connecting
tunnel. To her, this chamber seemed like a staging area,
with rubble pushed aside and piled out of the way to allow
entry to the other, larger tunnels leading to the more spa-
cious underground sites. Standing near one of those entrances was another security officer. Like all of the other
female members of the *Endeavour*'s security detail, she
wore black trousers and boots with a red tunic, rather than
the typical skirt uniform variant favored by many women
crew members aboard ship, with the notable exception of
Captain Khatami, who seemed to tolerate them and only
wore them when required.

"Commander Yataro," said the ensign, "Zane informed us you were coming." She indicated the tunnel
with the communicator in her hand. "That way, sir."

"What is the status of the survivors?" asked Yataro.

The ensign replied, "They've definitely had a rough
day, sir, but only one of them has critical injuries. Medics
should be on hand topside once we free him and the others
and get them to the surface."

Rideout frowned. "They're still stuck down here?
What's the holdup?"

"The antigrav unit they were using to move debris malfunctioned." The ensign gestured down the tunnel. "They're trying to repair it while some of the stronger guys are clearing rocks the hard way."

"Let's have a look at it," Rideout said, shining her light down the tunnel and setting off in that direction. With Yataro almost stepping on the backs of her heels, she led the way down the rugged, uneven passage, the darkness threatening to swallow them both, held at bay by her hand lamp. In the narrow tunnel she heard the chief engineer's breathing even more so than the sounds of his footfalls on the stone floor, and her own breath seemed to ring in her ears. She kept her eyes focused in front of her rather than letting her gaze wander about her surroundings. It took her a moment to realize that her anxiety had nothing to do with an irrational fear of enclosed spaces, but rather the very real possibility of another aftershock affecting these underground areas. What must the people waiting to be rescued be going through, sitting in the dark and hearing the sounds of rescue mere meters away, all the while knowing that another tremor or quake could happen at any time?

Shut up, Rideout chided herself. *You're not helping anyone.*

"There is light ahead," said Yataro, still walking right behind her, and when she glanced over her shoulder she saw that the engineer had turned off his own hand lamp.

"I take it you can see better in the dark than humans do?" she asked.

Yataro nodded. "Yes."

"Rub it in, why don't you."

"I am afraid I do not understand your choice of idiom."

"Don't worry. It wasn't that much of a joke anyway."

Rideout was able to make out the light from ahead of them now, as well, and switched off her hand lamp as she and Yataro rounded the last curve in the tunnel and emerged into a cavern that was perhaps half the size of the one they had left. Five Starfleet personnel, two dressed in standard duty uniforms while the other three wore olive-green jumpsuits like hers, were working in the chamber. One of the jumpsuits, Lieutenant Phu Dang, was kneeling next to what Rideout recognized as an antigravity unit of the model used to move large cargo containers and other large components or equipment with relative ease. The *Endeavour*'s assistant chief engineer looked frustrated as he waved a diagnostic scanner over the unit while holding a spanner in his other hand. Several meters away, the other four members of the group were working to maneuver out of the way stones of varying size. Rideout saw a gap between two larger boulders and what she thought might be the beam from a hand lamp moving about in the darkness beyond.

"Damn it," said Dang as Rideout and Yataro approached.

Moving toward him, Yataro said, "What is the issue, Lieutenant?"

Waving at the unit, Dang replied, "Some kind of short or defect in the power supply, sir. It's completely drained."

"Can it be recharged?" asked Rideout.

Dang shrugged. "Maybe, but we'd have to take it topside to one of the generators."

"May I take a look, sir?" Moving to stand on the unit's opposite side, Rideout knelt beside it and examined its open access panel. She saw scorch marks where the power cell connected to the relay points that then channeled energy to the antigrav plates as well as the unit's control pad. "This thing looks toasted."

"That's what I was thinking, Master Chief." Dang pushed back on his haunches until he was sitting on the cavern's stone floor. "I figure without swapping out the entire power relay, trying to charge it will just finish it for good."

Rideout considered her options, including a couple that were not in any of the technical manuals or specifications for the antigrav unit or any other piece of Starfleet technology, for that matter. "I think I have an idea, sir."

"Attempt to repair the unit," Yataro said. "I will assist the others."

Eyeing the chief engineer with no attempt to mask her skepticism, Rideout said, "No offense, Commander, but you don't look like the bodybuilding sort." She gestured to the unit. "I'll either have this up and running, or we'll go and get another one."

"The injured archaeologists need to be extracted as quickly as possible," replied Yataro. "Continue your repair efforts." Without saying anything else, he turned and headed to where the others were working to move aside the fallen rock.

"You don't know much about Lirins, do you?" asked Dang.

Rideout glanced over at the young engineer while fishing in the cargo pocket along her left leg. "I guess I don't."

Waving to where Yataro had joined the other *Endeavour* crew members, Dang smiled. "Look for yourself."

After a brief moment consulting with the security officers and engineers working to clear the blockage, Yataro began picking up and moving boulders that two or even three of the other crew members had been struggling to maneuver.

"Show off," said Rideout, snickering as she pulled from her pocket a short length of optical cabling with a stout U-shaped connector at one end. From her right hip pocket, she retrieved the type-1 phaser she had drawn from the ship's armory prior to beaming to the surface.

Dang, his expression one of confusion, prompted, "Master Chief?"

"Just a little improvisational engineering, Lieutenant," replied Rideout. After attaching the connector to the ports on the phaser that under normal circumstances allowed it to attach into the handgrip of the weapon's larger type-2 cousin, she took the other end of the cable and plugged it into the antigrav unit's charging interface.

"I've never seen a cable like that," said Dang.

Rideout grinned. "Something I came up with a couple of years ago. I needed a fast way to power up a portable computer workstation." She shrugged. "I did a tour on an *Archer*-class scout. When you don't have the supplies and other resources of a ship like the *Endeavor*, you learn to make do with what you can scrounge up."

"You weren't on the *Sagittarius*, were you?" The lieutenant shook his head. "No, I've known everyone who was assigned to that ship for the past three years."

"I wish I was that lucky." Checking the power levels on the phaser, she grimaced. "Unfortunately, when our ship crashed, it stayed crashed."

It took him a moment, but then Dang nodded in understanding. "You were on the *Huang Zhong*. I read about your last mission. That was . . . something else. I'm sorry about your shipmates."

"Thanks. I appreciate that," said Rideout, forcing a smile.

For her part, she still had a hard time believing some aspects of her last mission aboard the *U.S.S. Huang Zhong*. It had only been a few months since that ill-fated assignment, which had resulted in the loss of her ship as well as most of its crew, people she had called friends. Only she and two others had survived the *Zhong*'s crash landing on a planet that had been discovered inside an odd spatial rift that only allowed passage for a short time every few years. The Dolysians, a species indigenous to the rift's home star system, had figured out a way to use the rift, the planet, and its vast resources to establish a mining colony. Mineral ore extracted from the planet was readied for transport by the colonists, and during the period when the rift was open, the ore was shipped to the Dolysians' homeworld for use in energy production. Rideout and her fellow survivors were rescued and their injuries treated by members of the mining colony, where they had remained until the *U.S.S. Enterprise* arrived to investigate the crash. Despite the tragedy of the *Zhong*'s loss and the deaths of her friends, the incident had served to open formal relations between the Federation and the Dolysians.

I guess that's something.

As for Rideout herself, after undergoing the required rounds of physical examinations and mental health evaluations and even talking to a grief counselor, she had taken little time to reach the conclusion that the best thing she could do to benefit her own well-being was to get back to work. She had always been something of a drifter throughout her career, moving between assignments with no reservations while keeping in contact with her colleagues from previous tours of duty while easily making new friends wherever Starfleet saw fit to send her. When word was going around that the *Endeavour*'s entire engineering staff required replacing after the tumultuous events that had transpired in the Taurus Reach months earlier, Rideout had requested duty aboard the starship. She was eager for a change of scenery—so to speak—as well as a change of pace. Life on a cramped *Archer*-class scout had its moments, but she had no complaints with her new situation on a ship of the line. For one thing, it was nice to have her own cabin, and she definitely would not miss "hot bunking" as she had endured aboard the *Zhong*. The practice of sleeping in whichever of the ship's limited number of beds was available by virtue of individual crew member duty schedules was tolerable for brief periods, but it had been one of her least-favorite aspects of serving aboard such a small vessel. By comparison, the *Endeavour* was a spa in space.

"Okay, I'm ready to go," said Rideout as she finished assembling her makeshift solution and gave her handiwork one final inspection. She nodded toward Dang. "You might want to stand back, sir."

The engineer scowled. "Really?"

"Nah, not really." Without any other warning, Rideout flipped the antigrav's activation switch. There was a noticeable pop before a loud hum began emanating from the unit and its control pad flared to life. She smiled when the device pushed itself from the cavern floor and rose to hover a meter off the ground.

"Bingo," she said. "I figure it should last five or ten minutes before it blows up." When Dang cast a wary look in her direction, she added, "Just kidding." Satisfied with her efforts, Rideout maneuvered the antigrav over to where Yataro and the others had finished clearing all but the largest of the fallen rock. "Here you go, Commander. This should hold long enough to finish the job."

"Your timing is excellent, Master Chief," said the chief engineer before gesturing toward the last of the heavier stone. "Be my guest."

It took both hands to maneuver the antigrav into place, and as soon as it made contact with the sizable chunk of broken stone she had chosen, Rideout felt some initial resistance. Tapping the power level on the control pad was enough to stabilize the unit, and she grinned as she stepped backward with the harnessed rock now held in place.

"Nice!" said Dang. "I think I need you to teach me how to do that workaround."

Rideout set down the piece of rock and returned to the pile in search of another. "Piece of cake, sir." The antigrav and the muscles of the rest of the team made short work of the remaining blockage, and within moments Yataro and one of the security officers were helping the first of the trapped colonists through the newly created opening. The first person to come out was a disheveled female Starfleet lieutenant, her olive-green jumpsuit dirty and torn. She was favoring her left arm and there was blood on her face, and it took Rideout an extra moment to realize that it was green rather than red.

"Lieutenant," said Yataro, holding the woman's hand as she stepped over a few of the smaller rocks, "I am Commander Yataro from the *Starship Endeavour*. Besides your arm, do you have any other injuries?"

The woman shook her head. "Cook, sir. Colleen Cook. My arm's broken, but otherwise I think I'm okay." Rideout noted that the lieutenant sounded dazed. She likely had been shaken by enduring the alien ship's attack as well as the subsequent aftershocks, but there was something else; a haunted look in her eyes that told Rideout the other woman was not just rattled or injured, but also grief stricken.

Yataro said, "We have medics standing by to treat you, after which you will be transported to the colony where we have established a field hospital."

"My friends," replied Cook, her words little more than a mumble. Turning, she gestured toward the gap in the rubble. "Inside."

After guiding the other woman toward one of the waiting *Endeavour* security officers who would in turn escort her to the waiting medics, Rideout turned her attention to the gap between the rubble leading to the other victims. The first person she saw was an Andorian male, his azure-blue skin and his red Starfleet tunic marred with dirt. He sported numerous cuts and abrasions, and his shirt's left sleeve had been ripped away at the shoulder to serve as the bandage wrapped around his right leg.

"Ensign," said Rideout, reaching out with her free hand as she levered herself over a large piece of fractured stone and into the small chamber where the victims had been trapped. "You all right, sir?"

The Andorian offered a tired nod. "Yes, but Doctor Buntin has sustained a head injury and needs immediate attention."

"We're on it." Rideout moved to where the civilian archaeologist lay unconscious along the compact hollow's far wall. She and the Andorian, Ensign ch'Dran, carried him back to the opening where two more *Endeavour* security officers waited to help, then did the same for the fourth survivor, another civilian who had suffered a broken leg.

It was not until she turned her attention to the first of the less fortunate victims that Rideout realized that up to this moment, she had been positioning herself within the cramped cavern so that she did not have to look at the three bodies lying silent behind her. As she turned toward them, she forced herself to swallow the sudden lump of anxiety that had risen into her throat.

Hold it together, Rideout.

"That was T'Naal," said a voice behind her. It was Ensign ch'Dran, who despite his injured leg had once more maneuvered himself into the cavern to assist her. He gestured toward the body of a Vulcan woman. "She and Lieutenant Cook were friends. We all were friends."

"I'm sorry," Rideout said, stepping closer to the body. "We'll take good care of her, and the others."

Had it been a conscious decision to avoid looking at them until now? She did not want to believe that, but as her gaze lingered upon the deceased Vulcan who had suffered an obvious fatal head wound, her mind flooded with the haunting images of one of her shipmates, Greg Simon, who had suffered a similar fate aboard the *Huang Zhong*. As brutal as the scout ship's crash landing had been on the vessel itself, it had been no less forgiving on the fragile beings contained within it. Simon, an ensign fresh from Starfleet Academy and on his first deep space assignment, had simply been in the wrong place at the wrong moment when a section of the *Zhong*'s engineering overhead had buckled during the crash.

They worked in silence, moving the victims to the cavern's entrance, but after a moment ch'Dran asked, "Master Chief, are you all right?"

Blowing out her breath, Rideout reached up to wipe her forehead with her sleeve. "Yes, sir. I'm fine. I'm just . . . this is just bringing back a few unpleasant memories."

Retrieving Simon's body from the *Zhong*'s wreckage had been one of the most difficult tasks she had ever performed, as had notifying Simon's family of his tragic death. Though he had only been aboard ship for a few months, he and Rideout had struck up a fast friendship, perhaps because despite his outranking her, he had been forthright about his lack of experience and his desire to learn how things "were really done in the Fleet," as opposed to what he had learned in school. His effusive good humor had been as contagious as it was unrelenting, and hearing his ridiculous laugh at his own jokes was something she had missed.

He was gone, of course, and Rideout reminded herself, gone and beyond her ability to help. However, there were people here and now—both living and deceased—who needed her.

It was time to get her head back in the game and get back to work.

8

Finally, thought Ensign Adam Gaulke as he beheld the very large, very impressive door that marked the end of what was beginning to feel like a relentless, interminable hike through the depths of the alien vessel. *A change of scenery.*

"That is one hell of a door," he said, shining his light across the smooth metal circle set into a thick frame. He saw no seams or rivets, or any other hint that the hatch was not just one gigantic unmoving disk. Set into the bulkhead to the left of the door was an ovular control pad not unlike the one that he had seen at the airlock the boarding party had used to gain entry to the ship.

Gaulke turned to see his companion, Ensign Sa-Gameet, aiming a tricorder at the door. *"My scans are unable to penetrate the door or the walls of the adjoining section,"* reported the tall, lanky Efrosian. *"As for the hatch itself, it is magnetically sealed, and I am detecting no power being routed to this location. We should be able to disrupt the seal and open the door manually."*

"Might as well," Gaulke said. "It's either that, or we turn around and head back." The door represented the first variation in the vessel's interior design they had encountered since being dispatched by Commander Stano to investigate the ship. "According to the exterior schematics Lieutenant Klisiewicz gave us, there's still a ways to go before we reach the far edge of this sphere. So, we can go through this door, or look for another way around this section. I say we have a look. That's why we're here, right?"

Sa-Gameet nodded. *"Indeed."* Despite his suit's controlled environment, the ensign's stark white hair was matted with perspiration and lying flat atop his head, providing sharp contrast with his deep orange skin. His brilliant cobalt-blue eyes seemed to bore through Gaulke, their tint matching that of the control components mounted to the front of his suit.

Gesturing toward the door, Gaulke said, "All right, then. Work your magic."

Sa-Gameet returned his tricorder to his hip, pulling its strap taut and anchoring the device to the clip on his suit. From the satchel he carried, the engineer extracted a P-38 tool and placed it on the door near the control pad.

"Ready?" he asked, looking over his shoulder at Gaulke.

"Yeah." He looked to the other two members of their team, Ensign Anissa Cole from the science department and his fellow security officer, Ensign Guillermo Montes. "You two, cover us." As Cole and Montes drew their phasers and took up stations behind them, Gaulke joined Sa-Gameet at the door and placed his hand on the hatch's smooth surface. "Okay, let's give it a go then."

Sa-Gameet pressed the control on the P-38, and a moment later Gaulke felt a tremor in the door that was subtle yet still noticeable even through his glove.

"That should be sufficient," said the Efrosian as he

and Gaulke placed their hands on the door and began to exert force.

The door lurched once before snagging itself to a halt, creating a ten-centimeter gap that allowed Gaulke to peer into the darkness. Retrieving his hand lamp, he aimed it through the opening, but the light revealed nothing. Instead, it seemed to be swallowed by the darkness.

Once more consulting his tricorder, Sa-Gameet said, *"No life readings."*

"Okay, then," Gaulke replied. "Let's keep going." Now able to wrap his fingers around the door's edges, he set his feet and shoved. Working together, it took him and Sa-Gameet a second heave before the hatch gave way and rolled with ease into the adjoining bulkhead.

"A little too easy," Gaulke said as the door disappeared into the wall, leaving the team standing before the large, circular entrance. His nose itched and he wrinkled it in a futile attempt to quell the sensation.

Damned helmet.

"You are complaining?" asked Sa-Gameet.

Gaulke shrugged. "Let's just say that 'too easy' never seems to be true on missions like this, at least not in the time I've been with the *Endeavour*." Unlike Sa-Gameet and even Cole and Montes, Gaulke's tenure aboard the starship predated its current mission of exploration in the Taurus Reach. While his three companions were among the personnel who had been assigned to the crew in the wake of Operation Vanguard, as the ship was being repaired for its new assignment, Gaulke had come aboard while Captain Khatami and her crew already were involved in the highly classified project. The stresses of that brief yet intense time had almost been enough to push him toward reassignment, but Commander Stano had convinced him to stay. Turnover among the crew had been high, owing as much to individual desires to move on to a new station as a need to replace the numerous casualties the *Endeavour* had suffered at the Battle of Vanguard. "Continuity," Stano had called it, was vital in making sure the new replacements acclimated quickly with those members of the crew who had elected to stay on, in order to have the ship ready to undertake its new mission with as little disruption as possible. The first officer had made a compelling argument, and Gaulke and numerous others had elected to stay on with the *Endeavour.*

And it certainly hasn't been boring. Or easy, like this door.

Stepping across the threshold, Gaulke was the first to enter the room, with Sa-Gameet following him. Once Cole and Montes joined them, their four hand lamps worked to provide at least some illumination to the chamber.

"Reminds me of our hangar deck," Gaulke noted, eyeing the room's open space and high, curved ceiling. The bulkheads were covered with the same iridescent plating that had been used in the corridors they had just traversed. As for the room's length, that was hard to judge, as the beams from the team's hand lamps faded into the darkness without falling upon the chamber's far wall.

To his right, Cole said, *"Look at this,"* and Gaulke directed his light in her direction to see her standing before an array of furniture. Dozens of tables with attached benches, each of which obviously was anchored in some manner to the deck. Set into the bulkhead beyond the furniture was a workstation similar to the one Klisiewicz accessed near the airlock and like that console, this one also was inert.

"Designed for humanoid physiology," observed Sa-Gameet. *"This is consistent with everything else we have encountered."*

Then the lights came on with an abruptness that made Gaulke flinch.

"Damn it!" he exclaimed without thinking, his hand reaching for the phaser on his hip. The sudden activation of the room's lighting was accompanied by a noticeable hum from somewhere behind the bulkheads, or was it beneath the deck or over their heads? Gaulke stopped himself before he could brandish his weapon at the same time his suit's communicator chirped.

"Klisiewicz to boarding party. You'll be happy to know we've found a way into the ship's computer network, and we're accessing the main power systems. You should be seeing lights and other equipment coming online, and we should have life support and artificial gravity in a few minutes."

"I hope that means we can get out of these suits," said Ensign Montes, *"because I think I need to change my shorts."*

"Thanks for the update, Lieutenant," replied Gaulke into his communicator while doing his best to keep his tone level.

Klisiewicz continued, *"Lieutenant Tomkins also has a line on the dampening field that gave the* Endeavour *and the* Aephas *trouble. It's generated by a series of emitters scattered all along the ship's different spherical sections, but it can be controlled through a central relay. Tomkins thinks he can have that taken care of in short order."*

Sa-Gameet, his tricorder activated once more, said, *"The atmosphere is already well on its way to full pressurization in this section."*

"Gravity might take an extra minute or two," reported Klisiewicz over the open comm frequency. *"Their systems don't work quite like ours, so you might experience a bit of disorientation or queasiness when it kicks in. If I'm reading the specs right, the gravity in here is about one point one nine Earth standard, so the extra drag will take some getting used to. Watch your step, people."*

Gaulke said, "If the air's richer, I don't mind carrying a little extra weight. Good trade. We're continuing our investigation, Lieutenant."

"Acknowledged. Stay safe. Klisiewicz out."

The connection was severed, and within a few minutes Ensign Cole reported that the oxygen content of the room and surrounding section of the ship had been elevated to the point it was safe for the team to remove their helmets. Gaulke did so with relish, savoring the first taste of air that had not been recycling through his suit for the past two hours.

"A little stale," he noted, "but it won't kill us."

Once the team had removed their helmets and gloves, electing for the moment to remain wearing the rest of their suits in the event it became necessary to seal everything back up, Gaulke took in the rest of the expansive chamber.

Beyond the collection of tables, and lining opposite walls of the room, were racks of cylindrical containers.

"What've we got here?" Stepping toward the containers, he eyed Cole, who was examining another of the racks with her tricorder. "You picking up anything interesting?"

"The readings are muddled," Cole replied. "Whatever's in the surrounding metal is definitely interfering with our scans, but maybe it's some kind of protective measure for whatever's in these containers."

Gaulke shrugged. "Or it could be a defensive measure against attackers and prying eyes," he said. "You know, like ours."

"I prefer to assume positive intent until proven otherwise." She offered a small smile, but it vanished and her brow furrowed as she studied her tricorder readings. "Whoa."

"What is it?" asked Gaulke.

Now frowning, Cole adjusted her tricorder's controls. "I just picked up a spike in organic material readings. It wasn't there a second ago, but now it's definitely present. It's coming from at least some of these containers."

"Organic? Not a life sign?"

Cole shook her head. "I . . . I'm not sure." She stepped closer to the nearest rack of cylinders. "Readings are stronger now."

Resisting the urge to reach for his phaser, Gaulke turned to Montes. "Keep an eye on the door, just in case." He nodded to where Sa-Gameet was examining a console workstation he had found on the far bulkhead. "And keep him out of trouble too."

Ahead of him, Cole had moved still closer to the first section of containers. As he walked to join her, he noted that the opaque cylinders were stacked six high within the individual storage racks, each about a meter in height and maybe half that in diameter and fitted into the racks in such a way that there was no room for them to be affected by the ship's lack of gravity. "Okay, so what are these things?"

"My first thought is some kind of food storage," Cole replied. "The contents are a combination of amino acids, carbohydrates, fats, vitamins. The best description I can offer is . . . nutrient gravy."

Gaulke eyed her with skepticism. "Sounds delicious."

"It can't be any worse than some of the stuff that comes out of our food processors." When Gaulke released a groan of disapproval, she added, "By human standards, this stuff is completely edible."

"Pass," Gaulke said.

Cole adjusted her tricorder and Gaulke heard the pitch of the device's whine change, which was followed by the science officer frowning. "Wow. I just got a change in the readings. If I didn't know any better, I'd think the scan was agitating it, somehow, and now I'm getting indications of something else inside the containers." She made another adjustment to her tricorder's scan and Gaulke watched her expression change. "Okay, now it's settling down again. Weird."

"You think it's something you did?" asked Gaulke.

Her attention still focused on her tricorder, Cole replied, "No idea, and that other reading's gone too." She reached as though to make yet another adjustment to the unit, then stopped herself. "I can't tell what's actually blocking my scans, the cylinders or the stuff inside them."

A new sound reverberated through the deck plating beneath Gaulke's boots, and he felt his stomach heave as an unseen force seemed to reach up and grip him in an effort to pull him to the deck. He felt his face flush and a wave of nausea roll over him. Even with his gravity boots, he staggered and lost his grip on his hand lamp, which fell to the deck, bounced, and remained there. Sensing his balance slipping away, he flailed for a handhold and caught the edge of a nearby storage rack, and in his peripheral vision he saw Cole pitching forward, her feet still locked in place as she bent at the waist as though falling. Like him, she reached for something to steady herself but succeeded only in toppling several of the storage cylinders before collapsing to her knees. One container fell against her before tumbling to the deck, bouncing against the metal plating as its top gave way and released its contents. Viscous blue-green fluid washed across the floor, sloshing over Cole's hands and her legs.

"It seems Lieutenant Klisiewicz was successful in reestablishing the artificial gravity," said Sa-Gameet.

"No kidding." Disengaging his gravity boots, Gaulke extended his free hand to Cole. "Anissa? Are you okay?"

Cole grimaced. "You mean other than feeling like a cadet puking up on the first day of zero-g combat training? I feel great." Accepting Gaulke's proffered hand, she allowed him to pull her to her feet, at which point she deactivated her gravity boots before directing her attention to the broken container. "Looks like I made a mess."

"Adam!"

Jerking his head around at the sound of Montes shouting, Gaulke saw the security officer standing at the entrance to the room as the door cycled shut. To the ensign's right, Sa-Gameet stood before the previously dark and inoperative workstation that now was coming online, its array of seven display monitors and accompanying rows of controls and indicators flaring to life.

"What's happening?" asked Gaulke.

Sa-Gameet replied, "Now that power is being routed to this section, I was able to determine which controls activated this console. I did not, so far as I can tell, instruct the door to close."

"It had to be something," Montes countered. "I didn't touch a thing."

Behind them, Cole said, "It could be a protective measure." When the three men looked at her, she indicated the broken container and its spilled contents. "For example."

"Are you saying we've been contaminated with something?" asked Montes.

The science officer shook her head. "I didn't detect any indications of a contaminant or a pathogen."

"Assuming it's something you can pick up with a tricorder scan," said Gaulke. He gestured toward the puddle of blue gel.

"Always the optimist." Retrieving her tricorder and wiping away some of the fluid that had splashed across its black casing, she reactivated the unit and aimed it at the open cylinder and the spill. While he waited for her, Gaulke tapped his communicator control.

"Gaulke to Commander Stano." There was no response, or even an indication that his signal was being received. He repeated the call and heard nothing but dead air. "Gaulke to any team member." When that did not work, he even tried summoning the *Endeavour*, and achieved the same result.

Moving from the door toward Sa-Gameet, Montes asked, "Could the room be shielded?"

The Efrosian replied, "I detected no such readings when we conducted our initial scans. I will check again."

"Ensign Gaulke," said Cole. "There's something else in the container." When he turned back to once more face her, Gaulke saw that the science officer now was kneeling next to the meter-high container that still rested on its side, and she was holding her tricorder over a shapeless gray-white mass lying just inside the cylinder.

"What is that?" Gaulke asked, stepping closer. The thing looked to be about half again the size of his fist, and it was covered with fluid from the spilled container.

Cole said, "It's some sort of cnidarian species, more or less." She noted Gaulke's confused expression and added, "Basically a jellyfish, but my tricorder's picking up far greater neural activity than you'd find washing up on a beach somewhere."

"You're saying it's intelligent? Sentient?"

The science officer shrugged. "Could be. Looks that way. We should take one back to the *Endeavour* and run some tests."

"Captain Khatami will love that idea," replied Gaulke. "Let's not rush into anything. We should see if there's something in this ship's computer that can tell us more about this thing." Looking up at all of the cylinders sitting in their storage racks as well as the ones that had fallen to the floor, he grunted. "Now I really want to know how many of these things are in here." He turned back to Cole, but never got to ask his next question, as that was the moment the organism decided to move.

It was almost a blur as it sprang from the cylinder and landed on Cole. The science officer scrambled to her feet as the thing glided up her left arm to her shoulder. Gaulke, caught off guard, stared in shock for several seconds until the thing was moving over the collar of Cole's suit.

"Get it off of me!"

Move, damn it!

He had taken only the first step toward Cole when her entire body twitched and her eyes went wide before rolling back in her head. Both hands reached for her head as she twisted around, and Gaulke saw that the gray mass had affixed itself to the base of her skull, with four tentacles or appendages or something else he could not identify extending from its core and gripping the sides of Cole's neck. She cried out in shock and fright as Gaulke grabbed her arm. He heard boots running across the deck toward them, and an instant later Sa-Gameet and Montes were there, reaching for Cole and trying to prevent her body from convulsing.

Montes grimaced as he tried to keep hold of Cole's other arm. "What the hell is that thing?"

"Wait," said Sa-Gameet a moment later. "Something's happening."

Feeling Cole's muscles slacken beneath his grip, Gaulke studied her face and saw that her expression had gone blank. The pain and fear she had exhibited mere seconds earlier was gone. She looked . . .

"Anissa?" he prompted. "Anissa, are you all right?"

Cole opened her eyes, her arms rising slightly and away from her body, before she nodded. "I . . . it's okay. I feel . . . Adam, there's . . . something . . . she's . . . talking."

"She?" Montes repeated. "She who? Who's talking?"

Like a patient emerging from anesthesia, Cole blinked several times and a small, contented smile appeared. "Naqa. Naqa's talking to me. This is incredible."

"Naqa?" Gaulke eyed the thing on the back of her neck. "That's its name?"

"Yes." Her smile widening, Cole nodded. "Naqa. It's hard to describe, but I can hear her." She seemed to waver, and her hand reached out to grab Gaulke's forearm. "I feel dizzy. I need to sit down."

With Sa-Gameet's help, Gaulke directed her to one of the tables and its connected benches. He could not help staring at the thing now attached to her neck, and his first impulse was to tear the creature from her body. With no way to know how that action might affect Cole, he resisted the urge, but he could not help wondering what harm— if any—she was enduring from this seemingly parasitic coupling.

Now seated on one of the benches, Cole appeared to relax. "This feels strange." Her eyes narrowed as though she was lost in thought, then she added, "Naqa says she understands your concern and promises that she's not hurting me."

Montes asked, "Is she right? Is she hurting you?"

"No, not all. Naqa says not to worry and that she knows this can be unsettling to watch."

"Unsettling isn't the word for it," Gaulke snapped, not

caring about the concern creeping into his voice. "What are you feeling? Is it . . . is *Naqa* . . . controlling you?"

"I don't think it's that simple," Cole replied. "She's there, but I still feel . . . I've never felt anything like this. She seems genuinely happy that we're here. We'll explain everything."

It took Gaulke an extra second to realize what he had heard. "Wait, what? *We'll* explain everything? Who's 'we,' Anissa? Is she . . . is Naqa speaking through you?"

"She can."

Standing to Gaulke's left, Sa-Gameet said, "We should apprise Commander Stano of what has happened."

"Amen to that," added Montes.

Gaulke gestured to them. "Find a way to get that door open. Cut a hole through it if you have to, but I want out of here." Turning his attention back to Cole, he asked, "Are you all right, Anissa? Or, am I talking to Naqa? Or both of you?" To his surprise, she laughed.

"Adam, it's me. Naqa is simply with me now. I can hear her thoughts and she hears mine. It's a learning process for both of us. She says she's never encountered a species like ours before."

"Okay," Gaulke said. "So, what does she want?"

"They need our help. The ship has been dormant for a very long time, and its systems need to be restored. Naqa and the others are here to retrieve those they left behind on this world generations ago."

Gaulke, still processing all of this, frowned. "Okay, that seems reasonable, but why did Naqa have to take control of you to tell us this?"

"They need other bodies to communicate with those

who aren't like them," Cole replied. "Without such hosts, they can't do anything. They're helpless, Adam." She started to rise from the bench, prompting Gaulke to hold out his hand.

"Let's hang on a minute, Anissa. There's a lot to sort out here, don't you think? We need to tell Commander Stano about this, and she needs to tell the captain. We can help, but we don't know yet what all that might involve."

Cole nodded as she stood. "It's all right, Adam. Naqa understands your concerns, but she's already told me what to do."

The phaser in her hand was the last thing Gaulke saw before everything dissolved in a flash of blue-white light.

9

For the first time since arriving on Cantrel V, Yataro permitted himself to rest.

He did not so much sit as collapse upon the cargo container that had been left outside the temporary shelter designated for him and his engineering team, allowing himself to rest his back against the structure's sloping wall. Just that simple movement was enough to alleviate much of the day's strain, and the *Endeavour*'s chief engineer released a contented sigh. Though he knew his reprieve would be fleeting, he could still enjoy these few moments before he would return his attention to the numerous tasks and other matters demanding his attention.

"Commander?"

Only then realizing that his eyes had closed, Yataro opened them to see Lieutenant Phu Dang walking toward him. The engineer looked disheveled, and his hair and green jumpsuit were covered in a layer of fine dust. His skin had darkened beneath his eyes, a physical sign of fatigue that Yataro had learned to recognize during his earliest interactions with humans.

"What can I do for you, Lieutenant?"

The young engineer shook his head. "Nothing, sir. I was on my way to grab something to eat and wanted to know if I could bring you something."

Pondering that for a moment, Yataro shook his head. "I think that I will wait to eat until I return to the ship."

Dang smiled. "Are you sure, sir? You'll be missing out on some of the best reconstituted ham loaf that's been packaged in the last ten years. Maybe twenty."

Despite the extensive training he had received in preparation for leaving his homeworld of Liria to act as an envoy to Starfleet and the Federation, understanding various nuances of behavior inherent to different species remained an ongoing challenge for Yataro. Humans in particular carried with them a penchant for odd behavior in any number of areas, such as their propensity to inject humor into their various interactions with one another. Lieutenant Dang appeared to be most adept at this behavior. A native of Vietnam, one of Earth's smaller nation-states, Dang possessed a demeanor that his human colleagues described as "good-natured." The man seemed unshakable in his capacity to provide amusing observations in even the most trying of circumstances. Yataro was familiar with the concept, of course, and knew from observing such conduct that this ability, when employed with the proper balance of professionalism and bearing, often had a positive impact on the morale of those working in close proximity during stressful situations. Though humor was not unknown to the Lirin people, it was something that did not come with ease to Yataro. In the time he and Dang had worked together as leaders of the *Endeavour*'s engineering staff, Yataro had learned that his assistant was rather accomplished in this regard and had watched with no small amount of admiration as the lieutenant employed the tactic to great success.

"I appreciate your offer," Yataro said, "but for now I am content merely to rest. The available rations hold no appeal for me." Though he had worked with the *Endeavour*'s chief steward to program the ship's food processors to synthesize an acceptable selection of Lirin cuisine, no such options were available in the field ration packs such as those transported down with the rest of the landing party's supplies and equipment. His physiology did not react well to most of the foods preferred by humans, nor to much of the fare available to the starship's non-human crew members. It was a minor annoyance, and one easily rectified once he transported back to the *Endeavour*. Until then, water and the dietary supplements he had brought with him would suffice.

"You look tired, sir," said Dang, his expression one that Yataro recognized as concern. "Is there anything else you need?"

Yataro replied, "Perhaps a longer rest interval, but now this will have to suffice." A glance through the shelter's open doorway let him see that two other members of his engineering staff had found their way to cots. Another of the makesift beds beckoned, and he considered navigating what at this moment seemed a great distance separating him from the makeshift bed. It would, he decided, be a very easy feat to go to sleep right where he was. Of course, Starfleet protocol, to say nothing of personal pride, would prevent him from doing so, but that did not mean the thought wasn't tempting.

Reaching up to wipe his forehead with his uniform sleeve, Dang asked, "I suppose this isn't really the sort of thing you thought you'd be doing when you left your home planet, is it, sir?"

"I am not sure I understand your question," said Yataro.

"It's just that from what I understand of your civilization, every member serves a specific purpose. Is it true that you were bred for the sole intention of leaving your planet and representing your people to the rest of the Federation?"

"That is correct," replied the chief engineer. "I am only the third member of my species to leave my homeworld since Liria joined the Federation."

Dang nodded. "That's amazing. What did the other two do?"

"One served in Starfleet for a time, and the other acts as my people's representative on the Federation Council. When it was determined that Starfleet's ongoing exploration ventures were of great interest and benefit to Liria as well as all the worlds of the Federation, my government decided that more of our people should be active participants in such efforts. I am the first of that new group."

The lieutenant shook his head. "It seems like Starfleet could find something better for you than serving on a starship and dealing with situations like this."

"I requested starship duty," Yataro countered. "In fact, I specifically asked for assignment to the *Endeavour*. It has already been a far more rewarding experience than working in an office on Earth, a starbase, or even my homeworld. There is so much to do, so much to learn and discover. That is Starfleet's mandate, and we are here, at the forefront of that initiative." He paused, realizing that his emotions were welling up as he spoke. "It is exciting and an honor for me to represent my people."

Dang smiled. "I can only imagine." He gestured toward the shelter. "Our status report is due to Captain Khatami within the hour. I can take care of that, if you want to grab a few extra minutes' rest."

"I appreciate the offer," replied Yataro, "but I should be the one to submit the report. Take your meal. You have more than earned a respite. I will see to it before I return to the excavation site." He and his teams had spent the bulk of the afternoon clearing debris from the aftershock that had struck the area earlier in the day and caused several cave-ins within the site's underground areas. It was slow, methodical work as the engineers proceeded with caution deeper into the subterranean caverns and connecting passages, verifying the stability of the area as they moved. The last of the civilians and Starfleet personnel who had been missing since the alien ship's attack and the aftershock had been recovered and sent for medical treatment, leaving the rest of the archaeology team to assist Yataro and his people to continue cleaning up the site.

Turning his gaze toward the darkening sky, Dang said, "Has there been any word from the captain about the alien ship?"

Yataro replied, "There have been no updates since the boarding party was dispatched." The chief engineer was aware that even as he and the others worked down here, everyone's thoughts were on the mysterious vessel hanging above them in high orbit. Might it decide to launch another assault? There was no way to know.

The communicator in his jumpsuit's breast pocket chirped and Yataro retrieved the device, flipping open its cover. "Yataro here."

"Commander, this is Ensign Morrell," replied the voice of one of the *Endeavour*'s junior engineers. *"We've had a cave-in in sector four. A section of the tunnel connecting that area with the surface has collapsed."*

Pushing himself up from the cargo container, Yataro asked, "Are there any injuries?"

"None have been reported, sir, but we're still accounting for everyone. At last check, everyone had secured that area for the day. We'll have to clear this section again and verify its stability before allowing anyone else back down here."

Yataro said, "Let us account for everyone, and then we will halt operations until tomorrow. There is nothing in that section of the caverns that cannot wait until our people are better rested." He was not comfortable with anyone beginning another time-consuming clearing operation of the subterranean passages. Even with equipment to handle the laborious aspects of the task, most of the landing party had already been on duty for the bulk of the day. There would be time enough later.

"Sir," Morrell replied, *"there's something else down here that you need to see."*

Christine Rideout stared at the rubble littering the floor of the underground cavern. Earlier in the day, the piles of broken stone had formed the subterranean chamber's rear wall, but the rock had fallen away to reveal another wide, dark tunnel leading away even deeper beneath the dig site. One of the three portable field lamps positioned inside the cave had been caught by falling debris and damaged, its pair of bulbs extinguished. The other two lamps provided enough light to cast long shadows around the cavern as well as some light down the new tunnel.

"I'm no archaeologist," Rideout said, to no one in particular, "but I figure somebody's going to find this at least a little interesting, right?"

Standing next to her, Ensign Jonathan Morrell shrugged. "I'm not an archaeologist, either, and I think it's an attention-getter." The junior engineer gestured toward the new heaps of stone debris. "I'm just glad nobody was here when the wall decided to give way." He shook his head. "I don't get it. We scanned this whole area three hours ago, Master Chief, and there were no indications of any structural weaknesses. If there had been, we'd have sealed off the entire cavern."

It made no sense to Rideout, either. "I believe you, sir."

"I'll get a team together and we'll go over it again, just to be on the safe side." Sighing, Morrell waved again to the newly revealed tunnel. "And that too."

She resisted the urge to smile as she regarded the ensign, who seemed to her more like a teenager who had snuck out after curfew to meet up with friends, rather than a junior Starfleet officer and member of the *Endeavour*'s engineering staff. It was something she found herself noticing with increasing frequency in recent years, particularly after being promoted to her present rank. Rideout came from a long line of proud Starfleet enlisted personnel. More than one commanding officer had attempted to convince her to apply for a commission. Captain Khatami had remarked that her accepting assignment with the *Endeavour* was a sideways step, following her previous duty as chief engineer aboard the *Huang Zhong*. That ship had been a much different situation and crew dynamic, and she had no issues serving under Commander Yataro, from whom she knew she would learn a great deal as she undertook her first tour aboard a *Constitution*-class starship.

Rideout was aware that the *Endeavour* had already been involved in a number of missions here in the Taurus Reach—many of which remained classified—and that the ship along with the *Sagittarius* had taken the lead in a new initiative to further explore the region. Her orders had come through and she had arrived aboard just as both ships were completing upgrades and repairs after their first "exploration" assignment in this new area. Having read the official reports filed by the captains of both ships following that joint mission, Rideout knew she had made the right choice by requesting assignment to the *Endeavour*.

This is definitely where all the fun is.

"How far do you think this goes?" Rideout asked, nodding toward the new tunnel.

Taking the tricorder he had been carrying slung over his left shoulder, Morrell activated the unit and aimed it into the opening. The muted warbling of the device's scanner echoed in the cavern, and Rideout glimpsed strings of information scrolling across its miniature display. After a moment, the ensign frowned.

"It's hard to say, Master Chief. According to this, the

tunnel goes back at least thirty meters, and then looks to branch into at least three more, and there may even be another cavern down there." He frowned. "But after about fifty meters, the readings get pretty jumbled. It's almost like something's interfering with my scans."

Her gaze shifting between the ensign and the tunnel, Rideout asked, "Could it be natural interference from something in the rock?"

"Maybe, but our scans to this point haven't shown anything like that." Pressing another of the tricorder's controls, Morrell continued to direct the device toward the tunnel opening. "We'll check our readings against the schematics the colony's archaeology team made when they first surveyed the area, and compare the differences. It's possible this is just another section of tunnel they've already mapped."

The tricorder's whine was interrupted by a series of beeps that Rideout recognized as the unit's scans detecting something new. "What's that?"

Morrell's eyes narrowed as he consulted the tricorder's display. "I'm picking up an energy reading. It's faint, but it's there, and it's not consistent with our equipment, or anything belonging to the colony."

"What the hell could it be?" Rideout asked, her hand moving to rest on the familiar shape of the compact type-1 phaser tucked into the cargo pocket on her right hip. While the landing party's security contingent was carrying the larger, more powerful versions of the standard-issue weapon, she and most of the other engineers had opted for the smaller variant, which could be carried more easily along with the rest of their equipment. Now Rideout was beginning to wonder if she should have followed the security team's lead.

"I don't know what it is," Morrell replied, "but it's getting closer."

Instead of her phaser, Rideout pulled her communicator from another pocket and flipped it open. "Rideout to Lieutenant Brax."

A moment later, the voice of the *Endeavour*'s chief of security replied, *"Brax here. What can I do for you, Master Chief?"* An Edoan, the lieutenant's voice was high-pitched and possessed a raspy quality.

"We're still at the new section of tunnel, sir," Rideout replied. "Ensign Morrell's detecting an odd energy reading coming from deeper underground. We don't know yet what it is, but—"

"Look out!"

Rideout heard the warning just as she felt Morrell's hand against her back, pushing her down toward the ground before a shrill whine pierced the air. Something whipped past her cheek and she flinched, ducking away from it as she fell to the cavern's rough, uneven floor. There was the sound of glass and plastic popping and half of the chamber's light vanished as one of the field lamps was struck and knocked out of commission. Dropping to the ground, Rideout grunted in pain. Her communicator, jarred loose by the impact, skipped and bounced out of her reach. Before she could move to retrieve it, another sharp report echoed in the cavern, and this time Rideout saw a harsh green-yellow bolt of energy pass over her head.

"Son of a bitch!" she snapped, rolling to one side and scrambling to pull her phaser from her pocket. Next to her, Morrell had already brandished his own weapon and was aiming it at something she could not see.

Who the hell's shooting at us? And where the hell did they come from?

The questions rang in her ears along with the report from Morrell's phaser as he fired. Pushing herself to her feet, Rideout turned to face the tunnel, taking aim at the opening and for the first time seeing shadows moving inside the darkened passageway.

10

Sprinting around yet another in a series of curves in the underground tunnel, Ensign Kerry Zane slowed as the narrow passage opened into the larger cavern.

"This way!" he shouted over his shoulder. "In here."

Where the cavern previously had been illuminated by a set of portable work lights, now it was consumed by darkness save for the beam offered by Zane's hand lamp. He held the lamp alongside the phaser in his other hand, clearing the tunnel and moving to his right so that the other members of his security team could follow him. He inspected the chamber from left to right, his hand lamp and his phaser's muzzle tracking with his eyes as he searched for threats as well as Ensign Morrell and Master Chief Rideout. It had been less than two minutes since the chief's communication with Lieutenant Brax was interrupted by weapons fire, and the *Endeavour*'s security chief had wasted no time dispatching Zane and his team to this location.

There was no one here.

"Anybody see anything?" asked Zane. To his left, the two members of his team were spread to both sides of the tunnel junction, their backs to the rock wall as they mimicked his movements. Glancing in their direction, he saw two heads shaking. "Damn it. They were just here." With the newly exposed tunnel behind the collapsed cave wall, that meant there were three possible exits from this area. Zane and the others had not passed them heading in this direction, and no one had yet reported them as having arrived at the surface, which left only one option. "Berenato," he said, gesturing with his phaser toward the new tunnel opening. "Tricorder."

Ensign Joseph Berenato unlimbered the tricorder he carried slung across his body and activated it. The unit's whine filled the cavern as the junior security officer scanned the tunnel opening. "I'm picking up . . . wait." Zane heard him mutter something almost under his breath before adding, "I thought I had at least two life signs, but now there's nothing." He waved the tricorder in front of him. "Definitely residual traces of weapons fire in here, though; phasers, and something else I don't recognize." Turning to Zane, he asked, "Think they were ambushed?"

"Starting to look like it, don't you think?" Sidestepping around the cavern's perimeter, Zane maneuvered so that he could get a look down the mouth of the tunnel. "Question is, by who?" The first, obvious thought was that someone or something from the mysterious alien vessel currently orbiting Cantrel V must have transported to the planet without being detected by the *Endeavour*, the *Aephas*, or anyone else already down here, but Zane was finding that difficult to believe. "Check the work lights and see if they're still good."

"On it," replied Berenato, using his own hand lamp to guide him to where one of the field lights had fallen. "This one was shot out."

"As was this one," said Ensign Javokbi from where she stood next to a second light. The female Rigelian knelt beside the fallen equipment and directed her hand lamp to where it had shattered upon impact with the cavern's stone floor. "It appears to have been struck by a form of focused energy weapon, though perhaps not as advanced as our phasers."

Zane scowled. "That's not making me feel any better."

Well, you're the one who wanted the life of excitement.

After graduating third in his class at Starfleet Security School, Kerry Zane had been given his choice of assignments. This was following a brief stint with the security contingents assigned to the San Francisco Shipyards, during which he saw duty both on Earth as well as at the various orbital drydock complexes and other tenant organizations attached to the starship construction facility. That duty had provided him and other recent graduates with opportunities to acclimate to life in Starfleet beyond the Academy and follow-on schools, but like most eager young officers, Zane wanted a posting aboard a starship, preferably a ship of the line. News reports as well as security briefings and other correspondence was more than enough to convince him that the Starfleet's most advanced vessels—ships like the *Endeavour*, *Enterprise*, *Farragut*, and the *Exeter*—were where the action would be found.

Like many of his peers, his first choice had been the *Enterprise*, but scuttlebutt was that the ship was due for a return to Earth within the year, after which it would begin an extensive stem to stern refit. For its crew, that meant either reassignment or supporting the overhaul, which could take as long as three years to complete. Of the other starships with postings available, the *Endeavour* had stood out to Zane as showing great promise. The ship had seen action in the Taurus Reach while attached to Starbase 47 and reporting to Admiral Heihachiro Nogura, one of Starfleet's most revered flag officers. Though the starbase was gone and Nogura himself had been reassigned to Starfleet Headquarters back on Earth, the Taurus Reach remained, beckoning. That was enough to sell Zane on the *Endeavour*, and in the brief span of time that had passed since his reporting aboard, life and duty aboard the starship had been anything but mundane.

On the other hand, sometimes boring isn't so bad.

"Kerry, there's something else," said Berenato, his gaze once more focused on his tricorder. "Chief Rideout mentioned an energy reading before Lieutenant Brax lost contact with her. I'm not picking up anything like that, either. Whatever she and Morrell were seeing? It's gone."

Javokbi said, "Or, perhaps it is being concealed." When Zane and Berenato looked at her, the Rigelian added, "The energy readings Master Chief Petty Officer Rideout described were inconsistent with anything detected by any of our prior sensor sweeps, and none of the colonists have ever reported encountering anything similar in the time they have been here. Therefore, it seems reasonable to conclude that this new energy source has either only recently arrived beneath the surface, or else it has been here all along, but somehow able to avoid our scans."

"You keep talking like that," said Zane, "and I'm going to make you an honorary Vulcan." Despite his comment, he knew that Javokbi's observations were valid, and they served to heighten his own growing anxiety. "I'm not liking any of this. We're going to get some backup in here, and sweep every millimeter of this place until we get some answers." He was reaching for the communicator on his right hip when he detected movement to his right. Sweeping his hand lamp in that direction, Zane fixed the beam on a section of the cavern wall, his phaser now aiming at that spot.

Nothing was there.

"You okay?" asked Berenato, and Zane glanced over his shoulder to see the ensign stepping over a small rubble pile toward him.

Zane looked back to where his own light still shone on the cavern wall. Only bare rock looked back at him. "Yeah, I guess. I thought I saw something." He decided that his eyes must be falling victim to tricks being played by their own lights as well as the shadows themselves.

Then the shadows moved on their own. Again.

"There's somebody else in here!" Zane snapped, aiming his light and phaser at where he now was certain he had seen movement. Whatever it was, he realized it was moving away from his hand lamp beam, ghosts of motion teasing the edges of the darkness being chased aside by his light.

"To your right!" shouted Berenato, his warning punctuated by the sharp whine of his phaser. The cavern was bathed in a blue-white glow as the weapon discharged, and Zane saw the energy beam strike the rock wall.

"Ensign Zane!"

It was Javokbi, and she was firing her own phaser even before Zane could turn in response to her call. What he did see was her shot striking a dark, fleeting figure that had been darting among the larger stones near the section of collapsed wall. The blue beam hit its target in the upper torso, spinning it around and forcing it to stumble over a pile of rocks near the tunnel opening. It had been carrying something; a large, cylindrical object fell from its grip and clattered as it struck the cavern's stone floor.

Son of a . . . !

To his left, the darkness shifted and Zane swung his phaser in that direction, firing at the hint of movement that seemed to blend into the shadows. He glimpsed another figure dashing away from his light and tried to track it with the beam, but then there was nothing. There was no way whatever it was could have moved that fast. Zane fired in that direction and the phaser beam struck the cavern wall.

The wall—a section of it, anyway—*shimmered*.

Lasting only an instant, the effect was gone as abruptly as it appeared, and Zane's eyes narrowed as he realized what he had seen.

"They're using some kind of cloak!" he yelled, firing his weapon a second time at the wall. This time there was no reaction. "They're moving around us. Pull back!" Certain he detected yet more movement, Zane adjusted his aim, but then the air right in front of his face was wavering, and he felt a tingling sensation playing across his exposed skin.

Then something struck him in the face.

Light exploded in his vision as he cried out in pain, the force of the blow knocking him off his feet. He landed hard on the cave floor, his hand lamp striking a nearby rock and jolting from his grip. Managing to retain his hold on his phaser, Zane rolled to his left, ignoring the throbbing in his face and trying to find the source of the attack. Shouts of surprise echoed in the cavern, and he saw Berenato slumping to the ground. Then Zane felt hands on him, too many for him to fight, and the phaser was ripped from his grasp.

Despite his struggles, he was dragged to his feet, unable to see much due to the cavern's near darkness. His vision still blurred and his face still aching from the punch he had taken, Zane counted at least four bodies—humanoid, at least in most respects—pressing against his, preventing him from escaping and subduing his every attempt to shake free. Ahead of him, Zane saw Javokbi and Berenato restrained in similar fashion, with all three officers being guided toward the tunnel opening. Other figures stood at the threshold, some holding weapons while others carried items Zane could not identify.

"Let go of me!" he growled through gritted teeth, tensing his muscles and continuing to fight despite what felt like iron bands gripping his arms and shoulders. Then Zane felt another hand grab the back of his neck and push him forward with greater purpose. By now, Javokbi and Berenato were through the hole in the cavern wall and in the tunnel, which was almost pitch black. Only fleeting light from the team's dropped hand lamps cast any illumination, and even that seemed to be fading. Zane tried to examine his surroundings, to pick up any clues that might come in handy should he and the others manage to escape their captors, but there was nothing but the passage's stark, unyielding rock.

As the group reached what appeared to be a junction in the tunnel, one of the attackers—someone behind him—barked something Zane could not understand, and the group stopped its march. The sound of some kind of device powering up warbled in the confined space, and Zane jerked his head around in time to see the section of tunnel leading from the junction back to the cavern vanish, taking with it whatever light remained. Now in total darkness, Zane's eyes widened and he fought momentary disorientation as he attempted to get his bearings. All he could hear were the sounds of breathing, his own as well as those of the strangers holding him. Realizing that their only apparent avenue of escape was gone, Zane renewed his attempts to break his captors' hold on him.

"Joe!" he shouted, his voice all but deafening in the darkness. "Javokbi!" The grips on his arms, shoulders, and neck only seemed to strengthen.

Another punch came out of nowhere and crashed into the side of his head, and Kerry Zane's world went away.

Standing in front of the helm and navigation stations, arms folded as she stared at the main viewscreen, Atish Khatami felt an unsettling combination of annoyance and worry beginning to take hold in her gut. It required physical effort for her not to start pacing around the *Endeavour*'s bridge. She instead forced herself to stand still, her gaze fixed on the image of Lieutenant Brax, who looked to be standing inside one of the temporary shelters the landing party had erected at the dig location the Tài Shan colonists had designated as Beta Site. Behind the Edoan security chief were a trio of portable workstations and a pair of field tables, around which were gathered a half-dozen members of the *Endeavour*'s engineering and security teams.

"We have completed our initial sweep of the area, Captain," said Brax. *"There are no signs of the missing personnel, and we are at a loss to understand or explain what happened. My people are preparing to conduct a second search, and we will continue the effort until Ensign Zane and the others are found."*

"Any chance they were caught in another cave-in?" asked Khatami.

"We are exploring that possibility, Captain, but there appear to be no such indications." The lieutenant shook his oversized, orange-hued head, which always seemed as though it might topple off the narrow, elongated neck protruding from the collar of his red Starfleet tunic. The uniform had been custom-tailored to accommodate his physiology, which included a third arm extending from the front of his chest. Likewise, a third leg descended from his lower torso, providing him with added stability and agility. Very adept at his duties, Brax also was a formidable marksman, and Khatami had observed his skills on the ship's phaser range, where he had often conducted his regular recertification three times: once for each hand.

"What about those energy readings they reported?" Khatami asked. "Ensign Morrell and Master Chief Rideout said they were picking up some new energy source beneath the surface."

Again, the lieutenant shook his head. *"We have scanned for those, as well, Captain, and we are finding nothing."*

"They couldn't have vanished, Brax. Even if they're dead, you should be able to detect their bodies." Khatami regretted the callous comment the moment the words were past her lips, and she released a small sigh of mounting exasperation. "My apologies, Lieutenant. What do you think happened?" Before Brax could answer, another ensign in a red tunic stepped into the frame and handed the lieutenant a tricorder.

"One moment, Captain," the Edoan said. *"I have just been given some new information. Ensign Zapien has completed another scan of the area, and his tricorder detected residual evidence of phaser fire as well as another form of energy weapon with which I am unfamiliar."*

Khatami frowned. "A firefight? With whom?"

"Unknown, Captain."

Turning to the science station, Khatami regarded Kayla Iacovino, the junior science officer assigned to the bridge while Klisiewicz was off the *Endeavour*. "Ensign, have there been any signs of transporter activity from that alien ship? Or perhaps some kind of smaller landing craft? Anything?"

Iacovino shook her head. "No, Captain. Nothing like that. Whoever else is down there, they've been there all along. Or, if they did transport down from that ship, they did it before we got here."

None of this was making sense. Cantrel V had been surveyed and declared uninhabited well before the establishing of the Tài Shan colony. So far as Khatami knew and according to every report she had reviewed while en route here, the only people to visit the planet since the settlement's founding belonged to support vessels sent by Starfleet. Neither the Klingons nor any other interstellar power known to have assets in the Taurus Reach had shown any interest in the Cantrel system. Of course, this did not include the mysterious vessel that had come to make life interesting, but the identity of that ship's builders remained unknown.

So, who the hell else is down there?

"Brax," Khatami said, "I want all nonessential personnel out of the underground areas until further notice. Anyone who participates in your next search is to be armed or accompanied by our security people. We'll conduct a full-spectrum sensor sweep of the entire area to see if we can locate life signs or energy sources."

On the viewscreen, the Edoan nodded. *"Understood, Captain, but there are still colonists trapped in two different subterranean chambers. At last report, they should be extracted within the hour."*

"Fine, but then I want everyone out of there. I don't want to lose anyone else." She was unwilling to believe that Ensign Morrell and the other *Endeavour* personnel were dead rather than simply missing, but neither did she want to add more names to either list. That extended to the rest of her people working on the planet's surface, as well. Doctor Leone's latest status report indicated that those colonists requiring medical treatment had all been addressed, and the most serious cases had already been transported to the ship's sickbay to receive more extensive treatment than could be administered at the field clinic established by the landing party. At least in that respect, the situation facing the colony appeared to be stabilizing. Meanwhile, the most recent update from Commander

Mahmud al-Khaled detailed the *Aephas*'s ongoing repair efforts, which were continuing in slow but steady fashion. The commander had estimated another five to six hours before the most pressing repairs were completed, and that was with *Endeavour* engineers and other technicians providing assistance.

"Ensign Iacovino," said Khatami, "coordinate your efforts with Lieutenant Brax. Something down there doesn't seem to want us finding them, so whatever tricks you might have up your sleeve, now's the time to pull them out."

The young science officer smiled. "On it, Captain."

Khatami waited for Brax's image to fade from the viewscreen before allowing herself to sag against the helm and navigation console. Releasing another small sigh, she reached up to rub the bridge of her nose.

"You all right, Captain?" whispered her navigator, Lieutenant McCormack.

"Nothing a month's shore leave wouldn't cure," Khatami replied. "Remind me to do something about that once we're done here."

McCormack said, "I hear Argelius is nice this time of year."

"Sold." Khatami could feel the first hints of the headache she knew was coming. It was the sort of dull ache that asserted itself whenever she found herself feeling helpless while members of her crew were exposed to danger.

You think you'd be used to this sort of thing by now.

No sooner did the thought tease her than she corrected it. She did not want herself growing accustomed to sending her people into harm's way. On the contrary, when circumstances forced her to make such a decision, she wanted always to feel hesitation, perhaps even a bit of fear at the very idea. Only then could Khatami be sure that she never acted in cavalier fashion when it came to risking the safety of those under her command.

Of course, this also meant that she could count on those headaches, like the one now waiting to pounce on her.

Just another day at the office.

11

Stephen Klisiewicz swept his hand lamp's beam through the thin horizontal slot in the face of the large cylindrical vessel before him. The beam reflected off the transparent barrier set into the opening as it illuminated the container's interior and revealed yet another pair of closed eyes.

Hello? Is there anybody in there?

"Humanoid. Male," he said, verifying his guess against his tricorder's scan readings. "Species unknown. Age indeterminate." There were lines around the eyes and across the humanoid's forehead, and what hair there was featured a light gray or white pigment, matched by the color of the thick, unkempt mustache. As with the other cylinders he had inspected, this one's occupant was alive, though his metabolic functions had been slowed to a degree Klisiewicz had not seen even in the most advanced stasis chambers.

How long had he been in there, sleeping? The question again teased Klisiewicz, just as it had with each of the two dozen identical cylinders he had inspected to this point. Hundreds more, lining both sides of the massive room and stored on two separate levels, waited, each one containing a representative of the same humanoid species that the science officer did not recognize. Studying the person cradled inside the cylinder, Klisiewicz imagined for a moment that he could be roused from his slumber through sheer force of will. If he were a Vulcan or some other form of telepath, he might be able to reach through the metal coffin and into the suspended man's mind. What would he find in there? Tranquility, chaos, or perhaps nothing at all? Was the man dreaming?

"Lieutenant?"

Startled by the abrupt intrusion into his thoughts, Klisiewicz looked over his shoulder to where Commander Katherine Stano stood a few meters away. Like him and other members of the boarding party, the first officer had removed her environment suit and now wore an olive-green jumpsuit. A tricorder was slung across her chest and rested against her left hip, a type-2 phaser on her right hip.

"Sorry, Commander," replied Klisiewicz, clearing his throat. "I guess I let my mind drift for a moment." Blinking to push aside the remaining mental fog that had served to distract him, he asked, "Any word from the other teams?"

Stano nodded. "Gaulke finally reported in. They're on their way back. He says they didn't find anything interesting."

"At least they're okay." As with the commander and everyone else, Klisiewicz had been concerned when Ensign Adam Gaulke failed to make a scheduled check-in. After attempts to reach the security officer were unsuccessful, Stano had recalled the rest of the boarding party with the intention of launching a search, only to have Gaulke finally make contact a few minutes later. The ensign had reported entering an area of the alien vessel that seemed to act as a "dead zone" for their communicators, and it was not until he had attempted to make his regular update to Stano that he realized the problem and started backtracking until contact could be reestablished.

Waving to the row of cylinders Klisiewicz was inspecting, Stano asked, "Find anything interesting?"

"No variations in my readings. This one's just like all the others—in a state of deep hibernation for who knows how long."

Stepping away from Klisiewicz, Stano turned to study the rest of the immense room and its collection of hibernation chambers. "This place is enormous."

"We counted two hundred sixty cylinders," said Ensign Tropp as he walked toward them from another section of containers. "Based on the ship's layout, I wouldn't be surprised to find a similar chamber in each of the other spheres."

"The room's shielded from external scans," added Klisiewicz, "at least from anything like our tricorders. Combined with the ship's mendelevium hull, it's no wonder the *Endeavour* sensors didn't pick up any life readings." He gestured toward the cylinder. "Hell, they're barely registering now, and I'm an arm's length away."

"Any idea how they're controlled?" Stano asked.

Klisiewicz shook his head. "They're not controlled individually, if that's what you mean. No control pad or other instruments or obvious means of opening them." He gestured toward the far side of the room, where Lieutenant Ivan Tomkins was hunched over the control console he had discovered upon the team's entering the room. "Tomkins figures it's overseen by some kind of master control process via the ship's computer, but he hasn't found that part of the system yet." The man had more than proven his value since the team's arrival aboard ship. With main power restored, at least to most of the vessel's major sections, Tomkins had figured out how to engage and disengage the door security systems, which in theory now allowed the team access to any compartment on the ship. This had gone a long way toward facilitating the boarding party's inspection.

Stano stepped closer to one of the cylinders and peered through its slot. "Tropp, what about the people inside these things?"

"I've never encountered this particular species before, Commander," replied the medic. "Those I've scanned all appear to be in prime physical condition. If my readings are correct, they've been in hibernation for at least a century—probably more—but the long-term effects on their bodies would seem to be negligible. It's entirely possible that they could emerge from stasis and resume whatever they were doing before hibernation, with little to no trouble."

"Considering what this ship was able to do without a crew," Stano countered, "I'm not so sure I'm excited about these people waking up and going back to work."

"Commander!"

Tomkins's shouting from the other side of the room drew the trio's attention, and Klisiewicz could see that the console the engineer had been studying had come to life. Rows of controls, indicators, and displays now were active.

"What's going on?" asked Stano.

The engineer waved to the console. "The damned thing

just came on by itself, Commander. I was only scanning it with my tricorder and didn't touch a thing. I would've warned you first."

Walking toward the workstation, Klisiewicz asked, "Can you tell what it's doing? Are there other systems coming online?"

"Looks that way." Tomkins turned back to the console. "There are systems activating all through this sphere, and maybe the other ones too. Something big got tripped, that's for sure."

Footsteps on the metal deck plating behind them caught their attention, and Klisiewicz was relieved to see Ensign Gaulke and the other members of his search party entering the room. As with everyone else, they also had shed their environment suits and now wore green jump-suits.

"Gaulke," said Stano, watching as the ensign approached, flanked by Ensigns Sa-Gameet, Guillermo Montes, and Anissa Cole. "Good to see you and your team are okay."

Instead of the security officer, it was Cole who moved to stand before her, replying, "Hello, Commander. We apologize if you were startled by the abrupt activation of certain shipboard systems." She offered an odd smile. "That was our doing."

"You?" asked Klisiewicz, before exchanging glances with Stano. "You did this?"

Cole nodded. "Yes, Lieutenant."

"Explain, Ensign," said Stano. "What did you do?"

Her expression falling in response to the first officer's

question, Cole replied, "We've found something truly remarkable, Commander. Actually, that's not entirely accurate. It's not what we've found . . . it's *who*."

Stano frowned. "You've made contact with someone aboard this vessel?"

"We have."

"Who are they?" asked Klisiewicz. "Where are they?"

"And most importantly," Stano added, "why didn't you report this immediately?"

Cole turned her gaze to the first officer. "We're reporting to you now, Commander. We wanted to tell you in person so you could see—"

"Commander Stano," said Ensign Tropp from where he stood to the side of the new arrivals. The Denobulan medic's gaze was fixed on Cole and the others, concern evident on his face. "Ensign Cole and her companions appear to have been exposed to an unknown life-form."

"What?" The word all but burst from Klisiewicz's lips. "What are you talking about, Tropp?"

"Each of them is carrying an unidentified organism on the back of their neck. It's like nothing I've ever seen before."

Stano's first reaction to this was to reach for her phaser, but she stopped as Cole held out her hand. "Commander, wait. It's not what you think. Let us explain."

With her hand hovering over the phaser on her hip, Stano's reply was terse. "Very well, Ensign. Start explaining."

"They need our help," Cole said, holding up her hands. "Despite their advanced intellects, they need people, like us, to help them with all manner of physical tasks. Without a host, they're unable to even communicate with most other species. Please, let me show you." Keeping her hands out and away from her body, Cole turned around, allowing Stano and the others to see the gray mass on the back of her neck, just above her jumpsuit's collar and beneath the dark blond hair she had pulled into a tight bun atop her head. Klisiewicz could see it pulsing as it rested at the base of her skull, obviously alive, and with four appendages holding it in place in such a manner that it looked like a bulbous *X*.

"Dear God," Stano said.

Activating his tricorder, Tropp aimed it at Cole. "The creature has penetrated her skin with some kind of protuberance, Commander. My scans show an odd neurochemical balance, as though the organism is stimulating her cerebral cortex. I am also detecting elevated levels of epinephrine. From what I can tell, the effect is not harmful, at least physically."

"The others are the same?" asked Klisiewicz.

Gaulke replied, "Yes, Lieutenant. All four of us have been collected."

"Tomkins," Stano snapped. "Contact Ensign McMurray and tell him to get his team back here immediately."

The engineer replied, "On it, Commander."

Her right hand still poised near her phaser, Stano reached with her other hand to extract a communicator from a pocket of her jumpsuit and flipped it open. "Stano to *Endeavour*."

"I'm afraid that won't work, Commander," said Cole, her voice calm. "We have locked out communications to and from the ship."

Tomkins called out, "I can't raise McMurray, either. All comm frequencies are jammed. I'm not even getting static."

Stano, still holding her communicator near her mouth, glared at the young science officer. "If this is your way of telling me not to worry, Ensign, then you're not doing a very good job."

"I apologize, Commander. That's not my intention."

Klisiewicz asked, "Anissa, how are you feeling?"

"I feel wonderful, Lieutenant," Cole replied, and her smile returned. "I feel as though I have a true purpose."

Stepping closer, Klisiewicz resisted the temptation to scan her with his tricorder. Instead, he offered another question. "What can you tell us about the . . . whatever it is you brought with you?"

"Her name is Naqa. She's one of thousands of Lrondi aboard this ship."

"Lrondi," Stano repeated. "Never heard of them."

Klisiewicz shook his head. "Neither have I." He eyed Tropp. "Ensign?"

"No, Lieutenant," replied the Denobulan. "The species is new to me, as well."

Stano said, "Ensign, please tell . . . Naqa . . . that we're concerned for you and the others. We're worried that this . . . bonding . . . she's performed may be harmful to you."

"She can hear you, Commander," Cole said, "and you can speak directly to her. Think of me as a conduit. I help her go where she wants to go and do what she wants to do."

"Are you doing this against your will?" asked Klisiewicz. "Is she . . . ?"

Again, Cole's expression hardened. "The Lrondi are not parasites, Lieutenant. They do not feed on their hosts. Their nutritional needs are met in other ways. They are also very long-lived. By our standards, they're practically immortal."

"Practically?" asked Stano.

"They can be killed, certainly. They're not invulnerable to injury," Cole said. "But Naqa, like all Lrondi, ages at a very slow rate. Her cells simply regenerate in a manner similar to that seen in some species of jellyfish on Earth and other worlds. It's all rather complicated, but she's happy to explain it to you."

"Right now," Stano said, "I want Naqa to explain why the Lrondi are here and why they attacked Cantrel V."

Tension seemed to grip Cole for a moment before she answered, "That wasn't an attack. The Lrondi have answered a distress call and are engaging in a rescue operation. Thankfully, we have come just in time to help them. Now that we are here, we can be guided by the Lrondi to assist in the recovery of those on the planet who have awaited our return for generations. For that to happen, we will need to collect more hosts."

"You mean us?" asked Ensign Tomkins, who had moved to stand next to Stano.

Cole nodded. "At first, yes, but ultimately we have an entire crew to revive." She gestured toward the rows of cylinders. "For generations, the Pelopan have proven most helpful to us. It is their world we now orbit. Many were collected when my people visited this planet, but they were forced to leave, marooning scores of Lrondi, as well. We have come to rescue them."

"And to collect more Pelopan, as you called them?" asked Stano.

"Of course, Commander."

The first officer shook her head. "I don't think so. Ensign, from this point forward, you will take no further action without my orders. We need to inform Captain Khatami what's going on over here."

Again, Cole's smile returned. "This isn't your ship, Commander. You have no authority here. In this, I am guided by Naqa. She welcomes your assistance."

"If Naqa wants us to be friends," Stano said, "she can demonstrate good faith by releasing you and the others. Then we can update the captain and get direction from her."

Cole replied, "Naqa believes it's beneficial to remain bonded. Indeed, she believes we have much to learn from one another." Watching her talk, Klisiewicz noted the conflict in the ensign's eyes. She was, he surmised, fighting with Naqa on some internal level, perhaps laboring to convince the Lrondi to listen to Stano, while the organism pushed back. What must that be like, he wondered, to be caught in the midst of such a struggle?

"Naqa feels the bond is important," Cole said, and now Klisiewicz was certain he heard the strain in her voice, which now accompanied the apparent conflict in her eyes. Whatever was happening inside her mind, she was trying to fight it.

Stano stepped forward and pressed, "Ensign, are you able to break the bond yourself?"

"I do not want to."

"Phaser!"

Tomkins was the one to call the warning, and Klisiewicz reacted almost without thinking as he caught sight of
Ensign Gaulke reaching for the phaser on his hip. He was
bringing up the weapon but Tomkins was faster, drawing
his own phaser and firing. A blue beam of energy struck
Gaulke in the chest and the ensign sagged, stumbling
backward and falling stunned to the deck.

By then the room had erupted into chaos, with almost
everyone now pulling their weapons and either firing or
moving for cover. Only Ensign Tropp failed to draw his
phaser, and he paid for that hesitation as Sa-Gameet took
aim and fired. Caught in the open and empty-handed, the
Denobulan collapsed in a heap to the floor.

Stano, on the other hand, had seized the initiative,
opening fire on Montes, but the security officer was too
fast. He fired, moving away from the group and ducking
behind a row of hibernation cylinders. Sa-Gameet mimicked his actions, firing more to prevent pursuit than with
any real hope of hitting someone.

"You cannot interfere!" Cole shouted, trying to aim at
Stano, but Klisiewicz charged her, knocking the phaser
from her hand. The weapon skipped out of reach across
the deck, but Cole did not care. She turned on Klisiewicz,
swinging her fist toward his head. He ducked to avoid the
strike and she swung past him, carrying herself off balance. Trying to bring up his phaser, he realized he was too
slow as she lunged at him, rage burning in her eyes.

Blue energy washed over her, accompanied by the welcome sound of a phaser. Cole's body jerked in response to

the stun beam before she sagged forward and toppled into Klisiewicz, who grabbed her and kept her from falling to the deck.

More phaser fire erupted around them, lancing outward from where Gaulke and the others had sought cover deeper in the room. Stano took aim and returned volleys of her own, moving toward the door. "Klisiewicz, we have to get out of here!"

Lifting the unconscious Cole and settling her on his shoulder, Klisiewicz fired his phaser in the general area of where Sa-Gameet and Montes had retreated, then allowed Stano to cover him as he moved for the door. Once in the corridor, he stepped to the side and out of the line of fire as Tomkins dashed over the threshold, firing behind him as he ran. Stano was the last one out, and she hit the control pad to close the hatch. Once it cycled shut, she adjusted her phaser and fired at the pad, destroying it.

"I have no idea if that even worked," she said, trying to catch her breath, "so let's get the hell out of here."

Tomkins nodded. "Amen. Where are we going?"

"Good question," she said. "Anybody have any ideas?"

Still carrying Cole, Klisiewicz asked, "How about whatever passes for a bridge on this ship? Or engineering? Someplace where we can get access to the computer and the other onboard systems."

"I like the way he thinks," Tomkins said, keeping his gaze and his phaser trained on the door. "But what about the others? And what about contacting the *Endeavour* for help?"

Klisiewicz shifted Cole higher on his shoulder in a futile effort to get comfortable. "There's nothing we can do for them unless or until we can capture them, or figure out how to communicate with those things that are controlling them."

Stano gestured to the unconscious Cole. "Is that why you brought her along?"

"It seemed like a good idea at the time."

"I'd keep an eye on that thing, if I were you," warned Tomkins, pointing to the creature on Cole's neck. "No telling what it might do."

Klisiewicz tried shifting Cole's weight once more. "Yeah. No kidding, but at least it's a start toward figuring out what this is all about."

"Great," Stano said. "Any idea what to do next?"

Snorting, Klisiewicz shook his head. "The first thing we should do is find a place to hide. After that? I don't have the first damned clue."

12

Christine Rideout was certain that if left to its own devices, her brain would punch its way out of her skull.

"You okay?" asked a voice from somewhere above her, and Rideout opened her eyes to see Ensign Kerry Zane standing over her. He had a fresh bruise beneath his left eye, and the fabric of his red uniform tunic was torn at the right shoulder. Looking past him, Rideout realized that she was lying on her back, staring up at the stone ceiling of yet another cave.

Releasing a groan of fatigue laced with pain, Rideout pushed herself to a sitting position and promptly regretted that move. "Wow," she said, reaching up to massage her forehead, "this is my worst hangover since I was a cadet." When she looked up, she saw Zane eyeing her with obvious doubt in his eyes. "Okay, fine. It's my worst hangover since my last hangover. Stop judging me. You're not my mom."

Zane chuckled, extending his hand. Accepting his help, she allowed the security officer to pull her to her feet, then leaned on him as the room around her began to spin. She closed her eyes and drew a handful of deep breaths, while deciding that this really was her worst hangover since her Academy days.

"Why did I have to wake up?" Rideout grimaced, biting back queasiness. "Come to think of it, what put me to sleep?" With tentative fingers, she checked the welt on the back of her head. She must have earned that after striking the rock floor somewhere. It was tender to the touch, and she made a mental note to leave it the hell alone for a little while. After another moment, she was at least somewhat certain that she would not fall back down. She looked around the chamber and saw Ensign Jonathan Morrell as well as two members of Zane's security detachment, Ensigns Joseph Berenato and Javokbi. Though none of them appeared to have suffered any serious injuries, there were obvious bruises and cuts along with soiled and torn clothing.

"Are you all okay?"

Each of them nodded before Morrell asked, "What about you, Master Chief?"

"The good news is that I think I'm going to live, sir." Rideout blew out her breath. "The bad news is that I think I'll live." It took her an extra second to realize that none of her companions were carrying phasers, tricorders, or any other equipment, and Rideout's hands went to the pockets of her jumpsuit to confirm that her own weapon as well as her communicator and assorted tools and other items were gone.

"Where's our stuff?" she asked, looking around the cavern. "And where are we? What happened?" As she voiced the question, Rideout began remembering those last moments before everything had gone black. "Wait. We were attacked."

Zane replied, "That's a nice way of putting it." The ensign indicated Berenato and Javokbi. "We were ambushed. Whoever they are, they had some kind of cloaking ability. They were standing twenty meters from us, and we never knew they were there until it was too late."

"Cloaking tech might also explain why we never detected any energy sources down here," added Morrell. "However, the archaeologists who've been poking around never mentioned finding anything that might indicate that sort of technology."

"What about the weapons they used?" asked Berenato. "I don't remember seeing anything about that in any of the pre-mission briefings."

Javokbi replied, "The reports given to us for review indicated a level of technological advancement that seemed to preclude such weaponry." The Rigelian gestured as though to indicate the cavern as well as the rest of the dig site. "Nothing we have found here is in conflict with those reports."

"That likely means one of two things," said Zane. "Either everybody here has overlooked something incredibly obvious, or else someone else has decided to call this place home, for some reason. Now, if we're all sure nobody came from that ship up in orbit, then who the hell are we talking about, and where did they come from?"

Though she was listening to the conversation, Rideout also was diverting part of her attention to an investigation of the cavern. Something about their new surroundings had been bothering her since she had shaken off her lethargy, if not the annoying dull ache behind her eyes, and it was only now that she realized what had been begging to be noticed.

"Hey, am I the only one who sees that there doesn't appear to be any way out of this place?" When the others looked to her with varying expressions of confusion, she gestured around the chamber. "Look. No tunnels or air-shafts or other openings in the rock. How'd we get in here, and how are we supposed to get out?"

Zane frowned. "Damn good questions, Master Chief. Wish I had some answers to go with them." Stepping away from the group, he began taking a closer look at the nearby wall. "In addition to whatever cloaking ability they have, the people who attacked us also used something to seal up the entrance to the tunnel they dragged us into." He ran one hand across the wall's jagged, uneven surface. "What I don't know is whether they moved rock or some other substance into place, or if it was just a projection."

"Given the speed with which they were able to act," said Javokbi, "I believe it was a projection."

"I'm with her," added Berenato. "I remember a couple of their people carrying some kind of equipment. At first, I thought they might be weapons, but they seemed too bulky for that."

"Guys."

Something in Ensign Zane's tone triggered new worry in Rideout. When she glanced in his direction, it was to see the security officer staring not at the rock wall but instead something behind him—and her. Pivoting on her heel, she turned toward whatever had attracted his attention. That was when she felt her own jaw slacken.

Oh, holy . . .

"Please do not be alarmed," said the humanoid figure, one of a dozen standing along the cavern's far wall. She was dressed in what Rideout took to be a simple tan jump-suit not at all different from her own uniform, though it

offered no discernible pockets or insignia and seemed to
hang off her thin, lanky frame. Her companions sported
a variety of other clothing—unadorned shirts and trousers in an assortment of earth-toned colors. Rideout's first
impression was that the clothes were handmade, which
seemed to her at odds with the technology these people
had already demonstrated.

As for the humanoids themselves, most of them possessed physiques similar to that of the female who had
spoken: tall and thin, though nothing about their appearance suggested malnutrition. Their skin harbored a
greenish tinge, almost jade in color, and Rideout wondered if their blood might be copper-based rather than
iron, such as was the case with Vulcans, Romulans, and
a few other species. Some of the new arrivals were bald,
but those with long, dark hair wore it woven into a braid
and secured at the base of their necks. Their eyes, narrow
and white, lacked any obvious pupils, and it was this feature more than anything that seemed to accentuate their
intimidating appearance. Rideout also noticed that each
person appeared to be wearing something at the back of
their neck, but the cavern's dim lighting prevented her
from getting a better look. They also carried long, thin
staffs, with some kind of molded or manufactured handle
at one end, and held them in a manner that suggested to
Rideout rifles of some kind.

Despite the humanoid's calm demeanor, Rideout felt
her unease growing. It was a sensation mirrored by Zane
and the others, all of whom moved to stand next to her as
they beheld the new arrivals. As the senior officer present,
it fell to Zane to speak on behalf of the landing party, and

the ensign took a tentative step forward, holding his hands away from his body to indicate he was not a threat.

"My name is Zane. Ensign Kerry Zane."

The female humanoid fixed her gaze on him. "I am called Ivelan. You are the leader?"

Nodding, Zane replied, "In a manner of speaking." He gestured to Rideout and the others. "I'm responsible for these people, but I answer to other officers who will be looking for us, and they'll want to know why you've taken us hostage."

"We had to determine if your people are a threat, Ensign Kerry Zane," replied Ivelan. "That is also why we took possession of your weapons and equipment. One of your scanning devices emitted a frequency we found disruptive, so we were forced to take it. Once it has been examined and its harmful effects neutralized, it can be returned to you."

Zane raised his hands. "It's not our intention to harm you. We didn't even know there was anyone living underground here. Who are you? Are you descendants of this planet's original population?"

"Yes. We call ourselves the Pelopan. Our ancestors once lived above ground, in the cities you have undoubtedly seen and examined. We are the progeny of those who survived the conflict that ravaged our world generations ago."

"How are you able to understand us?" asked Berenato.

The humanoid turned her attention to him. "We have monitored your communications since your arrival, and we possess the ability to adapt to new linguistics. Your language is proving something of a challenge, but we have learned enough to communicate." She gestured to Javokbi. "You appear to be of a different species than your companions, so it stands to reason that you have your own language, and yet you understand one another."

The Rigelian replied, "Yes, my native tongue is quite different than those of my friends, but we all speak a common language that allows us to work together."

"Excellent." Before Zane or anyone else could continue, Ivelan raised her hand. "All of your questions will be answered in due course." She gestured for Zane and the others to step forward. "You will follow me." As she offered the declaration, the other members of her group maneuvered around the chamber, positioning themselves in a circle around the landing party. As though sensing Zane's unease, Ivelan said, "Do not be alarmed. I promise it is not our intention to harm you, unless you force us to defend ourselves."

"Where are you taking us?" asked Rideout. When everyone in the cavern turned to look at her, the master chief shrugged, her nervousness obvious by her widening eyes. "What? My mother told me never to talk to strangers."

Before Zane could respond, Ivelan replied, "You are to be taken to our Conclave, the ruling body of our people. Like you, they have many questions."

Though there was no menace in her voice, Rideout noted the way her companions moved closer, as though preparing to compel them by force to comply with Ivelan's instructions. Based on what they had already experienced from these people, she was not sure she and the rest of the landing party could fight their way out of this, and even if

they did, where would they go? Rideout had no idea where
they were taken after she was knocked unconscious. When
she exchanged looks with Zane, it was obvious that the
security officer had reached the same conclusion.

"We'll go with you," Zane said, returning his attention
to Ivelan, "and I promise we won't resist, but I'd like to
contact my superiors, to let them know we're unharmed."

Ivelan replied, "In due time, Ensign Kerry Zane." She
gestured to her companions before turning and walking
toward the cavern's far wall. Rideout fell in step behind
Zane as the ensign set off after her, with Morrell, Berenato, and Javokbi following. Rideout noted how the rest
of Ivelan's people formed an escort perimeter around
the landing party, though they at least were being polite
about it. Directing her gaze forward, she was in time to
see Ivelan stepping closer to the rock wall before her, but
instead of changing direction, she continued walking at
a steady pace. Just when Rideout thought the Pelopan
would stride face-first into the unyielding stone, she disappeared through it.

"Hologram?" asked Rideout, realizing only as the
word left her mouth that she had spoken it aloud.

Though he hesitated as Ivelan disappeared from view,
Zane continued forward without prodding from their escorts and Rideout watched him also vanish through what
appeared to be solid rock.

Well, damn. Here goes nothing.

She did not know what to expect as she stepped closer
to the wall. There was no sensation of an energy source
powering what had to be an electronic facade, though she
could not resist reaching out with one hand as though to

part a curtain. Only when her hand passed through the threshold to the hidden passage did she feel a warm tingle playing across her exposed skin, which she likened to that of a transporter beam. She passed through the illusion—or projection, or whatever the hell it was—and upon emerging from it she was greeted by yet another tunnel carved into the rock.

What were you expecting? Rainbows and unicorns? A nice sandy beach? Actually, that's not such a bad—

"This way," said Ivelan—who stood with Zane several meters ahead of her as Rideout got her bearings—before turning and continuing to lead the makeshift processional deeper into whatever subterranean lair these people called home. There was better lighting here, she realized, noting the circular lamps set into the tunnel's ceiling, and now that she was through the faux stone wall concealing this passage, she was aware of a low hum that suggested a power source.

Then she noticed the thing attached to Ivelan's neck.

It was partially hidden by her hair as well as the high collar of her single-piece garment. At first, Rideout thought it was just a natural part of the alien woman's obviously different physiology, but after a moment, the engineer was able to see that something was affixed to Ivelan's neck. Dull gray yet possessing a sheen that reflected the light from the work lamps, it appeared mostly as an amorphous mass, with two sinewy protrusions extending from its core that rested along the base of her skull. Watching the thing, Rideout saw that it pulsed with life, and even moved in rhythm with Ivelan's motions as she walked. Quick glances to the escorts flanking her told the engineer that they also carried similar—whatever they were—on their own necks. Instinct told Rideout that these things were not a normal part of the Pelopan's physiology, but something else altogether. Likewise, her gut also told her that any queries regarding the odd appendages would go unanswered.

It's not like these people are all that chatty, anyway.

Verifying that the other three members of the landing party had come through the entrance, Zane resumed following Ivelan. Despite her best efforts to keep track of the distance they traveled or the number of turns they made or the side tunnels they utilized, Rideout soon gave up any hope of remembering their route in the event they were able to make an escape. She settled for trying to identify and memorize key features as they traversed this chamber or that tunnel. Then even that effort fell away as they emerged from the passageway into the largest cavern she had seen since arriving on Cantrel V.

"Oh, wow," said Rideout, the words loud enough to make Ivelan turn and look in her direction, but the engineer ignored her as she took in their new surroundings. Like many of the tunnels they had navigated to get here, the immense grotto bore all the signs of having been carved from the rock by artificial means. Smooth walls rose toward a high curved ceiling, suspended from which were hundreds of light sources, spaced in such a way as to imply a night sky. An impressive feature, it was merely dressing for the remarkable scene dominating the cavern floor.

"An underground city?" asked Zane, still walking behind Ivelan. "Incredible."

It seemed to Rideout to be more a large town than a city, even a small one, despite its apparent size as indicated by the silhouettes of buildings and other structures stretching toward the massive cavern's far end. They had emerged from the connecting tunnel onto a ridge encircling the settlement at least several dozen meters above the cave's floor, by her reckoning. Most of the buildings seemed to share numerous similarities with respect to their exteriors, as though the same materials had been used to erect at least the major structures. In and around the buildings, Rideout could see people—all of them appearing to be of the same species as Ivelan and her companions.

"How many people do you think live down there?" she asked, looking to Zane.

The ensign shook his head. "Judging from the number and size of the buildings, I'd say a few thousand, at least. What I'm wondering is how such a large concentration of life-forms didn't show up on our sensors." He gestured toward the settlement. "They're producing energy too, and we didn't pick up that. However they're hiding it, they do it pretty damned well."

As she studied the scene, Zane's comments made Rideout realize that there appeared to be no form of transportation. No ground or other vehicles were visible, and despite what had to be a veritable hive of activity, very little in the way of ambient noise carried upward from the bottom of the immense chamber.

"How long have you lived down here?" she asked Ivelan. "You said you were descendants of those who once lived on the surface and who survived the war that destroyed it. Have you been down here since then?"

Instead of answering the question, the Pelopan gestured for them to continue following her. "This way."

"So, I guess it's not an interactive tour," Rideout said, rolling her eyes as she fell once more into step behind Zane. Ahead of the security officer, Ivelan followed the ridgeline until it ended at what looked to be a dull gray metal door set into a roughly circular opening in the rock wall. Ivelan pressed her hand against an oval, silver-colored plate that also was embedded in the stone, and the door slid upward, disappearing into the rock. Bright light emanated from the chamber beyond the opening, and Rideout caught glimpses of what might be furniture or other equipment she could not identify.

"What is this place?" asked Zane, and this time Rideout heard a harder edge in the ensign's voice.

Turning to face him, Ivelan replied, "This is where our Conclave gathers, Ensign Kerry Zane. You are to be taken before them."

"Look, we've complied with your demands to this point. If your leaders want to talk, they should really talk to my captain. She's the best person for something like this."

Ivelan smiled. "In due time."

Not liking the sound of that. Rideout felt her jaw tighten. *Not liking that at all.*

She was not alone with that feeling.

"Morrell! Wait!"

The warning came from behind her, and Rideout whirled around in time to see Ensign Jonathan Morrell lashing out at one of their Pelopan escorts. Surprised by the sudden attack, the alien was unable to defend himself as Morrell's fist smashed into the side of his head. The guard sagged, dropping to one knee and losing his grip on his weapon as the ensign turned and searched for another target. A second Pelopan was already moving toward him, raising the weapon he carried as though preparing to use it like a club. Morrell backpedaled from the guard, trying to put distance between himself and his opponent.

Raising her hands, Rideout shouted, "Look out!"

Morrell seemed to comprehend at the last possible instant that he was skirting danger as he backed toward the edge of the walking path, but by then his left foot was coming down on nothing but air. For what seemed like an eternity, Morrell hovered over the precipice, his arms moving in frantic windmill motions as he tried to maintain his balance. Lunging forward, Rideout extended her hands, racing toward him and knowing there was no way she would reach him in time.

Then, he was gone.

"No!" Rideout leaped forward, stretching her body to extend her reach, but he was gone even before she dropped to the ground. All that remained was the echo of the man's desperate, futile scream for help as he disappeared from the ledge. Rideout got there in time to see Morrell hit the sloping wall before sliding the rest of the way to the cavern floor. His fall attracted the attention of some few onlookers, many of whom were already running to where the ensign's unmoving body had come to rest.

"Damn it!" Rideout spat the words, smacking the stone beneath her with the flat of her hand. She had only known the engineer for a short time, but that brief interval had been enough to tell her that Jonathan Morrell had been

a young man possessed of great potential that would remain forever unrealized.

Son of a bitch!

Behind her, Rideout heard the scuffling of another
fight taking place behind her, and she rolled onto her side
to see Berenato and Javokbi struggling with other members of their escort detail. It was apparent that they also
had chosen to fight their guards, but the Pelopan and their
greater numbers made quick work of subduing both officers. Javokbi went down with a blow to the back of her
head, while Berenato was felled by an energy burst from
one guard's odd weapon. Rideout's initial fear that he had
been killed was mollified when she saw that he was still
breathing even as he lay on the ground.

"Stop."

The single word was spoken with such force that it
made Rideout flinch. Jerking her head around, she saw
Ivelan standing before the open doorway, holding out
one hand. Her expression had gone flat, and her eyes now
glowered at her before shifting to Zane and then to her
companions.

"That was as tragic as it was unnecessary," she said,
before gesturing to the escorts flanking Rideout and
Zane. "Bring them."

Rideout tensed as she felt the first hands grab her arms,
but it was obvious that she would not be able to overpower
the two Pelopan as they proceeded to guide her toward
Ivelan. Angry at Morrell's useless death, she still made
the attempt, if for nothing else than as a means of lashing out on the ill-fated ensign's behalf. Her movements
seemed not to faze the guards.

"Where are you taking us?" asked Zane, who also had tried without success to free himself.

Ivelan replied, "You have many questions, Ensign Kerry Zane. It is time to provide you with answers." As the Starfleet personnel were directed through the doorway, Rideout's first thought upon seeing this new chamber was that it looked and felt like a sickbay or medical lab. Everything was white or gray metal, illuminated either by overhead lighting or smaller lamps positioned next to work areas. What she took to be computer screens, each scrolling rows of information text in a script she did not recognize, occupied stations along the room's walls. There were other Pelopan in here, as well; she counted at least five, working with various pieces of the alien equipment. At the far end of the room was a row of upright translucent cylinders, each filled with a blue-green liquid and . . . something else.

The things on their necks.

Gray and all but shapeless, the gray, pulsing organisms floated in whatever solution sustained them within the cylinders. Frantic glances around the room told Rideout that each of the people working here had a similar lifeform affixed to them, nestled between the base of their skulls and their shoulder blades.

"What are those things?" asked Zane, pointing to the cylinders. "I don't understand."

Ivelan smiled. "You will. I promise you the process is harmless."

For the first time, Rideout noted that two of the cylinders held nothing but the jade fluid. Then she heard footsteps behind her and twisted her head to see another of the room's workers walking toward her and carrying one of the undulating blobs. She saw now that four of the sinewy appendages extended from its central mass, and all of them were moving as though reaching out toward her.

"Get that thing away from me!" Rideout barked, just as the thing leaped from the worker's hands and arced through the air toward her. She tried once more to free herself from her guards' grip, but her efforts were wasted as she felt the thing land on her right shoulder. One of the guards grabbed her head and turned away as the creature maneuvered itself toward the back of her head, then something warm and wet touched the bare skin of her neck.

Rideout screamed.

13

Your name is . . . Christine, yes?

The new presence probed at the edges of her consciousness, as though looking for an avenue in which to proceed inward. Despite the first endless panicked seconds and the initial sting of something making contact with the back of her neck, there was no pain. In fact, Rideout now felt a soothing warmth that seemed to course across her entire body. The terror that had all but consumed her as the creature touched her was gone. Her fatigue and earlier discomfort also had faded, and instead she now felt a sense of peace, though it remained tinged with anxiety as she struggled to comprehend what was happening.

Your name is Christine? The voice seemed so distant, and yet she turned, expecting to find the speaker standing beside her.

"Yes, that's my name."

Wait. Had she spoken the words aloud, or had they been uttered only within the confines of her own mind? Rideout could not be sure.

Standing in front of her, Ivelan extended a hand. "Do not be afraid, Christine. You are safe."

"I don't understand. What have you done to me?"

Ivelan smiled. "You have been collected. It was not our intention to frighten you, and for that, I apologize. We have no desire to harm you in any way."

Soon, you will be one with me. I am Sijaq, your collector.

Where was the voice coming from? Rideout looked around her, only now realizing that her escorts had released their holds on her. A few paces away and also standing unrestrained next to Ivelan was Kerry Zane. She saw that resting on his neck was another of the organisms, its muted gray skin contrasting with the ensign's bright red uniform tunic. Zane's expression was blank, at least until he noticed her looking in his direction. His features softened as he seemed to recognize her.

"Zane. Has he been . . . collected too?"

"Yes," replied Ivelan. "Doliri is his collector. Like you, he is unharmed and soon will understand everything."

"What about the others?"

"They will be collected, as well."

"Why?"

It is what we do. It is what we are.

The combination of voices competing for her attention was proving troublesome, and Rideout held up a hand. "What or who are you?"

We call ourselves the Lrondi.

"Is that supposed to mean something? I've never heard of your species."

Patience, Christine. Soon you will understand.

Her vision seemed to blur, and she lost sight of Zane, Ivelan, and the other Pelopan as light and color swirled together. There was no sense of dizziness or other adverse effects and within moments, the maelstrom that seemed to rage before her eyes began to subside. Objects once more took on form, though Rideout realized she was no longer in the lab or even anywhere in the mysterious underground caverns. Fear jolted through her as her vision cleared, and she found herself high above ground, as though floating in midair. It took her a moment to comprehend that she could only be looking at the surface of Cantrel V, and from this altitude the scars of war inflicted on this planet could not be denied. Impact craters littered the region, punctuating expansive swaths of what once had been lush green forests but now were little more than blackened wastelands. At the center of the devastation, standing as though in defiance of the utter destruction surrounding it, was an immense city growing outward from a single enormous metal spire to form a vast, brilliant circle. Even from far above it all, Rideout could see that the sprawling metropolis was *alive*. Vehicles moved along thoroughfares, through the air, and along waterways that tracked back to streams emanating from mountains encircling the thriving community.

"What is this?"

You see this world as we first beheld it, generations ago. When we arrived at this planet, the Pelopan were already locked in the inexorable grip of war. Entire cities were being annihilated. Whole populations were being wiped from existence. Upon our arrival, we were helpless to do anything save bear witness to the carnage.

The city disappeared as Rideout watched some form of projectile, long and lean and gleaming in the morning sunlight as it trailed fire and thick smoke, plummeting from the sky to strike the ground near the base of the enormous, beautiful spire. A white-hot ball of blinding light erupted, consuming everything in its path as it expanded from the point of impact. Buildings, vehicles, and even the tiny dots Rideout knew to be people were vaporized as the shock wave pushed outward across the ground and into the air. The magnificent tower that seemed to reach for the clouds crumbled, disappearing into the roiling flame and cloud of debris.

"Damn!"

Sijaq's voice rang in her ears, just as it seemed to reverberate through her very consciousness. *Despite their technological advancement, the Pelopan had not learned to balance such progress with the maturity required to evolve into a united, peaceful society.*

"That has a familiar ring to it."

Yes. I see from your thoughts that your own people, like so many other civilizations, endured harsh lessons as you learned to coexist with one another as well as other denizens of the cosmos.

"My thoughts?" Rideout felt her anxiety heighten. "You can read my thoughts?"

I can read what you are thinking at a given moment. As our bond strengthens, I soon will have access to all of your memories as well.

"I don't think I like this." Despite her initial apprehension, Rideout was surprised that she did not feel a compulsive need to repel what could only be described as an invasion not only of her privacy but of her very self. Why was that?

Below her, the scene shifted, and this time Rideout saw more of the airborne missiles, only now they appeared to be pushing themselves away from the planet and toward her. At the same time, swarms of small, gray spheres were descending from the sky, scattering as they approached the planet surface. She watched as many more of the spheres—many more than she could count—soared toward distant horizons.

Our arrival was met with suspicion and fear, and though there was at first little opposition, over time the warring Pelopan factions began focusing their dwindling reserves upon us as they realized what was happening.

"They found a common enemy: you." Now Rideout understood what the gray globes were: each must be carrying one or more Lrondi, bound for the surface in search of Pelopan to "collect."

That is precisely correct, Christine, Sijaq replied, and Rideout again was irritated at the easy way in which the alien seemed to be casually strolling through her thoughts. *By then, it was of course too late. We had already established a presence on the planet, and our collection efforts were well under way. The Pelopan resistance admittedly was greater than we were accustomed to facing. Their technology, though inferior to ours, still allowed them to push back against us for a time. It took years, as you measure time, and their efforts actually proved as damaging to themselves and this planet as the war they already had been fighting. In addition to the losses they had suffered as a result of their own conflict, we also were continuing to collect more of them.*

"Why? What brought you here in the first place?"

We had need of the world and the resources it offers. Despite the damage being inflicted upon it, this planet still offered us a sanctuary. So, too, did the Pelopan.

Once more, everything before Rideout's eyes dissolved

into a multihued jumble, and when her vision coalesced, it was to find herself standing amid the ruins of what had once been a great, thriving city. Was it the one she had just watched destroyed? Buildings, some of them standing despite considerable damage while others were little more than mountains of rubble, loomed all around her. Moving and working around the devastation were dozens of Pelopan; more than Rideout could easily count. Nearly everyone was engaged in some activity, from clearing debris—and no few number of bodies—to collecting equipment and other materials. Everything was being loaded into a small fleet of large, wheeled cargo vehicles.

Eventually, we collected a sufficient number of Pelopan to help turn the tide of the resistance. Once they began to understand that we meant them no harm and that in fact we needed them as much as they needed us in order to survive, their efforts at opposition faded.

"What does that mean?" Studying the Pelopan—male and female, adult and child—Rideout noted that each of them carried a Lrondi at the base of their neck. Every person here, and however many more she could not see, was so affected.

Not affected, Christine. Collected.

"Well, whatever the hell you call it," she snapped. "Why are you here? What do you want with the Pelopan?"

Only by joining with such beings can we survive. We rely on those we collect for our very existence, Christine. It has always been this way. At least, it has been this way for as long as any of us can remember.

"So, you just collect anyone you see as having value to you, and then impose your will upon them and make them do your bidding?" Rideout scowled. "Where I come from, we call that slavery."

That is an easy judgment to render, I admit.

"It's easy because it's true."

Our joining is mutually beneficial. We have not mistreated those we have collected here, not even after the Pelopan's efforts to kill us. Indeed, we have lifted up their civilization in many ways. We have accelerated their technological progression, helped to improve their understanding of engineering, science, and medicine. Even now, the Pelopan enjoy a greatly increased quality of life.

"But you didn't give them a choice."

We have no choice either. Our only option is to coexist with those we collect, or die.

Rideout braced herself as the scene before her shifted yet again, and now she found herself standing in the midst of what now was a gleaming, beautiful city. Unlike what she had just witnessed, the people here moved around her on what looked to be a crowded street, or sat at tables outside buildings. Sunlight reflected off glass and metal surfaces, and she even felt a cool breeze playing across her skin. Unlike the devastation she had seen mere moments ago, here everything exuded life and vitality.

"What is this place?" asked Rideout, studying her surroundings. Along with the wondrous testament of progress that was the city around them, these people seemed to have not a care in the world. They represented a race she did not recognize, their light orange skin and long, sinewy bodies all but nude save for wisps of light, loose-fitting clothing that sported vibrant colors and were as much works of art as they were items of fashion. None of the people moved with haste or urgency, and she saw a number of citizens relaxing in an adjacent park, enjoying a large pool at the center of the communal area or simply lying on the grass and basking in the warm sun. Others sat before large statues or other abstract works of art scattered throughout the park, and Rideout heard the sounds of what she took to be music coming from somewhere among the trees at the area's far end. Signs of technology were everywhere, from personal devices to larger equipment situated in kiosks or in the odd vehicle she saw moving through the thoroughfares.

These are the Vornal, inhabitants of another of the many planets we visited over uncounted generations. Unlike the Pelopan, the inhabitants of this planet had learned to live in peace with one another long ago. Their culture prospered as their attentions were focused on the improvement of life for all. In addition to their technological achievements, their devotion to the arts was of utmost importance to them. The Vornal's advancements in science and engineering were on a par with your own, Christine, and their world was one rich with resources. However, rather than journeying to the stars to seek even greater knowledge, they were content to remain on their own planet and continue the work of improving their civilization.

"And you collected them?"

Them, and many others like them.

Everything around her vanished again into a storm of blurred colors, and when her view cleared, she saw that she was standing in what appeared to be a massive industrial complex. The sounds of mechanization filled the air, peppered with a host of electronic tones and voices piped through an intercom as they relayed messages and information in a language she did not understand. Moving about the massive chamber—on the floor, on ladders, or on catwalks that formed a web around immense machinery—were numerous Vornal, only now there was one important difference: each of the people Rideout observed had a Lrondi attached to their neck.

"How long have you been doing this?" she asked. "Collecting people?" She could not help but notice that even with the Lrondi being carried by each of the factory workers, no one seemed to move as though in a catatonic state or daze. Just as with the prior scene on the city street, the people here looked to be full of life and purpose as they went about their various tasks.

I know only that it has been our way of existence for longer than any of our people can remember. Even with our protracted life spans, no Lrondi carries such memories.

"How long do you live?"

Thousands of your years.

"And you've always done this? Coexisted with other species against their will?"

It is not nearly so simple as that, Christine, though your reaction is understandable. According to the stories we have been told, there was a time when our form was similar to yours or the Pelopan. At some point uncounted generations ago, a mutation was introduced into our species, and over time we began evolving into our present form. We do not know what may have caused this change in our physiology. There are many theories, of course, ranging from natural evolution to some form of disease or other contamination. Despite our best efforts, no answer exists.

Rideout frowned, watching the alien factory workers move about the manufactured scene Sijaq was providing her. "What happened to the rest of your people? I'm no scientist, but it doesn't make sense that your entire civilization would change this way. At least not all at once."

You are correct. As you might imagine, the process unfolded over millions of years, though like you our species endured its share of global conflict which succeeded in erasing much of the historical data we had amassed. The truth of our origin and evolution is forever lost. All that we know is that it took considerable time for us to understand our abilities as collectors and how this was the means by which we could ensure our survival.

"You became dependent on the humanoid Lrondi," Rideout said.

In nearly every way. By joining with a host, we then could continue to carry out the tasks that are required to maintain our existence. Even as our intellect grew, our physiology continued changing over the countless generations until we arrived at the form you now see. Of course, there remained Lrondi who did not evolve in this manner, and in many respects we were two separate species. While our intellects far surpassed theirs, we of course lacked a physical form that was practical for so many things. Over time, our culture came to embrace this odd dichotomy and we thrived anew, until we realized that something else was happening to our people. Birth rates among the original Lrondi began falling—slowly at first, then at an alarming rate, until it became obvious that the entire species would eventually die out. We then were forced to find . . . suitable substitutes.

"Like the Pelopan."

Along with other species, yes. Dozens of space vessels, each carrying thousands of us, were dispatched to the stars in search of life-forms that could be brought back to our homeworld. Different species react to the collection process in different ways, and not every species we encountered was compatible, for a variety of reasons. Several races that could adapt still presented difficulties. Some were more resistant, and others were capable of circumventing collection altogether. The Pelopan were among the most promising of species we discovered, and it was our sincere hope that they would help to ensure that our civilization continued and thrived.

Despite her initial reaction to this bizarre paradigm, Rideout was forced to admit that the issue was far more complex than a simple master-servant relationship might imply. While remembering that the images she was seeing were provided by Sijaq and perhaps biased in favor of the Lrondi, nothing she had observed suggested that the Pelopan or the Vornal were being mistreated. Yes, the nature of their "coexistence" with the Lrondi could not be denied, but Rideout had read reports of other, similar species engaging in comparable practices where the targets of their actions fared much worse. She recalled an entry from the Starfleet data banks about a parasitic life-form encountered on the planet Deneva by the *U.S.S. Enterprise.* Captain Kirk and his crew had discovered the aliens had been migrating from system to system for centuries until they entered Federation space, attacking and forcing neural bonds with unwilling humanoid hosts in order to serve their needs. Those creatures had inflicted pain on their captives in order to instill obedience, a far cry from the Lrondi's supposed methods.

Of course, Rideout had to remind herself that she too was playing host to one such life-form, and there seemed to be no obvious debilitating effects. Was it because it was the simple truth, or was she just being manipulated to feel this way?

Hurting you would be counterproductive, Christine. We have no desire to hurt anyone.

"So, if I ask you to get the hell off my neck, you'll go pester someone else?"

We are attempting to help you understand us.

"I prefer a nice chat over coffee. Maybe breakfast." Sighing, she asked, "How many other species have you collected?"

I honestly do not know. We have had no contact with our homeworld since our departure, or with any of the other vessels sent out on similar missions, so we do not know if any of our efforts have been successful.

"So what happened here?" Even as she asked the question, Rideout was prepared for the next perspective change, anticipating the shift and sensing herself smiling when it happened. The factory and its Vornal workers disappeared into the onrushing burst of colors and when the visual storm subsided, her smile faded as she found herself standing in the middle of an expansive field of grass surrounded on all sides by high-rise buildings. All around her stood Pelopan as well as Vornal, and many of them carried Lrondi. The air here was thick and hazy, with plumes of brilliant blue smoke rising up from several points on the ground. It took Rideout a moment to realize that she was not experiencing any ill effects from the smoke, even though the Pelopan and Vornal around her seemed to be succumbing to it. Further, the Lrondi also seemed affected by the smoke, and she watched as several of them fell from the necks of their hosts and dropped to the ground, the reflective sheen of their outer skin growing dull and lifeless.

"They died?"

Yes. It was a desperate yet inspired attempt at resistance. Some of my people were captured by the Pelopan, and a group of their scientists was able to study these specimens and create a biological agent that could be used against us. It was crude, but effective, deployed first in key areas such as major cities and other large population centers, before the attacks spread around the planet. We were caught by surprise, and despite our best efforts, we soon came to realize that our efforts were in vain.

"They beat you back." Before her, numerous Pelopan stumbled about, or were sitting or lying on the grass, and around them lay the remains of what could only be dead Lrondi.

We were losing far too many of our people to the agent, and we were unable to devise any protection from it. The attacks became so frequent and intense that soon we had no choice but to withdraw, and as we did so, the Pelopan only increased their efforts.

Rideout floated once more above a city, only now the signs of devastation were evident. Piles of rubble were visible where she imagined mighty, even beautiful structures might once have stood. From this height, she was able to make out the movements of people, Pelopan citizens as well as a few Vornal, among the ruins. They were moving in large groups out of the city, heading toward distant mountains or the neighboring forests. She was able to see far more than just the immediate area, and it took her a moment to realize that she was rising ever higher into the air. Surface details of the city as well as the surrounding region were fading as they grew more distant, until clouds began to obscure her vision.

"What am I seeing?"

Our departure from this world. We had no choice, as the biological agent the Pelopan devised was simply too effective against us. It also proved devastating for our collected Vornal, who succumbed to the agent's effects. Those who were not evacuated from the planet died. I do not know about those who managed to escape.

This explained the presence of remains found by the archaeological teams working here on Cantrel V, Rideout realized. The Lrondi had guided Vornal they had acquired as indentured servants to facilitate collection of Pelopan specimens. She figured the Starfleet and civilian personnel assigned here would love this bit of intriguing information, provided she ever got a chance to tell them before they too were rounded up for use by the Lrondi.

Watching the scene play out before her even as her perceived altitude above the planet continued to increase, she asked, "If the planet had become poison to you, then why are you still here? Were you left behind?"

You are most perceptive, Christine.

There was a pause, and then Rideout saw that the vision Sijaq had conjured now placed her in space far above the planet. Her view of Cantrel V was similar to what she might expect to see out a porthole or on a viewscreen aboard the *Endeavour*.

The evacuation took place so quickly that only a portion of the Pelopan we had intended to collect was transported off the planet. Many were left behind, as were several hundred of us. A final message was transmitted, assuring us that we would be rescued once the situation here stabilized.

Stabilized? By the looks of things on the surface, Rideout surmised that the Lrondi might have different meanings for that particular word.

"How long ago did that happen?" she asked, guessing she already knew the answer to her question.

Approximately four hundred years, just as you have concluded.

"Still not used to that," she said. "So, you and a bunch of your buddies were left here to fend for yourselves, on a planet where the natives have been throwing poison at you. Now what?"

The only option available to us was to seek refuge wherever we might find it.

Her orbital view of Cantrel V disappeared, and she found herself standing on what she presumed to be the planet's surface. She was walking among a group of Pelopan, along with a handful of Vornal, and they were moving along a narrow path that wound through foothills leading toward the base of a large mountain. The shape of the mountain itself looked familiar, and Rideout realized it was one visible in the distance from the Beta Site excavation area.

We escaped the cities and other larger population centers that had been subjected to the biological agent and retreated into undeveloped areas, eventually moving into underground caverns. Here, we began establishing permanent settlements. We later learned that the agent possessed a limited viability, which was subject to any number of environmental factors.

"Why didn't you return to the surface once you realized it was safe?"

As we prefer such darker environs and also feared renewed attacks by Pelopan who remained on the surface, this seemed a sensible solution to our problem. We were not alone in our thinking. Other Pelopan who had not been collected soon also began retreating underground after conditions on the surface had begun to deteriorate as a consequence of their own war. The resulting environmental effects as well as food shortages and diseases ultimately succeeded in wiping out the last vestiges of Pelopan struggling to survive on the surface. Those who escaped underground were eventually collected and added to our group. Over time and while salvaging whatever components and remnants of their and our technology we could find, we began forging a new society down here and awaited rescue.

The group of marching Pelopan was gone, and Rideout found herself standing once more in the strange laboratory that had earlier greeted them. As before, Ivelan was watching her, an expression of genuine concern on her face. Rideout also saw Ensign Kerry Zane, along with Joseph Berenato and Javokbi, standing to one side, their expressions indicating they were under no distress, even though she saw the Lrondi resting at the base of each of their necks.

Rideout resisted the urge to reach to the back of her head and touch the Lrondi she felt there. As before, when she was first "collected," there was no pain, only a warmth where the creature nestled against her skin. Indeed, even the anxiety she had felt at the moment it had attached itself to her seemed to have faded.

Looking to Ivelan, she asked, "My friends are okay?"

"Of course, though Ensign Javokbi is proving to be more resistant to collection than you or your other companions, which likely is attributable to her neural pathways being somewhat different. It is most interesting."

"Yeah, that's one word for it." Rideout looked around the room. "I don't understand. Once the Lrondi got you down here, didn't you outnumber them?"

"For a time." Ivelan's white eyes narrowed as she smiled. "Eventually we learned to work together. The Lrondi have never mistreated us, and once it became clear to us that they needed us to survive, we learned to live in harmony."

"Are there any Pelopan who haven't been collected?"

"Of course. We still outnumber the surviving Lrondi."

Zane said, "Wait, you mean the Lrondi keep uncollected Pelopan here? Like cattle?"

"Given the Lrondi's much longer life spans, our host bodies eventually age, or fall victim to injury or disease, and die. Uncollected Pelopan continue to live and breed, until such time as they are needed."

"And your people just go along with this?" Rideout asked. "Willingly?"

"We soon came to recognize the advantages of alliance rather than opposition." Ivelan's smile faded. "This was good, in that as far as we know, we are all the Pelopan that remain. It is also good that you are here. Our numbers are dwindling. Birth rates have begun a noticeable decline, and we believe we may die out altogether within a few generations. New hosts will soon be needed, particularly if the Lrondi are unable to leave this planet. However, with your ship in orbit, there may be new options available to them."

"Oh, hell no," Rideout replied, allowing a tinge of irritation to lace her words. "There's no way you're getting aboard our ship."

Ivelan nodded in understanding. "You are concerned for the safety of your crew. Rest assured that they would remain unharmed, just as you have been."

"Doesn't matter," said Zane. "Our captain will figure out what you're up to and shut you down. You can count on it."

Your confidence in your captain is admirable, Sijaq said, her words echoing in Rideout's mind. *By the time she learns what we are, it will be too late.*

Rideout, for the first time since Sijaq had bonded with her, was trying to order the information tumbling around inside her mind. The act of playing host to the Lrondi, despite whatever steps might be taken to safeguard her health, still was taxing. However, no sooner did she focus on a single thought than she felt Sijaq's consciousness shadowing her own.

Another ship is here?

14

"*Endeavour*, come in. Are you reading this? *Endeavour*, do you copy?"

Stephen Klisiewicz watched as Katherine Stano, grunting in frustration, held her communicator as though considering whether to fling it away or perhaps attempt to crush it with her bare hands. Instead, she snapped closed the unit's cover and returned it to the hip pocket of her green coveralls.

"Comm's still jammed," she said, then closed her eyes and shook her head. "But, you probably knew that already." Releasing an exasperated sigh, Stano began pacing the length of the small room that now served as a temporary hiding place for her, Klisiewicz, and Lieutenant Ivan Tomkins as well as Ensign Anissa Cole. Klisiewicz sat on the edge of the bare metal bunk, next to where the young science officer lay unconscious. Another bunk was mounted atop hers, with two more bolted to the opposite bulkhead of what he had guessed to be some sort of crew or passenger berthing compartment. There was no bedding, nor anything stored in the tiny lockers set into the compartment's rear wall. Indeed, there was nothing to indicate the room had ever been occupied.

The team had found this place thanks to Tomkins, who had guided them through the bowels of the ship using a copy of the technical schematics he had managed to download to his tricorder after accessing the alien vessel's computer. The room offered a few advantages, namely that it was far away from the chamber they had escaped, and according to Tomkins was well away from what looked to be vital or possibly well-traveled areas of the ship.

It also has a door that locks, Klisiewicz mused, grateful for the respite, even if it was only for a short while. Though he prided himself on staying in excellent physical condition in accordance with Starfleet regulations, carrying the stunned Ensign Cole through the dizzying, unfamiliar passageways and past uncounted doorways and intersections while running from possible pursuit had begun to wear on him. The hiding place, no matter its size or level of comfort, was a welcome haven, for however long it lasted. Of course, even as Klisiewicz pondered that thought, his gaze drifted to the door, and he wondered when it might slide aside to admit Gaulke or someone else from the boarding party who now was compromised by the mysterious Lrondi.

Way to ruin a good thing, Lieutenant.

Stano only needed five paces to walk the length of the cramped room before she was forced to turn around. "Either we find a way to get around the jamming," she said after a moment, "or else we figure out how to use this ship's communications system, assuming it has one."

"Whichever way we go," replied Tomkins, "we're going to have to move from here to someplace with access to the computer or other onboard systems." He held up his tricorder. "But there may be a problem with that. According to my scans, there's been an increase in power being routed to that chamber with all the sleeping people. I think they're waking up those people, at least some of them."

Klisiewicz felt his stomach drop. "Reinforcements?"

Nodding, the engineer replied, "Could be."

"What about Ensign Grammell and the other team?" Stano asked. "I can't reach them with my communicator either. Any idea where they might be?"

"No." Tomkins closed the top of his tricorder. "I tried to find them when we were on the move, but they must be somewhere my scans can't penetrate. For all I know, they've been captured by the . . . by the whatever the hell those things are."

Stano reached up to rub her temples. "It's a sure bet they'll be looking for us, especially if they're bringing those people out of hibernation to help them. I guess the bright side of that is that they probably won't hurt our people if they find them."

"Of course they won't."

The new voice startled them, and Klisiewicz shifted on the bunk as he sensed Anissa Cole sitting up on the utilitarian sleeping berth. Her voice was groggy, and she was rubbing the back of her head as she swung her legs so that she could set her feet on the metal floor.

"Anissa?" asked Klisiewicz. He could not help noting that she had awakened far sooner than should have been possible, given the usual effects of a phaser's stun beam. Was the presence of the Lrondi providing some added benefit to her in that regard? "Are you all right?"

Cole nodded. "I think so. Naqa is also uninjured, though she tells me she's never been stunned before." She looked to Stano, who had moved to stand at the foot of the bunk. "I apologize for what happened, Commander. A few of Naqa's people let their fear and uncertainty guide their actions."

"I know you weren't entirely in control of your actions, Lieutenant," replied Stano. "Is that still the case?"

"Naqa is with me, and she also apologizes. This is a new experience for her. Yours is the first new species she and many of her people have seen for quite some time. This brings with it a new hope for the Lrondi."

"So, Naqa is guiding you now?" Klisiewicz asked. "Controlling you?"

Frowning, Cole said, "Yes, and no. It's hard to describe, Lieutenant. I feel her presence, directing me, but I feel as though I want to help her. I want to protect her. I guess I just took things too far. I lost my perspective."

"And now you have better perspective?" asked Stano.

"I do. Commander, the Lrondi don't want to hurt us. They are very thankful we've come to help."

Klisiewicz listened, thinking as Cole spoke that she sounded like someone who was reading prepared statements or even reciting propaganda. "You know this because Naqa tells you?"

"Yes. I hear her in my mind. At first it was just bits and pieces, like flashes of thought, but now it's closer to actual conversation." Pausing, Cole offered a smile. "In some ways, it almost feels like I'm talking to myself. Naqa says it's a learning process for her as well."

Stano said, "Ensign, if you're truly in control of yourself, then help us understand what they want. Be objective. Be the Starfleet officer I know you are, and help us figure this out."

"I understand." Cole shifted her gaze between the first officer and Klisiewicz. "I do believe her when she says they don't want to harm us."

"For the moment, we'll go with that," Stano replied. "What are their intentions?"

"They're waking up more Lrondi, as well as Pelopan. They need the Pelopan to operate this ship. Once they are ready, they will begin recovering their people from the planet, people they left behind generations ago."

Klisiewicz asked, "How do they know there's anyone down there to retrieve?"

"They don't. The Lrondi know only that they were forced to abandon many of their brothers and sisters. A promise was made to return for them, and now that promise has been fulfilled."

"Is it possible they're still alive, somewhere, and we just haven't detected them?" asked Stano.

Shrugging, Klisiewicz replied, "Anything's possible, Commander, but it's been centuries, at least."

Cole said, "The Lrondi are extremely long-lived, and they also had Pelopan hosts to assist them. Even after so much time, it is very likely that survivors will be found, along with the descendants of those Pelopan who initially were collected."

"Wouldn't the Pelopan have resisted?" asked Stano.

"Of course, but as with other races, they would eventually come to understand the benefits of mutual existence. Naqa says we too will learn to appreciate what they can offer us. She understands our concern and reluctance, of course."

"Make sure Naqa understands this," Stano said. "I don't like my people being taken against their will, and I don't like being cut off from my ship. If Naqa or anyone else wants to take a few steps toward earning my trust, addressing *those* concerns is a great place to start."

The blunt comments seemed to take Cole off guard, and she was quiet for a moment, as though collecting her thoughts. Klisiewicz then realized that was indeed what she was doing, only that she likely was gathering whatever Naqa was communicating to her.

"Of course," she said, after a moment. "Naqa says that the quickest and easiest way toward a full understanding of the Lrondi and what they face would be to collect—"

Stano cut her off. "No, that's not going to happen. To be honest, Ensign, my first instinct is to rip that thing from your neck, but I don't know if that will hurt you, or Naqa, but she's not getting any more of our people, and she's damned well not getting me. Like it or not, Ensign, you're the key to us understanding the Lrondi, so for now, I need you to hang in there and be our conduit."

"Naqa and her people actually appreciate what we've done so far, Commander. It was the ship's recognition of our life signs and our activity that triggered its system reactivation in the first place." She paused again, a frown darkening her features. "Naqa isn't saying anything more. It's almost like she's pulling back from me." Releasing a sigh, she closed her eyes. "Or, I could just be tired. I'm sorry, Commander."

For the first time, Stano's expression softened. "It's all right, Ensign. I can only imagine how hard this must be, but understand my position. My priority is the safety of our people, and I can't do that job if I don't know what's going on. You're the one who can best help with that."

Tears began welling up in the corners of Cole's eyes. "I'm jeopardizing the mission. I'm disappointing Naqa. I'm disappointing you."

Klisiewicz moved closer to her on the bunk. "Take it easy, Anissa." He took her hand, trying to offer some small display of comfort and understanding. "We'll get through this." Not for the first time, he wished Ensign Tropp were here, as it was obvious that Cole's bonding with Naqa was having an adverse effect on the ensign. Was it just the shock of this new experience, or was the connection having an actual adverse effect? He was no doctor, but without the *Endeavour*'s medical staff, Tropp was all they had, and he likely had also been collected by now.

After a moment spent in silence, Stano said, "We need to find a way to contact the *Endeavour*. Since our communicators are being jammed, that leaves this ship's systems."

"I can help you with that. I know that Naqa has been communicating with other Lrondi, trying to convince them that we mean them no harm. Maralom is their leader, and Naqa thinks that—"

The rest of her sentence was lost as a phaser beam rippled across her body. Cole went limp and she started to fall forward, only to be caught by Klisiewicz.

"What the hell?" asked Stano, turning to Tomkins. The engineer was standing near the door, phaser in hand. "Lieutenant?"

Tomkins pointed at Cole. "Naqa's been communicating with other Lrondi. Don't you get it? They speak with each other *telepathically*. She could have been telling her friends where we are."

"Son of a bitch," said Klisiewicz as he lowered Cole's body to the bunk. "He's right. We should move."

Stano, still glaring at Tomkins, said, "Any ideas?"

Already consulting his tricorder, the engineer nodded. "Okay, I think I've got something. If I'm reading these specs right, it's some kind of storage bay, not too far from here. We can relocate there, and it looks to have a reinforced hatch that can be sealed from inside."

Klisiewicz, using his tricorder to scan the Lrondi at the back of Cole's neck, said, "According to these readings, this thing is out too. No idea how long it'll last, though."

"We should keep her unconscious," Stano said. "Just to be on the safe side."

"As long as that translates to Naqa," replied Tomkins.

With Stano bringing up the rear and Klisiewicz once more carrying the stunned Cole, the engineer led the way down another series of turns and twists in the ship's corridors, the trio moving with as much speed and stealth as they could muster. In what felt like hours but in reality was less than ten minutes, Tomkins stopped before a large, reinforced hatch that bulged outward into the passageway. With the P-38 he pulled from his satchel, he opened the door and the group scrambled into the large room.

"Be it ever so humble," Tomkins said as he closed and

locked the door behind them. Looking around the room and its sparse contents, which consisted of a few dozen containers of varying shapes and sizes and all secured to the deck with metal bands, he added, "Not much here, but I'm guessing we won't be staying that long."

Stano gestured to the unconscious Cole. "Klisiewicz, you stay here with her. Tomkins, tell me those specs of yours can get us to a control center or even this thing's bridge."

After a moment studying his tricorder, the lieutenant replied, "I think I've got it, Commander. It's a bit of a walk, but I think I've found a route that will let us avoid what the schematics suggest are high-traffic areas."

"Good." Stano turned to Klisiewicz. "Lieutenant, keep the door locked until we get back. Once we reestablish communications, I'll contact you. After we update Captain Khatami on our situation, we'll start working on a way to get our people back, and maybe then we can find this Maralom and have a little chat."

Klisiewicz nodded. "Understood, Commander."

Stano and Tomkins disappeared back into the corridor, and he secured the hatch. Taking a moment to look around the room, he guessed it to be perhaps twice the size of the *Endeavour*'s crew lounge or gymnasium. Unlike the berthing area they had abandoned, this room offered no furnishings save for the deck itself. With a grunt of resignation, he maneuvered Cole so that she was lying near the wall in what he hoped was a comfortable position.

"We can never have just a simple, mundane mission, can we?" he said to no one. Looking at the insensate Cole, he tried to imagine what she must have been feeling at the moment of her bonding with Naqa. What was it like to possess another's thoughts and have them flow in parallel to your own? Did Cole have access to everything Naqa was thinking, or only what the Lrondi permitted her to know? There were so many questions, and the person best able to provide the answers he sought lay unconscious next to him.

With nothing more to do until Stano and Tomkins returned or contacted him—or he was found by other Lrondi-controlled Pelopan—Klisiewicz once more activated his tricorder and aimed it at the gray organism nestled at the back of Cole's neck. The thing pulsed or twitched, perhaps in reaction to his presence, but like Cole, it appeared down for the count.

"Doctor Leone would have a field day with you, my little friend," he said, studying the readings.

With a speed he would have thought impossible, the Lrondi moved.

Klisiewicz flinched, pushing himself away from Cole as the gray mass pushed itself from her neck and over her shoulder. He was trying to gain his footing when the thing seemed to launch from Cole's body, arcing through the air toward him. Holding up a hand, he felt something hit him in the chest. Two, three, four touches across his body, and he felt the thing sliding over his uniform. He tried to grab it, but its movements were a blur as it moved around his torso and up his back. Then something warm and wet touched the bare neck of his skin. Cole and the room around him disappeared in a blinding white explosion of light, and there was a rush in his ears as he felt his pulse quickening. His heart pounded as though it might drive itself from his chest.

"Wait!" he shouted, the word sounding faint and distant.

Then Klisiewicz heard nothing at all.

15

"I should've stayed in bed."

Standing to one side of the door so that she could cover it while Ivan Tomkins worked, Katherine Stano peered over her shoulder to where the engineer was standing before a control console. "Problems, Lieutenant?"

"Only the ones our ship seems to keep finding, Commander." He turned from the workstation, offering a smile that told her he was not airing real complaints, but instead was only hoping to lighten the moment. "If I'd known life could be this exciting on a ship of the line, I probably would've requested an assignment to somewhere safer. You know, the Romulan Neutral Zone, or something."

Despite the tension of the past few moments, Stano could not help smiling. She found it encouraging that Tomkins could maintain his humor in situations such as the one they now faced. It was a positive character trait, assuming it emanated from a confidence in his ability to complete the assigned mission, along with the trust he placed in his leaders and comrades. If it was based upon something else, such as recklessness or his having resigned himself to the futility of their current circumstances, then that might pose a problem.

Tomkins, thankfully, did not appear to be plagued by such feelings.

Gesturing to the console, Stano asked, "Any luck with

that thing? Internal sensors or something like that would be nice."

"They don't seem to have anything like that." Tomkins tapped the edge of the control panel with the heel of his hand. "I'm going to call that a good thing, considering the present circumstances. We sort of stick out now, you know. Meanwhile, I'm looking to see if I can't tap into their communications system. Maybe we can get a sense of what they're up to."

The workstation, active and interfaced with at least some of the alien ship's computer network, was a lucky find. Stano and Tomkins, attempting to make their way to what the engineer believed to be a communications or systems control room, had been forced to find cover upon realizing that they no longer were alone aboard the vessel. Pelopan now were moving about the ship, each carrying a Lrondi on his or her neck. As their appearance made them stand out from the taller, green-skinned Pelopan, they were forced to seek a safe haven while they regrouped.

"Scans from my tricorder should be good enough for us to avoid most run-ins with the locals," Stano said, "but I don't want to get caught somewhere with no place to hide." Examining the unit's readings, she frowned. "There's a lot of activity, but it looks to be concentrated in just a few areas, like the hibernation chamber and what we think might be their bridge. If they're ramping up various systems, they might have their hands full, at least for a while."

"But you know they'll be looking for us," Tomkins said, his attention again focused on the console.

Stano nodded. "And we haven't heard from Ensign Grammell or anyone from her team, so for now, we've got to assume they've been taken." She paused, casting a glance toward the deck. "Or worse."

"Already thinking along those lines," replied Tomkins. "With that in mind, I think we'd be smart to avoid what looks like this ship's main bridge and any sort of operations or control center. We need to find a secondary or tertiary access point; something they might only use as an auxiliary station or in an emergency." Holding his tricorder in one hand, the engineer began pressing keys and manipulating controls on the unfamiliar console in a sequence that to Stano appeared random.

"Tell me you're not just guessing."

"Nope." He smiled. "This interface is actually fairly intuitive, once you figure out the basics, though there are a few features that are definitely unique. For example, some processes are automated, while others have to be manually initiated. If I had to guess, I figure that was a power-saving measure, given that this ship looks to spend most of its time traveling at low warp velocities with a crew in hibernation, and also why certain systems only came online when they detected the presence of living beings. Us, for example. That dampening field wasn't just a defensive measure. We couldn't tell at the time, because those sections of the ship are heavily shielded, but it was actually drawing power from us to use for itself." Tomkins shook his head. "If we'd let it, the field would've drained us dry."

Stano said, "Good thing you shut it off, then."

"No kidding." Turning back to the console, the engineer added, "Oh, and I found out something else that's really interesting." He pointed toward the large, round depression positioned at the center of the console. "We've seen these on most of the workstations we've found. Guess what they are?"

"Coffee cup holder?"

Tomkins grinned. "Nice try. I scanned this one and found traces of Lrondi DNA." He said nothing else, and it took her an extra moment to connect the dots.

"A neural interface?"

"Looks that way. I've never seen anything this sophisticated, though. If it is an interface for the Lrondi, that means they could control this ship without help from humanoid hosts. Or maybe Lrondi who don't have hosts still help with ship operations." He ran his hand across the console. "I could spend years wandering around this ship and learning about everything it has to offer."

"Maybe later."

After another few moments spent entering commands, one of the console's display screens came to life, generating what Stano recognized as a technical schematic labeled in an indecipherable script. "I think I've got something, Commander." Tomkins tapped the screen. "If I'm reading this right, this is a communications array support substation. It definitely has access to both internal and external comm systems, so we should be able to broadcast from there if we can figure out how to make it work."

Stano nodded in approval. "And you can get us there without attracting too much attention?"

"I think so. There are some service corridors that move parallel to the main passageways and look to offer access to internal components and relays. Sort of like our Jefferies tubes, but bigger. I can't guarantee we won't run into anybody, but the odds are definitely in our favor."

Checking the setting on her phaser, Stano said, "All right, let's do it."

They moved to the door and Tomkins disengaged its lock. To Stano, the sound of the locking mechanism disengaging sounded loud enough to wake even hibernating Pelopan. The door's magnetic seal deactivated and slid aside.

Standing in the corridor outside the room was Ensign Adam Gaulke, flanked by Sa-Gameet and Guillermo Montes. All three carried phasers, which now were aimed at Stano's chest.

"Hello, Commander," said Gaulke, holding up a tricorder in his other hand. "We've been looking for you."

Stephen?

The voice echoed in Klisiewicz's mind, or did it? Looking around the berthing compartment, he saw only the unconscious form of Anissa Cole. Where were Commander Stano and Lieutenant Tomkins? He should know that answer, he realized. What was wrong with him?

You are disoriented, Stephen. This is normal for someone who has been collected.

"Collected?" Was he speaking aloud? It was difficult to be certain.

Yes. I am Naqa, your collector. Do not worry about the confusion. In time, it will pass.

"I don't remember what happened." He held up his

hands, which were empty. What had he been doing? Tricorder. Where was his tricorder? He was scanning something. Anissa. Ensign Cole. The thing on her neck. The Lrondi, Cole had called it. Naqa?

See? Your memories are returning.

"I'm dizzy." He tried to swallow, but his throat was dry, and his stomach felt uneasy. He wanted to lie down.

You are lying down, Stephen. You will feel better in a few moments.

He was already noticing an improvement in his condition as his stomach began to settle. "What did you do?"

A slight adjustment to your neurochemical balance. It is a natural effect of our bonding and helps minimize the shock of transition.

The dizziness was fading too. In fact, Klisiewicz now felt as though he had awakened from a restful sleep. He also was aware of Naqa's presence in his mind. Her thoughts were melding with his, and while each was a distinct entity, there also was a comfortable symmetry as they weaved in and around one another.

"This isn't what I expected."

The relationship between us and those we collect is unique for each bonding, Stephen. Even one who has been collected can find it difficult to describe the experience to another being. Anissa's responses were different from yours, and yet there still are similarities. It is a learning process for us as well as you. The longer we are bonded, the deeper our connection will be. Soon I will know you as well as you know yourself.

"Is that how we're able to understand each other?"

Yes. That also will continue to improve, the longer we are bonded. I am learning how to communicate using your language and knowledge. For example, I am what you would describe as the female of my species, which is why you now hear me as a feminine voice. I did that as a means of facilitating our interaction.

"Is that what this is? An 'interaction'? It feels like something more."

In time, it will be so much more. Anissa was only just beginning to understand this. I did not want to separate from her, but I knew that collecting you was the only way for you to see the truth for yourself.

Klisiewicz recalled the emotional turmoil that seemed to grip Ensign Cole while she was under Naqa's influence. "Her reaction was very strong. She had developed sincere feelings for you, even after such a short time."

I felt the same way about her, Stephen, just as I am learning to feel about you.

"I can sense that, but I don't understand how it can be happening so fast."

It is to our mutual benefit that we learn to trust each other as quickly as possible. My people have had to learn to engender trust from uncounted people on numerous worlds. They are all so different from one another, much like the diversity of your own crew and your Federation.

"You know about the Federation?"

Of course. I know everything Anissa knew, and I'm learning everything you know. We want to know more. You can help us with that, Stephen.

"I want to help." The statement came without hesitation. Klisiewicz sensed his unease at his abrupt bonding with Naqa fading with every passing moment. Her presence in his mind felt natural, rather than alien or intrusive. That was not wrong, was it?

I am happy you wish to help us, Stephen. I have already told the others, and they are also pleased. I hope all of your people will feel the same way. We are alike in many ways, as we too wish to help those in need.

"Like the Pelopan?"

Exactly. The Pelopan were waging war against one another, destroying their world and each other, but we helped to end their fighting. They were able to salvage their civilization and even improve it in some ways. In turn, they aided us during our time of need, and that remains true to this day. We care deeply for the Pelopan. We would be lost without them, as well as other species that have helped us.

"So the Pelopan were collected willingly?"

They saw the benefit of joining with us, for them as well as the Lrondi. This is true for all we collect. Do you not believe me?

"I'm not sure." The shock of bonding with Naqa had faded, but there remained fragments of memory from the moment she had touched him. Her presence had been undeniable, unstoppable as he felt the first tendrils of her consciousness beginning to blend with his own, but had she truly come to him uninvited? The question seemed odd now. "You're saying I'm still in control of my body and mind?"

Yes, but I am still here. So long as we are joined, I am here.

Was it his imagination, or did that sound like an evasion?

Our bonding is of mutual benefit, Stephen. Without hosts, my people are helpless, so to mistreat one who has been collected is unthinkable. For species like the Pelopan, we offer the same salvation they provide for us.

Sincerity and hope laced Naqa's every word, and Klisiewicz could not deny the comfort and security that seemed to wrap around him as she spoke. Her thoughts exuded reassurance and trust as they entwined his own, to the point where it felt as though they might be sharing the same ideas and emotions. It would be so easy to lose himself in this realm of tranquility and contentment.

"Lieutenant? Lieutenant Klisiewicz?"

It took him a moment to comprehend that the new voice was coming from somewhere else. The words were real, spoken aloud. He realized he was still in the berthing compartment looking up at the underside of the metal bunk. Turning his head, he saw Anissa Cole sitting next to him, concern evident in her face.

"Hi."

"Hello yourself," replied Cole. "Are you all right?"

Klisiewicz nodded. "I think so. I feel pretty good. Great, actually."

"Yeah, I figured that." She gestured to the back of her neck, then pointed to him. "That'll happen."

Tell Anissa that I miss our bond.

Unprepared for the abrupt suggestion, Klisiewicz blinked several times as he pushed himself to a sitting position. "Naqa says she misses you."

Cole's expression softened, and she leaned forward,

peering into his eyes as though attempting to see something inside them, or perhaps even beyond them. Nodding, she said, "I miss her, too, actually." Her eyes reddened, and she reached up to wipe them with her uniform sleeve. "I'm sorry. I wasn't expecting this, but once she was inside my head, there wasn't anything I could do."

Retrieving his tricorder from where it lay near his feet, Klisiewicz held up the device. "Do you mind? I'd like to scan you and compare the readings I took earlier, when you and Naqa were still bonded."

"Why not?" Shaking her head, she wiped her eyes again. "I guess I volunteered to be a science experiment the minute that thing latched on to me."

What does she mean, Stephen? Is it your intention to experiment on us?

Klisiewicz felt Naqa's anxiety translated as a sudden queasy feeling in his stomach. Dizziness returned, and he placed a hand on the bunk to steady himself.

"Wait, that's not what I meant!"

Cole grabbed his arm. "Lieutenant? What's wrong?"

As quickly as it had come, the feelings of discomfort were already subsiding. Drawing a deep breath, he patted Cole's hand on his forearm. "I think I'm okay. It was just . . . I think I must have upset Naqa."

"Then she made you feel better, right?"

Klisiewicz frowned, hearing the ensign's accusatory tone. "What do you mean?"

"You know what I mean. Think about it."

She is distraught, Stephen. She does not understand.

"Naqa's doing this to you," said Cole. "First she makes

you feel happy, then when you upset her, she turns it in the other direction." She pushed herself from the bunk. "That's how they control us, sir. They make it sound voluntary and a great deal for both of you, but you're still a puppet, and she's still pulling your strings."

She does not trust us, Stephen.

"A little while ago you were singing her praises," Klisiewicz countered. "What changed your mind?"

Cole tapped her temple with a finger. "Right. I changed my mind. I had it back to myself. She's messing around in your head, Lieutenant. We need to get her out of there."

She is jealous, because she was of no use to me. Not like you are.

"Naqa needs our help," Klisiewicz said, though he realized as he spoke the words that they somehow sounded wrong to him. They lacked conviction.

"*Needs* our help? You know what she's after, sir. Us. Our ship and its crew. She *wants* the Lrondi to collect all of us, because they *need* us just to survive. They are all but helpless without hosts to do things for them."

"You're out of line, Ensign." The words, including his apparent need to assert rank and authority, sounded hollow to his ears.

Undeterred, Cole pressed, "They know what the *Endeavour* can do. Naqa took that from my mind. They want the ship, and they want us to help them take it. We have to stop them, sir."

Stephen, she wants to hurt us!

Anger flooded his mind. He felt his pulse quicken. His eyes widened and his teeth began to ache as he clenched his jaw. Gripped by the need to flee and the desire to protect, every muscle in his body tensed. He did not realize his phaser was in his hand until his arm was raised and he was sighting down the weapon's length at Cole. The ensign held up her hands, backing away from him in panic.

"Sir!" she cried.

His finger tightened on the phaser's firing stud and blue energy sprang forth, striking Cole and sending her falling to the floor. She collapsed in an unmoving heap, lying on her side and facing away from him.

"No!" His arm shook with such force that the phaser fell from his hand, clattering to the deck. "Ensign!" He lunged toward her, dropping to one knee as he placed his hand on her face. "Anissa!" Moving his fingers to the side of her throat, he felt her pulse, and blew out his breath in relief.

"Why did you make me do that? What if the phaser hadn't been set to stun? I could have killed her."

She does not trust us, Stephen. She and others like her will interfere with what we have come here to do.

"What are you talking about?" Reaching for Cole's limp hand, Klisiewicz took it in both of his, cradling it.

We have brothers and sisters on the planet who have waited generations for us to rescue them. It is time for them to rejoin us, and for you to join us as well.

There was something rather humiliating about being escorted under guard by those under one's own command, Stano decided.

After relieving her and Tomkins of their weapons and

equipment, Ensign Gaulke set off into the bowels of the ship, leading the way and accompanied by his personal Lrondi accessory. With Sa-Gameet and Montes following behind them, Stano and Tomkins were guided by Gaulke around one last turn in yet another of the alien ship's seemingly unending corridors, arriving at a set of massive, reinforced double metal doors. The hatches began to part at Gaulke's approach, both sections recessing into the adjoining bulkheads. Despite their size and apparent weight, Stano heard little more than a faint hum as the doors moved.

"Wow," said Tomkins as he moved to stand beside her. "Have a look at that."

Beyond the threshold was a large oval-shaped room, the most eye-catching feature of which was the transparent dome that offered an unfettered view of open space. Curving, iridescent bulkheads rose more than two meters to meet the dome's lower edge. The northern hemisphere of Cantrel V was visible off to Stano's right, its mottled blue-green palette standing in sharp contrast to the blackness of space surrounding it.

As for the room itself, it was twice as large as the *Endeavour* bridge and teemed with activity at its numerous workstations, all of which resembled the same consoles the boarding party had encountered since their arrival. A dozen more stations were positioned along the room's perimeter, each one manned by a male or female Pelopan.

"It looks like all of them have been collected," Stanos said as Gaulke led them into the room, noting the gray masses resting on the necks of every person she could see.

"Not just them," replied Tomkins. He tapped her

on the shoulder and pointed toward the cluster of five workstations at the center of the room. "See anything interesting?"

It took her a moment for Stano to glean his meaning. Resting at the center of all five workstations was a Lrondi. Without hosts, the gray creatures lay in the consoles' circular depressions, their shapeless mass sitting in contradiction to the panel's smooth, regular lines.

"When Klisiewicz finds out he missed this, he's going to be pissed." Stano's comment made her think of her science officer and Ensign Cole. Were they still safe, having remained undiscovered by the Pelopan and their Lrondi masters? There was no way to know, at least for the moment.

"Commander, look," said Tomkins, who was gesturing again, this time to four figures standing with Pelopan at or near the different consoles. Each of them wore a Starfleet uniform.

"Hastert and McMurray," she said. "And Tropp and Ensign Grammell. I guess that answers the question of whether they were collected."

Gaulke marched toward the center of the room, past Ensigns Jay Hastert and Carlton McMurray. Stano noted that both junior officers acknowledged their approach and even smiled at her, as did Tropp. The Denobulan's long, wide smile seemed even more unnerving than normal to Stano, considering that he likely was not offering it of his own free will. This line of thinking was interrupted as Gaulke stopped before Ensign Angela Grammell.

"Commander," said the junior officer. "It's good to see

you." Unlike the last time Klisiewicz had seen her, the woman's long blond hair now hung freely about the shoulders of her Starfleet jumpsuit.

Her eyes narrowing, Stano replied, "Ensign. You appear . . . unharmed."

"I'm absolutely unharmed. All of us are, and we're grateful you weren't injured."

Tomkins asked, "Who's 'we'?"

"The rest of the landing party," Grammell replied. "And Maralom and the other Lrondi. There is so much to do, and they need our help."

"Where's the rest of the landing party?"

"Everyone is well and accounted for, Commander. A few of us are here, assisting as best we can. It's something of a learning process, but I think we're progressing well."

Offering a derisive snort, Tomkins said, "You assisted them rather well in finding us. That was thoughtful of you."

Grammell ignored the engineer. "Others are assisting in other areas, and everyone is acclimating very nicely."

"Sounds like we're all one big happy family," Stano snapped. As had happened earlier with Cole, she found herself losing patience with what she considered the patronizing way her people were speaking to her, albeit at the behest of the Lrondi controlling them.

Grammell seemed shaken by Stano's remark, and her expression hardened before she replied, "Our goal is to seek harmony for everyone, Commander."

"Whose goal, Ensign? Are you speaking to me, or is that your Lrondi master?"

"Maralom is not my master. I am speaking freely, out of a genuine desire to help the Lrondi and the Pelopan."

Stano felt Tomkins touch on her arm. "Maralom, Commander. Ensign Cole mentioned that name before."

"Yes," Grammell said. "Maralom has collected me. He is the leader, or what you would call the leader, of the Lrondi. He's most anxious to meet you. Since he collected me, he's seen the potential we offer, but he realizes I am a subordinate. It is you he wishes to speak to. He is quite long-lived, you know, a lifespan of more than a thousand years, and he prefers collecting younger hosts who are of a different comparable gender to his own. As he's told me, he believes he benefits from such a disparate perspective."

Stano's brow furrowed as she studied the ensign. "But he already has you. Why would he want to bond with me?" She believed she already knew the answer.

"A deeper understanding of our people and our civilization."

"And our ship," Tomkins added. "And its capabilities. I'm sure that'd be useful information."

Grammell nodded. "Maralom already possesses some of that information, but there is so much more to learn and so much we can do to help him and his people."

"It's just like Cole, Commander," Tomkins said. "She's talking like she's in a trance or she's been brainwashed. They're all a couple of steps short of joining a cult."

"That's a most offensive comparison, Lieutenant."

Stano countered, "Maybe, but it's also accurate. Now, what is it you want?"

By way of reply, Grammell turned back to her console and pressed a sequence of controls. Coalescing on the transparent dome was a depiction of the *Endeavour*, which began a slow rotation so that the image could be viewed from multiple angles.

"Yes, you want our ship," Stano said. "We've covered that."

Grammell replied, "We also want your help, Commander. With that help, we can continue to make a better life for ourselves and those we encounter."

"Sorry. Not interested."

A small, knowing smile spread across Grammell's face. "Soon, you will appreciate what we hope to do." She turned to Ensign Gaulke. "They are ready for collection. Have one of your people take them, then go and check on the rest of our people."

"I will take them," offered Ensign Tropp. "I would like to observe the collection process firsthand, anyway, for medical research purposes, of course.

Gaulke nodded. "Good."

"We'll see you soon, Commander," said Grammell as the Denobulan led them from the control room.

"Sure," replied Tomkins. "In hell, maybe."

The doors to the large nerve center closed behind them, but not before Stano got one last look at her people who remained under Lrondi control. Then Tropp gestured with his phaser toward a smaller corridor spurring off from the main passageway. They walked for perhaps a minute with the medic guiding from behind them before he uttered a single word.

"Stop."

Turning to face him, Stano eyed him with suspicion. "What now?"

"It is me, Commander," said Tropp. "I am not under Lrondi control."

Stano looked at the Denobulan in disbelief. "Are you serious?"

"Quite. For some reason, the collection process did not work. In fact, the Lrondi I carry seems to be in what you would call a 'daze.' It is conscious, yet it seems unable to guide me or compel me to any task. In fact, it appears quite susceptible to suggestion. I am at a loss to explain it, except that my physiology seems incompatible with their methods of control."

Tomkins smiled. "Hot damn."

"How can we believe you?" Stano asked. "This could be a trick of some kind."

Instead of answering, Tropp instead extended his hand and offered her his phaser.

Taking the phaser, Stano asked, "You're saying you can control it?"

"To a point, yes."

"An inside man," Tomkins said. "I love it. Of course, now the question is what do we do with you?"

The Denobulan offered a sly grin. "My dear lieutenant, I am devising a plan."

16

"Captain! I'm picking up a transmission from the alien ship."

Turning in her command chair, Atish Khatami watched as Lieutenant Hector Estrada used one hand to manipulate a series of controls on his communications console. The fingers of his other hand rested on the Feinberg receiver inserted into his left ear. He was seated so that he could divide his attention between his station and Khatami, and the captain watched his expression shift from surprise to confusion as he listened to whatever was being relayed to him by the ship's computer. A moment later, he looked in her direction, his right eyebrow arching in almost Vulcan fashion.

"It's being directed to the planet, not us."

Khatami frowned. "You're sure?"

"Absolutely." Estrada turned back to his console, tapping another series of keys before shaking his head. "And it's encrypted."

"So it's not coming from our people."

The communications officer shook his head. "I doubt it. Whatever's transmitting the signal isn't using any frequencies we employ, and that's before we talk about the encryption."

"Any bets this has something to do with whoever or whatever is responsible for our missing people?"

Estrada frowned. "First thing I thought of, Captain."

"Yeah. Me too." The lack of updates from the planet regarding the five members of her crew who had gone missing in the subterranean caverns was beginning to worry Khatami. What if one or more of them was injured? What if they had been taken prisoner by an as-yet-unidentified party? Brax's report about lingering traces from an unknown type of energy weapon was most disconcerting, given that—as far as anyone knew—Cantrel V was uninhabited save for the colony and those personnel from the *Endeavour* and the *Aephas* assisting in search and rescue operations. The alien ship had not been shown to have transported or otherwise delivered anyone to the surface, which left only one other obvious possibility: whoever or whatever was down there had been there all along.

"Any chance you can decrypt that message?" asked Khatami.

Pulling the communications receiver from his ear, Estrada replied, "With time, I should be able to crack at least some of it."

"Do it, but try to raise the boarding party again." Their inability to restore contact with Commander Stano and the others was troubling by itself, but this new wrinkle only served to heighten Khatami's unease.

After a moment spent hovering over his station, Estrada turned from the console, his expression dour. "Still no response from them."

Swiveling her chair so that she could see the bridge's main viewscreen and the image of the alien vessel it depicted, Khatami tapped the arms of her chair with her fingernails. "Any ideas about who they might be trying to contact?"

Estrada replied, "It's a wide-band broadcast, as though they don't even know who they're trying to contact."

"So, not the colony or our people on the ground."

"I doubt it, though I'm betting somebody's picking it up down there and wondering what the hell is going on."

"They can join the club." She sighed. "So, after this ship shows up and starts shooting, without anything resembling provocation, now it wants to talk to somebody down on the surface? It doesn't make any sense." Now more than ever, Khatami wanted to talk to Commander Stano or any other member of the boarding party. They had to be aware of the communications signal, but what else might be going on over there? Not for the first time, she offered a silent curse to the alien ship and its hull that blocked sensors, transporters, and now—it seemed—communications.

I do not like this. At all.

Rising from her chair, Khatami stepped from the command well and began a slow circuit of the bridge's perimeter workstations. Her crew members cast informal nods in her direction as she walked past them, having long ago grown accustomed to her habit of pacing while waiting, but comfortable in the knowledge that she would leave them to their duties. She studied the display monitors and indicators on every station, each providing its own tailored information regarding the current status of every major shipboard system. On the other hand, what none of the stations could tell her was what was happening over on the alien ship or down on the planet.

She resisted the urge to ask Estrada if there had been any updates from Commander Yataro, the senior officer of the *Endeavour* landing party providing assistance to the Tài Shan colony. According to his last report, the chief engineer was overseeing search efforts for the crew who had gone missing. Five of her people remained unaccounted for, along with a number of colonists and Starfleet personnel assigned to the Cantrel V expedition. Doctor Leone and his staff had completed the bulk of the medical treatments they had provided down on the surface, and had returned to the ship in order to monitor those patients requiring extended care for their injuries.

Missing people. People out of reach, and out of touch. *There are times when I really hate this job.*

"Captain," said Ensign Kayla Iacovino, who still manned the bridge's science station in the absence of Lieutenant Klisiewicz. The young science officer was leaning over the console's sensor controls, and she pushed herself away from the hooded viewer to face Khatami. "You need to see this."

Standing on the opposite side of the bridge, Khatami moved past the main viewscreen toward her. "What is it?"

"Sensors are picking up increased energy readings on the alien ship. They just started within the last thirty seconds, but there's no mistaking it."

Iacovino stepped aside, allowing Khatami to study the readings for herself. She bent over the viewer and reviewed the litany of information being routed here by the *Endeavour*'s sensor array, all of it presented in rapid, compressed fashion that served as an overview of the most current data being received. With practiced ease, she reached to the console without looking and began tapping controls to alter the flow of information, honing in on the indicators highlighting the other vessel's internal power readings.

"Definitely a spike," she said, stepping back from the viewer. "Any idea what's causing it? Could it be the boarding party?"

The ensign shrugged. "I honestly don't know yet, Captain. Maybe they've found the source of the communications disruption and are trying a work around?"

"That certainly sounds like something Commander Stano or Lieutenant Klisiewicz might try." Khatami knew that Klisiewicz in particular had no qualms about experimenting with unknown technology if he thought he might learn something from it. While that made him a first-rate science officer, one could not discount the possibility that his curiosity might trigger unexpected or unwanted consequences. Were they witnessing something like that now?

"Mister Estrada," said Khatami, "I need to speak with the boarding party. Sooner would be better than later."

The lieutenant turned in his seat, shaking his head. "We're still coming up dry, Captain. I've tried every trick I know, and now I've got engineering seeing if they can't somehow reconfigure our communications array. The ship's hull's a factor, but even if we channel more power to our transmissions, there's still something else working to disrupt our signals."

"We need a solution, Hector, or else I'll have to tie a note around your leg and launch you out an airlock."

With another glance toward the alien ship on the main viewscreen, Khatami was giving serious consideration to dispatching another team over there, if for nothing else than to make good on her initial, flippant idea of sending a runner to relay information. While not the most efficient method by any means, it at least held the virtue of accomplishing *something*, rather than leaving her to wait and wonder. At this point, she would accept just about anything that provided her more information.

Estrada grimaced. "If we can't figure this out, Captain, I'll volunteer to be the messenger."

"Don't think I won't hold you to that."

Klisiewicz entered the command center as though he had been living and working aboard the Lrondi ship for his entire life. It was not until he stepped through the formidable reinforced pressure hatches separating this chamber from the rest of the vessel that he realized he had made his way here without any prior knowledge of the room's location.

You are welcome, Stephen.

"I guess that answers one of my questions. Not only can you read my thoughts, sift through my memories, and guide my body, but you also can implant subliminal suggestions and information. That's going to take some getting used to." His interactions with Naqa were becoming easier as the bonding progressed. Though he was still keenly aware of her presence in his mind, she did not loom in the forefront of his consciousness as she had during the earliest moments of his collection. Now it was a sensation more akin to having someone standing behind him, watching his every move. Watching and judging, approving or condemning.

Stephen, our bond is nothing like that. As I have told you, we must work and live in harmony if we are to succeed.

Pausing just inside the entrance, Klisiewicz marveled at the wondrous, panoramic view of space afforded by the command center. The sight of Cantrel V hanging in the void before him was breathtaking, far more impressive than studying the image on a computer monitor or viewscreen. The room itself was awash with activity, and he noted Pelopan as well as members of his own crew moving about the chamber or working at different consoles. Standing at the center of a small circle of stations was Ensign Angela Grammell. Her hands were clasped behind her back, and she observed everything taking place around her with an air of authority he had never seen exuded by the junior security officer. When she looked up from the console she was studying, it was to greet him with a smile.

"Lieutenant Klisiewicz. It is good to see you."

Maralom, we have come as you requested, Naqa intoned.

Excellent, a new voice echoed in Klisiewicz's head. *We have much to discuss.*

"Okay," he said. "Getting a little crowded, if you know what I mean."

Forgive me, but time is of the essence. We require your assistance. Unlike Naqa, who always sounded gentle, almost soothing, during her interactions with him to this point, Maralom presented himself as an obvious authority figure, delivering his statements in terse, concise bursts. Despite this brusque manner, Klisiewicz was certain he sensed something between him and Naqa, as the thoughts and presence of both seemed to soften as they beheld each other in his mind.

Relationships between Lrondi are much more complex than you might imagine, Stephen. With our long life spans, our bonds transform uncounted times and reach a depth you may not even have a word to describe.

"Good to know," said Klisiewicz.

Stepping around the console, Grammell asked, "Where is Ensign Cole?"

Klisiewicz replied, "In the berthing compartment, where I left her. She's temporarily incapacitated, but she should be brought here. She may be of some assistance."

"I can retrieve her," said Ensign Tropp, whom the science officer had not noticed standing at one of the workstations just outside the room's central operations area.

Grammell nodded. "Very well. Bring Ensign Cole here."

At the mention of her name, Klisiewicz felt an ache in his stomach as he imagined her sprawled on the floor after he had stunned her at Naqa's bidding. He also sensed Naqa's reaction to his thinking about her. Was she . . . angry? Jealous? It was an odd, fleeting sensation that passed as quickly as it had come. Pushing aside the errant thoughts, he looked to Grammell.

"You summoned me here. Well, Maralom summoned me, so what do you want?"

We have begun attempting to contact our brothers

and sisters on the planet, Maralom replied. *They have awaited our return for generations, and it is long past time they were reunited with us. We fear your ships will attempt to interfere with our efforts.*

"If your efforts involve taking any of my people who are down there," Klisiewicz said, "or the colonists, or any of the native Pelopan, then yes, expect my ships to interfere."

That is why we must prepare to deal with them, but I have no wish to harm them.

Ignoring Maralom's voice in his head, Klisiewicz said to Grammell, "Then we should probably stop shooting at them."

"The initial attacks were the work of the ship's automated defense systems," said Ensign Adam Gaulke from where he stood at a control station along the command center's perimeter. "Those systems are able to act independently, modifying their responses as needed to perceived threats, but they can't devise new strategies." He gestured to the control consoles arrayed in a circle around Grammell, where Klisiewicz noted a Lrondi resting at the center of each workstation. "Now we have Pelopan and Lrondi overseeing those systems, but there is another issue."

Klisiewicz nodded in sudden understanding. "The Lrondi have no experience with this sort of thing."

"Neither do the Pelopan," replied Grammell. "In that regard, our crew is superior to them. The *Endeavour* can outrun and outmaneuver this ship, and we already know its weapons are capable of inflicting damage. However, this vessel's weapons also are formidable. A protracted battle might inflict irreparable harm to either ship. We wish to avoid this."

"We could hail the *Endeavour* and start a conversation," Klisiewicz said. "That'll avoid irreparable harm better than anything else I can think of."

Grammell said, "As you said, Captain Khatami won't stand by and allow us to proceed with our recovery plans on the planet."

"Again, not if it involves her crew or the colonists, or anybody else who's not actually willing to go with you." Klisiewicz felt Naqa recoiling as he spoke, and a feeling of discomfort was beginning to assert himself. Was something wrong?

We have no interest in seeing either ship damaged or destroyed, said Maralom. *Our absorption field is effective, but only at close range. It normally is used to drain the power from a ship that already has been disabled, but is not a real weapon when that vessel is still an active threat.*

"We could try increasing the range or the intensity of that field," Klisiewicz offered, realizing only as he spoke the words that he had not framed the statement in his mind before uttering it aloud. Naqa had beat him to it. "With sufficient power, you could drain the *Endeavour*'s shields or drain the plasma in its impulse engines. That would definitely get their attention."

"A tractor beam," said Gaulke. "We need a tractor beam. Something to latch on and hold them in place while the absorption field does the rest."

Naqa's voice sounded in his mind. *We do not possess*

such technology, but you do. You can show us how to adapt our technology for such a purpose.

"The absorption field emitters," said Grammell. "It's possible that some of them could be reconfigured to work as rudimentary tractor beams. They wouldn't be as precise as the *Endeavour*'s, but we'd have more of them, and we'd be able to channel more power to them."

"Like casting a net," said Klisiewicz. Why was it so easy to offer options for helping to fight against his own ship? Why was he not fighting the urge to do that? Why was he not fighting Naqa?

You are helping us, Stephen. You are helping us to avoid unnecessary violence.

"Is that what we're doing? When do we start helping you rescue those you left behind? What about helping the Pelopan, whose civilization you basically enslaved?"

We are not slavers, Stephen. That is not our way.

Maralom's voice carried over Naqa's. *Before our arrival, the Pelopan had already all but destroyed themselves. We brought hope, a chance at survival, and a new, better life. Instead, they turned their weapons on us.*

"Right," Klisiewicz replied. "They stopped fighting each other in order to fight you. What does that tell you?"

That they were extraordinarily shortsighted. Maralom's commanding tone had now acquired an air of arrogance. *Yes, some of the Pelopan understood what we offered and embraced the benefits of coexistence, but they were outnumbered by those who lacked such vision. It was this lack of clarity that ultimately cost them their world.*

"Yeah, I know all about the biological weapons they

used to drive you out, and how it eventually damaged the planet." Naqa had already been kind enough to share that bit of history with him. "Of course, you took a bunch of Pelopan with you when you left, and their descendants still serve you."

They are not our servants, Stephen.

"And they're not your equals." Klisiewicz gestured toward the Pelopan working around the command center. "They didn't choose to be here. Not really. You held their ancestors and allowed them to propagate their species in order to continue serving you. This is the only existence they've ever known."

Grammell eyed him with disdain. "You have known differently, Lieutenant. Would you consider your bond with us disagreeable?"

"I'll let you know when you let me break our bond."

No sooner did he speak the words than Klisiewicz felt as though he were being wrapped in a warm, soothing blanket. It was Naqa, of course, trying to rein him in. He could feel his resistance ebbing.

Our bond grows stronger, Stephen.

Maralom said, *We wish to share this with the rest of your people. Our coming together today might well be a turning point for us as well as your Federation.*

"Lieutenant," said Grammell, "think of what this means. We can serve as ambassadors for the Lrondi, spreading their message."

It was all so confusing to him. Klisiewicz could not understand how Maralom, Naqa, and the rest of the Lrondi could espouse such messages of love and mutual coexistence, and yet there was no denying that what they sought was control. Not control for its own sake, granted; their survival depended on living in harmony with other species that could assist them, but at what cost? And now he would be a part of it, acting against his will. He felt the desire—no, the need—to help Naqa and her people. It was vital that he assist them. Nothing would please him more.

"You want me to betray my ship and people," he managed to say. "Everyone on the planet."

Imagine the happiness you'll bring them, Stephen, Naqa coaxed. *The same kind of happiness you feel with me now.*

What was wrong with wanting to make people happy?

Klisiewicz said, "We need to get started identifying the emitters we want to reconfigure. The actual adjustments may take some time."

"Once they're online, and if we're able to trap the *Endeavour* and get their shields to drop," Grammell replied, "we can begin moving our people over."

Your transporters will be most helpful with this, Stephen. Such wondrous technology you have at your disposal.

"It'd be easier if we already had someone aboard," Klisiewicz said.

Maralom's voice reverberated among his thoughts. *Perhaps Commander Stano, once she has been collected.*

"No," Klisiewicz countered. "She would never return to the ship so long as any of our people were still here. It needs to be someone less conspicuous, but also someone who can get to Captain Khatami."

Perhaps we should go, Stephen.

Naqa is correct. Maralom's tone was resolute. *You are the ideal choice.*

"If it keeps people from getting hurt," Klisiewicz said, feeling pangs of guilt. They were quickly assuaged by more assurances from Naqa.

We cannot do this without you, Stephen.

Struggling to keep her intrusive thoughts at bay, he said, "We'll need some kind of diversion, a reason for them to want to beam me back."

"Do you have a suggestion?" asked Grammell.

Klisiewicz sighed. "Yeah, I think so."

17

The wail of red alert klaxons filled the *Endeavour* bridge. Khatami pushed herself from her seat, her gaze fixed on the main viewscreen and the alien ship.

"What's happening?"

Hunched over her sensor controls as though they were an extension of her own body, Ensign Kayla Iacovino replied, "Their power levels are increasing, Captain."

"Can you localize the source?"

"I'm trying. It looks like the main energy plant within each of the spheres, but the readings are still muddled. I think I might—" Iacovino jerked herself back from the viewer. "Captain! It's moving!"

On the viewscreen, Khatami could now see flares of energy visible from several small ports scattered across the alien vessel's hull.

Maneuvering thrusters.

"Full power to shields!" Khatami snapped as she moved toward her chair. "Weapons on standby!"

Behind her, Estrada said, "Captain, the *Aephas* is hailing us."

Khatami had been expecting that. At last report, the smaller ship was in the wrap-up stages of its repair efforts, which meant that it still was vulnerable in the event of a situation such as the one that appeared to be developing.

"Sensors are picking up power increases in propulsion

and weapons systems," reported Iacovino. Gripping the sensor viewer with both hands, the ensign turned from her station. "They're targeting us and the *Aephas!*"

Sitting at a console at the center of the command center, Klisiewicz scrutinized the streams of data coursing across the workstation's quartet of display screens. All of the alien script and most of the graphical representations appeared to him as little more than gibberish.

Do not worry, Stephen. Everything appears to be proceeding as we hoped.

It had been the same as far as manipulating the station's controls. Naqa had guided him through the proper commands, allowing him to receive updates from the suite of sensors arrayed around the massive ship. One of the few depictions he recognized on one screen was a computer-generated image of the alien vessel and its relative position to two other objects, which Klisiewicz understood to be the *Endeavour*, and the *Aephas* under the command of his friend Commander Mahmud al-Khaled. Guilt once more coursed through Klisiewicz at the thought of his actions pushing this vessel to attack his shipmates. Though the strikes needed to appear authentic so as not to arouse suspicion, all he could do was hope that Maralom and the other Lrondi overseeing the attack would heed his advice about not inflicting too much damage.

Stephen, I sense your feelings of distress.

"Of course I'm distressed. I'm trying to help you while making sure my friends don't get hurt. Isn't that what you want?"

"Lieutenant? Are you all right?"

Startled by the new voice, Klisiewicz looked up from his console at a young, brown-haired man wearing a blue Starfleet tunic standing at the adjacent station. It was Ensign Hastert, one of the newest additions to the *Endeavour*'s science department.

"Jay? I'm sorry." Shifting in his seat, he managed a small smile. "I guess you caught me lost in thought." He paused, thinking about possible meanings for that statement, then released a tired chuckle. "Sounds weird when I put it that way, doesn't it?"

"That it does, sir," replied the junior science officer. Klisiewicz noted the Lrondi affixed to the back of the other man's neck, whom Naqa had referred to as Tidan.

"How are you holding up?"

Hastert nodded. "Fine, sir, all things considered. They don't exactly train you for this sort of thing."

Understanding and sympathizing with the sentiment, Klisiewicz reminded himself that he had selected Hastert for this boarding party. According to the brief conversation they had exchanged before leaving the ship, it was the ensign's first landing party assignment since reporting aboard during the *Endeavour*'s most recent crew rotation.

"Hang in there," Klisiewicz said. "We'll figure this out, sooner or later."

With a smile, Hastert offered a mock salute. "Thank you, sir."

As the ensign returned to the station assigned to him by Ensign Angela Grammell and Maralom, Klisiewicz wondered about the influence Tidan might be exerting on him. Was it comforting, or just manipulating? Had the other man's relationship with his Lrondi handler grown the way his had with Naqa?

They are one, Stephen, just as we are.

A sequence of almost musical tones sounded from his workstation, and Klisiewicz's attention was drawn to an inset display on one of the console's status monitors. "We've damaged the *Endeavour*'s shields. Not significantly, but it will affect how Captain Khatami responds. She'll adjust her tactics to protect the weakened areas. Expect a counterattack from below."

We have lost several weapons ports on each of the spheres in that part of the ship. It will be difficult to defend against her attack.

"I know. I'm feeding new information to Ensign Grammell's station. We need to avoid inflicting so much damage that the captain elects to retreat, not if our diversion is going to work." Studying the displays for another moment, he nodded in approval. "All right. I think it's time to put the next phase of the plan into motion."

Are you certain this will work, Stephen?

"Once they pick up my distress call, you can believe they'll come running." His idea had been simple. Without the ability to transport to and from the *Endeavour* through the Lrondi vessel's thick mendelevium hull, his only recourse was to don his environment suit and exit the ship and call for help once outside. His story would have to sound convincing in order to ensure Captain Khatami's timely attempt at rescue. "I'll tell them my suit's damaged and I'm losing oxygen, and she'll fire everything she's got at this ship to clear a path to me."

You seem very confident.

"I know my captain. She'd fly through Hell for any one of her crew."

Klisiewicz left the command center and headed back into the convulsed network of passageways, Naqa once more making up for his complete lack of knowledge of the vessel's interior layout.

Do not worry, Stephen. You will never be lost with me.

True to her word, Naqa steered him to the room where he and the other members of the boarding party had left their environment suit. A quick survey of the equipment told Klisiewicz that everything appeared to be present, and when he inspected his own suit, he saw that it was in perfect working order.

We are truly going outside the ship?

"That's the plan."

I have never experienced anything like it.

"You're going to love it."

Klisiewicz noted that the environment suit was still just as uncomfortable as ever. Dressing in the protective garment without the aid of someone to double check its seals was a bit worrisome, but the suits were designed to be operated and maintained without the assistance of another person. Why did that knowledge not comfort him?

"I guess we'll just call this refresher training," he said to no one in particular, "with a pass-fail grade."

He was about to don his helmet when the door to the room cycled open, revealing Ensign Tropp. The Denobulan was not alone, however. Following him into the room was Anissa Cole.

"Tropp?" Klisiewicz said, making no effort to mask

his surprise. "Anissa? It's good to see you. I hope you're all right." He felt his cheeks flush with embarrassment. "I hope you'll forgive me for what happened. I didn't want to do that."

Cole nodded, her expression one of sympathy and understanding. "Believe me, I know."

"What are you doing here?"

And why is she here? Naqa seemed agitated, Klisiewicz thought. *She has not been collected, Stephen.*

"I thought you might need some assistance with your suit," replied Tropp. "Also, it's not advisable to undertake any extravehicular activity without a partner. Therefore, I volunteer to accompany you."

And what of Anissa?

"What are we supposed to do with her?" asked Klisiewicz, pointing to Cole.

"She can act as a distraction for us," Tropp said as he handed the ensign her environment suit. "Your plan is to tell Captain Khatami that your suit is malfunctioning, yes?" He pointed to Cole. "If they think it's her suit that's damaged, they'll focus their attention on her when we beam aboard, giving us a chance to take them by surprise."

Klisiewicz frowned. "That actually makes sense. A couple of extra seconds might be the difference between success and failure."

"Precisely."

Is this true, Stephen?

"Sure. They'll be caught off guard and worried about her. It might give us an opening to take control of the transporter or some other system." In truth, he was uncertain if the ploy would work, but it seemed harmless to try.

Cole made short work of donning her environment suit, and Tropp assisted her by checking seals and equipment. That Tropp was not getting dressed was not lost on Klisiewicz, or Naqa.

What is he doing? Why is he not putting on one of your suits? Why is she not resisting him?

"Naqa doesn't want me here, does she?" Cole asked. "She doesn't trust me."

She is dangerous.

Again, Klisiewicz felt the grip of anxiety beginning to close around him. His stomach lurched and his head pounded, and he nearly dropped his helmet.

"I can tell," said Cole. "She's hurting you because she's upset about me. She's trying to make you distrust me."

She is lying to you.

Tropp stepped closer. "Don't give in to her, Lieutenant. You can fight her."

What is he talking about? Fight me?

"Humans are different than the Pelopan," said Tropp. "Your brains are different, as are your neurochemical processes. You're still susceptible to the collection process, but you can resist it if you push hard enough."

What is he saying?

Cole gripped his arm. "Push her, Stephen. Fight her."

I do not understand.

"Fight, Lieutenant," said Tropp.

Why is he talking this way? Cejal, why do you allow this? Cejal?

"Cejal," Klisiewicz repeated.

Tropp replied, "My Lrondi collector, sir. He's not available at the moment."

"I don't understand."

"There's really no time right now, Lieutenant. We must be going."

Cole pulled on her helmet. "We need to move."

Stephen, you must stop this.

A wave of nausea rushed over Klisiewicz, and he was certain he might vomit all over his suit's open collar. "She's fighting me." He gritted his teeth, trying to force back the unwelcome sensations. "We have to hurry."

I cannot allow this. You are betraying us. You are betraying me.

There was a hiss near his left ear, and Klisiewicz felt Naqa shift on his neck, though she remained in place. Very noticeable, however, was the sudden loss of her thoughts and voice in his own mind.

Tropp stepped back into his field of vision, holding up a silver hypospray. "A mild sedative. It will not last long, but it should be enough for you to get outside and contact the *Endeavour*. You need to go."

"You're not coming?" asked Klisiewicz.

"No, Lieutenant. I'm still trying to help Commander Stano, but none of this will work if you are discovered before you can contact the ship."

Only partly hearing the Denobulan, Klisiewicz instead was searching his thoughts for signs of another mind. "Naqa? Are you there?"

Cole slapped him on the arm. "Stephen. We need to go. Now!"

An odd sense of longing now beginning to grip him, he allowed Cole to pull him after her as they headed for the airlock.

You couldn't wait thirty more minutes?

"It's altering its orbit," reported Lieutenant Molan lek Xav, calling out over his shoulder as he continued to report updated sensor information. He already had confirmed that numerous ports positioned at equidistant points along the alien ship's hull were maneuvering thrusters, and Mahmud al-Khaled watched the vessel on the bridge's main viewscreen as several of those thrusters flared to life. The results of that action now were visible as the ship attitude began to change.

"Route emergency power to the forward shields," ordered al-Khaled. Pushing himself from his command chair, he moved to stand behind the helm station. "Rodriguez, maintain our distance from that thing, and whatever you do, keep us facing that ship, no matter what."

Lieutenant Sasha Rodriguez nodded. "No problem, sir."

"And if you can angle us toward their damaged weapons ports, that'd be a nice bonus."

"I'll see what I can do."

Xav barked, "Reading a power surge. They are firing on the *Endeavour*!"

Al-Khaled looked up in time to see a barrage of writhing crimson energy bolts spit forth from a pair of the alien ship's weapons ports. Without being asked, Rodriguez tapped the control to shift the screen's image just as the last of the volleys slammed into the *Endeavour*'s deflector shields. The protective barrier flared with white-hot intensity at the points of impact even as the starship rolled to its left and arced away from the attack.

"Incoming fire!" shouted Rodriguez, who already was guiding the *Aephas* into an evasive maneuver. The image on the viewscreen flashed white at the same instant al-Khaled felt the deck tremor beneath his boots as the ship's defensive screens absorbed its own strike.

At the science station, Xav said, "Nicely done, Lieutenant. We only caught a glancing blow from that attack. Shield strength dropped two percent."

"Maintain evasive, Rodriguez," ordered al-Khaled. "Keep that ship in front of us. Xav. How's the *Endeavour*?"

The Tellarite replied, "They took a stronger hit than we did, but their shields appear to be holding."

Al-Khaled knew that a team from the *Endeavour* was still aboard the alien vessel and that communications with them had been lost. He figured Captain Khatami was all but chewing dilithium at the moment as she tried to restore contact with her people. Adding to that uncertainty was the new revelation that the alien ship was transmitting a signal toward the planet's surface, but its intended recipient remained unknown.

As for the *Aephas*, its shield generators were still undergoing last minute adjustments. Al-Khaled knew that excessive strain on those systems might nullify those hours the crew had expended on repairs after their previous skirmish. Although the *Aephas* had managed to get in its own hits, the enormous alien vessel still posed a significant threat, with only a handful of its weapons ports out of commission.

"Pzial," he said, "get me an update from engineering."

From where she sat at the bridge's communications station, Ensign Folanir Pzial replied, "Aye, sir."

"Targeting systems are tracking us and the *Endeavour* again," said Xav. "Sensors are registering continued power increase to the ship's weapons."

Al-Khaled asked, "What about that dampening field?"

"Still no indications that it has resumed operation," replied the science officer. "Perhaps the *Endeavour*'s boarding party found a way to disable it."

"Do you really think we're that lucky?"

Xav snorted. "Our joint history suggests that is unlikely."

"Always the optimist."

"They're coming after us, sir," reported Rodriguez. Her fingers were moving in frantic fashion across the helm console. "I'm adjusting our position to compensate."

Al-Khaled ordered, "Stand by weapons, but get ready to duck and run." Glancing down at the astrogator positioned at the top center of Rodriguez's helm console, he noted the positions of the *Aephas* and the *Endeavour* relative to the alien vessel. Both Starfleet ships were engaging in a series of minor evasive maneuvers, countering the movements of the larger craft. "It's trying to angle itself to aim some of its undamaged weapons at us, isn't it?"

"Looks that way, sir," replied Rodriguez. "So far, we're able to compensate."

"Updated report from engineering," Pzial called out.

"Commander Grace says that shield generators are at seventy-nine percent following that last strike and urges us to use caution." The Rigelian turned in her seat. "He sounds rather insistent on that last point, sir."

"Tell him no promises," replied al-Khaled as he returned to his seat. "He can yell at me about it later." He had just landed in his chair when Xav warned of the ship firing again. The effect was more pronounced this time despite Rodriguez's best efforts to dodge the new attack. Lights and monitors across the bridge flickered as the *Aephas*'s shields bore the brunt of the abuse.

Grace is going to kill me when this is over, assuming we live through it.

"I've got a lock on two weapons ports," said Rodriguez.

Al-Khaled replied, "Fire at will, Lieutenant."

With the alien craft looming on the viewscreen, the helm officer unleashed a pair of phaser strikes, and al-Khaled watched streaks of blue-white energy lance across open space, impacting against different points along the other vessel's hull.

Keeping her attention focused on her console, Rodriguez said, "That's two." The view of the alien ship changed again as she maneuvered the *Aephas* to maintain its forward-facing position and searched for new targets.

"The *Endeavour* has disabled three more," reported Xav.

"Good. That leaves us only about a hundred or so to go, right?" The image on the screen had settled once more on the massive vessel, with the *Endeavour* visible on its far side as the other starship continued to perform its own evasive maneuvers. "Is it just me," said al-Khaled, "or is this thing acting like it's lost or confused?" To him, the alien craft's movements seemed odd, as though whoever or whatever was controlling it was having difficulty adapting to the situation as its two opponents adjusted their own movements and tactics.

Rodriguez replied, "If you ask me, sir, I think it's acting in accordance with a largely pre-programmed set of responses. That or whoever's flying that thing is trying to learn it as they go. There's some basic strategy at work here, but nothing we can't defeat so long as we don't let it get in any lucky shots."

"I think you're right, Lieutenant." Al-Khaled pointed at the screen. "Let's test that theory. Give me a strafing run that feints us going starboard and then run us to port, along where we've already disabled some of its weapons." He was still aware of his ship's compromised state, but if they were dealing with automation rather than a living being who could alter and improvise its strategy as the skirmish continued, then he and Captain Khatami would possess a decisive advantage.

Here's hoping.

From over his right shoulder, Pzial said, "We are receiving an incoming transmission from the *Endeavour*."

"Let's have it."

A moment later, the voice of Captain Atish Khatami blared through the bridge's intercom. *"Commander, I know you're still dealing with repairs, but two against one looks to be better odds against this thing."*

"We're still here, Captain, and I was just thinking the same thing. How do you want to play it?"

"I've still got people over there, so I don't want to

stray too far. I just hope whatever's controlling that thing doesn't use that against me. We'll keep at it, targeting their weapons ports while trying to limit damage to other areas, but if we have to, we go for the throat, particularly if it looks like it might turn its sights on the planet again."

"Understood."

"Wait," Xav said, turning from his science station. "Sensors are picking up two life-forms outside the ship. They're humanoid, standing on the outer hull."

Frowning, al-Khaled asked, "Are you sure?"

The Tellarite nodded. "Absolutely."

"I am picking up a Starfleet communicator frequency, sir," reported Pzial. "It's being directed to the *Endeavour*."

Over the intercom, Khatami said, *"It's two of my people. They're sending a distress signal."*

Smacking the arm of his command chair with the heel of his hand, al-Khaled smiled. "All right. We were due for some good luck, weren't we?"

"The *Endeavour* will have to drop its shields to affect transport," offered Xav.

Al-Khaled nodded in understanding. This was not over just yet.

18

It was going to be close.

Khatami resisted the urge to lean back in her chair as the image on the main viewscreen rolled to the right, bringing the hull of the alien vessel into sharp relief. Under the adroit direction of Lieutenant Neelakanta, the *Endeavour* was moving into position for what Khatami hoped would be a fast and successful retrieval. Despite the ship's artificial gravity and inertial damping systems, Khatami still felt a twinge in her stomach in response to the starship's maneuvering.

Good thing I skipped lunch.

"Estrada," she said, "is the transporter room ready?"

The communications officer replied, "They're standing by, Captain."

Nodding at the report, Khatami kept her attention fixed on the viewscreen. The other ship had launched what she had felt was a rather lackadaisical attack on the *Endeavour* as well as the *Aephas*, leaving her to wonder who or what was responsible, and why this moment had been chosen for the engagement.

I won't know until I get Klisiewicz and Cole back.

This, of course, raised another point: Where was the rest of the boarding party? How had Lieutenant Klisiewicz and Ensign Cole become separated from Commander Stano and the others? Were there any injuries among her team? The report provided by Klisiewicz when he had contacted the *Endeavour* had offered precious little in the way of answers to those questions, and the situation was heightened by the fact that his environment suit had been damaged and compromised. Once both of them were back aboard the ship, Khatami would get more information and figure out what to do next.

One thing at a time.

"Closing to transporter range," reported her navigator, Lieutenant Marielise McCormack, from where she sat next to Neelakanta. She was hunched over her console, her attention riveted on the controls and indicators arrayed before her.

"How are we looking, Mister Neelakanta?" asked Khatami.

The Arcturian replied, "Maintaining course and speed." He seemed unfazed by the demands placed upon him as he maneuvered the ship into position. It was rare for him to lose his composure even in the face of imminent danger or crisis. Khatami had witnessed his formidable self-control in situations even more intense than the one they currently faced, and it was at times like these that she was grateful for his firm, steady hands guiding her ship.

At the science station, Ensign Iacovino reported, "Even this close, sensors are still compromised, but the ship is definitely reacting to our presence."

"Let it react," Khatami said. "We'll be in and out in a few more seconds." She hoped that sounded more confident to her crew than it did to her own ears. With the hull of the larger ship still interfering with sensors and communications as well as transporters, the only safe option for affecting a fast retrieval was to close the distance, which in turn placed the *Endeavour* in greater danger of attack as it made its approach. As though to emphasize the dangerous situation the starship was entering, Khatami felt the bridge shudder around her as the ship's deflector shields absorbed the impacts from yet another attack.

In front of her, Neelakanta called out, "Mark!"

"Drop shields! Transporter room, energize!"

Even as Khatami barked the order, Neelakanta was altering the *Endeavour*'s trajectory away from the alien vessel, and she could see his right hand hovering over one control in particular. A second later, the helm officer's fingers tapped that control and Khatami noted its corresponding indicator flash from red to green.

"Shields back up," he reported.

Khatami replied, "Excellent. Put some space between us. Mister Estrada, notify the *Aephas* to get clear of that thing. We'll regroup once we're out of its weapons range." Looking down at the intercom controls on the arm of her chair, she asked, "Transporter room, what's the story down there?"

"Affirmative, Captain. We got them both, safe and sound."

"The ship looks to be breaking off its attack, Captain," said Iacovino. "Once we moved out of its apparent weapons range, it's like it just lost interest."

"Don't bet on it," replied Khatami. Looking over her shoulder at Estrada, she asked, "Anything new on that signal it was broadcasting to the surface?"

The lieutenant swiveled his chair toward her and shook

his head. "It's still transmitting, Captain, but so far there's been no response or other action."

"Keep on it." Rising from her chair, Khatami pushed herself from the command well and toward the turbolift. "McCormack, take the conn, and make sure we keep a respectful distance from that ship. Estrada, whatever you and engineering are doing to get through the communications block, all of you need to step up your game. I'll be in the transporter room."

It was well past time to get some answers.

Klisiewicz's vision cleared as the beam faded, and he was relieved to see the *Endeavour*'s transporter room. His sigh of relief echoed inside his helmet.

Stepping around the transporter console, Chief Michael Hess was walking toward him, but Klisiewicz held up a hand.

"Don't," he said. "Notify security and Doctor Leone. I need to be put in isolation before I get out of this suit."

Hess stopped at the pair of steps leading to the transporter pad, his expression one of confusion. "I don't understand, sir. What's wrong?"

"Just do as he says," Cole snapped. "We need to quarantine him right now."

You have betrayed me, Stephen.

Naqa's presence reasserted itself in her mind with a force so great that it made Klisiewicz stumble backward. The wave of pain was enough to make his knees buckle, and he collapsed to the transporter pad.

"Cole, she's awake," he managed to force between gritted teeth.

"What's wrong, Lieutenant?" asked Hess, moving forward to help.

Cole held up her hands. "Chief! Stay back!"

The uppercut was enough to send Hess toppling off the transporter pad and down to the deck. Klisiewicz felt no pain in his gloved hand as he pushed himself to his feet.

You will pay for your betrayal, Stephen.

Feeling air escaping from his suit as he unfastened his collar's locking catches, Klisiewicz was removing his helmet as he felt Cole grab his arm.

"Stephen! No!" She tried to stop him as he stepped down from the transporter pad, but he whirled on her, his blood burning with rage.

I will make her pay.

Then, the door opened.

After running the length of the corridor leading from the turbolift that had deposited her on deck seven, Khatami slowed her pace as she arrived at the entrance to the transporter room. The doors parted at her approach, and she entered the room in time to see two figures dressed in environment suits. Ensign Anissa Cole stumbled away from Lieutenant Stephen Klisiewicz, and tripped over her own feet before sprawling across the transporter pad. Klisiewicz remained in place, his right hand gripping his helmet and his arm raised as though to strike Cole.

"What the hell . . . ?"

It was all Khatami could manage before Klisiewicz turned to face her. The ensign seemed to move like a silver automaton, as though confused or doubtful about what to do next. This odd hesitation lasted only a moment before Klisiewicz began crossing the room toward her.

"Stand fast, Lieutenant," Khatami snapped, but Klisiewicz did not heed her order. "I gave you an order, Klisiewicz."

Something's damned wrong here.

It was the only thing she had time to think before deciding to act. Rather than wait for Klisiewicz to reach her, Khatami seized the initiative. She closed the distance separating them, reaching for his suit's helmet connector bracket. Klisiewicz grunted in surprise as she jerked the bracket with her, twisting him to his left and placing his body between her and the fallen Master Chief Hess. Taking advantage of that fleeting moment of confusion, Khatami continued moving in a circle, pulling Klisiewicz with her. She felt him starting to resist and yanked harder, pulling him farther off his feet. He reached for her but she released her grip on him, using his own momentum to send him crashing to the floor. The helmet fell from his grip, clattering across the floor, and as Klisiewicz rolled onto his side, Khatami caught sight of the strange gray mass that appeared fixed to his neck. What was it? Some kind of parasite? How had it gotten there? Then the questions were forgotten as Klisiewicz began regaining his feet.

Khatami did not wait. The transporter room doors parted as she burst into the corridor. Her abrupt exit attracted the attention of a passing crew member who turned and leveled a shocked expression at her as she stopped herself from careening into the bulkhead on the other side of the passageway.

"Intruder alert!" she yelled. "Get security down here, right now!"

She turned at the sound of running footsteps, and she jerked herself to her right as Klisiewicz just missed colliding with her. He crashed into the wall, giving Khatami the moment she needed, and she kicked at the back of his legs. He dropped to his knees, still managing to swipe at her with one fist. Parrying that attack, she stepped in and punched him in the side of his head, toppling him to the deck. Appearing dazed from the hit, he was slow pushing himself to his feet, and Khatami was setting herself for another strike when the whine of a phaser pierced the corridor. The beam struck Klisiewicz's chest and his expression turned blank before he folded over and dropped unconscious to the deck.

"Captain!"

Turning toward the voice, Khatami saw Chief Petty Officer Lanier Wimmer approaching her, a type-1 phaser in his hand and aimed at the insensate Klisiewicz. The recreation officer stepped to within a couple of paces of the stunned lieutenant and leveled his weapon at him.

"Are you all right, Captain?"

Khatami pointed to Klisiewicz. "I'll be fine," she replied as she tried to bring her rapid breathing under control. "Watch that thing on his neck. If it moves, shoot it."

"What is it?" asked Wimmer.

The captain shook her head. "Damned if I know." Moving past the small group of crew members who had gathered in response to the commotion, she reached for a nearby intercom panel and thumbed its activation switch. "Khatami to bridge. Seal off transporter room two. In fact, evacuate and seal off this entire section. No one in or out without my order. I need another security team, and tell Doctor Leone to get down here too. Tell him contamination and isolation protocols are in effect as of right now."

"What's going on, Captain?" asked Lieutenant McCormack through the open intercom channel.

"Klisiewicz and Cole brought something with them from the alien ship. I don't know if they're dangerous or a contagion risk, so I'm not taking any chances."

"Security and Doctor Leone have been notified. They'll be there in a couple of minutes. Transporter room two is locked out, and we're evacuating the rest of that section now."

Casting a look at Wimmer, Khatami said, "Sorry, Chief. Looks like you're stuck with me for the time being."

"No problem, Captain. Just please don't punch me." The deadpan comment earned Wimmer a tired chuckle from Khatami.

"Fair enough." Returning her attention to the intercom, she said, "Bridge, what's the status on communications with the boarding party?"

McCormack replied, *"Mister Estrada's still working on it, Captain. Since Lieutenant Klisiewicz was able to contact us from outside that ship, Estrada's sure something has to be deliberately jamming our frequencies."*

"Then find me a frequency that isn't jammed, or tell Mister Estrada to suit up and be ready to take a walk. We need to find out if Commander Stano or any of the others have been affected by whatever this is." After a pause, she moved to the next item on her mental checklist. "What's the story with the ship itself?"

"We're still maintaining our distance, Captain. I had the Aephas *move to the other side of the planet so that Commander al-Khaled and his people could finish up their repairs. As for the ship, Ensign Iacovino picked up on something with regard to its attacks: it doesn't seem to want to move too far away from a point where it can monitor a particular section of the planet. It's continuing to broadcast its encrypted message, as though it's waiting for a reply."*

"We need to know who it's hoping will answer. I don't know how or why, but I'm convinced this ties to our missing people down there."

"Estrada's already assigned extra people to the decryption effort while he tries to get us communications with the boarding party."

Grunting in reluctant acknowledgment of that report, Khatami said, "Keep me informed. I'll be in sickbay."

"Are you all right, Captain?"

"I'm fine. I just want to know what the hell was brought aboard my ship, and if it's dangerous. For all we know, the entire boarding party's been affected."

Were her people even still alive?

19

Colleen Cook's arm ached.

Despite the outstanding treatment she had received thanks to the skills of the *Endeavour*'s medical staff, the bones in her left arm insisted on reminding her that they were there, beneath the surface of her skin and still in the process of completing the accelerated healing process. It was not her first time being subjected to the wonders of a bone knitter, and she knew that the discomfort would persist for a few days. Doctor Leone had advised her to get some rest, but that was impossible with everything still going on in space as well as on and beneath the surface of Cantrel V. People needed finding and questions needed answering, and Cook was determined to do her part in accomplishing all of that.

I probably should've taken a nap first, though. And maybe a shower.

In truth, she was happy to be out of the *Endeavour*'s sickbay and back to work. Being back aboard the starship had triggered a host of memories from her previous assignment, when the vessel was under Captain Zhao Sheng's command. Doctor Leone had lost none of the casual, dry wit that had been one of his many attributes, none of which superseded his abilities as a physician, and her solemn mood was eased upon seeing him at the aid station before her transport to the ship. Even Leone's ability to ease her grief had not been sufficient once Cook had arrived on the *Endeavour*, for it was there that many painful memories had resurfaced. Chief among them the circumstances that had resulted in the deaths of Zhao and other members of the ship's crew three years earlier.

The events of that day had been enough to push Cook and a handful of colleagues to request duty with another ship or ground posting, and it had taken her a while to come to terms with what she had witnessed on that tragic day. Seeing Captain Khatami in her role as Zhao's successor was at both upsetting and reassuring to Cook. The former, for how it brought forth memories of Captain Zhao, and the latter because she had known immediately that Khatami was more than up to the task of carrying on in Zhao's stead. That confidence in her former ship's current captain had not been enough to stop Cook from seeking a change of assignment, but it comforted her to know that Atish Khatami still occupied the center seat on the *Endeavour*'s bridge.

Likewise, the conflicting emotions had also served to steer Cook's thoughts in other, equally unpleasant directions. Lying in the patient recovery ward had only given her time to think about T'Naal. The passing of her friend was still a fresh wound, one she would endure for a while. Though Cook had only met the Vulcan upon being assigned to the Starfleet team on Cantrel V, the two had taken no time to mesh working styles in a way that complemented and supported each other. Although Cook had known and worked with other Vulcans in conjunction with her previous tours on other ships and starbases, T'Naal was the first she had been able to call a friend. In addition to their similar work styles, interests, and approaches to archaeology, the simple truth was that they had enjoyed each other's company. Granted, T'Naal might not have described it the same way, but the two had spent enough late nights sipping herbal tea and discussing any number of topics for Cook to know that T'Naal liked her and had valued those moments.

"I'm really going to miss you."

"Lieutenant?"

Looking up from the tricorder she was using to scan for life signs or any other readings that seemed out of place for a subterranean cavern, Cook realized she had spoken the sentiment aloud. With a start, she saw Lieutenant Brax, the *Endeavour*'s chief of security, walking across the chamber toward her. Watching him step first over a sizable boulder and then across a crevasse marring the stone floor, she noted that the Edoan's trilimbed physiology seemed ideally suited to navigating the uneven terrain of the caverns and tunnels.

"Yes?" she asked as Brax stepped closer, feeling her cheeks flush with embarrassment.

"You seem distracted," he said. "I wanted to verify that you are up to carrying out your duties. I know that you have only recently recovered from the injuries you sustained." When he smiled, the upturned corners of his thin mouth gave his countenance an appearance similar to that of ancient statues she had visited on Earth. It required effort not to chuckle as she made that sudden silent comparison.

Cook smiled. "It's an ongoing process." She held up her arm. "It only hurts when I laugh." At first, she thought Brax might not understand the joke, but instead he nodded.

"In my experience with humans, that is a common complaint."

It took her a moment to ponder the security chief's words, and she eyed him with uncertainty. "Was that a joke?"

"I sincerely hope so."

Allowing herself a small chuckle, Cook reached up to rub her forehead. "I apologize, Lieutenant. I guess I'm more tired than I thought, and I let my mind wander for a moment."

"I know that you suffered a personal tragedy," replied the security chief. "It is commendable that you want to assist us in this search, but I understand if you feel you need time to rest."

Cook shook her head. "No. I appreciate the concern, but I want to be here. I want to help find the others. T'Naal would do the same if our roles were reversed. Once everybody's found and safe, then I'll rest."

This seemed to satisfy Brax. "Very well. Carry on, Lieutenant."

Returning her attention to the tricorder and the matters at hand, Cook released a small sigh of relief, gratified that Brax had not seen fit to relieve her. She had volunteered to join the search effort that he was coordinating with several teams consisting of *Endeavour*, *Aephas*, and colony personnel moving through those underground areas that had been scanned and deemed safe. Cook and the others knew that there remained a continued risk of cave-ins and other problems in the event of another tremor, to say nothing of a full-scale earthquake. Then there was the possibility that the search teams might not be alone down here. Like the rest of the people engaged in the effort, she had been briefed on the circumstances surrounding the disappearance of Master Chief Petty Officer Rideout and another *Endeavour* engineer as well as Ensign Zane and two of his security officers.

Was that even possible? After all this time she and the other Starfleet science specialists had spent working alongside the Tài Shan colonists, had they all missed some clue or other sign that they were not alone on Cantrel V? It seemed unbelievable to Cook, but the energy readings reported by a few of the personnel who had gone missing were difficult to ignore.

What if it was true, and some as yet unknown group of beings had been here this whole time? Who were they? Where had they come from? Did they have any connection to the mysterious ship in orbit above the planet, as Captain Khatami believed? Had they been watching the colony? That unpleasant thought sent a chill coursing across Cook's skin.

As for Rideout, Zane, and the others, no life-sign readings had been detected, let alone any indications of remains or any other clue as to the whereabouts or condition of the five missing *Endeavour* crew. Likewise, no hints or suggestion of other life-forms had revealed themselves, according to the reports Brax had received from each of the dozen teams of people involved in the search. Also eluding them were any more instances of the odd energy readings noted by Master Chief Rideout during her last conversation with Brax. Whatever she and the other missing crew members had detected had so far not appeared on any tricorder scans, even with Cook and others manipulating and reconfiguring scanning frequencies in the hopes of finding something that might elude a normal sweep. Like everything else, these efforts had proven futile. Tensions were high and everyone was on alert, waiting for something to happen or for someone to show themselves. Every time Cook listened to Brax relay another status report to Captain Khatami, as he did at precise thirty-minute intervals, she heard the annoyance in the security chief's voice.

So, help him find something else to report.

"According to the map we've been able to piece together," Cook said, gesturing with her free hand to her tricorder, "we've covered all of the underground areas that we can navigate safely. There are still a few sections that are cut off thanks to cave-ins, but scans show nothing in those spots, either. It's like they just vanished."

Brax replied, "Even accounting for the scan interference from the rock itself, there are still a small number of sections we have not been able to search." The security chief had already given voice to the idea of using phasers or even a laser drill to gain access to those areas that at the moment were inaccessible, but he also was worried that such action might heighten the risk of a tunnel or cavern collapse. Cook had overheard his last report, in which he had expressed these points to Captain Khatami. She heard the *Endeavour*'s science officer—or, one of them—was at the moment doing her best to modify the starship's sensors in an attempt to circumvent the planet's natural interference.

"We've searched a much larger area than they should have been able to cover undetected," Cook said, "assuming none of them were injured. If they were injured, that reduces the ground they could traverse. Even then, you'd think they'd be calling for help, either with their communicators or just yelling at the top of their lungs. Of course, for that, they'd have to be . . ." She let the rest of the sentence die on her lips.

The Edoan shook his head. "If they had perished during one of the quakes, we would have found some indication of their remains in or near their last known location."

"What about the ground giving way?" Cook asked, realizing as she voiced the question the awful implication her words carried. "Could they have fallen through a hole or fissure to some deeper level, farther underground and beyond our scanning range?"

Brax replied, "We found no evidence of such a collapse. I am becoming convinced that they moved from their previous position, under their own power or via some other means, for reasons as yet unknown. If it is the latter, then this of course lends credence to the possibility of there being other persons at work here." The way he made the statement made Cook's gut twitch. It made the situation sound as though someone might be watching them right now, lurking in the shadows and waiting for an opportune moment to strike.

Cook heard Brax instruct the security team that had accompanied them into the caverns that they would soon be proceeding from this chamber into one of the connecting tunnels, on their way to their next designated search area. She reached to adjust the tricorder's scanning field for the transit through the narrow corridor, which would bring the unit into closer contact with the surrounding rock and the multitude of potentially disruptive mineral ores embedded within it. Tightening the scan radius might cause her to miss detecting something from a greater distance, but the increased intensity might allow the tricorder to pick up a reading that was closer yet perhaps concealed within a smaller chamber or cavity the search teams could have overlooked.

Wishful thinking?

At first, Cook thought she might have entered an incorrect setting, as the tricorder responded with an odd string of beeps and a spike in the unit's small, illuminated display. Frowning, she reached to enter the adjustments a second time and received the same result.

"What the hell's wrong with this thing?"

Behind her, Brax asked, "Is there a problem, Lieutenant?"

Cook studied the scan readings. "I'm not sure. My tricorder seems to be acting up. We've detected no traces of any energy signatures at all down here, but for a moment there was this small spike as I was refocusing the scan field. It's gone now, and I can't seem to reproduce the reading. It's almost as though . . ."

Oh. Damn.

"A dampening field," she snapped as she felt her hands

begin to tremble. "That has to be what's been messing with our readings. Someone or something's been using a dampening field down here."

Brax, brandishing type-2 phasers in two of his three hands, asked, "Are you certain?"

Still manipulating the tricorder's controls, Cook grunted in mounting annoyance. "As sure as I can be. It's one of the few things that makes any sense."

"Can you pinpoint the source?"

Cook grimaced. "Working on it." Even as she offered her reply, she felt goose bumps on her arms and a sense of trepidation beginning to grip her, and she was sure a twinge in her gut was trying to tell her something.

Yeah. It's time to go.

"Verify your readings, Lieutenant," ordered Brax. With his remaining hand, he reached for his communicator and flipped open its antenna grid. "Brax to all search parties," he said, and Cook noted that the security chief now spoke in a softer voice. "We have detected an anomalous energy reading at my present location. Lieutenant Cook will be transmitting information for you to adjust your tricorders in order to register this reading yourselves. All personnel are to remain on full alert and ready to defend yourselves should the need arise. Team leaders, coordinate your people and be ready to evacuate to the surface on my command. Acknowledge."

Listening to different members of the search party reporting in, Cook scowled as the readings on her tricorder shifted yet again. "Damn it. I've lost the reading. It was here a minute ago, and now it's gone." Adjusting the unit's controls did nothing to alter the results. "This doesn't make any sense. I just had it."

"Perhaps the tricorder is not the issue," Brax said, his voice low. "If you were able to detect some form of dampening effect, then it stands to reason that the originators of that interference are also aware of our presence."

"Is that your way of saying we should get the hell out of here?" Still holding her tricorder, Cook reached for the phaser on her hip. She had opted for the larger, more powerful type-2 model upon joining the search effort, leaving the smaller type-1 in a pocket of her jumpsuit.

Brax nodded. "I believe that would be prudent." Turning his attention to the three security officers who had accompanied him and Cook into the underground passages, he said, "We are leaving. Ensigns Gray and Wadsworth, you will cover our rear. I will take point. Ensign Drev, you stay with Lieutenant Cook."

A shadow fell across her tricorder, and Cook turned to see Ensign Kelor jilan Drev standing beside her. While not as burly as other Tellarites she had encountered, the young security officer still cut an imposing figure, stretching his red uniform tunic almost to its limit across his broad chest. His stout nose wiggled and his dark, deep-set eyes seemed to gleam as he regarded her. The phaser he carried seemed almost like a toy in his large hand. Like most Tellarites, Drev tended to say very little, though he nodded in greeting as he took up position next to her.

"Lieutenant."

The group began following Brax out of the cavern, with the Edoan setting a brisk pace as they made their way into the connecting tunnel. Each of the security officers carried a hand lamp, which they now used to illuminate the passage ahead of them. There were no other obvious openings leading from the tunnel and no places of possible concealment, and yet Cook could not shake the feeling that they were being watched. Was it intuition or simple paranoia? She could not be sure.

Ahead of her, Brax's communicator chirped and the security chief retrieved it with his one free hand. "Brax here."

"Lieutenant," said Captain Khatami, *"we've had something of a new development up here. There are definitely hostile life-forms aboard the alien ship, and we think that signal they've been transmitting toward the planet may be intended for someone or something affiliated with them. We don't know anything definitive yet, but not much else makes sense at this point."*

That would go a long way toward explaining many things, Cook decided.

Brax replied, "Captain, do you believe these life-forms may be connected to the disappearance of our missing crew members?"

"I'm certainly not ruling it out. Because of that, I want you and your people out of there. If there are more of these life-forms on the planet, they're dangerous. They're not humanoid, but they're able to take control of a humanoid host by latching on like a parasite and tapping into the cerebral cortex. Lieutenant Klisiewicz was beamed back to the ship after having been compromised. He's under sedation in sickbay right now, and Doctor Leone's trying

to figure out how to get the damned thing off. Until then, I want our people safe and accounted for. Return to the surface and rally at the camp, Lieutenant."

"What of Ensign Zane and the others?" asked Brax. As he walked, the team approached an intersection and he gestured with one of his phasers toward the new tunnel. A metal marker tag, affixed to the tunnel wall by one of the *Endeavour* security personnel, indicated this passage as a route to the surface. The code on the tag told Cook that they were less than fifty meters from the entrance to the underground areas.

"One thing at a time. For all we know, they've been compromised in similar fashion. It's already happened to other members of Commander Stano's team. We need to get a handle on this before we lose anyone else."

Brax nodded. "Acknowledged, Captain." The conversation concluded, the Edoan switched communicator frequencies and relayed Khatami's order to the other search teams. He was still doing that when the tunnel echoed with the whine of a phaser. Blue-white energy illuminated the passage, and Cook looked behind her to see Ensign Gray's silhouette highlighted against the flare of his weapon firing at . . . something. A fleeting shadow played across the rock wall as Gray fired again.

"We've got company back here!" the security officer shouted as his companion, Ensign Wadsworth, ran to assist him. Both men now were firing, the reports from their phasers amplified by the tunnel's narrow confines.

"There!"

Drev's single, terse word was enough to make Cook flinch just as she felt the Tellarite's other beefy hand close around her arm and pull her to one side. Drev's movements were almost a blur, his speed belying his bulk as he raised his phaser and fired. The blue energy beam streaked down the tunnel, and Cook saw it strike a figure that seemed to have appeared from the air itself. Succumbing to the phaser's stunning force, the new arrival dropped to the tunnel floor in a disjointed heap. Cook directed her hand lamp at the unmoving figure, not recognizing the species of humanoid. Who or what was it?

An indigenous inhabitant?

"Go!" shouted Brax, interrupting her thoughts and punctuating his order by firing both of the phasers he wielded as he directed the rest of the team into the connecting tunnel. Two more figures fell in the corridor, and Cook saw more shadows behind them, moving closer. Where had they all come from?

"Lieutenant!" she shouted as yet another figure emerged from the near darkness, and Cook was startled to see Ensign Kerry Zane running at Brax. His expression was one of anger as he charged the security chief, who did not hesitate before turning one of his phasers on Zane and firing. The ensign grunted, staggering forward before tripping on the uneven tunnel floor and collapsing to the ground.

"Take him!" Brax shouted, gesturing toward Drev before grabbing Cook's arm and propelling her into the smaller tunnel. Raising her phaser to cover both officers, she watched as Drev picked up the unconscious Zane with one hand and draped him over a muscular shoulder before the Tellarite turned and headed for the tunnel. Ensigns Gray and Wadsworth followed after them and she backpedaled as Brax brought up the rear. Once everyone was in the tunnel, Cook saw the security chief do something to adjust the settings on his phasers before taking aim with both weapons at the stone ceiling just above the tunnel entrance. He fired two quick bursts from each phaser, and harsh red energy beams sliced into the rock and chunks of rubble began raining down into the narrow passage, filling it and blocking the opening.

"That should slow their pursuit," Brax said, pushing her up the tunnel with his free hand. The run to the surface was short and fast, with the team covering the remaining fifty or so meters of dark, twisting tunnel in less than a minute. A pair of security guards was waiting at the entrance as Cook emerged from the passage with Brax right behind her.

"Seal it," ordered the security chief, gesturing to the tunnel opening, and the two security guards set to work with their phasers, collapsing the cave entrance in a matter of seconds. Opening his communicator, he called out, "Brax to all search teams. Report in."

As he set about the task of accounting for the rest of his people, Cook moved to where Ensign Drev had deposited Zane on the ground. The security officer was still unconscious, and for the first time she noted something gray and bulbous affixed to the back of his neck.

"What the hell is that?" she said, pointing to it.

The thing moved.

More than that, it shifted its position on Kerry's neck and all but launched itself, arcing through the air at Cook. She flinched, staggering backward and throwing up her hands to defend herself as something huge blocked her vision. It was Drev, grabbing her and pulling her around with him as he turned his back to the creature. Cook heard the Tellarite grunt in surprise and then he released her, pushing her away as he reached up and behind his head at something she could not see.

"Drev!" she shouted as the ensign flailed with both arms, and as he twisted his body she saw that the gray blob had with incredible speed maneuvered itself to the base of his neck. Drev released a roar of obvious pain before dropping to his knees, and Cook watched as four squat tentacles extending from the creature's central mass undulated as they seated themselves along the base of Drev's wide skull. Drev's expression flattened and he fell silent, his arms dropping to hang limply at his sides.

"Lieutenant! Stand clear!" Brax called out, and Cook saw the Edoan stepping closer, both phasers aimed at Drev. His third hand still held his communicator, which he raised. "Brax to *Endeavour*, we have a medical emergency. Ensign Drev has been . . . exposed to one of the parasites."

No sooner did Brax make his initial report than the thing sagged and fell from Drev's neck, tumbling without grace down the Tellarite's back and landing in the dirt next to him. Now separated from the creature, Drev wavered for a moment and held out his arms to steady himself, and Cook stepped forward to help him.

"Watch yourself," Brax warned, moving to Drev's opposite side and aiming his phasers at the unmoving creature.

"Brax, report," said Captain Khatami over the open communicator frequency. *"What's going on?"*

The Edoan frowned, exchanging a confused expression with Cook. "I honestly do not know, Captain. We have retrieved Ensign Zane, and he appears to have played host to one of the life-forms you describe. I was forced to subdue the ensign, and the creature subsequently attempted to . . . subvert Ensign Drev, but something went wrong. The creature is inert, possibly deceased."

"The thing obviously has poor taste in hosts," Drev mumbled, reaching up to rub the back of his neck. When he pulled his fingers away, Cook noted a drop of dark blood.

"Captain," Brax continued. "The situation here on the surface appears contained, at least for the moment. I wish to remain here and continue the search. The other missing crew members are likely still alive."

"I'll trust your judgment on the ground, Lieutenant, but put that thing in a sealed container and send it along with Zane and Drev back to the ship. Maybe they can provide additional information to Doctor Leone. I've instructed Administrator LeMons to secure the colony. No one in or out until we get this situation under control. I'm also starting an evacuation of nonessential personnel, but that's going to take some time. Start gathering our people at the Beta Site base camp. That'll be our rally point for beam-up."

"There's no way we cut off their only way to the surface," Cook said. "If they've been living here for any decent length of time, you have to believe they have tunnels and entrances all over the place."

Brax nodded. "We must proceed under the assumption that whoever attacked us will do so again, but we cannot leave people here unprotected." The Edoan's mouth thinned and his expression turned stern. "Until evacuation is completed, we will have to stand our ground."

20

Christine Rideout was furious.

"You didn't have to do that," she snapped, taking some small satisfaction as she felt Sijaq withdraw a bit from the forefront of her consciousness. For a moment, she was able to walk and think without the Lrondi's constant presence in her mind. She marched through the tunnel several paces behind a Pelopan male whose name she did not know. There were several dozen of them walking in column as they made their way deeper into the underground caverns. Ivelan was walking ahead of her, and somewhere behind her she knew that Ensigns Joseph Berenato and Javokbi also were part of the group, their own Lrondi guiding them just as Sijaq compelled her to keep pace with those around her.

"It was unfortunate," said Ivelan without turning to look at her, "but necessary. Now that they know we are here, we will have to act to protect ourselves."

Rideout had tried to convince the Lrondi collector that such action could be avoided and that an open and honest exchange of dialogue and ideas would prove far more beneficial. Despite her pleas and outright begging, neither Ivelan nor Sijaq had heeded her advice about avoiding confrontation with members of the *Endeavour* search parties or the colonists, and Rideout had borne witness to the skirmish. At least Sijaq had not felt compelled to force her into the fray as Kerry Zane had been compelled by Doliri, the Lrondi who had collected him. Rideout had no idea if the ensign had even survived the brief fight. When she'd last seen him, he was being hoisted onto the shoulder of a burly Tellarite security officer before he and the rest of the search party led by Lieutenant Brax had disappeared into another tunnel.

"Where are my friends?" she asked. "Did you hurt them?"

"No. They escaped to the surface. We are regrouping as we consider how next to proceed."

"Proceed? What does that mean? Are you going to attack them again? I told you they wouldn't hurt you if you just talked to them."

We could not afford the risk, Christine. There is simply too much at stake, particularly now, when we are at the cusp of salvation.

"You mean that ship?" Rideout made no effort to hide her contempt, which was impossible now, anyway, given Sijaq's presence in her mind. Rideout had listened with great interest to Sijaq's descriptions of the ship, based on the messages she and other Lrondi had received from the vessel hovering in orbit high above Cantrel V. She had been only somewhat surprised to learn that the ship was carrying a small contingent of Pelopan, descendants of a community taken from the planet generations ago. There also were thousands of Lrondi aboard the ship, the vast majority of them sustained by systems designed to support their physical forms. What must such an existence be like, Rideout had wondered. How did one not lose one's sanity after uncounted years spent in what amounted to suspended animation while still being aware of the passage of time? How formidable were the Lrondi and their advanced intellect, in order to persevere under such conditions? In some ways, Rideout found herself admiring Sijaq and those like her.

"If what you told me is true," she said, "you're going to need help even getting that far. You still need hosts for most of the Lrondi who are up there, right?"

Ivelan replied, "There are fewer available Pelopan than there are Lrondi. We will need to seek alternative hosts for collection if we are to support all of the Lrondi on the ship."

Rideout almost snorted. "Who are you planning to get? Now that my people have recovered Zane, they're going to know what's going on down here, or at least enough to take proper action to defend themselves if you decide to press things."

That remains to be seen. It is true that we cannot hear Doliri, but that does not mean he has been incapacitated. However, your point about your people possibly taking action against us is valid.

Releasing a sigh of irritation, Rideout replied, "Not *against* you. They'll defend themselves if they feel threatened, but they won't actively seek to hurt you, and you keep telling me you're not out to hurt anyone else. Aren't you all up in my brain right now? Can't you see I'm telling you the truth? I agreed to help you talk to them, didn't I? Wasn't that the point of going up there to meet them in the first place?"

We needed to learn what they know of the ship. Sijaq's voice had taken on something of a lecturing tone, which

Rideout found irritating. *The messages we have received indicate more of your people are aboard the ship. The Lrondi on that vessel represent what could very well be all that remains of our species. Once we are away from this planet, we will seek out other Lrondi, wherever they may be. Your people have the ability to interfere with that, so we must therefore know their intentions.*

"Again, you can ask them." Rideout could feel her temper rising as they emerged from the tunnel onto one of the pathways carved into the rock wall high above the cavern that for centuries had been home to Pelopan and Lrondi. An open area on the outskirts of the subterranean village now was the scene of a gathering. Dozens of Pelopan—male and female—were assembling there in groups of varying size. Many but not all of them carried what Rideout recognized as weapons similar to what she had seen other Pelopan carrying. "Ivelan, what's going on? What are you doing?"

Ivelan, her expression having grown somber, replied, "The only means we have of obtaining access to your vessel is through its people. For that, we must collect at least some of those on the surface."

"It doesn't have to be this way." Rideout tried to think of something else to say, but everything she considered seemed inadequate somehow. The Lrondi, through no real fault of their own, had become victims of destiny, and it could be argued that they had no choice if they were to ensure their continued existence, but why were they so unwilling to listen to reason? "The Lrondi ship shot at us first, remember? They fired on our colony, and then my ship. For someone who talks a lot about not wanting to hurt people, the Lrondi don't seem to mind hurting people."

We must protect ourselves if we are to avoid extinction. We have no other choice.

"Well, neither do my people. They don't want to hurt you, but you have to understand that they're not going to stand by and let you keep doing what you did to me." She looked to Ivelan, making no effort to hide her disbelief. "Was it really that easy to surrender your freedom? After everything I've learned about your people, you just let the Lrondi take you and use you?"

"The Lrondi saved my people," Ivelan replied. "It was the only way."

Rideout shook her head. "Well, not for my people. They won't submit to you, or allow you to collect them. It's simply not going to happen."

Then we will very quickly reach an impasse.

"That has to be one of the damnedest things I've ever seen, and at this point, that's saying a lot."

Standing next to Doctor Leone at the foot of the diagnostic bed in the *Endeavour*'s sickbay, arms crossed as she rubbed her chin, Atish Khatami studied the readouts on the wall-mounted monitor above the bed. The doctor had brought out a second neuroscanner and positioned it next to the bed, providing him—and her—with additional, more comprehensive information than could be gleaned from the bed's general display.

On the bed, contained within a transparent aluminum cylinder, sat a gray, mostly shapeless blob. Aside from the readings offered by the medical monitors, the small movements of its rubbery appendages and an infrequent, irregular pulsing of its central mass were the only outward indications that the thing was indeed a living creature. It had certainly seemed real enough to Ensign Kerry Zane, if the security officer's preliminary report was to be believed.

"If I'm reading your monitors correctly," Khatami said, "its neural activity is off the scale."

Leone nodded. "Its brain is almost as awesome as mine. The readings from this creature are largely in line with the scans we took of the one still attached to Lieutenant Klisiewicz. By every measure I can think to use, these Lrondi are most definitely sentient beings, just as Cole and Zane told us."

Zane, along with Ensign Kelor jilan Drev, had been beamed back to the ship after their encounter with what Khatami now knew to be Pelopan, the species indigenous to Cantrel V. Leone and his medical staff had already been dealing with Lieutenant Klisiewicz and Ensign Cole, both of whom along with Zane now occupied beds in the sickbay's patient ward while Leone tried to understand what had happened to them and what Klisiewicz was still enduring.

"How do they communicate?" Khatami asked.

"Beats me," replied the doctor. "Sign language?" He gestured toward the bed and its unusual occupant. "How many of those things did you say might be over on that ship?"

"Thousands, according to Cole." After the brief tussle

with Klisiewicz in the transporter room, Khatami had ordered the science officer along with Ensign Cole brought here to sickbay for observation, with Klisiewicz placed under restraints and guard. So far, neither he nor the organism attached to his neck had seen fit to make further trouble, but Khatami was taking no chances. Leone had spent the time since the incident hovering over his new patients, both human and alien alike.

Leone blew out his breath. "Still no luck getting hold of Stano or the others?"

Khatami shook her head. "No. Whatever's jamming our communications, it's giving Estrada and his people fits. I don't think I've ever seen him this frustrated." In the time the veteran officer had been with the *Endeavour*, Khatami had never seen him run into an issue or a problem he could not solve. That Hector Estrada had encountered this degree of difficulty said something about the complexity of the disruptive forces at work. "Whatever answers we're going to find, we'll have to find them on our own."

Following Leone back into the patient care ward while leaving Lieutenant Holly Amos to watch over their unusual guest, Khatami moved to stand beside the bed now occupied by Ensign Kerry Zane. The security officer was sitting up and obliterating the meal that had been provided to him. Upon noticing his captain's approach, Zane laid down his eating utensil and wiped his mouth with a napkin before setting that down on the tray attached to his bed.

"Captain," he said by way of greeting.

Khatami smiled. "Doctor Leone tells me you're going to be fine, Ensign, with no apparent ill effects from your experience." She nodded to the bed in the room's far corner, where Lieutenant Klisiewicz lay sedated and under guard, sealed within a transparent, airtight containment enclosure that had been installed on the bed. "We don't know yet about Klisiewicz." The unit, connected to the sickbay's computer interfaces, provided environmental control to its occupant while supplying medical telemetry to the wall monitors. Otherwise, Klisiewicz remained in a state of total isolation from the rest of sickbay and, indeed, the entire ship.

"He'll be okay, Captain," said Ensign Anissa Cole, who like Zane was sitting upright in her bed, though without the carnage of plowing through a recent meal. "Naqa won't hurt him. None of their people want to hurt us. Not really."

Khatami stared at the unconscious Klisiewicz and the organism resting at the base of his skull. "Naqa has an odd way of showing it."

Zane replied, "Cole's right, Captain. At least, for the most part. I can't speak for her or the others, but I feel fine, better than I have in a while, actually." He gestured toward his plate. "I was pretty hungry, though."

"Hungry enough to eat reconstituted meat loaf," said Leone. "Maybe I should keep you here a little longer and check your head again."

"What can either of you tell me about what you went through?" Khatami asked, ignoring the doctor. Despite her eagerness to talk with her people about what they had endured down on the planet and aboard the Lrondi ship, she had waited with strained patience as Leone verified that none of them had suffered lingering issues now that they had been freed of what Cole had called their "Lrondi collectors."

"They didn't hurt us, if that's what you're asking, Captain." He cast his gaze toward the tray before him, as though searching for the right words. "It's hard to describe, but in a lot of ways it was like talking to another voice in your head."

"But they had control over you," Leone replied. "Your actions. They could make you do things you didn't want to do."

His face flushing, Zane offered a small, embarrassed nod. "Yes, Doctor. They could make us do things we didn't want to do. When I attacked Lieutenant Brax, for example, that was all driven by Doliri."

"Doliri?" Khatami asked.

"My collector. Seems nice and harmless, right? There were times when it didn't feel like anything more than talking to myself," Zane said. Then, as though realizing how that might sound, he added, "You know, like when you're thinking about something and trying to work it out yourself—but someone else is controlling the other voice." He frowned. "No, that's not right. I'm sorry, Captain. I don't . . ."

Khatami held up a hand. "It's all right, Ensign. You don't have to apologize. It's not like you have a frame of reference for being possessed."

"That's not what happened, Captain," Cole said. "The Lrondi need us, but they don't want to hurt us in the process."

"They just don't give you a choice about it," replied Leone.

Cole's brow furrowed and she reached up to rub her forehead. "It's not that simple, Doctor. While the Lrondi could survive without hosts, they can't really exist without the help only hosts can provide. It's in their best interests to treat those hosts with care and even respect."

"And again," the doctor replied, "this would sound more exciting if the host had a vote."

Shifting his position on the bed, Zane said, "The Pelopan down on the planet—most of them, anyway—seemed okay with the arrangement. Of course, that could just be the result of them and their ancestors being under Lrondi control for centuries."

Khatami listened as Zane and Cole, often trading off points or bits of information, described the plight of the Lrondi. Their situations and individual experiences sounded similar in many ways, as each struggled to describe the mindset of the beings who had so manipulated them. The story of the Pelopan—a people caught up in the throes or aftermath of war before an advanced civilization saw fit to rescue them or lift them from their otherwise dire fate, was one that had played out on countless worlds across the galaxy. Even Earth had benefited from the timely arrival of visitors from a distant star, though it was fortunate that Earth had been found by the Vulcans, a people who sought cooperation and common pursuits, rather than someone seeking to impose their will.

Could the Lrondi be described this way? Yes, Khatami decided. And, no.

"Different species react to being collected in different

ways," Cole added. "Some are more accepting than others. The Pelopan were very resistant at first, but over time learned to live in harmony with the Lrondi."

Leone asked, "What about humans? How are the Lrondi taking to us?"

"They don't know yet how to deal with us," replied Zane, "or some of the other species represented by our crew. Humans, in general, seem able to resist the effects of collection, at least for a time." He nodded to Cole. "Like she said, the Pelopan were like that too, at first. Then there are other races that seem to give them problems. You saw what happened to Drev."

"Yeah," said Leone. "It's almost like he tasted bad, or something." When Khatami eyed him, the doctor added, "You know what I mean. Maybe Tellarites have something in their blood that the Lrondi don't like, or they're allergic. Drev checked out fine, but I took some samples from him and the Lrondi beamed back from the surface, and I'm running tests to see if anything interesting pops up."

"What about Rideout and the others who've been taken?" asked Khatami. "What's being done with them?"

Zane smiled. "The chief's been giving them hell, Captain. The whole time. I know I said it looked like humans could resist to a point? Well, she's been pushing that right back at them from the beginning." He paused again, once more hunting for the words. "They don't know if we're a threat, or someone who can help them."

"Or someone they can use," Leone said.

"There's that," Zane replied, "but it's not as though they're malevolent. At least, that's not how they see themselves."

Cole added, "For the Lrondi, it's a matter of simple survival, Captain. This is their existence now."

"I can sympathize to a point, Ensign," said Khatami, "and I appreciate that you both are attempting to speak as advocates for them, but I can't stand by while the Lrondi abduct my people." She looked to Cole. "Is that what they're trying to do? Capture my ship and 'collect' my crew?"

Her head drooping as her expression turned to one of embarrassment, Cole nodded. "Yes. They've seen that we represent many different species. With the Pelopan's numbers on the decline, they feel that we represent an unparalleled opportunity to find other races with whom they can coexist."

"And you see why I can't let that happen." Khatami sighed as she rubbed the bridge of her nose. "Ensign, it's obvious this isn't easy for you, but the simple fact is that no matter how pleasant the Lrondi make it for their victims, it's still slavery. The Pelopan on that planet and even on that ship might appear as willing participants, but bear in mind that they're descendants of those who were first taken involuntarily. This is the only life they've ever known."

Zane said, "That's exactly the feeling I got, Captain. It just seemed a foregone conclusion that the Pelopan and Lrondi lived together that way, for better or worse."

"Uh-oh," Leone said, grimacing. "Please don't tell me one of you is about to quote the Prime Directive."

"I don't know how or if the Prime Directive even applies here," Khatami snapped. Hearing how her words sounded, she placed a hand on the doctor's arm. "I'm sorry, Tony. The Prime Directive is a decent guideline with honorable intentions that keeps us from being the advanced race that takes advantage of other, lesser-developed civilizations, but it's also damned annoying at times. What am I supposed to do here? Let the Lrondi continue to use the Pelopan because that's the way we found them? Maybe the language says yes, but I'm not letting them take my people even if it means upsetting whatever society they've established here. That's not what the Prime Directive intended."

Cole said, "There are those who would disagree with you on that point, Captain."

"Well, they're not here. I am, and it's my call." She glared at Cole. "How do we free our people from Lrondi influence?"

"I'm not sure. Forcibly removing them could be harmful to the collected person."

Khatami gestured to Klisiewicz. "The Lrondi who controlled you, Naqa, transferred from you to him. She did that voluntarily, which means they can be removed without injuring the host. If they won't break the bond on their own, then we have to find a way to do it ourselves."

"What will that accomplish, Captain?"

"Once my people are free and safe, then we can discuss how to help the Lrondi, but it won't be something imposed upon us before any discussions or negotiations or requests for help are made. Whatever assistance we end up providing has to be consensual. The Prime Directive might give me fits over the Pelopan, but I'll be damned if my crew gets pulled into this against their will."

Nodding, Cole wiped a single tear from one corner

of her eye. "I understand, Captain. Just please don't hurt them."

"That's the last thing I want to do, Ensign, but the safety of my people has to come first." Before she could say anything else, the red alert klaxon began wailing, which was followed an instant later by the ship's intercom system flaring to life and the anxious voice of Lieutenant Marielise McCormack.

"Red alert! All hands to battle stations! Captain Khatami to the bridge!"

Khatami crossed the patient ward to the intercom panel mounted on the bulkhead next to the room's entrance and activated it. "Khatami here. Report."

"It's the alien ship, Captain! It's separating into sections and moving to intercept us!"

21

"You'd think he'd at least have left something for us to read."

Lost in her thoughts as she imagined and discarded various means of escaping their current predicament, Katherine Stano looked up from where she lay on one of the berthing compartment's two double-tier metal bunks, and allowed herself a small chuckle as she considered Lieutenant Ivan Tomkins's remark. "Or something to eat."

"Right?" Lying on the bunk along the cramped room's opposite wall with his hands clasped behind his head, Tomkins stared up at the underside of the bunk above him. "Of course, there's always the possibility that they figured out Tropp was faking. Or he found a way to blow his cover."

"Positive thoughts, Lieutenant," said Stano. While it was true that they had not seen Ensign Tropp since the Denobulan's startling revelation and after he brought them to this room to hide, it also was true that no one else had tried to break down the door. "He's probably biding his time, being patient, and waiting for an opportunity." After getting them to this compartment, Tropp had promised he would return with the means for Stano and Tomkins to bluff their way back into the command center in the hopes of seizing control of the facility. It was a long shot, Stano knew, but it was all they had.

Tomkins pushed himself to a sitting position. "I'm just saying that we should be ready for bad news, Commander. If they find us, they're going to want to put one of those Lrondi on us. I really don't want to do that. For one thing, I already have enough friends. Besides, that thing will just mess up the back of my hair. I like the back of my hair."

"Forgive me, Lieutenant," Stano said, stifling the urge to laugh again, "but I've never even noticed the back of your hair."

Any response the engineer might have offered was cut off by the sound of some kind of mechanism coming to life from somewhere in the depths of the ship. Everything in the room began to reverberate with a slight yet still noticeable tremble.

"What the hell is that?" Stano asked, not expecting any real response. Whatever was causing the tremors, it was unlike anything they had heard since coming aboard the Lrondi ship.

Tomkins was looking around the room. "I don't have the first damned idea, Commander. I can't tell if it's an engine, or what."

Further speculation was interrupted by the room's door cycling open. Stano drew the phaser Tropp had given her and aimed it at the entrance, only to lower it when the Denobulan was revealed. She saw his quick warning shake and hid the phaser behind her back as Tropp and another member of their boarding party, Ensign Trinh Van Son, entered the room. Each was carrying a black metallic cylinder that Stano recognized as the containers that had held Lrondi in their vats of nutrient fluid. One at a time, they placed their cylinders on the deck near the door.

"Commander," Tropp said, offering Stano a formal nod before looking to Tomkins. "Lieutenant. I trust you are well."

Wary of Trinh, who also had been collected and now carried a Lrondi on his neck, Stano replied, "As well as you might expect from a prisoner." To Trinh, she said, "Ensign? Are you all right?"

Trinh replied, "I feel fine, Commander, and perfectly fit for duty." He started to reach for the back of his neck, but stopped. "It's definitely an odd experience, but not unpleasant."

"I keep hearing that," said Tomkins.

Stano waved her hand to indicate the room and—by extension—the ship around them. "What's the racket about?"

Tropp smiled. "The ship's spherical sections are separating from the main spaceframe. I am told it is not a common maneuver, but it is performed under special circumstances."

"And those would be . . . what, exactly?" asked Tomkins.

"Four of the individual sections are being sent to subdue the *Endeavour* and the *Aephas*, while the fifth commences a landing on Cantrel V."

Stano's eyes widened. "It's starting. They're going to collect the people on the surface. Does that include the Tài Shan colony?"

"I would imagine so," replied Tropp. "However, that need not concern you now. First, we have other matters requiring attention. It is our hope that you find your collection as pleasing as the rest of our team. The effect is quite harmless."

Stano shook her head. "Pass." Was Tropp merely acting for Trinh's benefit, or was Tomkins right and the Denobulan was now really under Lrondi control?

"It will help to have an open mind, Commander," offered Trinh.

"Sorry, I'm not feeling particularly open-minded just now."

Releasing a sigh of apparent resignation, Tropp said, "That is unfortunate. We were so hoping you would be reasonable about this. I am afraid you leave me with no alternative." With one graceful, rapid movement, the medic drew his phaser and fired at Trinh. The ensign uttered a surprised gasp and fell forward, and Tomkins was quick enough to keep him from falling to the floor.

"Oh, wow, did you have me worried there for a minute," said the engineer as he maneuvered the unconscious ensign to one of the bunks before relieving the man of his phaser.

"I apologize for the subterfuge, Lieutenant," replied the medic as he moved to kneel beside Trinh. "It was necessary to keep up appearances."

"Speaking of that," Stano said, "do you want to tell me just how the hell you've managed to pull off all of this?"

Tropp shrugged. "Luck, fate, whatever you wish to call it, Commander. Apparently, my Lrondi handler, Cejal here, is relatively young and inexperienced. Unfortunately, he was paired with a mature and neurologically adept Denobulan, that being myself. I do not know if my cartilaginous spinal ridges prevented an adequate connection point, or if my brain works differently than any other species they have previously encountered. All I know is that I am simply not as affected by his suggestions."

"So, he doesn't have a grip on you?" asked Tomkins. "At all?"

"Oh, do not misunderstand me. I think he is somewhat charming. In fact, when the connection was unsuccessful and he wanted to give up, I convinced him to stay."

Stano felt her mouth fall open. "You what?"

"Denobulans initiate hallucinogenic experiences for fun and for mental exercise, Captain. 'Calisthenics for the mind,' if you will allow. I find it enhances mental relaxation and meditation." Again, Tropp offered a broad smile. "Cejal has been very entertaining."

"I don't even know how to respond to that," said Tomkins.

"The exercise has provided me with the perfect cover to move about the ship and interact with both the Lrondi and Pelopan. Maloram is very interested in you, Commander. Consequently, I was able to convince him and Ensign Grammell that I was the one best suited to oversee your collection."

Stano placed a hand on his shoulder. "Well played, Ensign." She gestured to where Trinh still lay unconscious on the bunk. "What about him?"

Instead of replying, Tropp opened the medical satchel he had been allowed to keep, and removed a dermal regenerator.

"Nobody's cut, Doc," said Tomkins.

"Indeed. However, I have discovered another use for it." Rolling Trinh onto his back, Tropp aimed the regenerator at the Lrondi still affixed to his neck and activated it. Though there was no visible beam, the effects were immediate as the gray mass began twitching and jerking.

"I'll be damned," said Stano.

"I am not causing any harm," Tropp replied as he continued to work. "I am merely agitating the creature so that it will see fit to withdraw from the ensign's neck."

The process took nearly a full minute, after which the Lrondi sagged and rolled away, falling from Trinh's neck and onto the metal bunk.

Tomkins nodded in approval. "Nice going, Doc."

"Due to the time required, this is not a practical means of treating someone unless we are not interrupted. If we can get to our people one at a time, we may be able to free them."

Stano shook her head. "We may not have time for that. Like you said, this ship is already moving to attack the *Endeavour* and the *Aephas*. We need to stop that."

"I do not believe the ships are in real danger," Tropp replied. "The Lrondi want them both intact, along with their crews."

"Yeah, but Captain Khatami isn't going to let that happen. She'll fight, and she'll go down fighting. We have to stop this before anybody gets hurt or worse."

Tomkins said, "We need to find a way to punch through the communications jam and get out a signal. The command center's our best option for taking control and keeping it."

"But what about the spheres?" Stano asked. "Tropp, you said they're separating."

The medic replied, "They are still overseen from the

command center. You may recall the Lrondi sitting atop consoles in the central control area? There is one Lrondi controlling the movements of each sphere. They are able to interface directly with each sphere's independent computer network."

"Disable those stations, and the spheres are out of action," said Tomkins.

Tropp nodded. "A reasonable assumption, Lieutenant." Picking up the apparently insensate Lrondi he had removed from Trinh, Tropp moved to one of the cylinders they had brought with them and opened its lid before depositing the limp gray mass inside it. From the other container, he extracted a pair of communicators and two additional phasers. "You may need these."

Satisfied with a phaser for each hand, Stano nodded. "Can you wake up Trinh? We'll need him too." As Tropp prepared a stimulant for the stunned security officer, she asked, "And can you get us back to the command center without being seen or stopped?"

"Most of the revived Pelopan are occupied with the current attacks and the landing. If we move quickly, we should be able to avoid encountering anyone."

In her mind, Stano envisioned the scene outside, with the Lrondi ship separating into its five spherical components, each one possessing enough weaponry to give the *Endeavour* and the *Aephas* a run for their money. Then there was the planet, with the Tài Shan colony as well as Starfleet personnel from both ships down there waiting for help. And what of the Pelopan and Lrondi who had called Cantrel V home for uncounted generations? What was to become of them, should Maloram and his people up here succeed? Would the Pelopan be taken from this world, consigned along with their descendants to exist merely in service to the Lrondi?

Not if we can help it.

"All right, let's get moving," said Stano. "We've got work to do."

The first shots came just as Colleen Cook was moving to board the shuttle transport.

Flinching at the sound of weapons fire, Cook looked beyond the perimeter of the Beta Site base camp to see figures running across the floor of the excavated area that was the center of the ongoing dig effort. The sun had set and darkness was looming, with shadows stretching across the ground and making it harder to see the far side of the crater. Piles of dirt and rock as well as temporary shelters, cargo containers, and other equipment scattered across the area now were obstacles impeding her vision, and offered cover or concealment for anyone attempting to advance toward the camp. Starfleet officers, nearly a dozen that she could see, had taken up defensive positions in front of the camp and near the crater's edge, and they had begun returning fire.

"Lieutenant Cook!"

She heard the call an instant before a hand patted her on the shoulder. It was Lieutenant Brax, armed once more with a phaser in two of his three hands. The Edoan was dividing his attention between her and the scene outside the camp, and she could see he was doing his best to maintain control of a situation that now was beginning to unravel.

"It appears we are out of time," he said. "Get aboard the shuttle. We are leaving as soon as I can recall the rest of our people."

Cook held up the phaser she carried in her right hand. "Let me help. Another pair of eyes might come in handy."

"I need someone to take charge of the shuttles in the event we are overrun," Brax replied, gesturing to where the second Tài Shan colony personnel transport sat, with members of the archaeology team scrambling to get aboard. "There are four people still in the camp's command post, along with one of my security people. Once they're here, it will only be me and my people on the perimeter. We will then make our final withdrawal."

The situation had been tense for more than an hour, since the skirmish in the underground caverns. Despite sealing each of the entrances from the dig site into the subterranean passages, Brax and Commander Yataro had concluded that the danger was far from contained. With the screening technology employed by the Lrondi and their Pelopan hosts—as they now had been identified thanks to information provided by Ensign Kerry Zane—it was possible and likely that there were other, concealed points of access that could be used in an attempt to attack the base camp. With fewer than two dozen people at his disposal, Brax had arranged them in a haphazard circle around the camp's perimeter, but that still left considerable holes in the hastily deployed defensive line.

Movement from one of the base camp's temporary shelters caught Cook's attention. Five figures, each of them carrying satchels and other bags, were running toward the shuttles. Four were dressed in civilian work clothes and overalls, with the fifth person wearing a Starfleet uniform bringing up the rear. He was gesturing and shouting directions for the group to head for the other shuttle.

"That is the last of them," Brax said, nodding in approval. "Lieutenant, make sure they all get aboard, then tell the pilot to lift off and head for the colony."

Cook nodded. "Aye, sir." The decision had been made not to attempt rendezvousing with the *Endeavour* or the *Aephas*, given the still unsafe situation in orbit with the Lrondi vessel. Transport under such conditions would be hazardous for the orbiting starships and perhaps even to people on the ground. The main colony, hundreds of kilometers away, would at least provide a temporary yet more secure shelter until such time as an evacuation could be completed, if the situation made such action necessary.

She started to jog across the open ground toward the transport when a salvo of energy bolts tore into the soil ahead of her. Stopping herself from running into the line of fire, Cook ducked and ran back for the other shuttle. She threw herself against the side of the vessel's hull, taking cover next to Brax, who was trying to peek around the aft edge of the transport in order to survey the area.

"Whoever took those shots was awfully close," she said. "Closer than I would've thought they'd make it this fast."

Beyond the shuttles and the camp's forward edge, the sounds of weapons fire stopped, and a moment later, Brax's communicator beeped. Removing the unit from his waist, he flipped open its cover. "Brax here."

"This is Ensign ch'Dran, sir," replied Zeturildtra ch'Dran, a member of the Starfleet field archaeology con-

tingent assigned to the Cantrel V expedition. *"Something odd is happening out here. We've just repelled two attempts to advance on our positions at the crater's edge, but now it seems as though the Pelopan have broken off their attacks."*

"Everyone is to hold their positions," Brax said. "I am on my way." After informing the pilots of both shuttles to have their crew and any security personnel to maintain their alert levels, the Edoan began running toward the perimeter. Without thinking about it, Cook set off after him, holding her tricorder against her hip and running almost at a sprint to keep up with him as he used his three legs to traverse the uneven terrain. It was not until he had reached the first of his security officers that Brax realized she had not remained at the shuttle. Instead of remarking on it, he turned his attention to Ensign ch'Dran.

"Where are they?" Brax asked, his attention focused on the crater. Looking past him, Cook saw the bodies of more than a dozen Pelopan lying on the ground. A lone figure was visible in the distance, running away from the fight and the lights cast off from the base camp, disappearing into the darkness.

Ch'dran replied, *"This was all they sent, sir. Given their tactics and numbers, I believe this was a probing action, designed to gauge our positions and search for weaknesses."*

"Or it's a distraction," Cook said, grabbing her tricorder and flipping open its cover. The unit flared to life, emitting its characteristic high-pitched whistle as she aimed it toward the crater. "I'm picking up twenty-eight life readings from the crater—fourteen Pelopan and fourteen Lrondi.

They're all unconscious." She began sweeping the tricorder in an arc, one hundred eighty degrees from left to right. "Nothing else." Adjusting the tricorder's scanning field, she continued her sweep, extending it past the edge of the crater and along the ridgeline leading toward the shuttles and the base camp. She looked past the handful of Starfleet security personnel manning defensive positions along that part of the perimeter, seeing nothing but open ground and the slope of a distant hill.

The scan readings flickered.

"Son of a bitch," she said. "Why didn't we think of this before?"

"What?" Brax asked, looking around the area.

Watching the indicators spike on her tricorder, Cook pointed with the hand still holding her phaser. "There!" Without waiting for Brax to say anything else, she fired, feeling the weapon's subtle vibrations as it released its energy. The blue-white beam lanced across the open space, seemingly aimed at nothing, but then she saw it flatten and expand as it washed over the body of a humanoid figure, who staggered and fell unconscious to the ground.

"The anomalous energy readings we detected earlier," Brax said. "They can use them to mask their movements."

22

Despite fighting with every iota of strength she could muster, Christine Rideout marched ever forward.

"We don't have to *do* this, Ivelan! They'll listen if you just talk to them. Let *me* talk to them. I can get my captain to listen."

Walking next to her on the advancing line, Ivelan shook her head. "Now is not the time for such dialogue, Christine."

Once the situation is under control, Sijaq added, her voice only serving to further anger Rideout, *we can consider such options.*

The line of three dozen Pelopan—there might have been more, but Rideout could not be certain—moved as one unit across the open terrain. Some of the Pelopan carried on their backs portable versions of the camouflage field generators they had used to conceal their presence underground. Others were hauling different containers, which Rideout knew held Lrondi waiting for hosts. The idea that she along with Ensigns Berenato and Javokbi were assisting in this assault, no matter how benign it might end up being, repulsed her. She strained against each step, willed her body to stop, but it ignored her demands.

Less than fifty meters ahead of them, she saw the Beta Site base camp with its collection of temporary shelters and other equipment as well as the pair of transport shuttles. Between the camp and the line of advancing Pelopan were a handful of people positioned behind or near some of the structures and stacked cargo containers. Judging by their behavior, the security guards saw or suspected nothing, telling Rideout that the camoflauge screens were working even against tricorder scans. She had not had an opportunity to examine the technology for herself, but there could be no denying its effectiveness.

"I won't hurt my friends," she said. "I won't. I've seen one crew die all around me, and I won't let you do it to another. I'll put my phaser to my own head and kill us both before I let you make me do that." Even as she spoke the words, she looked to her hand, seeing the phaser it held and feeling the weight of the weapon in her grip. It was set to stun, but could she adjust its power setting? That seemed a manageable feat. All it would take . . .

"I have no doubts that you would do that, Christine," replied Ivelan. "We do not wish to harm your friends, but we cannot allow them to interfere."

Our very existence is at stake.

Rideout had been arguing and pleading with Ivelan and Sijaq since returning to the surface, though her Lrondi collector had seen fit to ignore her for most of that time, making the entire exchange feel like nothing more than talking to herself. At another time and under other circumstances, she might have found this entire situation amusing. Now she was consumed by helpless rage as she felt her body obeying commands that were not her own. It was a grievous debasement of her very being she could never forgive.

It is saddening that you harbor these thoughts. We understand that you feel violated, but we have done our best to make the transition as comfortable as possible. It is always our hope that our collected will come to appreciate and even embrace our bonding.

"You still don't get it," Rideout replied. "It doesn't matter how nice you make it. You're still using me against my will. How can you not understand that?"

As we have told you, Christine, we understand it all too well. We simply have no choice if we are to survive.

The camp was closer now, close enough that she could make out the faces of a few of the Starfleet personnel taking up defensive positions. Even from this short distance, the Pelopan's advance was masked by the camouflage screens. Were they going to just walk over the camp and start collecting people? That was seeming more and more like how the scenario would play out. At the very least, by the time her colleagues from the *Endeavour* or the colony realized what was happening, it would be too late.

She heard the whine of a phaser and saw its harsh blue beam slicing through the increasing darkness. It struck a Pelopan several meters to her right, illuminating his body in a sheen of energy. Rideout watched him stumble and pitch forward, falling to the ground.

"They can see us!" shouted someone to her left.

From somewhere in front of her, another voice shouted, "Intruder alert, north side! All personnel engage!"

A latticework of phaser energy erupted from the camp, lancing across the open ground and seeking targets. Pelopan dodged and ducked, seeking protection that was woefully lacking. The Lrondi had placed too much

trust in their technology to conceal their movements, and
that now appeared to have been defeated, at least to some
degree. Phaser fire continued streaking across the field
bordering the camp, but Rideout sensed that the people
doing the shooting could still not see their targets. Behind the defensive line, she saw the shuttles closing their
hatches, and the whine of their propulsion systems was
growing louder. Standing amid the group of Starfleet officers scrambling to respond to this new threat, she saw the
familiar silhouette of Lieutenant Brax, gesturing toward
the shuttles and waving one of his three arms in the air
above his head.

"The transport vessels," Ivelan said, pointing to the
pair of ships. "They must not be allowed to leave."

Before Rideout understood what was happening, she
felt herself propelled forward, sprinting across the broken
ground past the first of the defensive positions and into the
camp itself.

"Chief!" a voice shouted, and she saw an *Endeavour*
security guard waving at her. He was an ensign, running
from one of the temporary shelters, and for the first time
Rideout realized she was visible to others. She had outrun
the Pelopan who had been flanking her and operating the
camouflage field generators.

"We've been looking all over for you!" the man
shouted, closing the distance.

Possessed like the rest of her body, the hand carrying
her phaser rose and aimed at the security officer, firing
before Rideout could comprehend the action. The beam
struck the man in the chest, and he tumbled backward,
falling to the ground.

"No!"

He is merely stunned, Christine.

Her eyes riveted to the fallen ensign, Rideout realized her other hand was moving to the phaser's power setting, and she could only watch as the level was increased from stun to lethal force. "You said you wouldn't hurt them. Damn you, Sijaq!"

Trust us.

The phaser rose and took aim again, this time on the rear of the nearest of the shuttle transports. Christine fought the motion, willed her arm to remain at her side, but it was no use. She watched the weapon focus on the shuttle's rear hull, near the vessel's propulsion unit, and she could only scream as the phaser fired. Striking the unprotected transport, the beam cut into the hull plating and produced an eruption of fire and sparks. There was a noticeable change in the pitch of the vessel's engine, and Rideout heard it starting to power down. A similar strike impacted the other shuttle as it was in the midst of taking off. It had risen several meters when the beam hit, tearing through its hull plating. The belch of fire and energy from inside the vessel was more powerful and the transport shuddered before its nose drooped and the craft fell to the ground. Rideout heard the rending of metal as the transport plowed into the soil, its frame crumpling but not collapsing. Though the drop had been of modest height, Rideout feared the craft's weight and the number of people likely crammed aboard would lead to numerous injuries, or worse.

"Damn it!" she shouted, aware that even this act of defiance was being resisted by Sijaq's thoughts rushing about in her head.

Her own actions had not gone unnoticed, and in short order Rideout found herself the focus of attention from multiple directions. Security officers and other personnel were moving in her direction, weapons aimed at her even as their wielders recognized her. Shock and confusion was evident in their faces, and Rideout thought she even saw one or two expressions of betrayal.

Without her conscious control, she felt her arm lifting again, the phaser rising to take aim.

"No, Sijaq! No! It's set to kill!" Seeing Ivelan standing nearby, she cast a desperate look in the Pelopan's direction. "Ivelan! Help me!"

Her arm stopped its motion, arrested with the phaser aimed at the ground. Was it her doing or her Lrondi controller? She could not move it any farther, but she did not care, so long as it was not pointed at a shipmate. Glaring at her hand, she willed it to drop the phaser, but the command went unheeded.

"Chief!" a voice shouted across the open field. One of the security officers, uncertain about what to do, was pointing his phaser at her as he stepped closer, and Rideout felt her own hand twitch. Behind her, she saw Brax and another Starfleet lieutenant—a woman she recognized as Colleen Cook, a member of the science team assigned to the Cantrel V mission—walking in her direction. Cook was holding a tricorder and sweeping the area ahead of her and Brax.

"This way!" Cook shouted. "They're coming from this direction!"

They can detect our protective veils. We must press forward, while we still ha—

Sijaq's words were lost in a flash of pain that shot from Rideout's neck and up into her skull. She released an involuntary scream, feeling Sijaq shifting on her back, and there was an odd rush of clarity in her mind, as though the Lrondi's hold on her was wavering. The pain rolled over her like the waves of an inbound tide, and she staggered as it hammered at her consciousness. What was happening?

Once more, she felt her hand and the phaser it wielded beginning to move.

"Sijaq, no!" Rideout heard her voice cracking. "Please don't make me hurt them." As Cook and the others drew closer, the intensity of her pain increased, and she realized in one brief, desperate moment that the sensation gripping her was in tandem with the warbling of Cook's tricorder. There was something about a tricorder. What was it?

A phaser blast struck nearby, and Rideout saw Ivelan fall. Her own hand twitched again, the muzzle of the phaser rising.

"No!" Seeing Brax and the others moving closer, she gritted her teeth, fighting the resistance that wanted to keep her from speaking to them. "Tricorder. Scans. Affects them!" Anything else was cut off by another rush of agony piercing her skull. "Sijaq!"

When the Lrondi said nothing, Rideout released a scream of frustration just before she began to feel the muscles in her hand relax. The phaser fell from her fingers, dropping to the dirt at her feet.

"Stun me!" she shouted, much to the surprise of Brax and the others closing on her. "Stun me now!" He had to know what she had endured, yes? Surely, Kerry Zane had warned their shipmates of the danger she and Berenato and Javokbi represented? "Stun all of us!"

Brax stepped into view, his weapon raised, and Rideout's skin warmed as she felt the tingle of energy of the phaser beam spreading over her before everything turned black.

Every muscle in Atish Khatami's neck, back, and shoulders was screaming at her, cursing her, and without doubt plotting some form of revenge.

She ignored it all, leaning forward in her captain's chair, gripping its armrests with such force that she was certain she could feel them giving way beneath her fingers. Listening to reports from members of her bridge crew as well as their short, clipped conversations with personnel in other areas of the ship was enough to keep her apprised of all the information flowing to and from the heart of the *Endeavour* as the starship readied itself for yet another confrontation with the Lrondi vessel.

Vessels, she reminded herself.

"Give me a tactical plot," she ordered. "Let me see everything."

Lieutenant Marielise McCormack, back at her navigator's station following Khatami's return to the bridge, entered the commands necessary to shift the image on the main viewscreen. It now displayed a computer-generated representation of the activity taking place above Cantrel V, which was depicted as a large green circle at the center of the schematic. Two blue dots, one each to represent the *Endeavour* and the *Aephas*, were moving apart from each other while still maintaining orbital distance from the planet, while somewhat larger red circles illustrated the positions of the five spheres that had separated from the framework of the Lrondi ship. Two spheres, designated "Alpha" and "Bravo" on the schematic, were giving chase to the *Aephas* as the science vessel headed toward the far side of the planet, while two more, "Charlie" and "Delta," were closing on the *Endeavour*'s position, but it was the fifth sphere, "Echo," which now held Khatami's attention.

"Helm, where's that one going off by itself?" she asked.

Consulting his instruments, Lieutenant Neelakanta replied, "It appears to be entering a trajectory that will allow it to make planetfall, Captain. Based on its course and speed, it may be getting into position to descend on the Tài Shan colony."

"Iacovino, can you confirm that?"

The junior science officer, who had been all but riveted to her sensor hood since Khatami had emerged from the turbolift, did not look up as she replied, "The sphere is decelerating, Captain. Mister Neelakanta is correct. It's preparing for atmospheric entry, and I don't see how it can be heading anywhere else but the colony."

"They're obviously not going to destroy it," said Khatami. "They could do that from up here. That can only mean one thing. The Lrondi and their Pelopan helpers are looking for more warm bodies." Now that she had been helped by Anissa Cole and Kerry Zane to understand the plight of the Lrondi and the dwindling number of this planet's indigenous population, there was no way she could not feel sympathy for the race of amorphous beings who were so dependent on other life-forms for their very existence. Still, that would not excuse what amounted to slavery for anyone the Lrondi decided were viable hosts.

"Separating the spheres has to be a ploy to keep us busy," said McCormack. "It's one thing to fight a single ship where we have greater maneuverability, but this is something else."

Eyeing the tactical schematic, Khatami shook her head. "We still have the speed and maneuverability advantage, but if the Lrondi on that ship have our people, then they know we won't leave anybody behind and unprotected down on the planet. They'll try to use that against us, so we need to get this situation under control as quickly as possible."

There was more to it, of course. As Anissa Cole had intimated, the Tài Shan colony and its diverse population of settlers offered the Lrondi an introduction to numerous new species, many of which likely would be compatible with the process that bonded a Lrondi collector to its host choice. The crews of the *Endeavour* and the *Aephas* provided an even greater sampling.

"Spheres Charlie and Delta are splitting off," reported McCormack. "They're trying to hem us in."

Khatami had already surmised this from studying both the viewscreen schematic as well as the astrogator positioned between the navigator and Neelakanta. "Bring us about, heading two eight one mark seven. Accelerate to half impulse."

In response to the order, Neelakanta looked over his shoulder at her. "Captain?"

"You heard me. Put us on a course right at them. I want

them to have to think about shooting if they're in each other's line of fire. Do it."

The Arcturian helm officer nodded. "Aye, Captain. Adjusting course . . . now."

"I don't think they like that," said Iacovino, glancing up from her console and toward the viewscreen. "They're adjusting course and speed, trying to compensate."

"Good," Khatami replied. "While they're thinking about that, target their weapons ports and fire at will."

Before the first barrage of phasers could be unleashed, Khatami felt the entire ship tremble around her. There was a distinct shift in the pitch of the *Endeavour*'s impulse drive, and every light, screen, and indicator on the bridge flickered or blinked. Even the main viewscreen's image distorted and dissolved, static beginning to eat away at the display's edges.

"Uh-oh," said McCormack.

"Sensors are picking up that dampening field," Iacovino reported. "Wait, this is different. The frequencies and signal strength aren't the same as before."

Keeping her gaze fixed on the viewscreen, Khatami waited for the science officer to elaborate, and when that did not happen after several seconds, she prompted, "Ensign?"

"They've reconfigured the emitters that were channeling the field, Captain." Iacovino turned from her console. "They've been modified to function as simple yet effective tractor beams."

"Helm, evasive!" Khatami all but shouted the order even as Neelakanta was reacting to the new information. With his hands moving as though possessed of their own

will, the helm officer guided the *Endeavour* out of its previous course and toward relative safety.

McCormack called out, "They're coming about and
accelerating."

Behind Khatami, Lieutenant Hector Estrada said,
"Captain, we're receiving an emergency call from Lieutenant Brax."

"On speakers," Khatami ordered, and a moment later
the bridge's communications system crackled to life, followed by the voice of her security chief.

*"Captain, we are in need of assistance. Both trans-
ports at the Beta Site have been disabled. I have sixty
people down here in need of evacuation. We are being
attacked and in danger of being overrun."*

Khatami gritted her teeth, hating what she was forced
to say. "We're a little busy up here, Lieutenant. You'll have
to hold your ground for a bit longer."

"Captain!" shouted another voice. *"This is Lieutenant
Cook. I think we've got a way to deal with the Lrondi. It
looks like certain tricorder scan frequencies are disruptive to them. It causes them pain or produces some kind
of neurochemical imbalance that affects their bond with
their hosts."*

Her focus divided between the evolving tactical situation between the *Endeavour* and the Lrondi spheres and
this new revelation, Khatami scowled. "Are you sure?"

*"It seems to be having an effect, but only at close
range. We're not even sure—"* The rest of her report was
cut off by the sounds of weapons fire blasting through the
open channel before Brax's voice returned.

"We are taking renewed enemy fire, Captain. Please send assistance as soon as possible."

"Working on it, Mister Brax."

The bridge lighting sputtered yet again, and Khatami felt her stomach lurch as even the ship's inertial damping and artificial gravity systems seemed affected by the proximity of the Lrondi spheres. Then the deck heaved and pitched to starboard as something slammed into the *Endeavour*'s deflector shields, prompting a new onslaught of alert warnings.

"Captain," McCormack said, "they're attempting another bracketing maneuver."

"Increase to full impulse and continue evasive. Helm, the instant you get a clean shot, you take it." Casting a look over her shoulder to Estrada, Khatami asked, "What about the *Aephas*?"

23

The first salvo was enough to push Mahmud al-Khaled out of his chair.

Throwing his hands out in front of him was enough to arrest his fall, as he caught hold of Lieutenant Sasha Rodriguez's chair. Still off-balance, he dropped and slammed his knee against the raised deck plating beneath the helm officer's seat. Rodriguez, still reeling from the impact against the *Aephas*'s shields, was almost toppled from her seat as al-Khaled fought to keep from being tossed to the floor.

"Direct impact to our rear shields," reported Lieutenant Xav. "Shield strength down to eighty-six percent."

"What about main power?" asked al-Khaled, grimacing at the pain in his knee as he regained his footing.

The Tellarite boomed, "Ninety-three percent and falling. Whatever they did over there, it was rather ingenious."

"Yeah, that's one way to put it." Al-Khaled was still working to absorb the information supplied by Captain Khatami regarding the Lrondi ship, the mysterious cnidaria-like species that were its masters, and the race of beings controlled by the Lrondi. Then had come the newest revelation that someone aboard the alien vessel had figured out a way to generate tractor beams. Had a member of the *Endeavour* crew been forced to act against his or her shipmates by rendering such aid? Trying to imagine being placed in such a position, with one's body or mind compelled to act without regard for its owner's will, was almost sickening to contemplate.

"They're coming around again," said Rodriguez, her attention fixed on her console. "Trying to hem us in."

Al-Khaled ordered, "Route emergency power to rear deflectors." Glancing at the astrogator on the helm officer's console, he asked, "Xav, what about that fifth sphere? Still heading for the planet?"

"Affirmative." The burly science officer nodded toward the viewscreen, where a tactical plot showed the *Aephas*'s position relative to the *Endeavour* and the five spheres that until ten minutes ago comprised the Lrondi ship. "Each sphere is acting independently. If a computer program is guiding them, then even with oversight it is still a remarkable piece of software."

Al-Khaled frowned. "You can admire it later, assuming we live long enough to send you over there. I'm betting the answer's simpler than that, and that the Lrondi revived more Pelopan to control each sphere independently." Now the question was whether he should risk the *Aephas*—repaired, though still sub par so far as its operational status—against the sphere moving to enter Cantrel V's atmosphere. According to the brief, terse update he had received from Khatami just as the alien vessel was making its move, the Lrondi did not just want the Tài Shan colonists, but the *Endeavour* and *Aephas* crews, as well.

Not if I have anything to say about it.

As though taunting him and his unspoken bravado, the *Aephas* shuddered around him for a second time, though the intensity of the impact of weapons fire against the ship's shields was lesser this time.

"That could've been a lot worse," he said, still gripping the back of Rodriguez's chair. "Nice work, Lieutenant."

The helm officer did not acknowledge the compliment, but instead pushed the *Aephas* into a series of evasive maneuvers that caused the view of Cantrel V to tumble up and around the edge of the main viewscreen. Despite artificial gravity and inertial suppression systems, al-Khaled felt dizziness threatening to snare him in its grip.

"Where *did* you learn to fly, anyway?"

"You mean they have courses for this?"

Xav, his face once more buried in his sensor hood, said, "Shields holding at ninety percent after routing emergency power." The Tellarite snorted. "I suppose now would not be the best time to inform you that Commander Grace is expressing concern about the renewed strain to the shield generators."

"No, it wouldn't." Returning to his command chair, al-Khaled said, "Helm, continue evasive. Keep us away from those tractor beams." He already had reasoned that in its compromised condition, the *Aephas* likely would not be able to fend off any concentrated attack on its power systems were it to become snared and made vulnerable to the Lrondi ship's dampening field. He cast a glance over his shoulder. "Ensign Pzial, open an audio channel to the *Endeavour*."

A moment later, the Rigelian communications officer turned in her seat. "I have Captain Khatami on audio, sir."

"Captain," al-Khaled said in greeting, raising his voice, "I'm sure you've seen what the Lrondi are up to."

The *Endeavour*'s commander replied, *"Yes. Any ideas?"*

"If we stay up here, we're not going to be much good for much longer, but we might be able to do something about that fifth sphere. Maybe get in front of it or find some other way to force it to alter course."

"You want to play chicken with that thing?"

Al-Khaled shrugged, though Khatami of course could not see that response. "We have to try something. Anything to give the colonists a chance to make a run for it."

"Agreed. I just wish I had a better idea. My people think we might be able to disable enough emitters on the other spheres to knock out their tractor beams and maybe that dampening field. I'm having my navigator send you coordinates. Plot an evasive course to that mark. We'll take it from there."

"You're going to go four against one?"

"Want to trade jobs?"

As Rodriguez fed the new coordinates to the helm, the rest of the crew prepared for their latest and perhaps craziest encounter with the alien ship. Al-Khaled was thinking ahead to the inevitable moment when the *Aephas* stood toe to toe with the other vessel and wondered what the *Aephas* might do at that point. Was there anything that could be done?

Hell of a time to ask such a stupid question, Commander.

"Doctor Leone!"

Doing his best to avoid getting tossed around his sickbay as the *Endeavour* absorbed yet another strike against its shields, Anthony Leone still managed to smack his elbow against the side of the bed in his patient care ward. Once more, the overhead lighting as well as each bed's medical monitor and accompanying equipment protested the assault, and the monitor above Stephen Klisiewicz's bed even reset itself. Leone cursed the equipment, knowing it would take a moment to reinitialize and reacquire the information being fed to it by the bed's array of sensors. Capping off everything was another red alert klaxon whining and generally serving to worsen Leone's already foul mood.

"Amos, are you all right?" he shouted over the alarm, seeing his nurse collecting herself as she rose to a sitting position on the deck.

Nodding, Lieutenant Holly Amos pushed herself to her feet and brushed off her uniform. "I'm fine, Doctor." After silencing the alert siren but leaving the red warning light to flash above the doors leading from sickbay, the nurse moved to where Ensigns Kerry Zane and Anissa Cole stood, having vacated their beds in the patient ward once the shooting had started.

"Are you two okay?"

Zane nodded. "Fine, Lieutenant. Nothing personal, but I'd rather be anywhere but here."

"I understand," Amos replied, offering a sympathetic smile. Zane in particular was ready to vacate sickbay and return to duty, even if just to pitch in with damage control efforts should the need arise, but Leone had opted to keep both officers here for continued observation. He hoped either or both of them might help shed additional insight into Klisiewicz, who remained sedated and restrained on his own bed.

"How is he?" Cole asked, gesturing to Klisiewicz.

Leone consulted the monitor, which had completed its reset and once more was displaying information pertaining to the science officer's current condition. "He's catching up on his beauty sleep." The ship rumbled around them again, though the effect this time was far less intense than the previous shake-up. Still, the doctor noted the change in the *Endeavour*'s engines as the starship continued through whatever hellish maneuvers its captain was foisting upon it. "I really hate it when the shooting starts."

"Amen to that, Doctor," said Amos.

The whistle of the ship's intercom echoed through the room, followed by the voice of Atish Khatami. *"This is the captain. As of now, power to all nonessential systems is being routed to propulsion, weapons, and defenses. Other than life support, power will be reallocated as required without further warning. Hang on, people. This is going to get rough. Khatami out."*

Cole said, "She sounds tense."

"There's an understatement," replied Leone. The dampening field being generated by the Lrondi vessel had been a problem before, but now that the alien ship had opted to go on the offensive, the field's effects across the *Endeavour* were being felt to an even greater degree. Even without the field, the other ship still possessed greater firepower than the *Endeavour* and the *Aephas* combined. The one advantage the starships might have now was the experience of their respective commanders. Despite her rapid promotion to captain in the wake of her predecessor's untimely death, Atish Khatami had proven herself in battle numerous times, against Klingons, Tholians, and even some adversaries best left forgotten. Were he a betting man, Leone would put his chips on Khatami every time.

Movement from the bed pulled Leone's attention from its medical monitors, and he saw that Klisiewicz was beginning to stir. The science officer's eyes were fluttering, and he was attempting to move his arms, both of which were restrained.

"Hand me that neural scanner," Leone said, pointing to a cart situated near the bed. Amos retrieved the instrument and handed it to him, and the doctor began waving it over Klisiewicz's head. "Readings are spiking. It's like his brain is being stimulated." His eyes narrowed as he considered the Lrondi on the lieutenant's neck, then reconfigured the scanner. "Maybe his friend was already awake, and she's trying to juice up Mister Klisiewicz, here." Completing his adjustments, Leone again activated the scanner and brought it to bear.

Klisiewicz's eyes opened wide, and his entire body spasmed.

"Nurse!" Leone said, taking an involuntary step back. "Prepare another sedative. We may have to put him out again." The scanner still flashing in his hand, the doctor moved closer again, and Klisiewicz reacted in kind. His features had contorted in what could only be pain, and even the attached Lrondi was beginning to make its own independent movements.

Then the restraints around Klisiewicz's arms gave way.

"Watch out!" Leone shouted, throwing up an arm to prevent Amos from getting any closer as Klisiewicz pushed against the top of the containment unit's transparent shell. Not designed to confine an unruly patient, the enclosure gave way with little resistance and clattered to the floor. Klisiewicz sat up in the bed, reaching for the restraints still binding his legs as Leone pulled Amos back with him toward the door. Seeing the intercom panel to his right, he slammed his hand against its activation switch.

"Sickbay to security. I need help down here right now!"

Klisiewicz had freed his legs and was twisting his body to get off the bed when he was met by the entire mass of Ensign Kerry Zane. The security officer plowed into him at a dead run, sending both men toppling onto and over the bed and crashing to the floor on its opposite side. Zane rolled to his feet, giving himself room as Klisiewicz pushed himself from the floor.

"Don't hurt him!" shouted Cole. "It's not his fault."

Zane grunted. "I know. *Believe me*, I know." Keeping his attention on Klisiewicz, he added, "Sorry about this, Lieutenant."

"I understand," replied the science officer, and Leone saw the conflict and pain in the other man's eyes. He did not want to fight. He did not want to resist, but his will was being subverted, and there was no way to stop that.

Or was there?

"The scanner," he said, holding up the device in his left hand as Klisiewicz lashed out at Zane. "I'll be damned."

Zane deflected the science officer's attack with the ease born of training and experience, and pushed him away to create some space between them. "I don't want to hurt you, sir." Raising his voice, he said, "If you can hear me in there, stop pushing him to do this. There's nowhere for you to go now. It's over."

"Her name is Naqa," Cole offered. To Leone, she said, "We noted some strange effects in the Lrondi with our tricorders, but weren't able to make anything of it."

Leone nodded. "Right." After Khatami had told him about Lieutenant Colleen Cook's frantic report from the planet surface about her tricorder causing distress to the Lrondi, Leone had attempted to duplicate the effect here with no success. Then the firefight with the Lrondi ship had begun, requiring him to see to his patients as the *Endeavour* went on red alert.

So what's stopping you now?

"I must speak with the captain," Klisiewicz said. "Naqa's people on the ship want to collect you. Even if you stop me, they'll still come. The *Endeavour* won't hold out forever against their defenses." As if supporting this declaration, the ship trembled yet again under the force of another strike against its shields. Lights blinked and dimmed, and the starship's engines once more groaned in protest.

Aiming the scanner at Klisiewicz, Leone stepped forward and activated it. The response was immediate, with the lieutenant stopping his advance on Zane and staggering until he collided with a nearby bed. His eyes screwed shut, and he reached for his head, gripping it in both hands as he released a cry of pain. Then his body jerked and twisted and Leone saw the Lrondi fall from his neck, dropping to the floor and beginning to skitter across the carpet toward the room's far corner. Now freed of the creature's influence, Klisiewicz sagged against the bed, and Zane rushed to his side to keep him from falling to the floor. Leone, stepping around the dazed science officer, followed after the Lrondi.

"Doctor, please!" Cole shouted. "Be careful!"

Holding the scanner before him like a phaser, Leone closed the distance, and the Lrondi retreated even farther. The doors behind him slid aside and two security officers ran into the room, phasers drawn, and he waved his free hand at the Lrondi.

"Stun it! Now!"

Stepping around the doctor, one of the security guards leveled his phaser and fired. The weapon's high whine filled the room as the soft blue-white beam struck the gray mass and it immediately slumped against the bulkhead.

"All right," Leone said, scowling as he deactivated the scanner and tossed it on the nearby bed. "I think having my sickbay turned into a shooting gallery is cause for a day off, right?" He waved to Amos. "Nurse, get me a portable containment unit. I want this one locked up next to her buddy in the other room." When the ship shuddered around them once more, he reached for the bed to steady himself. "In the meantime, let's see if we can't put what we just learned to use."

24

Reluctant as she may have been to fire a phaser an hour ago, Colleen Cook had put aside such reservations.

Her weapon whined yet again as she sighted on an incoming Pelopan, dropping him in a disjointed heap to the dirt. That made eleven—or was it twelve—intruders she had dispatched, but what had started as a frenetic clash had slowed since Master Chief Rideout's sudden appearance and now that the attackers had lost their element of surprise.

"I think they're pulling back," she said, using her uniform sleeve to wipe sweat from her face. The air was dry and she tasted dust, which was everywhere. Her next shower, she decided, would last no less than three consecutive duty shifts.

Kneeling beside her just inside the doorway to one of the Beta Site base camp's temporary shelters, Lieutenant Commander Yataro pressed himself against the structure's wall paneling and used it for concealment as he searched for new threats. The dim illumination offered by spotlights around the camp made the violet hue of his skin seem almost black, highlighted by his bulbous blue eyes. "Agreed, but I do not believe they are simply abandoning their attack. It is obvious that we hold value for them."

"Right," Cook said. That the Lrondi and their Pelopan hosts felt the need to probe and strike at the base camp spoke volumes, but it seemed their resolve was faltering. How many Pelopan had been sent against the camp? Thirty to forty, so far as Cook could tell, but that number was shaky given the assailants' ability to mask their movements. Though instructions had been sent to all personnel on how to make the tricorder adjustments necessary to detect the presence of the dampening screens, there was only so much individuals could do while fending off attacks from multiple directions.

"Any word from the *Endeavour* or the *Aephas*?" asked Cook, searching the now oppressive darkness for hints of movement that might reveal the presence of Pelopan intruders.

The Lirin chief engineer shook his oversized head. "No. At last report, they were engaging the components of the Lrondi vessel, and one component was preparing to make planetfall near the colony."

Movement from her left made Cook shift her position and take aim at the approaching figure, but she lowered her phaser upon recognizing Lieutenant Brax bounding toward her. His trio of legs allowed him extra purchase on what had become something of an obstacle course in the camp's compound, with cargo containers, equipment, and other debris littering the ground. The Edoan made his way to them and crouched in the doorway next to Yataro. In the hand that did not carry a phaser, Brax held up his communicator.

"I have been in contact with Colony Administrator LeMons. They are engaged in evacuation operations and cannot spare another transport."

More weapons fire, this time more distant, still made Cook flinch. "How much longer before they're ready to leave?"

"Administrator LeMons and I agree that the Lrondi sphere will arrive before all of their colonists are safely away."

Yataro said, "We must do something."

"There is very little we can do here at the moment, though the *Aephas* and the *Endeavour* are deploying a new plan to delay or repel the planetary landing."

Cook asked, "And how long will that take? We can't hold these guys off forever." Though she had no way of keeping an accurate count, she had tallied no fewer than a dozen Starfleet personnel that she had seen injured during the firefight. The Pelopan weapons, though no match for Starfleet phasers, were brutally effective, if the wounds Cook had observed were to be believed. She had seen two *Endeavour* medics rushing back and forth across the compound, frantically attempting to treat the wounded, but time was not on their side as the Pelopan continued to press their attack.

Brax's communicator beeped and he flipped it open. "Brax here."

"Lieutenant, this is Commander al-Khaled on the Aephas. *Captain Khatami is rather busy right now, but she asked me to relay you a message: that scan frequency your people detected as having an effect on the Lrondi? Doctor Leone has isolated it."* He rattled off several numbers in rapid succession, almost too fast for Cook to follow as she made the necessary adjustments to her

tricorder. *"You can configure your tricorders and communicators to broadcast a signal that should disrupt the Lrondi's hold on their hosts."*

"That's great," Cook said.

Yataro countered, "Perhaps not. Coordinating such an effort among our remaining people would be problematic, and the effective range of the signal would be limited."

"Then you need to find a way to boost the signal, people. I'd love to—" The rest of al-Khaled's comments was obliterated by a burst of static erupting from the speaker grill of Brax's communicator. When the disruption faded, the commander was still there, but his voice now sounded more shaky. *"We're taking fire. Good luck. Al-Khaled out."*

Cook felt a tingle of excitement as an idea presented itself. "The comm shack. There's a public address system installed around the camp. We could broadcast the signal that way."

Shouts of warning were filtering across the compound from somewhere near the camp's forward edge, and Cook looked up to see several men and women, most in Starfleet red but a few in civilian attire, waving as though signaling people in the camp.

"Here they come! Get ready!"

"If we're going to do this," said, Cook, "it's probably now or never."

Brax nodded. "Agreed. You two head to the communications shack. I will assist those on the line." Not waiting even for an acknowledgment, the security chief dashed off, heading toward the perimeter.

Checking the power level on her phaser, Cook glanced

over her shoulder to where Christine Rideout lay uncon-
scious on the shelter's floor. She had not stirred since
Brax had stunned her and moved her inside the shelter.
She hated the thought of leaving the other woman here
alone, especially as she still was playing host to one of the
Lrondi, but there was little time to waste.

Looking at Yataro, Cook asked, "Ready, Commander?"

"There is nothing to be gained by remaining here."
The Lirin rose to his feet and used his massive left hand
to lever himself through the open doorway and out of
the shelter. He set such a pace that Cook was required to
run in order to keep up. With an agility that seemed in
stark contrast to his tall, lanky frame, the chief engineer
bounded between cargo containers and other shelters, his
head sweeping from left to right as he searched for possible threats. She flinched as they both reached another of
the shelters assigned as billet space, dropping to one knee
as weapons fire erupted from somewhere behind them.
Illuminated by spotlights positioned near the camp's perimeter was Lieutenant Brax, firing phasers in both hands
at targets Cook could not see.

"It's starting to get crazy in here again."

Yataro nodded, consulting the tricorder he had been
carrying slung from his left shoulder. "Scans show more
incoming Pelopan life-forms. Another twenty to forty."
He deactivated the unit. "That number, if reliable, gives
them the tactical advantage."

"Tell me about it."

Without warning, Yataro reached out and put his hand
on her head, pushing her to the ground. His phaser whined

mere centimeters above her, and the weapon's flash was almost blinding in the near darkness. She heard the sound of two bodies crashing to the earth; when the commander released her, she saw that two more Pelopan were now sprawled unconscious on the ground.

"Thanks," she said, feeling a sudden wave of relief wash over her.

"My pleasure."

When they arrived at the communications shack, they found it empty. In the haste to prepare for evacuation, all of the comm equipment had been considered expendable. A quick survey of the field computer console perched along one wall of the shelter told Cook that the equipment was still active and functioning. Moving to the console, she began flipping the switches needed to tie into the public address system.

"Lieutenant!"

Cook heard the warning at the same time she heard footsteps behind her. Near the entrance, Yataro turned in time to greet the first Pelopan—a female—as the intruder rushed him. Her body collided with his and both of them fell crashing to the floor. A nearby chair was pushed aside as Yataro kicked and jerked his body in an attempt to roll atop the Pelopan, who was stronger and more nimble despite her smaller size compared to the Lirin. His attacker still maintained a grip on the rifle she had been carrying, and in seconds the pair separated as she brought up the weapon's muzzle.

"The signal!" Yataro shouted, lunging forward and thrusting his arm up and under the rifle's barrel. Its muzzle was pushed upward just as the Pelopan pulled its trigger and a deafening roar rolled through the shelter as the weapon fired. Cook's ears rang from the report, and she ducked to avoid being shot, but by then Yataro had knocked away the rifle and was lashing out at its wielder. "Lieutenant!"

Grabbing at the console's intercom pickup, Cook activated her tricorder.

Rideout was certain her head was coming apart.

Christine! The pain!

Sijaq's frantic pleas seemed to ricochet around in her mind as the piercing whine exploding all around her drilled into her skull. Rideout covered her ears with her hands, but it was useless. The sound, whatever it was, enveloped her. It felt as though it was seeping through her very skin and penetrating her bones.

Every heartbeat stretched as though to infinity. Her vision blurred, and she felt her balance give way. No sooner did she push herself to her feet than she collaped again, her knees impacting against the floor before she collapsed forward and curled into a fetal ball that was useless to ward off the ceaseless assault. Something warm and wet dribbled between her fingers. Rideout could not hear the scream she knew had to be bursting from her lungs, and then her breath caught in her throat. Still, the sound did not stop.

The pain! Christine! It hurts! Make it stop! Make them stop! This is unbearable! Where is it coming from?

Even Sijaq's agonized wails were swept away as the whine continued, and then . . .

And then . . .

A sudden chasm opened in her mind. The jumbled maelstrom that was her consciousness as besieged by another waned, until all that was left were her unasked questions and unspoken entreaties for the pain to stop, and . . . nothing.

Sijaq was gone. Completely.

The first thing Rideout noticed was that the thunderous assault on her senses had diminished. It was still there, but it no longer carried its former power. She pulled her hands from her ears, seeing the trace amounts of blood on her fingers. Her ears pounded. Her entire body was one enormous ache. Uncoiling herself from her protective ball, she stretched sore muscles and drew air deep into her lungs. Every breath was fire.

"Chief. Chief Rideout?"

It took her an extra moment to grasp that the voice was not coming from inside her skull. Lifting her head, she looked around and recognized that she was lying on the floor of a Starfleet-issue temporary shelter. Why or how she had ended up here were mysteries she hoped might be solved by whoever was calling her name. Blinking away the last of her disorientation, she rolled onto her side— and regretted that move. A groan escaped her lips, and she reached to rub her temples.

Worst hangover ever.

Realizing the unbidden thought was her own made her smile. She pushed herself to a sitting position and heard footsteps scraping along the shelter's floor. A shadow fell across her, and she looked up to see Ensign Joseph Berenato crouching next to her. Dark circles underscored his bloodshot eyes, and there was dust in the bristle of his unshaven cheeks, neck, and jaw line. Also apparent was his lack of a Lrondi on the back of his neck.

"Do I look as bad as you look?" she asked.

"No, but I bet you feel as bad as I do. Are you all right?"

Rideout grunted as she allowed Berenato to pull her to her feet. "I'll live. Maybe." It was not until she was standing that she comprehended why she felt odd, and her hand reached for the back of her neck.

Nothing was there. Sijaq was gone.

"Where is she?" Rideout glanced around the compartment, searching for the Lrondi who had controlled her. She saw a shapeless gray mass lying on the floor beneath a nearby table. It did not move, and Rideout felt her gut twitch at the possibility that Sijaq might be . . .

No!

"It's okay," Berenato said, reaching out to place a hand on her arm. "They're alive. I checked. They've been stunned or something. That signal we heard had to be what did it."

Kneeling beside the Lrondi, Rideout laid a hand atop it and felt its warmth as well as a gentle pulsing beneath her fingers, and she released a gratified sigh. Only then did she realize the feelings she was displaying for this creature, this thing that had held her against her will and taken control of her mind and her very sense of self.

What the hell am I supposed to do now?

Lying on her side on the opposite side of the shelter was Ensign Javokbi. Ivelan was next to her, and both appeared unconscious. Rideout noticed that like herself and Berenato, neither of them hosted a Lrondi any longer.

"They're both over there," said Berenato, pointing to the far corner where two more gray masses lay unmoving. "Looks like they reacted the same way to whatever that was."

Checking Javokbi and Ivelan, Rideout asked, "Why are they still out of it?"

Berenato replied, "No telling. Ivelan mentioned before that different species take to collection in different ways. Maybe her and Javokbi's physiologies were more sensitive to the signal that freed us."

The door to the shelter opened, and a sliver of light shone into the room. It was obscured by a figure that stepped into the compartment: Lieutenant Brax. Rideout smiled when she saw that the Edoan was followed by Lieutenant Cook as well as Lieutenant Commander Yataro.

"You have no idea how happy I am to see you," she said, feeling relief flooding over her.

Cook replied, "Not as happy as we are to see you."

"What happened?"

"The Pelopan have been incapacitated," said Brax, his voice high and clipped, which Rideout knew was a tone he adopted when he was pleased. "The signal generated by Lieutenant Cook had the desired effect. The Pelopan hosts have been freed of their Lrondi counterparts, but the transition appears to have been a shock to their systems. Most of them are unconscious, and my security teams are moving them to the field hospital."

Rideout asked, "What about the Lrondi?"

"They are being contained in one of the shelters until we can figure out what to do with them," replied Yataro.

Stepping past the new arrivals, Rideout exited the shelter and onto the open ground. The light she had seen through the door was coming from one of the numerous portable lamps positioned around the camp. Scattered in and around the shelters, other equipment, Starfleet officers, and civilian colonists were dozens of Pelopan, many of them unconscious but a few stumbling about, uncertainty and confusion evident on their faces. Rideout could sympathize. Her connection with Sijaq could be measured in hours, whereas the Pelopan likely had known almost nothing else for the majority of their lives. The shock of such an unexpected and abrupt transition might be too much for some of them to bear.

"What do we do now?" she said as the others joined her from inside the shelter.

Brax replied, "This is not over just yet."

25

The energy bolt chewed into the bulkhead centimeters in front of Katherine Stano's face, close enough for her to feel its heat on her cheeks. She flinched, squeezing shut her eyes as bits of hot metal peppered her face and uniform. Throwing up one arm to protect herself, she backed away from the point of impact, hearing shouts of alarm and the sounds of heavy footfalls on deck plating.

"Back! Get back!" she yelled, raising the phaser in her other hand and firing blindly down the corridor as she backpedaled around a corner. The weapon's whine filled the narrow corridor and she saw the light from its beam even through her closed eyelids. She had set the phaser to wide-beam stun in the hopes that it would give her an edge against the greater number of Pelopan they might encounter. It was a good tactic in theory, but as she staggered backward, Stano realized that it would only work if she aimed the weapon at least in the vicinity of her intended target, rather than at a defenseless floor or ceiling.

Damn it!

More fire from the Pelopan energy rifles howled in the passageway, and Stano felt the rounds burrowing into the wall she was using to support herself.

"Watch out, Commander!" she heard Ivan Tomkins shout from behind her. She felt a hand on her shoulder, pressing her down, and she dropped to one knee before another phaser fired past her. Sounds of someone stumbling into bulkheads and falling to the deck echoed in the corridor.

Wiping at her face to verify that no hot shrapnel had stuck to her skin, she pushed herself to her feet. "Thanks, Lieutenant." Glancing over her shoulder, she asked, "Everyone all right?" In addition to Tomkins, Ensigns Tropp and Trinh Van Son replied that they were uninjured, but the strain of their advance was evident on their faces. Though she had not been keeping strict count, the pair of Pelopan Tomkins had just dispatched put them somewhere in the neighborhood of two dozen they had encountered and dealt with in similar fashion. "It's getting a bit crowded out here."

Despite the apparent critical tasks taking place in the command center, there still seemed to be a number of Pelopan moving about the ship. It was obvious that Maloram was preparing to receive more Lrondi and Pelopan from Cantrel V. Laying siege to Tài Shan would also require additional personnel, as would dealing with the crews of the *Endeavour* and the *Aephas*.

Over my dead body.

Above them, the recessed lighting conduits running along the ceiling flickered yet again. It was happening with greater frequency as the ship marshaled its power reserves for planetfall. Stano had noted the slight pitch in the deck, which likely corresponded to course corrections as the vessel aligned itself for entering the atmosphere, and the maneuvers were beginning to tax inertial damping and artificial gravity systems.

Seeing the look of concern on Trinh's face, Stano asked, "Ensign? Are you sure you're okay?"

The young security officer nodded. "Yes, Commander."

Stano recalled from her review of his service record that Trinh, a recent addition to the *Endeavour*'s crew, came from a family with a long tradition of Starfleet service. This was his first deep-space assignment.

"This is your first mission off the ship, isn't it?" she asked.

"That's right." He offered a small, weak smile. "Heck of a way to start."

Clapping him on the shoulder, Tomkins said, "Let's be sure to finish strong, all right, then?"

"Aye, aye, Lieutenant."

Satisfied, Stano used her sleeve to wipe sweat from her forehead. "All right, we're almost there, so let's go and get this over with." Still brandishing phasers in both hands, she led the way from the team's temporary hiding place. This was the last stretch of corridor separating them from the entrance to the command center, with no more places to hide. There was only one direction to go.

Of course, the hatch was guarded.

With Tomkins at her side, Stano emerged from the corridor with both phasers up and firing. Both of them had their weapons set for wide-field stun, blanketing the entire hall leading to the command center. Six Pelopan stationed at different points along the passage slumped and fell, succumbing to the phasers before even having a chance to raise their weapons in defense.

"Piyii!"

The piercing cry startled Stano and made her duck to

her right, but she was not fast enough to avoid the large green arm that slammed down onto her left hand, forcing the phaser from her grip and sending the weapon clattering across the deck. Stano rolled away from the attack, sensing the Pelopan lunging after her. Tomkins twisted his body around and attempted to take aim but the alien was faster, sweeping her arm across his face. His head snapped back, and he toppled to the deck, almost taking out Stano's knees as she scrambled to regain her own balance and defend herself.

"Commander!" shouted Trinh, firing his own phaser at the Pelopan but missing as the large female jumped toward Stano. The first officer ducked left, avoiding the tackle as her assailant dropped to the ground. It was obvious that the Pelopan had no real fighting experience and instead was merely running and swinging with wild abandon in the hopes of landing a damaging blow. The female rolled onto her side and began pushing herself to her feet as Stano tried to angle herself to fire the phaser she still held in her right hand, but a shot from another weapon, Tropp's, was enough to send her dropping back in a heap to the floor.

"I'm about done with this vacation," Tomkins said, punctuating the remark with a grunt of pain. Blood ran from a gash on his left cheek, but he otherwise appeared uninjured.

"You all right?" asked Stano as she retrieved her dropped phaser.

The engineer nodded. "I'll live."

Ahead of them, the command center awaited.

"Pretty thick door," said Tomkins. "Think they heard us?"

Tropp replied, "No, but you can be sure the Lrondi guiding the actions of the Pelopan we have encountered so far have at least attempted to warn others of our approach."

"Now he tells us." Tomkins forced a humorless snort as he checked his phaser. "So, how do we get inside?"

"Allow me," said Tropp, advancing toward the control pad set into the bulkhead to the right of the hatch. The pad consisted of more than a dozen controls, each shaped differently from the others and possessing its own unique color. Almost too fast for Stano's eyes to follow, the medic pressed eleven keys in rapid succession.

"I'm going right," she said, hearing the door's lock disengaging. "Tomkins, left, Tropp right, Trinh left. Stun anything that's not the four of us. We'll apologize to our people later."

Showtime.

The door had opened just enough to admit a person when Stano charged ahead, sidestepping to her right as she entered the room and putting the bulkhead to her back. Arms raised and covering a ninety-degree arc in front of her, she started firing with both phasers. Pelopan bodies started dropping with her first shots as she swept the weapons from left to right, subjecting everything in front of her to the wide-field stun blast. While able to cover a larger area with a single shot, the setting weakened the beam's strength and reduced its effective range. It also meant that anyone fast enough to duck behind a console or other cover might avoid getting caught by the phasers' effects.

Ensign Adam Gaulke was the first *Endeavour* crew member to go down, caught by a beam fired either from Tomkins or Ensign Trinh. Jay Hastert and Carlton McMurray followed suit, and Stano stunned Ensign Guillermo Montes. That only left Ensign Sa-Gameet, but after engaging a few rounds with Tomkins, the lieutenant was able to drop the Efrosian engineer.

By now, the team was receiving return fire from elsewhere in the room. Stano ducked behind a nearby workstation as the bolt from a Pelopan weapon drilled into the wall above her. Then she heard a scream of pain and jerked her head to see Trinh thrown against the bulkhead behind him before he slid in a disjointed heap to the floor, an ugly scorch mark visible on his left shoulder.

"No!" Stano yelled, rising from behind the station and firing both phasers in the direction of Trinh's shooter. The male Pelopan crumpled in the face of the stun beam, and Stano was already searching for a new target. Moving around a support stanchion, she leveled her phasers at the face of Angela Grammell.

"You're too late, Commander," said the ensign from where she stood with a console separating them, her voice carrying a weight and authority that was out of character for the normally quiet, reserved security officer. Stano was certain the voice she was hearing had to be channeling Grammell's Lrondi collector, Maralom.

Grammell gestured upward to the command center dome, where Cantrel V loomed large in the window; far

closer than it had been during her last visit, and it seemed
to be getting bigger with every passing second. Displayed
upon the dome's transparent material were numerous
computer displays, offering a litany of information Stano
could not begin to comprehend.

"We can still end this, Grammell," she said, her phasers unmoving as she aimed them at the ensign's chest. "Or
am I talking to Maralom now?"

"Maralom hears you. He does not believe you."

Her speed was uncanny, launching herself over the
console and at Stano before the first officer could react.
By the time she started to move, Grammell was on her,
crashing into her and sending both women tumbling to
the deck. The phaser in her left hand was knocked away,
and Grammell's hands clamped around her right wrist,
twisting it up and around until Stano was forced to drop
that weapon as well. Pivoting into the hold Grammell was
trying to use, Stano jammed her elbow into the ensign's
chest, knocking out her wind and forcing her to lose her
grip. Stano took advantage of the break to kick at the ensign's knees but the other woman was faster. In a heartbeat she was in Stano's face, one hand grabbing her hair
and pulling back her head as the other latched onto her
throat. Flailing for anything to hold on to, Stano's hands
landed on something warm and wet: Maralom, on the
back of Grammell's neck.

Stano pulled the Lrondi free.

A gut-wrenching scream filled the air as Grammell's
body began to convulse, and she fell away from Stano before stumbling into a nearby console and falling to the

floor. Her hands reached for the back of her neck, where a small gray protuberance was still visible, piercing her skin and leaking a viscous pinkish fluid.

The Lrondi in Stano's hand was squirming, and she saw more of the fluid seeping from where the appendance should have been. Instinct made her drop the flailing creature and it rolled and twitched on the deck plating while making no sounds. She heard footsteps behind her and then Tropp was there, leveling his phaser at the Lrondi and firing. The stun beam enveloped the spasming gray mass, and it became still.

"Maralom!" Grammell shouted, her voice racked with agony. "No! He's gone. I can't feel him anymore! What did you do?"

"Commander," said Tomkins, "look at this." He was gesturing toward the set of five control consoles at the center of the room, each still occupied by a Lrondi. Their gray bodies pulsed and twitched at differing intervals as they communed with the ship's computer network, and Stano tried to imagine the technology necessary for them to interface with the system on such an intimate level.

It made her head hurt.

The fits were growing more pronounced, to the point that they were reacting in a manner similar to Maralom. First one, then the others, abruptly separated from their consoles, their bodies growing limp as they rolled or fell from the stations to the floor.

"What the hell just happened?" Stano asked.

From where he knelt next to Grammell, Tropp replied, "They appear to be reacting to the loss of Maralom. The

Lrondi are linked, after all. Perhaps they too felt the pain of his separation from Ensign Grammell."

On the floor, Grammell was crying. Tears ran down her face, and she was thrashing her head from side to side. "He's totally alone! Give him to me!"

"Tropp," Stano prompted, and the medic responded by administering a sedative from his medical kit. The hiss of the hypospray preceded Grammell's body relaxing and her eyes closing. In a moment, she was unconscious.

Looking around the room, Stano saw that everyone in the command center had been dispatched. Her eyes fell on the unmoving form of Ensign Trinh as she saw Tropp moving toward him. "Is he . . . ?"

Tomkins said, "Tropp thinks he can treat him here. It'd be better if we could get him back to the ship, but he should pull through okay."

"First things first: Secure that hatch. Nobody in or out until this is over, one way or another." She looked up at the displays superimposed on the dome. "Does any of that make any sense to you?"

"If I'm reading it right, the *Endeavour* and the *Aephas* look to be holding their own," Tomkins replied. "But the big issue is the sphere we're on. It's still maneuvering for a landing."

Without warning, the displays vanished, which was followed by consoles all around the command room beginning to blink, flicker, and offer audible alarms of varying pitch and volume.

"What's going on?" Stano asked.

Running to the console nearest to him, Tomkins began

manipulating controls. "I can make out some of this, but not all. I can't tell what's happening." He hooked a thumb to the consoles that had been operated by the Lrondi. "Those guys must've done something when they pulled out of the system."

Stano felt her heart racing.

Please tell me they didn't trigger a damned self-destruct.

Another strike against the shields. Another alarm sounding. Another damage assessment.

How much more punishment could her ship take? Atish Khatami asked herself the question yet again as the *Endeavour* shook beneath the force of another attack. Once more, she shook in her command chair as the starship weathered yet another pounding.

"What's the story on Echo?" she asked, using the name given to the fifth sphere.

Ensign Iacovino said, "Course unchanged, Captain." She lifted her head from her sensor viewer to consult another indicator on her console. "They should enter the atmosphere in just under two minutes."

"Where are the colonists with their evacuation?"

"Still under way," replied the science officer. "They're not going to make it."

Damn.

The fifth sphere was the one her people had boarded, and it now was the object of Commander al-Khaled's focus on the *Aephas*. According to Ensign Cole, Stano and the others had been captured by their Pelopan servants. Even if Khatami could shake off the attacks from the four spheres chasing the *Endeavour*, any action she might take with the *Aephas* against Echo to prevent the vessel from completing its mission put Stano and the others at risk. Ten Starfleet lives on that ship along with those of the Pelopan and Lrondi, balanced against hundreds of people on the planet below, and however many more on the other spheres. From a tactical perspective, there was only one option.

"Captain," said Lieutenant Neelakanta from the helm, "they're moving to box us in again." On the main viewscreen, the image illustrated the *Endeavour*'s position against that of the four spheres hunting it. The Lrondi ships were approaching from different angles despite her helm officer's valiant efforts to keep them at bay.

"Main power is at fifty-three percent and falling," reported Iacovino. "Shields are at twenty-eight percent and falling. If they manage to hem us in, that'll be it, Captain."

"Stand by to go to warp," Khatami said. "We need some breathing space while we still have a chance to get some." She had refused to break orbit and run, not wanting to abandon her people on the surface or on the Lrondi ship, but losing the *Endeavour* now would doom them and the rest of her crew. If she wanted to stay in the fight, she needed to retreat, at least for a few precious moments. "Notify Commander al-Khaled of our intentions." She was about to order Neelakanta to take the ship to warp speed when she watched the tactical image on the viewscreen change. The four spheres, which had been moving to intercept and corral the *Endeavour*, were slowing even as her own ship continued its evasive maneuvers.

"They've stopped firing," reported Iacovino. "And I'm reading a power falloff in their dampening field and tractor beam emitters."

Khatami scowled. "Are you sure?"

"No doubt about it, Captain." Still peering into her sensor viewer, the science officer added, "Echo has halted its descent. It's holding its present altitude above the atmosphere."

The other four spheres also had fallen into something of a formation, holding their current position as the *Endeavour* continued to pull away.

"Captain," said Lieutenant Estrada from the communications station, "we're being hailed. It's . . . it's Commander Stano!"

Unable to prevent the smile from warming her face, Khatami shook her head. "Put her through."

"*Captain?*" called her first officer through the ship's intercom.

"It's nice to hear your voice, Commander. What the hell did you do over there?"

"We've taken control of their bridge, and as you may have noticed, everything is sort of holding in neutral for the moment. The best way to put it is that at least some of the Lrondi have had a meltdown of sorts over here. They've checked out and left everything in a sort of wait state, so we'd sure appreciate it if Commander Yataro or al-Khaled or any of those super-smart engineers could come over here and help us find the off switch."

26

Standing at the edge of the crater, Khatami watched as dozens of personnel, some dressed in Starfleet uniforms while many more were dressed in numerous variations of civilian work attire, milled over and around the dig site. Notable among the different groups were the varying number of Pelopan. While many stood at the periphery of such gatherings, some few were participating in the moving of equipment or assembly of shelters or any of several tasks currently unfolding across the site. In just the last four hours, the number of temporary shelters and other modular buildings had tripled, along with all manner of equipment containers as well as loading and excavation equipment. She had already inspected the main Beta Site camp and was pleased to see that most of the debris and other clutter from the previous evening's skirmish had been cleared away. The camp was up and running again, a hive of activity that was the focal point for everything that would happen here today, and for many more days to come.

"Never point a bored engineer toward a problem you only want fixed," a male voice said from behind her. "Fixing's never good enough."

Khatami smiled as Commander Mahmud al-Khaled approached, along with Katherine Stano, Chief Christine

Rideout, and the Pelopan the chief had identified as Ivelan. While al-Khaled and Khatami's people all wore crisp, clean Starfleet uniforms, Ivelan wore a flowing, cream white dress that left one shoulder bare and accented her brilliant jade skin. Her dark hair was pulled back into an elaborate style that sat atop her head, giving her an almost regal appearance.

"Captain," Stano said, nodding in greeting. "Figured you'd get some fresh air?"

"My first officer has a habit of keeping me cooped up on the ship. This might be the closest thing to shore leave I'll likely get for months."

Rideout said, "You're certainly welcome to stay, Captain. It's not like we won't have plenty to do."

"I think Starfleet Command would have something to say about that, Chief. However, I commend you for volunteering to remain here until a proper Starfleet support team can be sent. Considering everything you went through, that's a pretty noble act." In addition to Rideout, Khatami was aware that Lieutenant Ivan Tomkins and a handful of other *Endeavour* crew members had stepped forward, requesting temporary duty with the Starfleet detachment assigned to support the Tài Shan colony. After the events of the past days, the ongoing repair work to the colony as well as new efforts to support the liberated Pelopan would require more personnel. To that end, Starfleet had ordered Commander al-Khaled and the *Aephas* to remain on station until relief arrived. "I'm sure the colonists will be grateful for the extra hands."

Al-Khaled said, "As am I. Good to have you aboard, Chief."

"Just promise you'll be coming back to us," added Stano. "Good help's just so hard to find, you know."

Looking uncomfortable with the praise, Rideout nodded. "I appreciate that, all of you. As for the why?" She looked to Ivelan, and placed a hand on the Pelopan's arm. "I spent a lot of time trying to convince her that we could help her people, hers and the Lrondi. I figure the best way to prove it is to do exactly that." Pausing, she cast her gaze toward the dry soil. "Besides, I know what it's like to have your whole life change around you, and to have new friends there to help you when you need it most. I thought I'd keep that going."

Ivelan smiled. "Christine is a worthy representative of your crew, Captain. We are honored by her presence."

Surveying the scene around them, Khatami once more eyed the numbers of Pelopan either observing tasks in progress or pitching in to help. "It's really something to see. I'm amazed that the Pelopan seem to be handling the transition so well."

Ivelan said, "Bonding with our Lrondi collectors did not inhibit our intellects, Captain. After all, it was not just our bodies they needed to survive, but also our knowledge and our skills. When my people were first collected, we were enduring the aftermath of unremitting conflict, and the Lrondi guided us from that, and helped us rebuild our society. Indeed, we forged a new society with them. As much as we helped the Lrondi, they too assisted us in so many ways. Yes, this transition has been and will continue to be difficult, but I feel that with the aid and guidance of people like Christine and Commander al-Khaled, we will be ready to face that challenge."

"It's your world," said al-Khaled. "We're just here to help you reclaim it."

Stano asked, "What about the Lrondi?"

"Some of them requested to remain here with us," Ivelan replied, "and many of my people have asked to be collected in order to facilitate their living among us. Still others have requested to travel with those already on the ship. There are many among my people who want to help the Lrondi, either upon returning to their home or building a new one. Apparently, many Lrondi aboard the ship experienced the shock of Maralom's abrupt separation from your Ensign Grammell. Those aftereffects continue to be felt. I am told that Maralom may never recover."

"That wasn't my intention," Stano said, her expression falling. "I really didn't want to hurt him. It was more an accident than anything else."

Khatami replied, "It wasn't your fault, Commander. You couldn't have known."

"I know." Stano cleared her throat. "That doesn't make it any easier, though."

Ivelan said, "One unexpected benefit is the willingness of many Lrondi to work with us as equals." She smiled. "It is an interesting situation, but one from which I feel we can all benefit. There will be controls in place, of course, but I believe the Lrondi are sincere in wanting to live with us in true harmony, where all have equal voice."

Khatami pondered the Pelopan's comments, and wondered if perhaps they were colored by too much optimism. Could the Lrondi so easily adapt to this radical change in the nature of their very existence? The captain wanted to believe so, but the doubt lingered.

"Most will still be departing aboard their ship," she said, "bound for their homeworld, or whatever's left of it. Mister Klisiewicz was able to plot a trajectory based on their original course and according to his calculations, it will take decades at the ship's top speed to get there. The Lrondi have no idea what they'll find when they arrive."

Al-Khaled added, "They're also leaving behind many components of their technology, which the Pelopan learned to use over the generations."

"They have been quite generous in this regard," Ivelan said. "With such resources, and all of us working together, I believe our new society will thrive."

Khatami could not help but admire the Pelopan woman, whom fate had seen fit to place in the position of representing her entire species on an interstellar stage. "After everything your people have been through, after everything they endured thanks to the Lrondi, and you have it in your heart to forgive them. I don't know that I could be so magnanimous."

"The simple truth is that my people survived because of the Lrondi. They cannot help what they became, or what was required for their existence to continue. For all they took from us, they gave us so much in return, and now you also are giving us so much more. I hope you will visit us again one day, Captain, to see what your efforts have put into motion."

Now it was time for Khatami to be uncomfortable with such commendation. "Thank you, Ivelan. I'll keep your invitation in mind. It'll definitely be interesting to see what you're able to accomplish before we return." She nodded to Rideout. "Besides, I have to come back for my people." Pausing, she cast her gaze toward the sky. "But for now, I'm afraid we have our own work to do."

Plenty of interesting things out there, too.

"Are you worried it's going to start moving?"

Oblivious to this point with respect to the evening rush of the officer's mess, Stephen Klisiewicz looked up from his plate of stir-fried chicken and vegetables—in truth a reasonable facsimile of that meal as interpreted by the *Endeavour*'s food synthesizers. Standing beside his table was Anthony Leone, smirking at him as he held his own tray of alleged food.

Returning the smile, Klisiewicz said, "Actually, I think this is one of the more trustworthy selections from my diet card."

"Glad to hear it, Lieutenant. I hear the guy who reviews and approves those things has impeccable taste, if he does say so himself." He glanced down at his tray. "Of course, it's not as good once it gets cold."

Klisiewicz straightened in his chair. "Sorry, Doctor. I'm sorry if I held you up."

With an exaggerated rolling of his eyes, Leone replied, "Where I come from, Mister Klisiewicz, that's called a verbal cue. It's a socialization thing, and it can't be a subtle one because even I've picked up on it. The appropriate response is to offer an invitation to sit down."

Stifling a laugh, Klisiewicz indicated the chair on the table's opposite side. "Where are my manners? Doctor Leone, would you care to join me?"

"I thought you'd never ask." Setting down his tray,

Leone pulled out the proffered chair and threw one leg over its back before sitting down. "It's getting harder all the time to get a dinner date around here."

"Again, I apologize." Using his fork to poke at his chicken—which did not move—Klisiewicz said, "I guess I'm just not feeling sociable at the moment."

Resting his elbows on the table, Leone leaned forward. "Are you just saying that, Lieutenant, or are you really feeling that way?"

"Am I allowed to say a little of both?"

The doctor shrugged. "You're allowed to say whatever you like." Pausing long enough to take a bite of his meal, he spoke around a mouthful of carrots. "Here's a funny thing: Did you know that I can program the computer to track each time someone uses a food slot, what he or she orders, and when? For example, I can set it to tell me when a particular member of the crew is eating at a particular location, like his quarters or one of the lounges or mess halls. Pretty handy, huh?"

"If not a little creepy." Eyeing Leone with no small amount of wariness, Klisiewicz asked, "Why didn't you just tell me you wanted to talk? Invite me for something to eat or call me down for a drink? I mean, you invite the captain for a drink all the time, and she doesn't even drink."

"Again, we're talking about customary social skills," Leone said, "and there's only a certain range of them that work for me, and they only work with certain people." With his fork, he gestured first to Klisiewicz, then to himself, then to the table separating them. "This, I like."

Klisiewicz swallowed another bite of chicken. "Fair enough. So, what do you want to talk about?"

"I saw that the Lrondi ship is finally on its way."

"Indeed it is." The science officer had watched the massive vessel's departure from his station on the bridge. According to the trajectory he had plotted, it would take nearly twenty years to reach the Lrondi homeworld, which lay in an area of space beyond anything the Federation had charted. Perhaps one day, some future Starfleet vessel and crew would be able to learn what the Lrondi found once they finally reached their home.

"I've been making the rounds among the crew who had a direct experience with the Lrondi. You're the last one on my list."

Tapping his empty fork on his plate, Klisiewicz said, "I see. Learned anything?"

"As you've probably guessed, different people had different reactions. Take Tropp, for example. I can ditch the usual doctor-patient confidentiality bit, because he's discussed it openly. The guy turned it into a game or something. He let that Lrondi pull out every neurochemical trick in the book, including triggering some hallucinations that sounded borderline psychotic to me." He grimaced. "Thanks to him, we'll have a pretty entertaining report for Starfleet Medical."

Klisiewicz said, "I never had a hallucination." A tinge of sadness welled up within him as he recalled his experience with Naqa. "It wasn't . . . it wasn't like that."

"It's okay to tell me what you were feeling."

"No, I get it." Klisiewicz shifted in his seat. "I'm not sure how to describe it. I guess—for now, anyway—I'll say that you just had to be there."

"Okay," Leone said. "Just asking."

"What about the others?"

"They're all over the place," replied the doctor. "No one suffered any physical effects, and each person's emotional responses are different, of course. Ensign Grammell probably had the worst time of it, given how she was separated from her Lrondi handler. There was some initial trauma, but she seems to be recovering. It might take her a while, but I don't think there will be any lasting negative effects."

Klisiewicz frowned. "Negative effects?" He was uncertain what to even make of such a statement. "Does that mean something positive could come from what we went through?"

"Doctor Leone?"

Both men looked up as Anissa Cole approached their table. It was the first time Klisiewicz had seen her since their return from the Lrondi ship. His memories of the fight in the transporter room were hazy, to say nothing of everything that took place after that.

"Anissa," he said, rising from his seat. "Hi."

Leone also stood. "Ensign Cole, this is a pleasant surprise."

"It is?" Her expression turned to confusion. "I was responding to your message about meeting you down here as soon as possible?"

"Oh, that." Leone reached for his tray. "Well, I appreciate you coming on short notice. Please, sit down. I was just speaking with the lieutenant here about recent events."

Crossing his arms, Klisiewicz said, "And about social invitations, as it happens." He waited until Cole sat before returning to his chair.

"I ought to be heading back to sickbay," Leone said, his smile giving him the appearance of a child who's just broken a piece of his mother's fine china. "I'm sure somebody's dying or something. You two catch up." With that serving as his farewell, Leone walked away, disposing of his tray before heading out of the mess.

"Subtle, isn't he?" Cole asked.

Klisiewicz chuckled. "Like a warp core breach. How are you feeling?"

"Well, you know," Cole replied. She paused, a small smile teasing the corners of her mouth. "Actually, you *do* know, don't you?"

"Yeah." Klisiewicz nodded. "Yeah, I guess I do. I don't know what to say or how to describe it." He drew a breath. "I miss her. I miss Naqa." While the raw emotional turmoil he had endured with Naqa had already started to fade, he still felt a pang of separation. How long would that stay with him?

Reaching across the table, she took his hand in hers. "I miss her, too, and I wonder if she misses me."

"Yes." Klisiewicz squeezed her hand. "Yes, that's it. I know this sounds crazy, but I've never felt that sort of connection before. Not just with another person, but with anything."

Cole sighed. "Neither have I."

"And now part of me is wondering if I'll ever feel that way again, about anything or anyone. The problem is that I don't know if it was real, or just Naqa manipulating me."

"Now that she's gone," Cole said, "it feels like there's a hole in my soul."

A sudden, odd thought occurred to Klisiewicz, and he

snorted at the imagery it conjured. "It feels like the worst breakup I ever had. Worse than Rhonda Ross back in fifth grade."

The comment evoked his intended reaction as Cole laughed. "You're kidding. Fifth grade is still your worst breakup?"

"She dumped me when her family moved away that summer. Didn't even say goodbye. Transporters, and real-time communications all the way out to Pluto, but she never even told me where she was going. I hated her until I graduated from the Academy."

It was Cole's turn to squeeze his hand. "You realize we basically broke up with the same person, right?" This time, their shared laughter was enough to turn heads at several tables throughout the mess, and she covered her mouth.

Once they had regained control of themselves, she looked at him. Her smile was infectious, Klisiewicz thought, and he was sure that if she allowed him, he could lose himself forever in her eyes.

"Doctor Leone made the right call here," Cole said, after a moment. "Didn't he?"

"Yeah," said Klisiewicz, "but whatever you do, don't tell him. We'll never hear the end of it."

ACKNOWLEDGMENTS

Once again, we thank our editors at Pocket Books for continuing to let us play in this little corner of the *Star Trek* universe we've created with our good friend and fellow word pusher, David Mack. After all, playing in the sandbox is even more fun when they let us bring a few of our own toys.

Speaking of Mister Mack, we raise our glass to our partner in mischief perpetrated against the written word. The three of us continue to have more fun with *Star Trek: Seekers* than should be allowed by law.

Thanks are due once again to Rob Caswell, the gifted artisan who has provided yet another mouthwatering piece of cover art for this latest *Seekers* installment. This series wouldn't even be here if not for his imagination, and we're grateful that his skills are brought to bear for each new book.

Lastly, we thank you, our readers who've continued to support us and these new missions into the Taurus Reach. You keep readin' 'em, and we'll keep writin' 'em.

ABOUT THE AUTHORS

Dayton Ward has been modified to fit this medium, to write in the space allotted, and has been edited for content. Reader discretion is advised.

Visit Dayton on the web at www.daytonward.com.

Kevin Dilmore is universally specific and easily sendable. If you have questions about postage rates, contact your local post office.